PENGUIN BOOKS

Tom Clancy's Power and Empire

Thirty years ago Tom Clancy was a Maryland insurance broker with a passion for naval history. Years before, he had been an English major at Baltimore's Loyola College and had always dreamed of writing a novel. His first effort, *The Hunt for Red October*, sold briskly as a result of rave reviews, then catapulted on to the *New York Times* bestseller list after President Reagan pronounced it 'the perfect yarn'. From that day forward, Clancy established himself as an undisputed master at blending exceptional realism and authenticity, intricate plotting, and razor-sharp suspense. He passed away in October 2013.

A retired Chief Deputy US Marshal, Marc Cameron spent nearly thirty years in law enforcement. His assignments have taken him from Alaska to Manhattan, Canada to Mexico and dozens of points in between. He holds a second-degree black belt in ju-jitsu and is a certified scuba diver and man-tracker. An avid adventure motorcyclist, Cameron's books heavily feature bikes and bikers – from OSI Agent Jericho Quinn's beloved BMW GS to Harley Davidsons, Royal Enfields, Ducatis and . . . almost everything on two wheels. Cameron lives in Alaska with his wife, Blue Heeler dog and BMW GS motorcycle.

Also by Tom Clancy

FICTION

NON-FICTION

Tom Clancy's
Power and Empire

MARC CAMERON

PENGUIN BOOKS

PENGUIN BOOKS

UK | USA | Canada | Ireland | Australia
India | New Zealand | South Africa

Penguin Books is part of the Penguin Random House group of companies
whose addresses can be found at global.penguinrandomhouse.com

First published in the United States of America by G. P. Putnam's Sons 2017
First published in Great Britain by Michael Joseph 2017
Published in Penguin Books 2018
002

Set in 12.5/14.75 pt Garamond MT Std
Typeset by Jouve (UK), Milton Keynes
Maps by Jeffrey L. Ward
Printed and bound in Great Britain by Clays Ltd, Elcograf S.p.A.

A CIP catalogue record for this book is available from the British Library

ISBN: 978–1–405–93447–3

www.greenpenguin.co.uk

MIX
Paper from
responsible sources
FSC® C018179

Penguin Random House is committed to a
sustainable future for our business, our readers
and our planet. This book is made from Forest
Stewardship Council® certified paper.

Principal Characters

US COAST GUARD AIR STATION PORT ANGELES
Lieutenant Commander Andrew Slaznik: MH-65
Dolphin helicopter pilot
Petty Officer 2nd Class Lance Kitchen: Dolphin
rescue swimmer

CYCLONE-CLASS PATROL SHIP USS *ROGUE*
Lieutenant Commander Jimmy Akana: Captain
Petty Officer 2nd Class Raymond Cooper: RQ-20
Puma operator

VBSS RHIB CREW USS *ROGUE*
Lieutenant Junior Grade Steven Gitlin
Chief Petty Officer Bill Knight
Chief Petty Officer Bobby Rose
Petty Officer Peavy
Petty Officer Ridgeway

USS *MERIWETHER*
Dave Holloway: Captain

PEOPLE'S REPUBLIC OF CHINA
Zhao Chengzhi: General secretary of the Chinese
Communist Party
Huang Ju: Colonel, Central Security Bureau; President Zhao's principal protection officer
Li Zhengsheng: Foreign minister
Xu Jinlong: Lieutenant general, People's Liberation
Army; director of Central Security Bureau

Ma Xiannian: General, People's Liberation Army

Long Yun: Colonel, Central Security Bureau; Foreign Minister Li's principal protective officer

TEXAS

Eddie Feng: Taiwanese journalist

Magdalena Rojas: Thirteen-year-old victim of sex trafficking

Blanca Limón: Thirteen-year-old victim of sex trafficking

Ernie Pacheco, aka Matarife (The Slaughterer)

Lupe: 'Bottom girl' who works for Matarife

Emilio Zambrano: Upper boss in cartel

Roy Calderon: Texas Department of Public Safety trooper

Kelsey Callahan: FBI special agent, commander of the Dallas Crimes Against Children Task Force

John Olson: Special Agent, FBI, on CAC Task Force

That city is well fortified which has a wall of men instead of brick.

— LYCURGUS

I shall not waste my days in trying to prolong them. I shall use my time.

— JACK LONDON

Prologue

A dozen men clad in bright orange coveralls and white hardhats swarmed the decks of *CGSL Orion*, the 396-meter flagship of China Global Shipping Lines, like ants. The hollow thud of metal box against metal box rattled the air, adding a bass note to the scream of gears and the whine of spinning cable drums. Gargantuan orange gantry cranes towering fifty meters above dipped and rose, then dipped again, their noses swinging back and forth from dock to ship with payloads of white, green, blue, or red metal containers known as TEUs, or twenty-foot equivalent units.

Gao Tian, chief of the ants, stood on the concrete docks of Dalian. This was one of the busiest container hubs in China, and the mountain of TEUs stacked beside the huge vessel made the man look and feel minuscule. He waved his good arm and spoke into the radio clipped to a loop on the chest of his coveralls. The broad smile across his face belied the frenetic pace of the activity around him. Far too busy with their own tasks, none of the other dockworkers looked up to pay any attention to his flailing arm, but they listened intently to his voice over their respective radios. His job was to coordinate and make certain the loading went quickly and safely; of all the people on the docks, Gao was intimately familiar with the dangers.

Each year, almost three-quarters of a billion of these ubiquitous metal containers – roughly 24 trillion pounds of cargo – moved around the world via tractor-trailer, locomotive, and cargo ship. Roughly 180 million TEUs came from China, and well over 10 million of those came through the Port of Dalian – on ships much like *Orion*.

The job of a dockworker was stressful enough, but Gao Tian found it difficult to concentrate, considering his recent upturn of fortune.

Gao was forty-one years old, with thinning black hair and a round face that naturally relaxed into a smile – a co-worker had remarked that he always looked as though he'd just relieved himself in the swimming pool. He was not a big man, nor was he particularly strong. In truth, Gao had many reasons to be unhappy. His right hand had been crushed in an accident three years earlier when a turnbuckle on a piece of lashing gear had snapped. The sudden loss of tension allowed the TEU to shift just a few inches – but those few inches were enough. Three fingers of his right hand had been sacrificed to the ship, his bone and flesh smeared between the steel bulkhead and the fifty-thousand-pound metal box, like so much red-currant jelly.

Gao's thumb and remaining finger were of little use. He could, at least, hook the antenna of his radio and depress the talk button, allowing him to direct the activity of the crane operators and the dozen orange-clad stevedores, ensuring that the stacks of TEUs were loaded correctly and efficiently. Gao earned no more pay as the chief coordinator, but, given his useless hand, he counted himself lucky that the dock manager gave him a job at all.

And besides, it made sense that the men who did the hardest and most dangerous work received a few more yuan a day than someone who merely stood on the dock and talked into his radio.

Other men in the crew might eventually move up and become true supervisors with offices of their own, but that was not to be for Gao. In all his years, he had never strayed farther than a hundred kilometers from his birthplace of Dalian – and then only to visit his wife's mother, who lived on a small piece of cooperative land north of the city.

He'd grown content enough with his lot – and then the man with the red eye had come to visit him. Three weeks ago, the man had offered a considerable sum of money to see that a certain TEU was loaded into a certain spot aboard a certain ship. To Gao's astonishment, this arrangement happened twice more, and each time the man had given him an envelope of money along with verbal instructions. He made Gao repeat the number of the desired TEU and would not allow him to write it down.

Today, the man with the red eye wanted two TEUs – PBCU-112128-1 and PBCU-112128-2 – loaded together, well aft of the stacks, low and near the centerline of the ship.

CGSL Orion was classified as an Ultra Large Container Vessel, or ULCV. Almost four hundred meters in length and with a draft of sixteen meters, the ship was deep enough to stack eighteen TEUs from the bottom of the hold to the topmost box above deck. Twenty-three TEUs could be arranged side by side across her fifty-three-meter beam. One TEU looked much like any other, so the chalky blue box with unobtrusive white X's painted at each corner would soon blend with the 16,000 other boxes aboard the ship, all similarly muted in color, that were stacked over, under, and around it. PBCU-112128-1 and PBCU-112128-2 were not particularly difficult to remember, which was a good thing, because Gao was already thinking of how he was going to spend the extra money the man with the red eye had given him. Nine hundred yuan, roughly equivalent to a hundred and fifty US dollars, each time he helped arrange a spot for a container that was going on the ship anyway. It was a tidy sum for someone making seven thousand yuan per month.

Gao suspected his benefactor worked for a triad and wanted his container of drugs or other illicit material stowed deep in the middle of the thousands of containers on the vessel, thus lessening the possibility of search by authorities. Gao was a moral man, opposed to narcotics, but nine hundred yuan was nine hundred yuan, and he rationalized that he did not know with any degree of certainty what was in the container. The man with the red eye had assured him that he wanted only to hasten the unloading process when his container reached its destination. So Gao took the man at his word and kept the money, with a conscience as cloudy as his benefactor's eye. He was able to slightly assuage his guilt by thinking about how he might spend the newest installment of nine hundred yuan.

Keeping well clear of the swinging cables and flying TEUs, Gao followed the man's instructions and located PBCU-112128-1 and PBCU-112128-2 in the stacks. He located the barcode on each container and checked them with the scanner he kept secured to a lanyard at his waist. He then coordinated between the operator of the second gantry crane and the stevedores working aft of *Orion*'s exhaust stack and bridge house to guide the chalky blue TEUs into place. The entire process – from the time Gao first pressed the talk key on his radio with his surviving finger to the moment the locking cams on the lashing hardware were turned at each corner of the two containers, locking them together, seven layers from the bottom deck, ten rows aft of the raised white bridge castle and eleven across from the starboard rail – took just under six minutes.

His task complete, Gao began to move his arm again. He spoke into the radio, directing the crane operators and stevedores as they continued to fill *Orion*, none the wiser to his deal with the red-eyed man. The chief of the ants smiled, nine hundred yuan richer, and thought about the pigs he could now purchase for his mother-in-law. He liked his mother-in-law. She was a good and gentle woman, well deserving of some new pigs.

Hands clasped behind the small of his back, General Xu Jinlong of the Central Security Bureau leaned in to peer through the tripod-mounted camera over the rooftops of the Chunhe residential district and industrial buildings situated along the Port of Dalian. A soldier at the core, Xu was thick across the shoulders, with the big hands and muscular forearms of a man who spent more time in the field than the office. Two other men flanked him, one close and relaxed, ready to take orders or give counsel. The other, a youthful man wearing a pair of black sunglasses, had positioned himself back a few steps. His hands were folded in front of him, his head slightly bowed, as he waited to be bidden forward.

All three men stood in the shade of a small copse of walnut trees on a gravel apron off Zhongnan Road, just north of Haizhiyun Park and Laohutan Scenic Area. Many varieties of protected birds and plant life were abundant in these woods, so passers-by paid little attention to the powerful eight-hundred-millimeter telephoto lens that protruded like a cannon from the front of the digital camera. The camera itself was superfluous; it was only there to give the lens credibility. The last thing the general wanted was a digital record of any of his activities. He had not come to capture the beauty of Laohutan's numerous waterfalls or magnificent root carvings. His interest at the moment lay northward, down the hill toward the sea and the intense activity along the Dalian docks.

Charged with protecting the highest political leaders in China, the duties of the Central Security Bureau were akin to those of the US Secret Service. Operatives in the CSB, however, put much more emphasis on the word *secret*, particularly those operatives under the command of General Xu.

Xu stood motionless, eye to the camera, studying the scene with rapt concentration. The dark suit the fifty-six-year-old man customarily wore allowed him to blend in among the hordes of similarly dressed businessmen and government officials around his offices in central Beijing. But Beijing was four hundred sixty kilometers away and a suit would have drawn unwanted attention as he stood on the side of the roadway on the coast of the Yellow Sea. He dressed instead in light khaki slacks and a white shirt with the sleeves rolled up against the unseasonably hot and muggy September. A beige photographer's vest of light-weight nylon hid the Taurus semiautomatic pistol tucked inside the waist of the khakis. The men with him were similarly dressed. But the young CSB operative named Tan wore dark glasses to cover a severely bloodshot eye. All three men were tall and fit, as those tasked with the protection of other men needed to be.

Both the general and his protégé, a man named Long Yun, had come up through the officers' corps of the People's Liberation Army, Long following Xu by a decade. Another ten years younger than Long, Tan began his professional life in the People's Armed Police. He'd shown great promise until the blood vessels around the pupil of his right eye began to burst every time he sneezed. Rigorous testing revealed his vision was still fine, but Xu found the thing hideous and looked for assignments that would keep the man out of his line of sight. It was the general who had suggested Tan wear dark glasses, even on cloudy days or indoors. It would not do to have the general secretary or some other party dignitary thinking one of the men who protected him was half blind or, worse yet, half drunk.

Xu used a handkerchief to wipe the sweat from a high forehead. He spoke without looking up from the camera. 'Comrade Tan, do you trust this cripple dockworker of yours?'

Tan's shoes crunched in the gravel as he took a half-step forward. 'I do, General,' he said. 'I have conducted three transactions in all, one week apart. In the first two, I chose a container at random, each from a lot heading to the

7

United States. Over this three-week span, Gao Tian has mentioned our arrangement to no one, not even his wife.'

'Astounding,' Xu said, and gasped, mockingly, though he doubted that Tan had caught the inflection. What man in his right mind would confide a sudden windfall of money to his wife, of all people?

General Xu stood up from the tripod, arching his back, feeling it pop and snap. In retrospect, it was a mistake to use someone from his own staff for the negotiations, but he would never admit it out loud. The matter of the container ship *Orion* had been conceived and decided prior to his arrangement with the man known as Coronet. Other operations would be far more tidy – and less likely to connect to Xu or his organization.

'The gods gave men mouths,' the general said. 'And in my experience, men have a difficult time knowing when to keep those mouths shut. This endeavor must be handled with the utmost discretion and secrecy. We cannot afford for your man to speak of this . . . ever.' He looked at Tan. 'Do you understand?'

'Of course,' the younger man said, but Xu doubted this was true.

'You must kill him,' the general clarified.

Tan blanched at the order, proving Xu's suspicions correct.

'Of course,' the young man said again.

'Today,' Xu added. It was tedious how everything had to be spelled out for this one.

Tan braced to attention and gave a curt nod. 'Of . . . course,' he said again, stammering, as if any more appropriate words had flown from his brain.

8

The general sighed, exhausted by the conversation. He tipped his head toward the tripod. 'Retrieve the lens and gear,' he said. 'But be certain you are careful as you put it away. The people's money should not be wasted by shoddy handling of equipment.'

Before Tan had a chance to repeat himself yet again, Xu turned to Long Yun and gave a knowing glance toward the car.

Long Yun settled in behind the wheel as the general took his customary spot in the backseat, on the right side, so the two men could more easily communicate. Outside, Tan blustered on the gravel pad as he packed the camera equipment, no doubt made more nervous by his boss's watchful eye through the tinted window.

'Follow this witless egg,' Xu instructed Long Yun. 'When he has killed the cripple, silence him as well. I am afraid your man Tan lacks the constitution for matters of delicacy and discretion. If the fool on the docks has not yet bragged to his friends, then someone will most certainly have witnessed him meeting a man with such a hideous eye. That ship will reach the United States in two weeks. I'm confident there will not be much left after . . . the incident, but the Americans are known to be extremely thorough. There can be absolutely nothing to link *Orion* to this office. Do I make myself clear?'

Long Yun turned and grinned at the general.

'Of course,' he said.

I

Jack Ryan, Jr, sat behind the wheel of a dusty Ford Taurus and rubbed a hand through his dark brown beard, trying not to think about his growing need to pee. The car sat parked for the fourth time in seven hours, and Ryan rested both hands on the steering wheel, staring into the darkness. Dallas, Texas, had a reputation for being muggy, even in fall, but this September night had turned out cool, allowing the two men in the Taurus to keep their windows rolled up most of the way and the AC turned off.

Just two years old, the dented Ford looked to be in much worse shape than it actually was. The Taurus was one of the few models that could be a police car, or, with a quick coat of rattle-can black and some judiciously applied dents to the doors and fenders, become a ratty beater that those same police would see as a meth fleet vehicle. Despite being in dependable shape mechanically, this particular car stank like bad cheese and dirty gym socks – blending well into this seedy South Dallas neighborhood.

A quick Internet search had revealed that the intersection not three blocks away was among the top five most likely spots in Dallas to get stabbed. There'd been no stabbings tonight as far as Ryan knew, but the night was still young. The sound of bottles breaking on pavement not too far down the street signaled that a cutting, at the very least, was a distinct possibility.

Ryan tapped the steering wheel with his thumbs and looked at his watch. His need for relief was going to reach critical mass in the next few minutes. He had a Gatorade bottle in the backseat, stashed there for surveillance emergencies, but he really hoped to get out and stretch his legs for a minute – even if it was behind a stinking dumpster that overflowed with pizza boxes in an alley littered with broken syringes and used condoms.

During the forty-two minutes they'd been parked between the back door of a Mexican grocery and a store that sold sewing machines – of all things – Jack had seen a half-dozen guys – all Asian – go into the Casita Roja strip club across the street. Over the course of those same forty-two minutes, he'd watched a homeless dude stagger by and vomit all over himself, a graffiti artist tag the back of the sewing-machine shop, and two hookers entertain clients as they stood against the rough brick wall beside the dumpster, accompanied by a halo of moths fluttering under the sad glow of a feeble streetlamp.

'If you could see me now, Mother dear,' Ryan mumbled to himself, tapping the Taurus's armrest.

'You say something?' Bartosz 'Midas' Jankowski asked from the passenger seat. Like Jack, he was bearded and wore a loose button-down shirt with short sleeves to cover the Smith & Wesson M&P Shield pistol tucked inside his waistband, as well as the loop of copper wire he wore low around his neck. Hollywood would have everyone believe the entire communication package, including the mic and radio, could be wrapped up and fit into the tiny bit of plastic worn inside the ear. Ryan wished it were that simple. There were tiny mics, but they still required a radio and some kind of power source. Campus members used a Profilo wire near-field neck-loop mic and a small flesh-tone earpiece. A house-built voice-activated intercom system obviated the use of a PTT switch. The whole shebang ran off a Motorola radio about the size of a fat deck of playing cards.

'Just thinking about this sexy life of a spy,' Ryan said. 'I'm going to need to take a leak in a few.'

Four other sets of ears listened to the conversation over the encrypted net. Ryan had hoped Midas might admit he needed a relief break as well, to make him feel a little more human in his time of need. No such luck. Jankowski was relatively new to The Campus, but Jack had been on enough ops with the retired Delta Force commander to know he possessed a bladder the size of a watermelon.

'I went an hour ago,' Domingo 'Ding' Chavez's voice came over Jack's earpiece, gloating a little. 'When I slapped the microphone up.'

Chavez, a senior member of The Campus – and a former CIA officer – had made an educated guess about their target's next stop, and arrived in just enough time to stick a magnetic hi-gain microphone to the light fixture outside the doors of the Casita Roja. About the size of a matchbox, the little mic broadcast on the scrambled radio frequency of the team's net. It was surprising what useful intelligence could be picked up from people just before they walked through the door of an unfamiliar location. Even when alone, they sometimes just blurted out things to themselves.

Chavez continued to rub it in. 'I had me a few sips of a

cold one while I was inside. Had to blend in, you know, go with the flow.' He made no comment about the nude girls gyrating on the stage. His father-in-law, The Campus's director of operations, John Clark – a legend in the intelligence community – happened to be working overwatch on this op from the roof of a payday loan place halfway up the block with a good view of both the front door of Casita Roja and Ryan's Taurus. He was listening on the same net.

Ryan sighed. 'Maybe I should go in and try to get a listen on what our guy's talking about.'

'Negative,' Clark said. 'We have the tracker on his car and we're up on his phone. Right now we're just building patterns.'

Chavez spoke through a barely concealed chuckle. ''*Mano*, a white guy like you would stand out in there.'

Ding had a master's degree in international relations, but he could turn on his East LA accent at the drop of a hat.

'Hold up,' Clark said. As the boss, his radio was primary and had the ability to override any chatter – which he frequently did. 'Two Asian males coming out the main entrance now.'

Jack threw his own monocular scope to his eye and got a good look at the two men. In their early twenties, with short cropped hair, both wore faded jeans. Loose white wife-beater shirts displayed arms and shoulders covered with tattoos. They loitered by the doors, each lighting up a cigarette. Ryan could make out the print of a pistol stuffed down the front of one guy's jeans, barely hidden under his shirt. The team had already identified several members of the Sun Yee On triad. Casita Roja was a strip club run by Tres Equis, a small cell of the Sinaloa Cartel known for the three figurative X's formed by a single bullet hole between the two dead eyes of their victims. Since the capture of Joaquín 'El Chapo' Guzmán, factions of the cartel were becoming even more bloody – if more violence than that brought on by the Sinaloa was even possible.

It made sense that everyone in the club would be packing. The men out front spoke in rapid Mandarin – which to Ryan made them sound highly pissed about something.

Midas cocked his head to one side, listening. The Chinese men took a couple cursory looks up and down the street, saw nothing to alarm them, and settled in to smoke and joke. They finished their cigarettes, stood outside, and then talked for two more minutes before going back inside, as if on a time clock.

'I'm guessing those two are triad,' Ryan said.

Midas gave a slow nod. 'Sounds like these Sun Yee On assholes are into some heavy shit with Tres Equis. Prostitution, drugs, you name it. According to these guys, they're supplying the Mexicans precursor chemicals to cook up some meth. My Mandarin's a little rusty, but I'm pretty sure I heard "red phosphorus" in there.'

Clark concurred. 'Thought I caught that.' He wasn't fluent in Mandarin, but he'd been around long enough to pick up more than a few words and suss out the interspersed English. 'Any mention of Eddie Feng?'

'Nope,' Midas said.

Their target, Eddie Feng, was a Taiwanese national. Apart from being addicted to strip clubs and lap dancers, he called himself a reporter for a rag called *Zhenhua Ribao* – *True Word Daily*. This online journal specialized in juicy exposés about the secret lives of the political elite in the People's Republic of China. The *ZRB* was, at best, sensationalized click-bait. At worst, it was just plain fake news.

Gerry Hendley, CEO of Hendley Associates, the financial arbitrage firm and white-side face of The Campus's clandestine activity, would never have approved the unwarranted surveillance of a bona fide journalist. But Eddie Feng was more of an entertainer and propagandist. Feng did, however, appear to have stumbled on something going on with Taiwanese operatives and the PRC.

Jack had found the tenuous connection while comparing some chatter on an Internet forum for the Confucius Institute at the University of Maryland. According to several U of M students, *True Word Daily* had run an article about the bombing of an unfinished subway tunnel on the outskirts of Beijing. There was a lot of detail in the article – at least the translation Jack read – details only someone familiar with the investigation or the person or group who did the bombing would know. Ryan happened to be privy to the same information in the form of a People's Armed Police transmission grab by Fort Meade. This Feng guy was getting too much right about events that would be embarrassing to the ChiComs to be blowing smoke. The PRC hadn't released anything about the subway bombing to the media yet. There was no chatter of it anywhere but for the NSA intercept – and Eddie Feng's article.

Jack had taken his analysis to John Clark, who'd done some research of his own before calling Ryan into a meeting with Gerry – who'd okayed a more intrusive operation. Gavin Biery, IT director for Hendley Associates, would pull up Eddie Feng's bank records, phone history, and anything else he could hack into – which was, according to Biery, 'every digital jot and tittle' there was on the man.

It turned out Eddie Feng had made a recent payment of two thousand dollars to a guy named Fernando Perez Gomez, a car dealer in South Dallas who the Texas Department of Public Safety Gang Intelligence database said had ties to the Tres Equis offshoot of Sinaloa – and a second two thousand dollars to a Sun Yee On triad boss, a recent arrival to Plano, Texas, from Taiwan.

The information was thin, but considering the underworld players involved, and the fact that Eddie Feng had somehow gotten his hands on the information about the Beijing subway bombing, Clark and Hendley had agreed to spool up a short operation and use Eddie Feng as an 'unwitting agent.' Feng would do the hard work, continuing to develop his sources and extracting information from them while they watched from afar and took notes. The Campus team would merely follow him during his investigation, see where he went, and who he met, and learn if he came up with any more useful intel from behind the Bamboo Curtain.

Biery had located Feng when his phone pinged a cell tower in Houston, but by the time the team had spun up and the Hendley Associates Gulfstream was in the air from Washington Reagan, Feng had already moved north. It didn't take him long, though, to get down to business in the Fort Worth–Dallas metroplex. In the past seven hours, the team had followed him to four different strip clubs. None of them were particularly high-class joints, but Casita Roja was definitely the worst. What's more, the club was located in an area of town where a couple bearded white guys like Jack Junior and Midas Jankowski stood out like . . . well, like bearded white guys in the barrio.

Ryan looked at the front door of the club, then back to Midas. 'They say anything else useful?'

'Not really,' Midas said. 'Other than the meth ingredients, they mostly talked about girls and shit.'

Adara Sherman, another member of The Campus's operational cadre who was conversant in Mandarin, came over the net. 'One of them has a girlfriend who dances in this hellhole,' she said.

John Clark spoke next. 'Did the skinny one mention something about a Camaro?'

'He did,' Adara said, obviously impressed.

'Damn,' Ryan said. 'Am I the only one who's not fluent in a bunch of other languages besides English?'

Ding Chavez, John Clark, Adara Sherman, and Dominic Caruso all answered back in turn.

'*Sí.*'

'*Da.*'

'*Oui.*'

'*Hai.*'

Midas turned and looked at Ryan from the passenger seat, giving a little shrug in the darkness.

'Yep,' he said.

'Looks like I need Rosetta Stone or a multilingual girlfriend,' Jack muttered, reaching over the seat to grab the Gatorade bottle. He started to pop off and say something else, but he caught movement out the rear glass as he turned.

He froze.

'John,' he said. 'You got a visual on our six? I've got movement out our back window.'

Clark's slightly muffled voice came back a moment later, giving a play-by-play. Ryan could visualize the man's cheek welded to the comb of his suppressed .308 Winchester model 70, his eye peering through the reticle of a night-vision scope.

'Two Hispanic males,' Clark said. 'One female. Males have pistols tucked in their pants . . . One is carrying a cane or stick . . . Scratch that. It's a golf club . . . The males just left the girl standing at the wall. They're creeping your way, Jack, ten meters and closing.'

'We're moving in from the west,' Chavez said. He was in the crew-cab pickup with Adara, a little more than a block away.

Dom was parked farther out, five blocks up the street in the direction of the next nearest strip club with Hispanic or Asian ties. The location was another educated guess, since Eddie Feng had been working, more or less, along a zigzagging line of such places all day.

'Stay sharp,' Clark hissed. 'These guys are moving slow, tactical . . . Always a chance they could be undercover cops – hang on, the female decided she's coming with them now . . .' From the tone of his voice it was clear he remained on his rifle.

Clark exhaled fast, like a boxer taking a body blow.

'Shit! Not cops. Guy with the golf club just whipped the shit out of the girl.'

''Bout time to unass the car, partner,' Midas said, drawing his sidearm.

'Hold up,' Jack said, his hand on the ignition. 'I got an idea.'

'They're coming up on either side,' Clark said.

He could see the man on his side moving up now, almost at the back of the Taurus.

Ryan looked across the center console at Midas. 'Fling your door open on my mark.'

Midas grinned. 'I like your style.'

Ryan turned the key as the image of a man filled his side mirror. He used his left hand to push his door wide open while at the same moment using his right to throw the Taurus into reverse.

The engine roared to life. Tires chattered on the grimy asphalt and the car shot backward down the alley. The open doors acted like wings catching the two approaching men, knocking them off their feet and dragging them along with the car. Ryan stomped the brakes just after impact. Physics and inertia kept the doors traveling rearward, slamming them shut and pinching the two men between the unforgiving pieces of steel.

Ryan and Midas bolted out of the Taurus on top of their respective assailants. Ryan's was unconscious but still breathing. The broken shaft of a golf club stuck from his right thigh. Midas's man was a little more coherent, but the retired Delta operator solved that by bouncing the man's head off the doorpost.

Ryan and Midas each secured the pistols and did a quick pat-down for other weapons before calling 'clear.'

'No movement from Casita Roja,' Clark said, his voice cool and detached, as if they were still on routine surveillance. 'Ryan, Midas, pull those guys back behind the sewing-machine shop. Ding, you and Adara check on the girl.'

Gravel crunched as Chavez rolled up with Adara Sherman and loaded an unconscious Asian female into their ratty four-door Silverado. Adara's sure voice came over the radio. She'd served as a Navy corpsman in a past life and had seen more than her fair share of wounds and death. 'The girl's still alive, but that asshole broke her nose. Pretty sure her orbital bone is shattered. Good chance she'll have some swelling in her brain.'

'Parkland Hospital is just south of us,' Dom Caruso said. It was his job to keep up with things like emergency rooms and police stations during this rolling surveillance. He gave the complete address of Parkland.

'Roll up to the emergency department,' Clark said. 'Watch for surveillance cameras but drop her off by the door and haul ass out of there before anyone sees you. They'll be used to it around here.'

'Roger that,' Ding said.

Adara climbed into the backseat with the unconscious woman and the pickup backed out of the alley, taking a quick but quiet left toward Parkland Hospital.

'Don't forget to grab her ID,' Clark said. He didn't have to say it would come in handy to build their picture of Eddie Feng's web of associates.

'Way ahead of you, boss,' Adara said. 'No ID, but she does have some kind of brand on the side of her neck. It's covered with blood, but I'll get a photo.'

Clark came over the net again. 'You about done, Jack? We could have company anytime.'

'Just about,' Ryan said.

Both he and Midas donned blue nitrile gloves and leaned the unconscious men against the graffiti-covered back wall of the sewing-machine shop. Neither man carried ID, which was not surprising. Tattoos identifying them both as Tres Equis affiliates were clearly visible on their necks and shoulders.

Ryan and Midas took the rolls of cash from each man's pocket to make it look like a robbery and jumped back into the Taurus. They'd voucher the money and turn it over to Gerry Hendley, who'd find some charity that needed it. Four and a half minutes after Ryan first saw the men coming up behind them, wind whistled through the bent doorframes as he sped toward Harry Hines Boulevard.

'I'll be right behind you,' Clark said. 'We'll stay up on the phone and check in tomorrow. This guy has an inside scoop on a terrorist action in the PRC and now he's involved with drug cartels and the Sun Yee On triad. Something's going on here, boys and girls. I don't know what it is yet, but it's enough to do some more digging into Eddie Feng.'

2

Captain Leong Tang, a thirty-two-year veteran of China Global Shipping Lines, pressed the small of his weary back against a leaning post on the bridge of *Orion*. It was dark outside, but his running lights pushed back the night and illuminated the expansive deck of the great ship.

The big low-pressure system whirling up from the south-west had chased *Orion* across the 124 line and into the mouth of the Strait of Juan de Fuca two hours before. The Canadians controlled the separation of shipping traffic up to roughly the 124th meridian of longitude, but when inbound traffic passed Cape Flattery, US Coast Guard Vessel Traffic Services took control. Seattle Traffic already knew they were coming, even before they took over from the Canadians. Like every legal commercial ship on the seas, *Orion*'s automated information system broadcast a unique identifier. Much like an air traffic controller, the vessel traffic coordinator called in periodically to make *Orion* aware of other commercial vessels, logging tugs, or some other such hazard. Shipping was an around-the-clock business, but Captain Leong could relax and sip his coffee here, even amid the blow outside. Compared to Shanghai, the strait was comparatively dead this time of night. The young woman working VTS was all business but cordial enough. She understood Leong's English – which many other people didn't, no matter how much he studied.

Leong consulted the electronic chart plotter above his console, leaned in to make out the numbers, then nodded to himself. They'd make Ediz Hook in just over an hour. There, they would pick up the pilot who'd drive the ship the rest of the way into the Port of Seattle.

He took a sip of Sumatran coffee from a ceramic mug that bore the image of a blue-and-silver Dallas Cowboys football helmet. He was not a fan of the team or the game. He only kept the mug because, though it signified something so uniquely American, it had MADE IN CHINA etched on the underside. Culturally, Captain Leong should have been drinking tea, but the rigors and travels of a sea captain's life had simply taught him to know better. Chinese tea had a place among women and gentle souls, but sea captains needed coffee, and Captain Leong preferred beans from Sumatra, made even smoother when drunk from his made-in-China Dallas Cowboys mug.

He'd departed Dalian fifteen days before, steaming his way down the eastern coast along the Yellow Sea to make stops in the ports of Tianjin and Qingdao. He topped off his ship at the frenetic Port of Shanghai with six thousand more TEUs filled with buttons, eyeglasses, smartphones, dinnerware, and countless other shiny trinkets bound for American consumers. There were, no doubt, a few drugs and an illicit weapon or two hidden in some of the containers, but the captain was a freight man, not a smuggler.

Anything illegal on board was the fault of the shipper, not the ship.

Captain Leong and his crew of thirty-one souls – seven officers and twenty-four 'ratings,' or able-bodied seamen – had steamed *Orion* out of the busiest seaport in the world at precisely midnight. Navigating the heavily used sea lanes was made easier for the monstrous ship by a harbor pilot and two tugboats. They left under cover of darkness, not because they wanted to hide anything, but because that's when the last TEU was secured to the deck and the final piece of paperwork was signed and stamped by port officials. Captain Leong wanted his ship loading, unloading, or sailing. Anything else was wasted time – and money.

At 165,000 tons, and fifty meters longer than an American *Nimitz*-class aircraft carrier, *Orion* required a great deal of space for the basic maneuvers of simply stopping and turning. Two tugboats worked in concert with the Shanghai pilot on board to assist her in negotiating the crowded waters of the harbor, one ready to bump the side, the other with a steering cable off the ship's stern. They cleared the entrance in less than an hour. The pilot exited through the bunker door below the bridge castle and hopped onto one of the tugs, leaving the huge vessel to her own devices and the crew's good seamanship.

Orion's powerful Wärtsilä diesel pushed her northeast on glassy seas at a steady twenty-two knots. The design of his mammoth container vessel made it impossible for Captain Leong to see the water directly around his ship, but he could imagine *Orion*'s bulbous bow pushing up a frothy white wake on either side. A British sailor would say she'd 'taken the bone in her teeth.'

The crew had watched the sparkling lights of Shanghai grow dim and finally wink out behind them, leaving them alone in the purple night. Shortly after sunrise, *Orion* sailed below the southern Japanese island of Kyushu to catch the dark waters of the Kuroshio Current. Similar to the Gulf

Stream of the Atlantic, the Kuroshio flowed up from the equator, pushing her warm waters north and east – and saving Captain Leong and his company precious fuel.

The massive ship moved through several squalls as it reached the halfway point of the journey. Then, for the next three days, Captain Leong watched the radar above his helm as a giant blob of low pressure brought cooler temperatures and confused seas. Exposed to the westerlies of the open Pacific, the strait offered little protection from the wind and waves. By the time they crossed the 124, gusts were forty knots and sustained winds had reached thirty. Waves were three and four meters high, but that was okay. Leong's ship was big, and cut through four-meter waves like they were barely even there. It was too dark to see the shore of Washington's Olympic Peninsula or his starboard side, but he could almost pick up the hint of sawdust and sap from the endless mountain forests. He liked the Pacific Northwest. There was a quietness to the place that calmed him, even in heavy seas.

Safely tucked inside the heated bridge, the captain yawned in spite of the nasty blow outside. Any fool could drive a boat on calm waters. It took a real seaman to save fuel in a storm, aboard a box carrying boxes that were filled with boxes.

Leong Tang supposed boys in every country that was bordered by a sea were somehow beckoned by the lure of salt and wind and adventure. But there was no lure in boxes. The captain hardly even noticed them anymore. They were merely gray or blue or red blobs that he looked over and around to try to catch a glimpse of the horizon or the lights of the next port.

He had no idea what was in any of the containers. There was, of course, a manifest, but the modern ship's master found himself buried under mountains of paperwork between ports, and Leong simply didn't have the time – or the inclination – to read it. Dangerous goods were noted, refrigerated containers were stowed together – and, unless another dozen Fujianese stowaways had hidden themselves away in one of the TEUs as they had the year before, there shouldn't be anything alive in any of the containers.

While the TEU had changed the nature of shipping, progress had changed the inside of the modern seagoing vessel. *Orion*'s helm was not the beefy wooden wheel of Leong's seafaring forefathers, but high-impact plastic – and most of the steering was done through the computer and a small bump lever. A bank of screens above the helm displayed the radar, the ECDIS electronic charts, a depth sounder, radio frequency, a tachometer, and the AIS. This Automatic Identifications System broadcast the ship's name, speed, and heading to port authorities, passing ships, and if they were savvy enough to have the app for their smartphones, pirates.

Fortunately, Seattle had no pirates, but for the company that pumped the shit from the ships' holding tanks. Their prices were outrageous.

With all the soulless plastic, the only nod toward a more traditional helm was the half-sphere compass, its magnetic correction noted on a metal plate affixed to the plastic beside it.

It cost just over one American penny to ship a can of beer across the Pacific, but with that efficiency came the loss of soul. Lightning-quick unloading and loading made it impossible for Leong to give his men liberty in all but a very few ports. And even then, most of them would not be able to make it past the razor-wire fences that cordoned off the MARSEC area of the docks.

It seemed to Captain Leong that he'd sailed out of one port when sailing had provided him an exotic life of adventure, and then, over the course of that single voyage, while he was not paying attention, it had become a job. Storms like this at least made him feel like a sailor.

And still, the job did have its good points. He did have a few quiet moments to read. The Chinese government frowned on organized religion, but a decade earlier, a zealous dockworker in the Philippines had gifted him a small copy of the King James Bible – and he'd read it many times.

'Better to dwell in the corner of a roof than in a wide house with a brawling woman,' the Proverb said. And when Captain Leong thought about his sniping wife, his life at sea seemed less like the corner of a roof than it actually was.

Leong heard the squeak of the hatch behind him and turned to see Goos, the Balinese steward, enter with a platter of fresh doughnuts. At seventeen, Goos – short for Bagus, meaning 'handsome' in Bali – was by far the youngest pair of hands on the ship. In Leong's estimation, he was also the brightest.

'Captain,' the boy said in English, giving him a polite nod.

'Goos,' Leong said, toasting the air with his Dallas Cowboys mug.

The boy spoke passable Mandarin, but he was attempting to learn English – the international language of commerce — and it helped Leong and his first officer to try to teach him. It was good practice for the times they needed to communicate via the radio with VTS.

Goos held up the doughnuts. 'Mr Hao . . . cook . . . doughnut,' he said.

'Good English,' the captain said. 'I like doughnuts.'

Goos smiled. 'I like doughnuts.'

The captain closed his eyes to breathe in the heady smell of the fried dough. He opened his mouth to speak but was cut off by a loud pop. At first he thought some piece of gear had fallen outside, but a violent shudder ran through the length of entire ship, as if they'd run aground.

Leong's eyes shot open. He set the coffee mug in the slot beside his leaning post and scanned the instruments. The depth sounder showed 119 fathoms — more than seven hundred feet. Perhaps they'd hit something. Countless TEUs went overboard each year. Most sank shortly after hitting the water, but some lurked just below the surface like drifting reefs. Perhaps *Orion* had struck one of them, or even a flotilla of logs. Her hull was thick and made to withstand such an impact, but any strike was reason to worry.

Half a breath later, a massive explosion rocked the aft decks. The bank of windows along the rear of the bridge castle shattered from the oncoming shockwave. Bits of glass peppered the men like a shotgun blast. Leong grabbed young Goos by the collar and dragged him behind the captain's chair, out of the path of flying debris. First Officer Su was already there.

Outside, heavy containers shot skyward like so many children's toys, disappearing into the darkness to fall into the sea or crashing back down on the rail to burst and spill their clothing and electronics into the water. Leong couldn't feel the blood from the wounds running down his cheek, but he saw tiny cubes of shatterproof glass embedded in Su's face. Goos's black hair was covered in the stuff.

Windows gone, the gale outside moaned in, whipping through the cabin, lifting papers and ripping away the warmth. The smell of burning plastic and the sharp, acidic odor of molten metal flowed in on the back of the wind.

The aft deck lights had gone dark, but Leong watched in horror as a pillar of white fire five meters wide shot like a geyser from among what was left of the TEUs, illuminating the ship as if it were midday.

The captain looked away from the stunning brightness and clapped his hands to clear First Officer Su from his stupor.

'Call Engineering and get a report,' he said. 'There will surely be injuries. Goos, get on the intercom and tell Mr Huang to stand by in the galley.' Huang had trained as a medic in the PLA Navy and was the closest thing to a doctor on board the ship.

Alarms sounded amid the moaning gale and the shouts of terrified men. Stack after stack of shipping containers listed heavily to starboard. Lashing rods snapped, cracking like gunfire, and the boxes toppled one by one into the angry sea. Wind whipped the heavy black smoke, at once making it easier for Leong to see the carnage and fanning the flames.

The white pillar continued to roar upward from the bowels of the ship.

Warning lights on the console changed from green to red, flashing urgently as system after system failed.

The ship's intercom broke squelch and the breathless voice of Jimmy, a Filipino deck rating, filled the bridge.

'Captain,' the man stammered in English. 'I . . . need help, sir . . .'

Goos reached up for the microphone and passed it off to the captain.

'Where are you?' Leong asked.

'Engineering . . .'

'I must speak with Mr Duan.'

Leong's English was good, but in times like these, he preferred to talk to a native of China. Duan was the engineer, the man with the training to understand the questions Leong needed to have answered.

'That . . . that is not possible,' the deck rating said. 'Mr Duan is . . . gone.'

'Gone?' Leong whispered. He put a hand on top of his head in dismay. Outside, containers continued to fall over the rails on both sides and a fearsome groan ran the length of the ship. Leong imagined some awful beast had escaped a TEU and was now running rampant down below.

Jimmy grew more breathless with every word, choking back sobs. 'I . . . I was helping him change a filter . . . then it . . .' He coughed, probably from smoke. 'There were many explosions from above and then . . . the most terrible noise. Captain, do you believe in Hell?'

'I do not,' Leong said, willing himself to remain calm. It did no good to scream at times like this. He prodded the terrified man. 'What happened, Jimmy?'

'A ball of white fire . . . It just dropped.'

'Through the ceiling?' Leong said.

'Yes. From above the compartment just aft of the Wärt.' The rating used the nickname for the engine.

'And Mr Duan?' Leong whispered.

'He . . . fell, sir.'

'Fell?' Leong gasped. 'He is injured?'

'You do not understand,' the rating said. 'The fire burned through the deck. Mr Duan fell into the . . .' The man sniffed, obviously trying to compose himself. 'Captain, the deck melted beneath his feet. He is gone.'

'Okay,' Leong said, trying to imagine the unimaginable scene. 'Get out of there.'

'I cannot, Captain.' Another gasp turned into a frightened whimper. 'The fire . . . it was very bright. I saw Mr Duan fall, but I cannot see anything. The flames are close. I feel the heat. I will fall if I try to move.'

'Stay where you are,' the captain said. It was no wonder the man was terrified. 'I will send someone to collect you.'

'Please . . . hur –'

The line filled with static, then went dead.

Leong's head snapped up to look at Su. The first officer had pulled a thick binder labeled FIRE PROCEDURES from below the console and thumbed through it with trembling fingers.

'Wen!' the captain said, calling the addled man by his given name in an effort to steady him. 'Put that away and go to Engineering. Remind everyone you see to put on their life vests. Some will forget in these moments of confusion.'

The first officer gave a curt nod, then, grabbing his own life jacket from a compartment under the navigation table, ducked his head and moved to the hatch leading to the aft deck.

Goos looked back and forth from the open hatch to the captain. 'I will go with him,' he said, waiting for permission.

The captain nodded, picking up the radio phone.

'Goos!' he said as the young Balinese steward started down the stairs to the aft passageway. The boy turned, only his head above the deck. 'A white flame means a metal fire. Make certain to use the dry Class D extinguishers only. Water will make it worse. And put on a life vest!'

The boy scrambled back up the stairs to retrieve a life jacket from the locker below the console.

A tremendous roar filled the night air. As if to lend credence to the captain's fears, the shriek of rending metal carried in from the aft decks. A shower of white-hot sparks shot skyward out of the gaping hole. The body of a man dressed in flame-retardant coveralls followed, pushed upward on a geyser of steam and flames. Leong watched helplessly as the man fell straight back down, into the same fiery pit from which he'd come.

Now he believed in Hell.

He turned to Goos. The boy was paler now, his chin quivering. He'd seen the whole thing.

'Go,' Leong said, hoping the boy would understand the instructions given in Mandarin. 'Keep your –'

Something heavy hit him in the head. He saw Goos's terrified face, and then nothing.

Goos had watched in horror as the shard of metal from a ripped container whirred in like a sawblade and struck Captain Leong in the back of the head. Goos ducked instinctively, and when he looked up, the poor man was face down in a pool of blood and shattered glass.

The boy found himself alone on the bridge. He grabbed the intercom to call for the first officer, but it was dead. The gale moaned outside, rain and wind whipping through the shattered windows.

The radio microphone hung from the console on a coiled cord, swaying with the heaving motion of the ship.

Goos had been on the bridge during man-overboard drills. He knew how to work the radio. And if there was ever a time to call for help, it was now. What he did not know was how to speak English.

He stayed low as he reached for the dangling mic, hiding behind the captain's chair to keep from meeting the same fate.

Goos depressed the key on the side of the mic and said the only words he knew that would get help coming his way:

'Mayday, mayday . . . Man overboard . . .'

A female voice crackled over the radio a moment later. 'US Coast Guard Seattle Sector, ship calling mayday, please say your location.'

'Yes!' Goos said, happy to hear a voice. 'Yes! Man overboard! Please to help us!'

A horrible clatter rose from the belly of the ship, as if a dragon had gotten loose in the engine room. A moment later, the clatter abated and the steady thrum of the Wärt fell silent. Powerless, *Orion* shuddered and began to turn broadside to the waves, at the mercy of the gale.

Out on the demolished deck, rain did little to beat back the wall of fire, now fanned by a wicked wind. Metal groaned and men screamed. The bow began to lift as the aft portion of the ship wallowed lower in the water, flooding compartment by mangled compartment.

Goos felt the ship rise under him and huddled among the glass and debris on the floor of the wheelhouse, clutching his knees to his chest and trying to focus on the female voice speaking on the radio. He didn't understand her, but he prayed she was sending help.

3

The straits operator, Petty Officer 3rd Class Barb Pennington, leaned back in the swivel chair, scanning the dotted traffic lanes on the six color monitors above her workstation in the Seattle Vessel Traffic Services. It was late and she'd just taken a sip of coffee when a terrified voice crackled into her headset. She rocked forward immediately, as if getting nearer to her computer screens would help her hear better.

'Chinese container ship *Orion* reporting a man overboard, Chief,' Petty Officer Pennington said as her supervisor walked up beside her. 'AIS shows him two miles west of Pillar Point. I spoke with the vessel captain at 0114 hours when he crossed the 124 line. It sounds like a different person making the report. I was able to get him to switch to channel 16, but he's not responding to any other questions.'

The watch supervisor nodded. 'Man overboard. Understood.' He passed the call to the command duty officer in the Joint Harbor Operations Center on the other side of the frosted glass wall.

The CDO, Chief Petty Officer George Rodriguez, assigned a JHOC operations specialist named Sally Fry to monitor the call through Rescue 21, an advanced maritime C4 (computing, command, control, and communications) program. Rescue 21 used a variety of fixed towers to vector

36

the ship's position each time it transmitted, superimposing a line of position on a digital chart. Best case scenario, the transmission hit multiple towers and took the 'search' out of search and rescue, but even one tower would put the distressed vessel somewhere along that given line.

In a calm but authoritative voice belying her junior status and twenty-three years of age, Petty Officer Fry engaged the young man at the other end of the radio in a conversation during which he said little but 'Man overboard' and 'Please to help.'

Both the straits operator and the operations specialist were female, and the transfer went so smoothly that the person reporting the mayday never knew he'd been passed from Vessel Traffic Services to the rescue management side of the JHOC house.

A time clock began the moment the command duty officer became aware of the distress call.

Chief Rodriguez looked across his workstation and nodded at the Operations Unit specialist, who returned the nod, letting the chief know he was already building a case in Search and Rescue Optimal Planning System. Among many other nuanced factors, SAROPS accounted for pre-distress vessel movement, present wind speed, and water currents, generating an estimated location of the vessel when rescue assets arrived.

Next, Rodriguez picked up the phone and activated Air Station Port Angeles to spin up their B-Zero response crew and get the ready-helo flying toward *Orion*. Anyone watching the process might have thought the call happened simultaneously with his other actions – and they would not be far from wrong. As command duty officer,

Chief Rodriguez had the authority to send assets before even notifying his boss, the search-and-rescue mission coordinator.

The SMC made it crystal clear. When it came to SAR, the initial response of the US Coast Guard was to 'go there.'

The junior duty officer at Coast Guard Air Station Port Angeles answered the phone on the first ring. CDO Rodriguez passed on the information to the JDO, who repeated it back, then hung up and pressed the extension for the senior duty officer, Lieutenant Commander Andrew Slaznik, pilot in command of the B-Zero response helicopter.

Each Coast Guard air station in the United States had at least one B-Zero response crew on duty at any given time. They slept next to the hangar and were ready to deploy inside a thirty-minute window. Each SDO had his or her own way of doing things, and this one liked to be called prior to the SAR launch alarm being activated.

The SDO answered quickly for so early in the morning. 'This is Mr Slaznik,' he said, his words thick with sleep. The pilots were accustomed to these middle-of-the-night calls. Lieutenant Commander Slaznik seemed to live for them.

The JDO relayed the scant information regarding *Orion*'s man-overboard report and the SDO repeated it back to assure the petty officer he was awake and moving.

'Let's go ahead and wake up the crew,' he added, before hanging up.

The SAR alarm wailed a moment later, wresting his co-pilot, Lieutenant Becky Crumb, from a deep sleep in the adjacent room. Slaznik called her cell phone, just to

CONTAINER SHIP *ORION*
IN THE STRAIT OF JUAN DE FUCA

N

CANADA
USA

VICTORIA

CGSL ORION   Strait of Juan de Fuca

PORT ANGELES
COAST GUARD STATION

Pacific
Ocean

SEATTLE

© 2017 Jeffrey L. Ward

make sure she heard the siren, and said in his best Arnold Schwarzenegger voice, 'Get to the choppa!'

The flight mechanic and rescue swimmer slept in a building closer to the hangar and nearer to the alarm.

Slaznik splashed cold water on his face and smoothed the bed head out of his dark hair. He sat on the edge of his rack while he pulled up local weather and any Notices to Airmen on the Electronic Flight Bag program on his iPad. Winds gusting to forty with heavy rain in the strait. He groaned. As a helicopter pilot, he didn't mind the wind. In fact, wind helped him with his hover when the bird was heavy, but it wreaked havoc on the hoist cable and made the rescue swimmer's job all the more difficult. And his swimmer on this crew was a newbie, fresh out of thirteen weeks' training. They'd gone out earlier that day on a jumper from the Tacoma Narrows Bridge, but locals had fished the body out before they got there, so it wasn't a real call-out. The kid had handled himself well, asked good questions during the CRM open conversation Slaznik encouraged during any mission. This was going to be different. The kid was going to get wet. The weather was skosh, but it was a good thing he was going to cut his teeth on a simple man-in-the-water operation.

Firsthand experience in cold water cajoled the SDO along in his routine. People who fell off ships rarely wore any sort of protective suit – and without any protection, the window for survival began to close at an extremely rapid rate.

Slaznik would check the weather again before he launched. Marginal weather at the station often sucked severely farther west in the strait. He pushed a speed-dial number on his cell and made his first call the OPS boss at home, holding the phone to his ear with a shoulder while he stepped into his Switlik dry suit.

It was a goofy thing and he didn't admit it to anyone other than his wife, but he loved that orange suit. Wearing it along with the black SAR Warrior survival vest made him feel like a superhero.

He didn't mind getting up in the middle of the night. Like his five-year-old son said, that's when superheroes were needed the most.

Andy Slaznik had known he would someday become a pilot from the moment he saw his first crop duster growl overhead to drop a marker at the end of a row on four hundred acres of canola at his grandfather's farm. He was nine years old, and his family had been visiting his mother's parents in southern Alberta. The Piper Pawnee Brave had seemed low enough to reach up and touch.

Andy begged his granddad to make the hour drive to the Lethbridge city library, where he checked out as many books on aviation as he could fit in his scrawny arms – and then devoured them all in three days. His room back in Boise became a gallery of plastic models, and he bored his friends to tears with an intricate and ever-growing knowledge of each and every aircraft that hung from the spackled ceiling on bits of sewing thread.

An uncanny memory and a natural knack for math worked in concert to give Slaznik an SAT score of 1464. Midway through his junior year, he began the lengthy application process to both the United States Air Force Academy and the United States Military Academy at West Point. His GPA, superior SAT score, and a sub-two-minute 800-meter time on his high school track team got him accepted to weeklong programs at each school during the summer break before he was a senior.

The Air Force liaison from nearby Mountain Home AFB took one look at the boy's stats and pushed him hard to keep his sights firmly fixed on the Wild Blue U. But a guidance counselor suggested he might consider the Coast Guard Academy. She told him that because of its smaller class size, the USCGA was considered more selective. She then said maybe he should forget it. It might be a great deal of work with such a slim chance of being accepted.

The challenge alone appealed to Andrew's competitive nature. He liked to prove he could excel at the hard stuff. He knew that the Navy and the Coast Guard both had aircraft – and some hotshot pilots – but they also had boats, a lot of boats. Andrew didn't want to do boats. He wanted to fly. And besides, the Air Force liaison kept reminding him that if he ever wanted to be an astronaut, he needed to go with the Zoomies.

In the end, it was the guidance counselor's thrown gauntlet that found Andrew Slaznik sitting with a class of thirty-four other AIM summer-program cadet wannabes in New London, Connecticut, listening to various old-timers answer questions about their respective jobs. The discussion was informative enough, but there was far too much talk about boats. Andrew found his mind wandering, thinking about how cool it would be to tell his friends he was an astronaut.

And then a tall, gangly, redheaded MH-65 Dolphin helicopter pilot took the microphone. He'd been last on the program – and, looking back, Andrew understood why.

None of the other pros wanted to follow this guy. The pilot regaled the eager young students with stories of killer winds and night flights over mountainous seas. To hear this guy tell it, he got into hairy situations every other day.

It was Andrew who asked the final question of the night, and even as he spoke, he felt his mind drift again, pondering what the guys at Colorado Springs had to offer him. Surely the Air Force had hundreds of pilots with swagger and stories like this guy.

Andrew stood to ask the question. 'Sir,' he said. 'How many people would you say you've saved over the course of your career?'

The redheaded chopper pilot was a lieutenant commander. Probably in his early thirties, still a few years away from making O-5, where he'd be forced into grad school and flying a desk more than his bird. He listened to the question, then leaned back in his chair and stared at the ceiling for a few seconds, moving his fingers over his thumb as if counting. After a moment, he looked up at Andrew and clarified.

'Do you mean pulled some retired granddad with a bad case of food poisoning off a cruise ship or literally plucked somebody from the jaws of a watery death?'

The cadet wannabes all chuckled.

'Let's go with plucked from the jaws of death,' Andrew said, thinking maybe he'd hit a nerve.

The pilot gave a humble shrug. 'Thirty-seven,' he said.

The room grew quiet as a church.

Andrew Slaznik returned to Boise, where, later that year, he received congressional nominations for both USAFA and West Point. He was formally accepted to

43

each school. The Air Force Academy sent an early admission letter in an effort to preempt him from accepting another offer. But five weeks after he graduated high school, and to the chagrin of the Air Force liaison from Mountain Home, his parents dropped him in New London, Connecticut, for Reporting day – colloquially called 'R-day' – at the United States Coast Guard Academy.

Cadet Slaznik memorized every word of Reef Points – the pocket-sized cadet bible of Coast Guard general knowledge – gritted his teeth through the seven-week horror show of 'Swab Summer,' and plowed through the rest of his freshman year. Four years later, after learning not to be such a self-important ass, he graduated third from the top of his class with a degree in mechanical engineering – and a tolerance for boats.

With a fresh set of ensign boards on his shoulders, Slaznik's academic standing opened the door to flight school, and, after a battery of rigorous physical tests and an in-depth background where OPM investigators asked with complete sincerity if his mother's family had ever urged him to spy for the Canadians, he was admitted to rotary wing training at Naval Air Station Pensacola. He finished up training in his Coast Guard air frame in Mobile, Alabama.

And even now, Lieutenant Commander Andrew Slaznik got chills every time he walked with a swagger out to the flight line and his own MH-65 Dolphin, because few weeks went by that he didn't have an opportunity to pluck someone from the jaws of death.

4

Dressed in his orange dry suit, Lieutenant Commander Slaznik logged in to the Aviation Logistics Management Information System across from the watch captain's desk to check maintenance records. The air station had three MH-65s, but it was a rare moment when at least one wasn't undergoing some kind of maintenance. The Coast Guard seemed to operate under the 'have three to make one' rule when it came to helicopters. In this case, two birds were operational, so Slaznik flipped a coin and signed out 6521. He made a second call to the OPS boss, who'd already touched bases with JHOC and been informed there was also a forty-seven-foot response boat out of Neah Bay near the mouth of the strait, responding to the mayday. Co-pilot Lieutenant Becky Crumb was already outside doing the preflight and starting the helo. She was quick and efficient, which was good, because now that he knew surface assets were on the way, Slaznik's competitive nature kicked into high gear. He knew the boat crews in Neah Bay, and they were every bit as competitive. Not a bad thing, really. The guy in the water didn't much care who got there first.

Eighteen minutes from the JDO's call, the two pilots walked through a steady rain and climbed into their orange bird – sometimes called 'Tupperwolf' or 'Plastic Fantastic' by other, less discerning pilots – and began their instrument checks. Slaznik preferred to sit in the left seat and run the radios while he flew, but Crumb was new and not yet hoist-qualified, so Slaznik took the right side. The flight mech and rescue swimmer got themselves situated in the back. Eight minutes after that, Slaznik flipped down his ANVIZ 9 night-vision goggles and called Whidbey Island Approach to request clearance to take off to the west, advising them he had Information Bravo.

With flight clearance given, he added throttle and pulled up the collective to bring the Dolphin into a hover. The seventy-mile-per-hour rotor wash drove the rain into the ever-present goose crap on the runway, throwing it into the upwash and spattering green slime across the windscreen.

'That is so nasty,' Lieutenant Crumb muttered, before depressing the microphone and transmitting to the JHOC.

'Rescue 6521 departing Air Station Port Angeles with four souls on board. ETA Pillar Point fourteen minutes . . .'

Lieutenant Commander Slaznik checked with the rest of his crew, who each gave him a thumbs-up. 6521's tail came up slightly and she shuddered, like a racehorse in the gates. 'Gauges in the green,' Slaznik said, performing one final scan of his instruments an instant before he eased the cyclic forward to scoot down the runway. 'This looks, smells, and feels like a helicopter. We're on the go.'

In the rearmost seat of Rescue 6521, mounted almost flush to the deck, Rescue Swimmer Lance Kitchen checked his gear for the second time since boarding the aircraft. He was five-feet-ten, 172 pounds. At twenty-four, and a recent graduate of the monumentally strenuous thirteen-week Coast Guard Rescue Swimmer School in Elizabeth City,

North Carolina, he was in the best shape of his life. The darkness was nothing to him now. Dangling on a spinning cable above an angry sea was second nature. Black water and big waves called his name. What he feared was failure – more specifically, any failure brought about because of something he missed.

Unlike the other members of the SAR crew, Petty Officer 2nd Class Kitchen's gear reflected the fact that he planned to get in the water. A scuba mask and snorkel were affixed to the top of his windsurfing helmet, along with a strobe that would allow the pilots to keep him in sight in heavy seas. His black Triton swimmer vest harness contained, among other things, a regulator and small pony bottle of air, a Benchmade automatic knife, a 405 personal locator beacon, and a waterproof Icom radio with an earpiece. An EMT paramedic, he'd leave the bulk of his trauma gear on the chopper to utilize once he got the guy in the basket and hoisted him up. Heavy rubber jet fins hung from a clip on his high-visibility orange DUI dry suit. He'd slip them on when they got to the scene, just before he attached himself to the hoist.

With the gear and mind-set checks complete, Kitchen sat back in his seat and looked at the Seiko dive watch on his wrist. Eleven minutes out. One man in the water. Simple. He could do this.

Tilda Pederson, the captain of *Ocean Treasure*, was on the bridge when she heard *Orion*'s initial mayday broadcast on 22 Alpha, the communications channel with Seattle VTS. The luxury cruise ship was returning from a twenty-five-day round-trip cruise to Hawaii. She was making twenty-four knots in order to pick up her pilot near Port Angeles and make her berthing time of 0700.

She put a pair of blue marine binoculars to her eyes and looked at the orange glow on the water ahead. 'Man overboard,' she repeated, half to herself.

'Captain,' Alberto said. 'The radar shows what appear to be multiple small craft suddenly in the water.'

Pederson lowered the binoculars. 'Small craft? How many?'

'At least thirty by my count. They completely surround the *Orion*. I would guess she's losing containers overboard.'

'A fair assessment.' Pederson studied the multiple blips on the radar. They looked like a swarm of silver dots around the much larger vessel. An orange glow now filled the horizon ahead. Pederson's binoculars went back up to her eyes. 'Alberto,' she said, 'keep a weather eye for floating containers, but bring us up to best speed. That ship is on fire.'

Fourteen miles to the east of *Ocean Treasure*, Slaznik and Crumb flipped up their NVGs at the sudden brightness in front of their helicopter.

'Holy shit!' Kitchen said, surveying the conflagration in the water ahead.

'Man overboard my ass,' the flight mech said, nose pressed to the helicopter's window as they made a tight circle over the carnage. The bulbous bow of the container ship pointed upward while the stern was completely submerged, like an enormous whale slipping backward into the water. The ship itself was on fire, but if that weren't bad enough, floating oil and diesel surrounded the rear portion in a wall of flames.

JHOC comms center squawked over the radio. 'Rescue 6521, we're getting reports of a vessel fire off Pillar Point . . .'

Slaznik swung wide, flying slowly around the burning ship, assessing the situation.

Crumb craned her neck as they went around. 'I count eleven souls up on the forepeak,' she said.

'At least three in the water,' the flight mech said. 'Thirty yards off the bow. I don't think they're in Gumby suits.'

Slaznik brought the Dolphin around for another pass, burning a few more pounds of fuel to give him more hover time, while he briefed JHOC and requested more assets.

Slaznik keyed the intercom. 'The 47 is still twenty-two minutes out. Lots of fire down there, Kitchen. How do you feel about going down in flames?'

The swimmer strained at his harness, wanting to get out of the helicopter. 'Looks good around the bow, boss,' he said. 'I say we kick out our crew raft to give the survivors something to hang on to while I get started.'

Lieutenant Crumb's voice came over the intercom. 'That ship's going down fast. Two more just did a Peter Pan off the bow.'

The helicopter was finally light enough to hover within regs, so Slaznik reduced power, utilizing the wind as he descended toward the waves. Rain pelted the windscreen. The gale roared in as the flight mechanic slid open the side door. The RAT OUT – radar altimeter alarm – sounded at forty feet above the water. Twelve-to-sixteen-foot waves and unpredictable winds kept him hovering there. The radios were blowing up with chatter from JHOC,

Whidbey Island, and an assortment of responding surface vessels.

Slaznik had chosen a lone survivor floundering a good thirty meters from the others on the port side of the vessel, reasoning that this one was alone and had probably been in the water longer than those who were grouped together.

Ninety seconds later, the flight mechanic lowered Kitchen down toward the surface on the hoist. The basket went down next and came up with a survivor, dazed and shaking but very much alive. Kitchen sent up five more, one after the other.

The 47 arrived but was soon busy at the wallowing stern, picking its way through floating containers and pools of fire. The Coast Guard boat crew had already pulled in two survivors and were heading toward a pocket of at least two more who appeared to be stuck behind a wall of flaming diesel.

Lieutenant Crump tapped the console. 'Commander, we're nearing bingo fuel.'

The MH-65 had a flight window of about two hours and twenty minutes – and a requirement that she come back with at least twenty minutes of reserve fuel. Pillar Point was slightly closer to Neah Bay to the west than it was to Port Angeles. Landing in Neah Bay for fuel would get the survivors on the ground for treatment sooner, extend Slaznik's available flight time by a precious few minutes, and get him back into action.

He raised the rescue swimmer on the radio.

'We're packed to the gills up here,' Slaznik said, looking out his window at Kitchen, who rode the frothy waves in the seventy-mile-per hour prop wash. The swimmer worked steadily to try to keep ten survivors together around the small six-person flight-crew raft they'd kicked out of the helicopter. None of the survivors spoke English, and Slaznik was sure it was a lot like herding cats down there. 'You good to hold down the fort? We have to go and offload these survivors.'

Kitchen didn't hesitate. 'Roger that. We'll be here when you get back.'

Slaznik spoke into the radio as he added power, gaining altitude.

'Coast Guard Neah Bay, Rescue 6521 heading to you with six survivors. The flight mech will fill you in on their condition. Break. Kitchen, you hold tight. We'll be back in a flash.'

Petty Officer Kitchen used the stiff jet fins to kick through the chop, directing the panicked seamen toward the crew raft he'd dropped out of the helicopter. The raft was meant for only six passengers, but Kitchen would stack them in like cordwood to await rescue from either the 47 boat from Neah Bay or 6521 when they returned. The bright yellow raft riding the waves should have been self-explanatory, but if Kitchen had learned anything about rescue operations, it was that cold and drowning men were unpredictable. He used hand signals and, when needed, physical force to direct the seamen. He'd already elbowed a particularly aggressive one in the solar plexus when the guy had tried to climb on top of him and use him as a human ladder to board the bobbing life raft. A couple of the men – one looked as if he was still a teenager – had the sense to hang on to the outer rings and direct their shipmates, calling out amid the wind and spray.

Behind them, the mammoth ship groaned and hissed, shooting jets of spray into the air from every crack and ruptured seam as she slid deeper into the water. Kitchen could have imagined the seven hundred feet of blackness below him, the possibility of being crushed between half-submerged shipping containers that were tossed around in the mountainous waves. He could have focused on the fact that he was alone in the middle of an unforgiving sea with ten men who were about to claw one another's eyes out in an effort to keep from drowning. But he didn't.

He was too busy.

5

Jack Ryan awoke at four fifty-one a.m., a full thirty-nine minutes before he got up on a normal day – but then, as President of the United States, *normal* was a subjective term.

Cathy was out of town with the kids, performing cataract surgeries in Nepal. School wasn't exactly in full swing, but it had already started for the year, and Ryan wasn't too happy about Katie and Kyle missing the first few weeks. Katie had pointed out that while she fully agreed that school was important, a deep understanding of world culture was also crucial. Travel to Nepal, she reasoned, would add to that understanding in a way no classroom could. 'China canceled travel visas for people that wanted to go there, just to keep the Tibetans from sneaking into India, Dad! Don't you want me to visit someplace the ChiComs say is off-limits?' Ryan's wife bristled at the use of 'ChiComs,' and he'd had to remind Katie it wasn't especially diplomatic for the President's daughter to use the word in reference to the communist Chinese – no matter what she might overhear him saying in the White House.

His daughter's logic was sound and emotional – leaving Ryan to live in mortal fear that she would decide to be an attorney. So the kids went with Cathy to Nepal – and Jack Ryan found himself alone.

He arched his back, ticking through the myriad old injuries that stitched his body. He had more than a few, and some woke up slower than others. Sitting up against his pillow, he glanced at the bedside table and the five-by-seven photograph of his wife and him on the docks at Annapolis. They were standing with his old friend and mentor, the late Admiral James Greer. The photo customarily occupied a place of honor on top of his cherrywood dresser, but it was Ryan's favorite picture of Cathy, so he moved it to the side table whenever she went out of town.

Ryan reached for his glasses and stood, wincing when his feet hit the carpet. He cast another glance at the photograph, getting a clearer view now. Jeez, his hair was so dark back then. 'That's just like you, Cathy,' he mumbled, 'going off to restore poor people's vision when I need you here to rub my aching foot.'

With his wife performing medical miracles and no opportunity to engage in what the Secret Service euphemistically referred to as 'discussing the situation in Belgrade,' Ryan was up and seated on the rowing machine in the residence gym by 5:05. An hour later found him showered and dressed in a pair of gray wool slacks and a white French-cuffed shirt that had been laid out for him while he was in the gym. He left the blood-red power tie on the bed, preferring to wait until he finished breakfast before he consigned himself to the noose.

The Navy steward, a young petty officer named Martinez, followed Ryan's location in the residence by watching a lighted panel that indicated POTUS's whereabouts as he moved across the pressure-sensitive pads under the carpet of the bedroom, gym, shower, and back to the bedroom. Accustomed to the President's schedule, the steward had breakfast ready on a side table in his study by the time he was dressed.

The First Lady had given strict instructions to the White House chef that her husband's breakfasts should consist of oatmeal, skim milk, and raisins during her absence. Ryan quickly countermanded that order, offering a presidential pardon to whatever punishments his wife might dole out if she ever discovered he was eating a buttered croissant and two poached eggs.

Ryan spread the front page of *The Wall Street Journal* beside his plate on the white linen tablecloth. He'd heard it said that when it came to food, the eye ate first – but he'd always preferred to let his eyes work independently of his plate. He read and hardly looked at his food but to plot the correct aim with his fork. Twenty minutes later, he carried the unfinished pages of the *Journal*, along with the *Post* and *The New York Times*, to a more comfortable chair. He could have gone into the office, but when he went in, others thought they had to come in, and he saw no reason to get everyone else spun up just because his wife was in Nepal.

Ahead of schedule, he allowed himself to linger a little over the papers and sip his coffee while he enjoyed some thinking time in the quiet of morning. In no time, things would speed up to their usual breakneck pace and he would have to start making decisions, 'wielding his cosmic power for good,' his chief of staff would say. Ryan laughed at the thought. As a boy, growing up in the house with his policeman father, power had smelled like Hoppes No. 9 gun oil and strong coffee. Here in the White House it smelled like freshly pressed linen . . . and strong coffee.

Ryan glanced at his watch, then rationalized away six more minutes to limber his analytical mind on half the *Wall Street Journal*'s crossword before digging into the Presidential Daily Brief.

The PDB was a collection of highly classified executive summaries that the Office of the Director of National Intelligence deemed worthy of his review. It contained everything from hard intelligence to rumors that, while patently false, were likely to incite unrest or instability in parts of the world where the United States had strategic or humanitarian interests. Charged with the deconfliction and information sharing between the seventeen US intelligence agencies, it was the responsibility of the ODNI to have a finger on the pulse of important world events – and to boil them down into the PDB.

Ryan preferred a BLUF report – Bottom Line Up Front. He wanted a simple executive summary of straight facts – even when those facts were about rumors – and would drill down on the specifics in face-to-face national security briefings. He'd cut his teeth in the intelligence community as an analyst, playing what-if games with world events, and could spend hours delving into the nuances of a single issue – and enjoying the hell out of it. But he wasn't in the rank and file of the IC anymore. The problems facing the office of President came at near lightning speed from all points of the compass and at all hours of the day. Ryan was forced into the role of a generalist, relying on subject-matter experts to work through the in-depth analysis and strategy.

Theoretically, the PDB allowed him to stay a move or two ahead and decide where to put his pieces on the board. This morning's brief was straightforward, with the same parts of the world devolving into their continued spiral toward chaos, while other parts – admittedly fewer than he wished for – continued to emerge into newer, more robust economies. According to the briefing folder in front of him, the world was just as safe – or every bit as dangerous – as it had been the day before.

At seven-forty a.m., Ryan snugged his red tie into a semi-uniform single Windsor and stuffed the PDB into the same leather briefcase he'd been carrying for years. He downed the last of his delicious Navy coffee – a phrase that did not come easily to the mind of a former Marine – and walked out of the West Sitting Hall to meet an earnest young Secret Service agent who was posted there.

'Good morning, Tina,' he said.

Special Agent Tina Jordan gave him an exuberant smile, though she was coming to the end of her shift just as he was beginning his.

'Good morning, Mr President.' Then, quietly, she raised her sleeve to her lips and whispered, 'SWORDS-MAN is on the elevator.'

She stepped into a small alcove and pushed the button on the elevator that would take them down to the ground floor, where they hung a right to begin on Ryan's three-minute walking commute to the office.

Ryan entered the Oval from the Rose Garden, the door opened by the agent who knew how to overcome the security device in the handle. He found his daily calendar printed on a single sheet of paper that was centered perfectly on the middle of his desk where his lead secretary had placed it shortly after she'd arrived at seven-thirty.

Ryan pressed the intercom button on his phone. She already knew he was there, because she too had a light board indicating his location.

'Good morning, Betty.'

'Good morning, Mr President,' his secretary said. 'What can I do for you?'

'Director Foley and Secretary Adler should be here in a few minutes. Go ahead and send them in when they arrive.'

'DNI Foley is here now, sir,' Betty said.

A moment later, the director of national intelligence entered from the secretarial suite outside the Oval. Ryan had known Mary Pat and her husband, Ed, since their days at CIA together. They'd dodged innumerable crises, weathered the ones that were unavoidable, and together walked barefoot over the broken glass of some of the most tragic events in recent history. She was more than a member of his inner circle, she was a friend – and in Washington, friends were as rare as genuine statesmen.

They saw each other at least four times a week, but Ryan still stood when she entered. He winced when he put weight on his foot, tried to hide it – and failed. Mary Pat gave him a narrow look. She opened her mouth to say something, but Scott Adler, the secretary of state, came in, followed by Jay Canfield, the director of the Central Intelligence Agency. Arnie van Damm, Ryan's chief of staff, entered from the adjoining door to his own office – the only person in the White House able to enter the Oval unseen and unimpeded. Arnie had served as chief of staff to three presidents. Ryan was the polar opposite of a politician, leaving Arnie to handle the annoying – and, frankly, unfathomable – part of the job that allowed him to get elected so he could make the decisions the country needed him to make. Jack picked his clubs and hit the ball, but Arnie told him the lay of the course.

Ryan made his way to his favorite chair in front of the fireplace and waved the others to sit on either of the two off-white couches in the middle of the Oval Office. His advisers had all staked out their customary spots for these meetings long ago – and he felt sorry for anyone new to the cabinet who happened to take the wrong seat. The thought of it brought a smile to his face and a question to his mind.

'Not national security-related,' he said, 'but you guys have your ears to the ground out there more than I do. What do you hear about Dehart's nomination?'

Ryan had recently put Mark Dehart, senior congressman from Pennsylvania, forward as his pick for secretary of homeland security, an office recently vacated by the resignation of Andrew Zilko.

Van Damm gave a slight shrug, the way he did when something was a non-issue. 'That guy squeaks he's so clean,' he said. 'Confirmation sounds like a foregone conclusion.'

The door opened again and Bob Burgess, secretary of defense, stepped in. He scanned the seated group, checked his watch, and then shook his head. 'I apologize for being only five minutes early, Mr President.'

Ryan smiled, nodding to the Navy steward with the service cart rolling in behind Burgess. 'You beat the coffee,' he said. 'That's something, I guess. We're just getting started.'

Ryan thanked the steward – who was already his

co-conspirator in the less-healthy breakfast scandal – and, as was his custom, poured everyone's coffee himself. Rather than standing, he simply held the cups out for his advisers to get up and take. No one appeared to mind.

The meeting breezed along, hitting the high points about Russia, the Ukraine, immigration, and, on the home front, the possibility that the Fed was going to raise interest rates.

'And that brings us to the latest FONOP,' van Damm said. As CoS, it was his job to keep the momentum going on the meeting, but always with an eye on his boss. FONOP was the acronym for Freedom of Navigation Operation. With China continuing to make what much of the world felt were absurd maritime claims in the South China Sea, the United States in general, and Ryan in particular, felt it important to show that not everyone agreed with those claims. To that end, several times each month, US Navy vessels, typically destroyers or littoral combat ships, innocently sailed within the twelve-mile line surrounding several of the disputed islands and reefs – without asking permission. The movements themselves had become almost commonplace. Within the last month, harassment by Chinese vessels and planes had reached new and alarming proportions.

'Sounds like the PRC got their feelings especially hurt on this one,' Ryan mused, perusing his written brief.

The SecDef nodded. 'That would be a correct assessment, Mr President. LCS *San Antonio* sailed eleven miles off Woody Island in the Paracels on her way to Phuket, Thailand. As you know, the ChiComs have surface-to-air missiles on Woody, so the island is of particular interest to us. Two J-10 fighters off the Woody airstrip buzzed the

LCS a half a dozen times. Commander Roger Reese, skipper of the *San Antonio*, reported encounters with multiple Chinese vessels, including a PLA Navy guided missile frigate that stayed on their tail all the way to the mouth of Patong Bay. Reese followed international protocols, utilizing the Code for Unplanned Encounters at Sea and hailed the ships to declare intentions and avoid miscommunications. Three large fish processors attempted a blockade, without a doubt at the behest of the PLA Navy. Commander Reese apparently plays a better game of chicken and they eventually got out of the way.'

Ryan nodded. 'Good for Commander Reese.'

Burgess said, 'ChiComs accused him of "illegal and dangerously provocative" actions, as usual.'

'I'm a little concerned about the optics on these FONOPs,' SecState Adler said.

Burgess suppressed a scoff, but just barely. 'The optics here are perfect, Scott. These patrols make it absolutely clear to the new Chinese president what the administration thinks of the Great Wall of Sand he's continuing to dredge up.'

Ryan looked at the secretary of state and shrugged. 'Bob's got a point,' he said.

Adler took a sip of his coffee and shook his head. 'Don't misunderstand me, sir. I'm referring to the optics presented to the Chinese public, not President Zhao and the party mandarins.'

'Pun intended,' Ryan said, arms crossed, chin on his fist.

'Absolutely, Mr President.' Adler grinned. He too had been with Ryan since the beginning – and his opinion was invaluable, even when Ryan didn't agree with it, often for that very reason.

'But in all seriousness,' Adler said, 'it's a brave new world out there. Everyone with a smartphone is an on-the-scene reporter. The Communist Party of China has worked very hard to gain back the hearts of the population after President Wei lost control and killed himself before he could be arrested. They're doing that by whipping up a nationalist fervor. Xinhua is running multiple stories this morning about the "illegal encroachment" of American warships into their waters over which China has "indisputable sovereignty" – complete with photographs of the *San Antonio* that were presumably taken from the Chinese guided missile frigate.'

Mary Pat raised her pen and conceded the secretary of state's point. 'Weibo is abuzz with nationalist fervor.'

Ryan mulled that over but said nothing. State controlled, Xinhua News ran nothing that was not filtered and approved by the Communist Party. Weibo was the micro-blogging site that was the Chinese answer to Twitter.

DCIA Jay Canfield added, 'There are more than a few folks in the micro-blogosphere calling our actions nothing less than an act of war.'

'That's not unusual,' Burgess said. 'Ninety-nine-point-nine-nine percent of those buzzing voices are, no doubt, spewing forth from columns of Terra Byta warriors marching in lockstep in some information warfare battalion or 50 Cent Army in a Beijing warehouse – or working directly for the Ministry of State Security. In any case, this nationalism is likely voiced by the same government propaganda machine that submits stories to Xinhua. As you just pointed out, it wasn't too long ago that a large part of the PRC's population was so fed up with the Communist Party that they threatened to storm the Zhongnanhai and drag their bastard leaders to the guillotine.'

Mary Pat raised an eyebrow. 'The guillotine?'

Burgess shrugged but held his ground. 'The sword, the firing squad . . . You know what I mean.'

Ryan sighed. 'President Zhao's relatively new, but my read is that he's made of much tougher stuff than Wei ever was. He's a princeling – and with that comes a certain amount of old-guard support among the Central Committee. He appears to be using that support to gobble up power like Pac-Man, all while he sees to the rebuilding of national pride along with the thousands of acres of new islands in the SCS. People can be fed up with the party and still have a hell of a lot of contempt for us.'

'True enough,' the secretary of state said. 'I'm just saying that it's one thing for the party to know you mean business, but the broad media coverage of our warship sailing through what the average Chinese citizen views as their waters could force President Zhao to respond. He can't afford to appear to be letting his power slip. As Bob says, Zhongnanhai leadership knows all too well what happens if the masses smell blood in the water. I'm in no way suggesting that Freedom of Navigation exercises are a bad thing. But the optics are something to be aware of.'

'Interesting stuff,' Ryan said. 'But nothing here is surprising. Maybe this FONOP will be nothing more than a little bump under the tires of our week.'

Mary Pat scoffed. 'I'm sorry, sir,' she said, 'but did I ever tell you about the tiny little tick bite that put me in the hospital for a week when I was ten years old?' She pulled back the collar of her silk blouse to reveal a dime-sized scar on her neck. 'Sometimes it's the little things that scare me the most.'

'There's that old Chinese curse,' Burgess said. 'May you live in interesting times.'

Ryan sat back in his chair. 'I think Bobby Kennedy just made that one up.'

Burgess started to add something, but Ryan said, 'Optics noted.' He was ready to move on. 'Scott, put together the usual statement reiterating our position that the US Navy and US merchant ships have been operating freely in the South China Sea for many decades – and we don't intend to leave anytime soon. Note that LCS *San Antonio* was on an innocent and routine mission to visit our friends in Thailand. And have someone leak informally to the Chinese ambassador that I'm pretty pissed about the way they hid behind a bunch of innocent fishermen and put them in danger.'

Adler made a note in his folio. 'Yes, Mr President.'

Ryan looked at the DNI. Her lips were pursed in thought, eyes twinkling and narrow. They'd worked together long enough that he knew when she was chewing on something that might interest him.

He prodded. 'What is it, Mary Pat?'

She gave an almost imperceptible nod, as if still working through a thought.

'A game of chicken only works if neither party knows when the other will flinch,' she said. 'It wasn't too many months ago that you demonstrated to China that you are willing to – excuse me, but there's no other way to say it – bomb the shit out of them. It was only a building that time, but you've made your resolve crystal clear. An increase in hostilities, even to bolster nationalism, is incredibly danger-ous. All due respect, Mr President, but playing chicken with you is akin to driving into a brick wall. Stupid men do not become the paramount leader of the People's Republic of China. President Zhao has to know that you will not get out of the way.'

Adler looked up from his notes. 'Are you saying Zhao is knowingly trying to foment an actual shooting war?'

The DNI shook her head. 'I'm saying there's some-thing strange going on in the PRC. I can't put my finger on it. But it is strange.'

Ryan paused for a moment, eyes fixed on the Reming-ton bronze beyond his desk. The others in the room knew when he was thinking, and they gave him the space to do so by looking down at the folios in their laps and keeping quiet. Mary Pat was right. He'd never been much of a yielder when it came to games of chicken. Now, though, he played the game with other people's kids. It didn't ne-cessarily mean he was more likely to flinch. It did, however, make him careful never to start such a game himself.

'Scott,' he said, 'get on the horn with your counterparts in and around Southeast Asia over the next few days. You can start with Australia and Japan. They certainly have big dogs in this fight over the SCS. Let them know we appreciate what they are doing, but it wouldn't hurt our feelings if they ramped up their own movements in these waters. They don't have to go out of their way to piss off the Chinese, but they shouldn't be tippytoeing around to avoid them, either.'

'A unified front,' Secretary Burgess said. 'Wouldn't that be nice?'

'Yes, it would,' the President said. 'And I'll do my part by bringing up the issue during bilateral meetings while we're in Tokyo.' He eyed van Damm over his glasses. 'I do have meetings with both the Japanese and Australian PMs, right?'

'You do,' the CoS said.

Ryan looked forward to the G20 Summit. It was supposed to be about the economy. What wasn't, after all? But world leaders, being who they were, discussed whatever they damn well pleased when they got together. Ryan enjoyed the face-to-face meetings. Statesmanship between leaders with competing agendas was often sorely lacking, even in his own country – hell, especially in his own country.

Van Damm flipped through several pages in his folder. 'The final advance team is in Tokyo now. Last-minute changes will be doable, of course, especially if you and State need any follow-on talks with Australia and Japan – but the Secret Service won't be too keen on it. I'm pretty sure they'd just as soon drive you around Tokyo in an Abrams tank.'

The White House Advance Office went out at least three times before any presidential travel such as to the G20. The first trip, five months prior to the event, was called the survey. The second, known as a pre-advance, occurred a month or so before the actual event. A final advance took place three weeks later, a week prior to the President's arrival. By pre-advance time, the big hurdles such as where they would park the nineteen aircraft and hundreds of vehicles had all been roughed out, allowing the advance team to drill down on the inevitable crisis issues that always came up.

'And don't forget the PRC,' Ryan said, nodding. 'I want to sit down face-to-face with President Zhao at least once. Maybe keep this game of chicken from progressing any further. It would be nice if I could point out our unified front with –'

Betty's voice came over the intercom, cutting him off.

'Mr President,' she said. 'I'm sorry to interrupt you, but Commander Forrestal is here. He says it's urgent.'

Interruptions like this were not uncommon. When not in the Oval Office, every person in the room was tied to a government-issue BlackBerry or iPhone – the 'intelligence umbilicus,' Mary Pat called it. But each of them left their smartphone in a basket at the secretary's desk just outside before entering the Oval. There were secure phones in compartments inside the Oval Office furniture if anyone needed to make a call pursuant to a meeting.

Betty had a copy of the President's calendar. She knew how long his appointments were scheduled to last – and her ability to ascertain if some issue just absolutely could not wait bordered on a superpower.

6

Commander Robby Forrestal stepped into the Oval a moment later, standing by the door until the President motioned him the rest of the way in. Bald as an egg, he had an angular jaw and runner's build that suited his Navy service dress whites – the summer uniform he'd wear through September. The placard of ribbons on his chest said he'd served in conflicts involving Afghanistan, Iran, and China. It never ceased to move Ryan how much time in action these young servicemen now faced before they were thirty-five. It was a sobering thought, since for too many years it had been a nod from him that sent them there.

Three minutes later Commander Forrestal finished his initial Bottom Line Up Front briefing regarding the explosion and eventual sinking of China Global Shipping Lines' *Orion*. He took a step back, waiting for discussion and questions. As a former national security adviser himself, Ryan knew how to conduct a briefing, and Forrestal was one of the best.

'Casualties?' Ryan asked.

'Preliminary information reports four dead,' Forrestal said. 'But the ship's manifest says there were thirty-two souls on board – and only twenty-two of those are accounted for.'

Ryan took a long breath and gave a pensive shake of his head. 'Six more . . .'

'Still missing, Mr President,' Forrestal said. 'Coast Guard has a Mandarin speaker from Seattle on scene at the command post now. I'll have more information for you in short order.'

Ryan read the one-page executive summary Commander Forrestal had provided. 'Forty-knot winds and sixteen-foot seas . . .'

'Yes, sir,' Forrestal said. 'We're fortunate they were able to save the twenty-two, considering the conditions. The search for the six missing crewmen is still ongoing. I have to admit, the Coasties are doing an incredible job here.'

'High praise from a Navy man.' Ryan smiled. 'So they're diverting traffic up through Canada?'

'Yes, sir,' Forrestal said. 'The strait is twenty miles wide at some points, but given the weather, it's impossible to tell how many containers are floating around beneath the surface. One of the Coast Guard 45s out of Port Angeles has already hit one. The crew is okay, but their vessel is in-op.'

Ryan checked his watch. 'It'll be getting light out there by now at this time of year. That'll help, but I'd imagine it's a circus. A ship that large, there's bound to be a lot of oil and diesel floating around.'

'True enough, Mr President,' Forrestal said. 'The district captain has raised the MARSEC level and instituted a standoff zone. If there's anything good about the weather, it's that most of the looky-loos are staying off the water. EPA officials out of Seattle are on scene. We should have the preliminary environmental assessment anytime.'

'As bad as the weather is, it would be nothing for a modern container ship to negotiate.' Ryan tapped the paper with his forefinger to underscore his point. 'What caused this ship to sink?'

'According to the Mandarin speaker, the crewmen are claiming a series of explosions.'

Burgess couldn't contain himself. 'In the engine room?'

'That's unknown,' Forrestal said, before turning back to Ryan. 'Nothing but WAGs so far, Mr President.' Commander Forrestal had been around long enough to know that Ryan had enough information flying across his desk; he didn't have time for Wild-Ass Guesses.

'Very well,' Ryan said. 'Keep us informed.'

'Thank you, Mr President.' Forrestal turned to go, but Ryan stopped him, calling him by his first name, to take the tone of the meeting down a notch.

'Thank you, Robby,' the president said. 'Didn't your son have a football game last weekend?'

The commander smiled. 'He did, sir. Ran for a total of sixty-four yards.'

'Not bad for an eleven-year-old in Pop Warner,' Ryan said. 'Be careful, the Patriot scouts will be looking at him before he knows it.'

'I'll tell him you said that, sir,' Forrestal said, excusing himself with a broad grin. Not everyone got to pass on kudos to their kid from the President of the United States.

Ryan turned back to his advisers once the door was shut.

'A bomb?' Secretary Burgess said. 'Diesel engines don't usually explode.'

Scott Adler gave a slow shake of his head. 'That's one possibility,' he said. 'The explosion could very easily have been a reaction of some chemicals in one of the containers. We'll have to look at the manifest. In any case, this incident creates another problem that piles onto the issues I mentioned regarding the FONOP. I'm happy the Coast Guard was so quick to respond, but our rescue of twenty-two Chinese seamen is just another thing to make President Zhao look weak. His ships can't even make it to Seattle without the evil capitalists lending a hand . . .'

'You know,' Mary Pat said, nodding, 'it's a poor state of affairs, but he's right.'

'Maybe,' Ryan said. 'All of you get into this and see what you can find out regarding terror threats toward Chinese shipping.'

'And specific threats toward us from the ChiComs,' Burgess added.

'That too, Bob,' Ryan said. 'Although I sincerely hope any specific threats would have floated to the top already.'

Ryan stood to show the briefing was at an end. He was careful not to put any weight on his heel.

Ryan waited for everyone, including Arnie van Damm, to file out and their respective doors to close behind them before he hobbled toward his desk. He'd nearly made it when Mary Pat stuck her head back inside.

'I saw you limping, Jack,' she said, affecting the motherly voice she'd used on him when they were in the CIA together. MP was one of an extremely close cohort who still addressed him by his given name – but even she rarely did it in the Oval Office. She opened her hand to reveal a golf ball with the presidential seal in her open palm. 'I got this from the stash of tchotchkes Betty gives out to visitors when they can't get in to see you. Ed had a bout with plantar fasciitis a couple years ago. It's nothing to be ashamed of.'

Ryan leaned back in his chair, his eyebrows raised.

'Getting old isn't for wusses,' he said.

'You're not a wuss,' Mary Pat said. 'You're an invalid.'

Ryan sighed again. 'Yeah, well, don't spread that around. Press gets word I have a toothache and the markets drop fifty points.'

'I will treat your condition as highly classified,' Mary Pat said, and then tossed him the ball. 'You're supposed to take off your shoe and roll this around under the arch of your foot. It works wonders.'

Ryan looked back and forth from the golf ball to his aching foot.

'Well,' Mary Pat said, glancing at her watch, 'my boss expects me to get some work done today. I'll leave you to your rehab.'

Alone again, Ryan glanced at the paper copy of his schedule on the center of his desk. It was not uncommon for the document to be vague, as the President's daily schedule was posted on the White House website. Betty or Arnie usually added a little handwritten commentary for him in the margins of his copy. This morning, his nine o'clock simply said: *Meeting*.

He'd just pressed his intercom when the door opened and his secretary stuck her head in. The woman's prescience really did border on a superpower.

'What's next, Betty?'

'Special Agent Montgomery, Mr President, the new special agent in charge of your protection detail. He asked for five minutes to introduce himself.'

Grouchy from the pain in his heel, Ryan dropped the

golf ball on the carpet and began to roll it around under his foot. 'I liked Joe,' he muttered. 'We got along well. He was good at his job. Why couldn't they just leave me Joe?' Ryan glanced up at his secretary's passive face. It was the closest she would ever come to chastising him – even when he deserved it.

'Lovely dress, Betty,' he said, by way of apology for his sulking.

'Thank you, Mr President,' she said. 'Special Agent O'Hearn will do a fine job as deputy director.' She raised her eyebrows and tilted her head like a mom, telling him to give the liver and onions a chance. 'This Montgomery fellow seems like a very nice man.'

'Send him in,' Ryan said.

Betty placed a file folder in the center of Ryan's desk and excused herself with a benign smile.

Prepared by the Secret Service, the folder contained the new agent's photo, work history, and biography. Ryan had asked them to include his detail agents' shooting scores and short bios of their families as well. It was the analyst in him. He'd already read Montgomery's file but left his copy in the residence on the mile-high stack of briefs, budgets, and political ballyhoo he had to read every day along with the PDB.

Special Agent in Charge Gary Montgomery stepped in a moment later, wearing an expensive gray wool suit. His charcoal-colored hair was cut neat and short, just long enough to part. Ryan smiled. Everyone got a haircut and bought a new suit for their first meeting in this office – if they had the time. He remembered his first time in the Oval and shuddered a little.

Ryan guessed the agent at around six-three and well over two hundred pounds – with the ferocious look and thick neck of a guy you'd want protecting you when the shit hit the fan. People in the private sector – and even other countries – tended to hire their bodyguards by the pound, but the US Secret Service was different. The agency understood that big didn't necessarily mean competent.

Ryan had been around long enough to know that at some point in their careers, virtually all agents in the Secret Service had to punch their tickets by working on some kind of protection; the best were assigned to PPD – Presidential Protection Detail. But even those assignments could range from any one of a variety of positions – advance agent scouting locations prior to the President's arrival, outer perimeter, countersurveillance, or lowly post-stander at any of dozens of doors at any given venue.

While Ryan respected the entire agency, the SAIC and the principal detail agents who worked within arm's reach – 'inside the bubble,' they called it – were the best of the best. PPD agents didn't have to be large in stature – but they did have to be extremely good at their job. From all accounts, Gary Montgomery was both. It said something about the man that he now stood in Ryan's office with a gun under his suitcoat. Not many people in the world got to do that. The file said his range scores were near perfect with both his SIG Sauer pistol and the MP5 SMG. There was a lightness to the way he stood, with his large hands hanging easily at his sides, as if he knew right where they were if he needed them. The bio said he'd boxed at the University of Michigan, so it made sense that he would be self-assured. Still, it would take months to develop the relationship Ryan had with Joe O'Hearn. And the level of understanding shared between him and Andrea Price-O'Day – forget about it.

'Welcome to the Big Show,' Ryan said, referring to what the agents themselves called PPD. His eyes narrowed as he studied the new addition to his detail. 'We've met before . . .'

Montgomery possessed a disarming smile for such a ferocious-looking man. 'I was warned you had an incredible memory, Mr President.'

'So we have met?'

'Not officially,' Montgomery said. 'I served as whip of the VP detail shortly after Special Agent Price-O'Day became SAIC on yours.'

Ryan sighed. Andrea Price-O'Day was one tough human being. She'd picked him up and dusted him off – both figuratively and literally – during his first moments as President. That was what? A million years ago? Not many agents in the Secret Service could say they'd gotten a field promotion from the President to lead PPD – but then, considering the carnage that had led up to that promotion, no one wanted that kind of bragging rights. The longtime agent in charge of his detail, Andrea had retired after injuries sustained protecting him in Mexico City. Ryan was sure Montgomery knew the story.

'The VP detail?' Ryan mused, instead of boring the agent with bloody memories. *The Little Show with free parking.*' The Naval Observatory, home to the VPOTUS, offered agents a place to park – something not available to them at the White House.

'You know your Secret Service culture, sir,' Montgomery said.

'Just enough to get me in trouble.' Ryan closed the file folder. 'Welcome aboard, Gary.'

'Thank you, Mr President,' Montgomery said. 'I thought I should stop by and introduce myself before I get started in case you had any questions.'

'You're not handling the Tokyo advance for the G20?' Ryan asked.

'No, sir,' Montgomery said. 'I've assigned Assistant Special Agent in Charge Flynn. I thought it more important I stay here and get my feet planted firmly in the detail. It allows me to get to know you and your idiosyncrasies so that I can better prot –'

Ryan's head snapped up. 'I have idiosyncrasies?'

'You do, sir,' Montgomery said.

'Name one.'

Montgomery's hands hung still and relaxed. He cocked his head to one side. If he was nervous, he didn't show it.

'For starters,' he said. 'You test your agents.'

'This isn't a test.'

'Of course not, Mr President.'

Ryan smiled in spite of the pain in his foot. This guy was direct. Direct was good. 'Well, maybe it is a test, but it's a good-natured test. I'm sure we'll get to know one another well enough.'

'Very well,' Montgomery said, taking that as a dismissal. He paused at the door to the secretaries' office, then shook his head as if thinking better of something. At least he'd picked the right door; agents had been known to walk into the personal study. 'I beg your pardon, Mr President, but I happened to overhear DNI Foley mention that you might have a bout of plantar fasciitis going on. I don't know if you are aware of this, sir, but that particular malady is also known as "policeman's foot." Protective agents are on our feet for long hours, standing post and whatnot. I feel your pain, Mr President, and I have some tried-and-true remedies if you're interested.'

Ryan thought for a moment, then motioned to the leather chairs in front of the Resolute desk and leaned forward, all ears.

This Montgomery guy might work out after all.

7

Three Hours Earlier

Magdalena Rojas leaned her head against the window in the backseat of her pimp's Chrysler 300 sedan and wondered if tonight might possibly be the beginning of a different chapter in her life.

She was a small thing, bony at the knees and elbows, and not quite five feet tall. Parrot wanted his girls to look nice, so he gave her plenty of makeup and a brush when she needed to tame her wayward black hair. Even that was thinner than it had been. Others might not be able to tell, but she could. She'd been beautiful once. Her father had told her so when she was little. Other men in her home country used to say it all the time – and mean it. But the men she went with now hardly even took the time to speak. Some of them were scared of her. Those were the worst. They had to hurt her to be real men.

Magdalena could not understand how a grown man could be so frightened of a thirteen-year-old girl.

She touched the outline of the item in the pocket of her nylon gym shorts and felt a flicker of hope. It had been so long since she'd possessed any hope at all that even a hint of the emotion caused a deep and abiding pain in her chest.

Parrot wasn't driving. He'd gone ahead in a different

vehicle. That was something. His long dreads made him look like the Predator from the movies and he had to be one of the meanest pimps in the known universe – at least that's what Blanca said, and she was his favorite. And because she was his favorite, he'd chopped the shit out of her when she pissed him off – that's what he called a whipping, getting *chopped*.

Didn't nobody wanna get chopped by Parrot.

Magdalena had nearly fainted when she saw how bad he'd hurt his favorite, especially considering what she now carried hidden in her pocket. But Parrot had decided to let Reggie drive the girls home because he looked more like a college kid than a pimp and the cops wouldn't hassle him so much. Reggie might have looked like a college kid, but he was almost as mean as Parrot. He was just sneakier about it.

The Chrysler's leather seats were freezing and Magdalena wanted to ask Reggie to turn up the heat. It was cold outside and Parrot hadn't told them they'd be going all the way south of Dallas, so she'd worn only her usual gym shorts and tank top. Reggie kept looking at her in the rearview mirror and licking his lips, so she decided to put up with the cold.

She'd hoped to see some stars on the drive back home, but Parrot told Reggie to stay in the city where the lights were bright and there was more traffic so the car would blend in. It was better for all of them, the pimp told Magdalena, because if he or Reggie got arrested, then they'd all get arrested. That's the way cops did things in the United States. They arrested you and put you in with other whores who might have a sharpened toothbrush with them. He said those whores would stab you in the eye because they thought you looked more beautiful than they did. Parrot was mean, but Magdalena believed him because she'd seen girls who'd been stabbed in jail. They weren't beautiful anymore, but she thought they probably had been, once.

She gave up on seeing any stars and let her head loll to the side so she could check on Blanca.

Her friend lay in the seat next to her, asleep now but breathing fitfully. She wasn't much bigger than Magdalena, and one of her johns had gotten rough tonight and dislocated her shoulder. She'd bitten the man and Parrot had chopped her with the buckle end of his belt – probably broken some ribs to go along with her shoulder. That was how he taught them. Sleep in too long – feel the belt. Catch the clap from some guy for doing your job – get a couple shots of antibiotics, then get chopped because Parrot was pissed you let yourself get sick. Magdalena had gotten used to the sound of the last few inches of leather slithering out of the loops on the bastard's jeans. Sure, the beat-downs left marks, but some men even got turned on by a few bruises. The doctor who gave them their shots sure as shit didn't care.

And anyway, the doc was in on it, just like Reggie, the guy who looked like a college kid.

Reggie had offered to let Magdalena sit up front with him tonight and even choose the radio station. She'd declined, saying she wanted to rest – but no amount of rest was enough for the work she had to do at the bar tomorrow and the next day . . . and the day after that.

She looked at the sleeping girl beside her and shook her head. *Pobrecita*, poor little thing. Blanca had fallen into

80

this life accidentally. She deserved pity. Magdalena was different. She had chosen this life – or, at least, that's what her mother told her.

Jacó, Costa Rica, sprawled across the lap of the jungle-covered Talamanca Mountains at the mouth of the Gulf of Nicoya, faces the open waters of the Pacific. The picturesque village is famous for three things: incredible surfing, expatriate *norteamericanos*, and legal prostitution.

For most of his adult life, Miguel Rojas ran a small zip-line business that catered to affluent tourists. It did not make him wealthy, but Miguel could support his family and still have time to walk along the beach with his three daughters, including his favorite, Magdalena – until the cable parted and sent him plunging into the deep jungle gorge below. Miguel had not died immediately. There were many medical expenses, as well as the eventual cost of the funeral. His wife's job cleaning rooms at the Hotel Cocal & Casino was not enough to cover the crushing weight of it all.

A month after the funeral, Magdalena's mother sat her down and explained to her that as the eldest of the three Rojas daughters, it fell to Magdalena to 'open her kitchen,' so the family could pay its debts and her younger sisters could continue to go to school.

Prostitution was not only legal in Jacó, but culturally sanctioned. Procreation recreation was, in fact, one of the driving forces of the local economy. Internet travel sites extolled the beauty and variety of the surfing and the young women. Cocaine was plentiful, as was rampant theft and street crime, but there was also good food, dancing, copious amounts of liquor, and hundreds of girls who worked the restaurants, clubs, and bars – without scary pimps looking over their shoulders.

These working girls made enough money during the tourist season that they had savings to spend during the lull, buying food, shopping for clothing, eating at local cafés, until the surfers – or men with more sinister motives – returned to the village. A girl who worked hard and didn't get played into lowering her prices for handsome but hard-luck beach boys could make enough money to support a family and have a few nice things of her own.

At her mother's prompting, Magdalena opened her kitchen four months before she turned thirteen. She didn't look any older than she was. In fact, people often thought she was younger than her ten-year-old sister – but the men who hired her seemed to prefer it that way. The age of consent in Jacó was sixteen, but the authorities were more interested in catching speeders and they made it clear that they would leave the girls alone unless they were under twelve.

Magdalena looked like she was ten – and no policeman ever bothered her.

Opening her 'kitchen' for business turned out to be grueling work, and she spent the first three weeks in constant tears. But a lot of money was coming in, and her mother told her she'd get used to it in time. That is what women did. They got used to it.

Magdalena entertained many men – but instead of a pimp, she had her mother to contend with. Where other girls went to the hair salon every two weeks and had someone else to do their nails, Magdalena's mother insisted she paint her own nails and do her own hair. Other girls shared apartments and ate at cafés, but Magdalena took her meals at home and tried to sleep during the day while she listened to her sisters argue over their lessons or the handsome boys who talked to them at school.

Then Dorian had come to Jacó. He was a businessman with a kind smile. Magdalena was hanging out at a place called the Monkey Bar when she saw him. It was a slow night and he was handsome. He wore no wedding ring – she always added fifty dollars to her price if they had a wedding ring. She offered him an hour for a hundred American dollars. He made a counteroffer of five hundred for a three-hour date. She told him he was foolish, so he raised his offer to one thousand dollars a night – and they ended up spending the entire week together. She told her mother about him, but passed along only five hundred dollars to her each morning and kept the other five hundred in her shoe until she got to her room. At the end of the week, Dorian surprised her by asking if she wanted to go to the United States. She was beautiful enough to be a model and he would be willing to buy her some better clothes and be her manager. He said she could make a lot more money in the United States standing in front of a camera than she did in Jacó lying on her back.

Her mother smelled a fortune in the deal and signed a letter to the American immigration authorities allowing Magdalena to accompany their family friend, Dorian, to the United States on a short vacation. She made Magdalena promise to write every week and, of course, send a remittance home to help take care of her little sisters.

All had seemed fine on the airplane. People were still watching. But Dorian put on his wedding ring as soon as they reached Dallas. He hardly spoke to Magdalena at all, instead keeping her prisoner in a hotel at the edge of the city, while he did lines of cocaine and Oxy he bought from some guy in the next room. He took back the money he'd paid her in Jacó and never bought her any nice clothes. The only camera she ever saw was hooked up to the Internet, and he put her in front of that – a lot.

Dorian sold her to another man a week later, for enough money to pay for his entire vacation, including the money she'd given her mother, and then went back home to his wife.

Magdalena Rojas changed hands three times before being sold to Parrot, who already owned Blanca. She knew Parrot reported to someone else and probably gave him a piece of the money his girls brought in. He was mean, all right, but he didn't seem smart enough to run a business by himself. Whoever that other person was, Magdalena never saw him. She was too busy staying alive.

The girls spent their days trying to sleep, and their nights bouncing between a biker bar and a couple different massage parlors in South Fort Worth.

Magdalena was nowhere near strong enough to give a decent massage, but she went through the motions for the guys that came to get massages – mongers, they called them. They got their fake massages, and then pretended the rest of it was all her idea.

Parrot or Reggie took them to the doctor every other Wednesday, where they got checkups and antibiotics. The doctor was old, with very cold hands, and Magdalena hated him even worse than she hated the stinking bikers or the mongers who came to the massage parlors. The doctor was supposed to be nice and only pretended to be.

Every so often, Parrot would get a call on one of his mobiles, and they would take a road trip in his Chrysler. Magdalena and Blanca had been to the Super Bowl and Mardi Gras and even the State Fair . . . well, cheap hotels near the Super Bowl, and Mardi Gras, and the State Fair. The ceiling of one cheap motel room was much like any other, but at least she got a road trip, and sometimes they got to meet a few other girls.

Tonight, Parrot had set up a private event with a bunch of Asian guys somewhere south of Dallas. The event had gone long, and there was no traffic to speak of on the roads. Reggie was starting to get twitchy and drove slower than the limit. He kept his eyes glued to the road so he didn't appear to be drunk.

Magdalena hoped he didn't get them all arrested. She didn't want to get stabbed with a sharpened toothbrush – especially not tonight.

She didn't mind Asians, but her last guy of the night was an odd one. She'd been so tired, and incredibly sore by the time she got around to him. He must have noticed, because he said he only wanted to sleep. He'd paid for two hours and just talked to her until he fell asleep, ten minutes into his time. Sometimes guys all but passed out when they finished with her, and she would usually just be still and try to grab a little rest until Parrot banged on the door.

This guy was weird, and she wondered what he'd want her to do when he woke up. He'd talked about all kinds of stuff – the places he'd been, the dangerous stuff he'd seen – like he was a spy or something. Magdalena had been carried away by his fantastical stories. She'd lain there beside him staring at the ceiling until his breathing became more rhythmic and she knew that he was asleep. She began to wonder what it would be like to be a spy, and once the man began to snore, she slipped out of the bed and snooped through his small backpack. The pack contained some wadded clothing, a camera, and a bunch of papers she couldn't read – messy for a spy. She wrinkled her nose when she saw the loose toothbrush among the dirty clothes, covered in hairs and tiny bits of lint. That was just nasty.

Magdalena had stolen things before, usually small amounts of money that the johns wouldn't miss. She'd taken a watch once, but she'd been caught and Parrot chopped her bad for that. She'd never taken anything as useless as a thumb drive. She had no access to a computer, no way to know what information the device held. But she reasoned that if this man was indeed a spy, the contents of such a drive would be very valuable – and might keep the police from putting her in jail with the other whores if she got arrested. With her heart in her throat, she shoved the drive into the pocket of her short shorts and climbed back into bed. The odd man stirred, whispered something in her ear, and threw an arm over her shoulder. He woke from his two-hundred-dollar nap an hour later and shooed her out the door, pretending for Parrot that she'd been good at her job. Maybe he was nice, maybe he'd just been too tired to be cruel. Men were strange – and though she was only thirteen, Magdalena was old enough to know that she would never understand them.

She'd told Blanca about her odd spy. She even told her

about the thumb drive. The other girl was smart enough but could never focus on important things.

Magdalena felt herself slide forward on the slick seat. Her heart lurched into her throat as the car turned off the main highway. Reggie got out and fooled with a chain a minute before pushing open a big iron gate. He sat behind the wheel again without speaking. The tires rumbled over a metal cattle guard.

Magdalena peered over the back of the seat and out at the headlights as they played across the deserted gravel road. She rocked back and forth, about to jump out of her own skin.

'Why are we stopping here?'

Reggie shrugged. 'Parrot told me to drop you off.'

'And Blanca, too, right? You're coming back?'

'Nope, sweetheart,' Reggie said. 'Just you. She's too banged up for this job.'

Magdalena could see the lights from the big house on the hill now. She'd never been here before, but she'd heard about it from Parrot when he was trying to scare her. If there was a spot worse than the massage parlors and biker bars where she worked, then this was sure as shit that place.

She began to sob. 'But for how long?'

Reggie looked in the rearview mirror like he expected the tears. Every girl cried when they brought her here.

'I don't know, sweetheart,' he said. 'I'm just doin' what Parrot tells me.'

Blanca was awake now. She too began to sob when she realized where they were.

'Are we . . .?'

Magdalena shook her head. 'Not you,' she said. 'Just me.' She took the thumb drive from her pocket and pressed it into her friend's hand, careful not to let Reggie see what she was doing.

She whispered directly into Blanca's ear.

'Take this.'

'I can't,' Blanca said. 'What if they find it on me? I'm hurt bad. I can't get chopped no more. It would kill me.'

'Just take it,' Magdalena pleaded. 'Stash it under my cot.'

'You keep it.'

Magdalena gave her friend's hand a squeeze and nodded at the red-brick house. A dozen black lampposts fringed the circular driveway. The glow of pool lights illuminated the trees on the far side of the big garage. It was fancy, but that didn't make what happened inside any less horrible.

'They'll take away all my clothes,' she said. Her throat was so tight she could hardly speak. 'You have to help me.' She curled Blanca's fingers around the thumb drive and patted the girl's fist. 'This is important. I'm sure of it. Maybe it will even save us.'

Blanca's mouth hung open as she stared at the huge house. The front door opened and a Hispanic woman in her early thirties walked out to stand under a brick archway in the porchlight. A white tank top barely concealed sagging breasts and a muffin top overflowed the waist of her skinny jeans. She held a twisted leather quirt made from a dried bull penis. The cruel thing even had a name, Ratón, or Mouse. It was as long as her leg, and it had the power to flay skin.

The woman's name was Lupe and she was the bottom bitch here – what Parrot called the senior girl of any operation, the one who'd been around the longest, survived all the chopping, and somehow kept enough of her teeth to hold on to the boss's affections. Some men wanted innocence, but those girls never got to be in charge. They were just kids, used until they broke and then thrown away. There were always more kids. It was the girls like Lupe who became the bosses, girls who exuded equal parts danger and sex – just enough to be interesting. Though she was small, Magdalena was constantly on guard against giving off too much danger. Not physically, but because she was smart – and that scared men more than anything.

Lupe leered at the car as they pulled up. She'd been through it all herself. She had to know how hard it was, but instead of understanding, she was vindictive and deceitful, enforcing the boss's orders and using her position to keep the other girls in line. Fiercely jealous, she was known to apply her rawhide mouse with great effect to the back and legs of girls who didn't obey her quickly enough – or simply for fun.

Chest heaving, choking on her sobs, Magdalena cringed as Lupe tapped the cruel whip against her leg. The terrible woman would go hard on her, since the boss had apparently asked for her specifically. Bottom bitches were always the cruelest to girls they thought might pose a threat to their status. Magdalena had often thought that if her mother had joined the life, she would have been the bottom bitch.

Blanca finally relented and took the thumb drive, stuffing it into her own pocket before Lupe could see. Sobbing in earnest now, she wrapped her arms around her friend, speaking without caring if Reggie heard her or not.

'What if you do not come back?'

Reggie flung open the door, ready to drag her out if she didn't leave on her own.

Magdalena closed her eyes and whispered, 'Then save yourself.'

8

Texas Department of Public Safety trooper Roy Calderon had already ended his shift and made it home once today. He'd just snuggled down against his wife's pregnant belly at their small three-bedroom house in Mansfield when dispatch called his cell about an overturned cattle trailer at the 287/67 junction. The accident investigation and subsequent report had taken the better part of three hours.

Now on the way home a second time, Calderon thought about calling his wife to tell her he was fifty minutes out – the baby was probably keeping her up, anyway – but decided he'd better not, just in case she'd been able to drift off. Thinking about her made him smile. He hoped the kid was a redhead like her.

The trooper rarely had time to listen to the good-time radio during a normal shift. He preferred to keep his mind on the job between traffic stops, but there were no cars on the road this late – or this early, considering the fact that the sun would be up in a couple hours. The night was wonderfully cool, so he rolled down the windows on his Ford Mustang interceptor and turned up the volume on the AM to let *Coast to Coast* blast conspiracy theories into the darkness.

He caught the glimpse of taillights fifteen miles south of the Mansfield city limits. Trained to be inquisitive when it came to vehicles on 'his' highway, Calderon stomped on the gas. The Mustang's V-8 roared to life, throwing him back into his seat like a good interceptor should. The other car was going slow – too slow, really – and the Mustang closed the distance in a matter of seconds. The trooper silenced the good-time radio out of habit and fell in behind the vehicle.

The car, a maroon Chrysler 300, kept a constant speed of sixty-three miles an hour, two miles an hour less than the posted limit. It bumped the center line a couple times but didn't cross it, and that could have been a function of trooperitis. Nobody could drive a quarter-mile without committing some kind of violation, least of all someone with a black-and-white staring at them in the rearview mirror. Still, there was a gnawing in Trooper Calderon's gut that came from one part experience and two parts instinct – something about this particular vehicle – that made him want to do a little more investigation.

He asked Ellis County to run the license plate, gave the dispatcher his location, then decided to follow it for another minute or so. This guy hadn't really done anything wrong. Calderon was exhausted, and he wanted to get home to his wife's pregnant belly.

Then the face of a young girl popped up in the rear window. She hadn't given him a long look. In fact, the face vanished as quickly as it had appeared, as if someone had ordered her away.

Calderon had seven years on with the Texas Department of Public Safety. Way back during his field-training days, a senior trooper in the Highway Patrol had once told him that only three kinds of people were out during the wee hours of the night – cops, paperboys, and assholes. Thousands of violator contacts over those seven years – many of them after dark – had proven the notion.

Ellis County came back over the radio and said the LP was registered to a guy named Carlos Villanueva, aka Parrot. The dispatcher was on the ball and had already run a triple-I, checking Villanueva's criminal history as well as any outstanding warrants. He wasn't wanted, but his record showed two convictions for driving while intoxicated.

Calderon followed the car for another mile, thinking about the girl – and whoever it was that ordered her out of the window.

'That's too nice a car for a paperboy, asshole,' he muttered, and flipped on his red-and-blues.

Troopers in the Texas Highway Patrol are endowed with buckets of swagger by the time they graduate the DPS Academy in Austin. But swagger could get you killed if it wasn't backed up with good procedure. As tired as he was, Calderon was careful and precise as he prepared to make the stop.

He gave Ellis County his new location and followed the Chrysler over to the right shoulder, stopping far enough back that the other car's rear license plate was just visible over the front of the Mustang's hood. He cheated the cruiser over a few feet to offer a little cover from traffic coming up behind him. Instead of walking up immediately, he flipped on the white, forward-facing halogens on the interceptor's light bar. These 'takedowns' flooded the back of the vehicle with bright light. Never one to engage in a fair fight when it came to his own safety, Calderon did one better and turned the dash-mounted spotlight so it hit the rearview mirror, effectively blinding the driver to his approach.

Then, instead of going up on the driver's side, the trooper skirted around behind the Mustang so as not to cross in front of his own headlights, and made his approach on the right shoulder. He thought the guy with the peach-colored polo shirt was going to crap himself, he jumped so bad when Calderon tapped on the window with the butt of his flashlight.

Once the driver got over his initial shock, he blinked up at the trooper but kept both hands on the wheel. A lone girl was seated directly behind the driver. She was tiny – just a child, really – with long hair hanging down and obscuring her face. This was surely the girl he'd seen in the rear window. She pretended to be asleep, but her breath was uneven.

One hand on the butt of his SIG Sauer pistol, the trooper motioned with his flashlight for the driver to roll down the window. It came down with a motorized whine.

'Good evening, Trooper,' the guy at the wheel said.

He didn't look like a Parrot.

'Morning,' the trooper said, getting a better view of the Chrysler's interior with the periphery of his flashlight's beam now that the window was down. He didn't say anything else for a long moment.

'Is everything okay?' the driver said, right on cue. Nature wasn't the only thing to abhor a vacuum. People – especially guilty people – hated silence.

'You tell me,' Calderon said.

'I'm fine,' the driver said.

'Are you Parrot?'

'I . . . where did you hear that name?' His hands began to slide down the sides of the steering wheel.

Calderon wagged his flashlight at the guy's lap. 'Scares me when you do that,' he said, grinning. The beam of his light illuminated an empty condom wrapper at the driver's feet. Calderon shot a quick glance at the girl in the backseat. The grin bled from his face.

'Scares *you*?' the driver said.

'Do me a favor and keep your hands on the wheel until I tell you.'

The driver nodded but didn't say anything.

'So,' Calderon asked again, 'are you Parrot?'

'Parrot loaned me his car,' the driver said. 'My name's Reggie Tipton.'

'Is this your daughter, Mr Tipton?'

Reggie gave a forced smile. 'No.'

'Who is she?'

A long pause.

'She's Parrot's niece,' Reggie said. 'I'm taking her to visit her aunt.' His hands started to slide down the wheel until Calderon wagged his light again.

'Parrot's sister?'

'No,' Reggie said. 'The girl's aunt.'

'Parrot's sister-in-law?'

Reggie shook his head.

The trooper raised an eyebrow. 'Parrot's wife?'

'No, *her* aunt,' Reggie said, looking up toward the ceiling, exasperated. 'She's not related to Parrot.'

Calderon nodded. 'I get it,' he said.

Reggie finally caught on to his mistake. 'I mean . . . Parrot just calls her his niece.'

'Okay,' the trooper said. 'That makes sense.' The hairs on the back of his neck were already on end. 'Had anything to drink tonight?'

Reggie's shoulders slumped, visibly relaxing at the new line of questioning. He shook his head. 'Not a drop, Trooper.'

'This is just a routine stop,' Calderon said. 'You crossed the center line a couple times back there, so if you haven't been drinking, I'll just write you a warning.'

'Thank you,' Reggie said, relaxing even more.

'I just need to see your license and insurance and I'll get you on your way.'

'Can I move my hands to get my wallet?'

'Anything down there I should be worried about?'

The girl in the backseat glanced up and shook her head, then pretended to be asleep again.

'No.' Reggie gave a nervous chuckle. 'Nothing that I know of.' He moved slowly, pulling his driver's license out of his wallet with trembling fingers, and then leaning across the passenger seat to pass it through the open window.

The girl behind him looked up again. Her hair fell away and Calderon was horrified to see the thick layers of makeup around her eyes and cheeks. It was smudged and streaked, as if she'd been crying. She was hardly old enough for a bra, but the lace straps of a lacy black one peeked from under her pink tank top. It was cold enough to hang meat inside the car, but the poor kid had on nothing but skimpy gym shorts and the thin shirt.

The trooper hoped he managed to hide his surprise. 'What's your name, hon?'

Tipton jumped at the question. He shot a glance over

his shoulder, not bothering to conceal his anger. His leg began to bounce.

'Her name's Mag . . . I mean Blanca,' Tipton whispered.

'Hi, Blanca,' Calderon said. He kept one eye on the driver but offered the child his best smile. It was difficult enough not to look imposing in the gray-green Highway Patrol uniform and Stetson. 'My name's Roy. How old are you?'

'She's thirteen,' Reggie said. 'She doesn't have a license or anything. Look, if you don't mind –'

Calderon put the light directly in the driver's eyes while his right hand drew his SIG. 'Reggie,' he said, his voice raspy and tight. 'Keep your hands where I can see them. Shut your mouth and get out of the car.'

Tipton's hands dropped as if to open the door but went to his lap instead.

Calderon saw the black metal of the pistol glint in the beam of his flashlight, and fired two quick shots from his SIG. Tactically, he should have stepped to the rear to keep more of the Chrysler between him and the shooter, but that would have put the girl directly in the line of fire, so he stepped backward, firing as he moved.

Tipton wasn't smart, but he was committed, and he managed to get off four shots from his nine-millimeter before the third of Calderon's .357 SIG rounds struck him below the right eye, ending the fight.

Calderon kept his SIG Sauer still trained on the dead man while he reached for his radio with his left hand.

'Shots fired, Dispatch,' he said into the mic, sounding more excited than he wanted to. He yanked open the passenger door and pulled the gun out of Tipton's hand.

Suddenly woozy, Calderon grabbed the door post to steady himself. He looked at Blanca. 'Are you okay, hon?'

'Yes,' she said, pointing at him. 'But you . . . you are bleeding.'

The Ellis County Sheriff's Office dispatch came back over the radio. 'Three SO units rolling your direction,' the dispatcher said. 'Paramedics also en route.'

'Ten-four,' Calderon said. He slid to the ground, leaning against the door. 'Tell them to hurry. Suspect's down. And I'm losing a lot of blood.'

Three minutes later found Roy Calderon lying in the dark on the gravel shoulder of the road. The young girl cradled his head in her lap. The odor of road tar and the sweet smell of newly cut hay from the field on the other side of the fence reminded him he was still alive – for the moment. Blanca Limón pressed her hand against the wound in his neck, slowing the flow of blood.

'Are you going to arrest me?' the girl asked.

Trooper Calderon gave a tired sigh. He was incredibly thirsty, and he knew that wasn't a good sign. 'You're just a kid,' he said. 'I don't arrest kids.'

The little girl sobbed quietly, her trembling lips set in a grim line as if she didn't believe him.

'Parrot told us all the police would put us in jail with the other whores.'

Calderon's heart broke. 'I would never,' he whispered. 'Besides, you're saving my life.'

The girl nodded again at that. 'My name is Blanca Limón.'

Calderon licked his lips. He could hear sirens now. 'Good to meet you, Blanca Limón.'

'More police are coming,' she said. 'Do you think they will put me in jail with the other whores?'

'No.' Calderon coughed, wincing at the movement. 'And you're not a whore.'

'But I am.' Blanca's crying grew more intense as the sirens got closer. 'I have . . . I have something that maybe I can use to make a deal.'

'You don't need to deal.'

'Maybe that is so.' She sniffed. 'But maybe not. My friend was with a man earlier tonight –'

The trooper began to cough again, cutting her off. He closed his eyes and regained control. 'Sorry,' he said. 'Go ahead. You were with a man . . .'

'My friend,' the girl said, then stopped. She looked down at him as if coming to some conclusion. 'Yes . . . I was with a man last night. I think this man is a spy.'

'Really?' Calderon stifled a smile, humoring her, a little kid telling fantastical stories. 'A spy, you say?' The sound of approaching sirens grew louder. *Dear God*, Calderon thought, *please let that be the ambulance.* 'Did this man hurt you?'

The girl hesitated, blowing out a long breath as if to regain her composure. 'Yes,' she said. 'They all do.' She looked over her shoulder, then back at Calderon. 'My father used to watch many spy movies and this man bragged about doing things I think real spies must do. He fell asleep after he . . . finished. That is when I stole the thumb drive from his computer.'

'Really?' Calderon coughed again.

'You do not believe me?' Blanca said.

Calderon groaned. 'Of course I believe you.'

'Well, I did steal it,' Blanca said. 'Maybe I can give it to you and you will help my friend. Awful people have her now. And I am worried for what they will do to her.'

Calderon felt himself drifting off. He licked his lips, willing his eyes to stay open, to stay awake for the ambulance. 'Not . . . a very good spy . . . if he let you steal his thumb drive.'

Blanca slumped. 'She told me he was a spy . . .'

The trooper coughed. 'What?'

'Nothing,' Blanca said.

'I'll tell someone to help your friend,' Calderon said. The paramedics rolled up, and just like that, it began to rain cop cars. 'And I promise to check out that guy for you. What's his name?'

A tear rolled down Blanca Limón's filthy cheek.

'Eddie Feng,' she said.

9

The large earth-tone painting of the Great Wall above the paramount leader's head hid a single bullet hole in the wood paneling. The thick beige carpet, too, concealed evidence of violent death. Everyone in the room knew the story of the previous president, including Colonel Huang Ju of the Central Security Bureau, but they rarely spoke his name.

Standing against the wall, out of the way but close enough to act, the colonel sensed there was something very wrong in the room, something that went far beyond any violence from the past. No, this was a new threat, and like a good protective officer, Huang could smell danger in the air.

A Chinese container ship had sunk in US waters – and it was the feeling of some in this room that America was somehow to blame. Tensions were high among the advisers – and when tensions ran high around the general secretary, the man he was charged with protecting, Colonel Huang Ju paid close attention.

The commander of the 1st Squadron of the 1st Group of the Central Safeguard Regiment – sometimes referred to as Regiment 61889 – stood to the right of the polished mahogany doorway inside the paramount leader's spacious office. His senses were raw, as if they'd been rubbed with coarse sandpaper. Huang was tall and trim, with thick black hair long enough to part yet short enough that the gray around his temples was difficult to notice. His face was serene as stone, a very sharp and dangerous stone, but a stone nonetheless.

Those charged with the protection of others were often described as willing to take a bullet for their principal. Like the American Secret Service, rather than seek cover during times of attack, they were trained to make themselves larger targets. That was indeed something Colonel Huang had vowed to do, but there was much more to protection than simply absorbing bullets intended for one's protectee. His primary duty was one of *vicarious concern*; he worried over the many dangers that lurked both without and within, so the paramount leader did not have to think of such things.

Though officially a member of an army regiment, Huang wore a white shirt and dark suit nearly identical to the white shirts and dark suits worn by three of the other five men in the inner office. Everyone else in the room ranked exponentially higher than Colonel Huang, but under his dark suit jacket was a Taurus PT 709 nine-millimeter pistol. None of the other men were armed, and, as Chairman Mao had so rightly pointed out, political power 'grows from the barrel of a gun.'

Some twenty feet from Colonel Huang, beyond the seated guests, the paramount leader sat behind his expansive desk. Zhao Chengzhi was at once the general secretary of the Communist Party, president of China, and chairman of the Central Military Commission. Thick black hair, normally combed up in the front, hung down over a pallid forehead. It was late evening, and his long workday was beginning to take its toll.

Zhao's mahogany desk was cluttered with file folders. There was a white telephone for general calls and a monstrous red phone with twin handsets that he used to contact ranking ministers of government as well as any one of several dozen state-run businesses. A photo of the general secretary's wife sat to his immediate right, though this and the unruly stack of files had been removed when Zhao had given his New Year's address to the nation.

Huang could not help but notice that the general secretary, normally a quiet and serene man, shifted a great deal in his seat, as if he were uncomfortably warm.

General Ma, the vice chairman of the Central Military Commission, and Admiral Qian, commander of the PLA Navy, each wore the uniform of their respective office, festooned with enough medals as to form protective breast plates for the two men. The general and the admiral were both possessed of the heavy jowls and swollen bellies that seemed to go with high command, attributes Huang swore he would never possess.

At forty-two, Huang Ju was a working colonel, still striving to be out in front of his team instead of slumped behind a desk preparing schedules and checking pay books. It was his responsibility to guard the life of the most powerful man in China. That meant he could not afford the frequent banquets and trappings of office life that other men of his station might enjoy. The general secretary kept long hours, and so did those who protected him. Huang led by example, and he made certain every close-protection officer under his command was given the opportunity to exercise and practice weekly to stay proficient in both firearms and defensive tactics.

This meeting had been going on for an hour. President Zhao shifted often in his seat but listened intently while his advisers offered up their counsel.

In addition to the two military men, State Premier Cao and Foreign Minister Li were also present. Huang did not trust any of the men, but he trusted no one beyond himself when it came to the safety and security of his charge. His job was to suspect – and he came by it naturally.

The general secretary leaned forward, elbows on the table. There was a trace of sweat on the man's brow, though the air-conditioning kept the office relatively cool compared to the humid outside temperatures. For the past hour, the topic of discussion had been about nothing but the sinking of *Orion*. Colonel Huang, of course, was not consulted, but present only to make certain none of the other men did anything to harm Zhao – and to put a bullet in their head if they tried.

'The idea makes no sense,' the general secretary said. 'Does anyone truly believe the Americans are stupid enough to sink a Chinese ship off their own coast – and then prove themselves magnanimous enough to rescue our personnel?'

General Ma gave a sullen nod. 'It would be a mistake to put anything past the American CIA. I would not be surprised if they were behind the bombing of the subway construction site.'

The foreign minister interjected. 'We are referring to that as a gas explosion, are we not?'

'Of course, of course,' Ma said. 'But we in this room are all aware Uyghur separatists were behind it – financed by the Americans, no doubt.'

The general secretary raised an eyebrow. 'The bombing of the new subway tunnel was obviously a terrorist act. This matter of *Orion*, however . . . Is it not more likely that some bureaucrat cut corners during safety inspections? Perhaps someone accepted bribes to line his own pockets and those overlooked violations caused the explosion and eventual sinking of our container ship.'

Zhao's anti-corruption initiative had already seen top executives from six state-run companies and several prominent party leaders, including a PLA general, thrown into prison. Three of the executives had been convicted of crimes stemming from the shoddy workmanship of an apartment building in Shanghai that collapsed, killing forty-nine. The men were given the death penalty but received the customary two-year probationary period whereby they might, with good behavior, have their sentences commuted. Zhao made it clear that he was not pleased with that loophole in the law. He was more than passionate about the topic.

Admiral Qian spoke next. 'The sea is over a hundred fathoms deep where *Orion* was lost, so there it will be impossible to look at any physical evidence. And we all know that the Americans will cover up any relevant facts.'

'Can any of the twenty-two survivors fill in the missing pieces?' Zhao asked.

'Perhaps,' General Ma said. 'But that leads to a question. What if the United States *is* behind this?'

'We will cross that river if we come to it,' the general secretary said.

Premier Cao spoke next. 'That the Americans trespass into our territorial waters is bad enough. Now we must kowtow to the Ryan regime and thank him for rescuing men on a ship they likely sank.'

Zhao scoffed at that. 'Do you imply that allowing our seamen to be saved will be seen as a weakness?'

The admiral, general, and premier nodded in unison. Foreign Minister Li sat and smiled, taking no position, which was, Colonel Huang thought, in and of itself a position.

'More than a few have taken to Weibo to show their displeasure at American meddling,' Premier Cao said.

'More than a few?'

'Thousands,' Cao said.

'A dog barks at something,' Zhao said, quoting a proverb, 'and the other dogs bark at him.'

'But they all bark,' General Ma said. 'There is danger enough in that.'

'This is true,' Zhao said, 'but I tend to give the people of China more credit. In any case, what would you have had me do? Call the President of the United States and tell him to let our sailors drown? That is flawed thinking, gentlemen. I have no love lost for the Americans or Jack Ryan, but I will not presume to give the man so much power over our country as to dictate who we will and will not allow to be rescued.'

The premier gave a solemn tip of his head. He was, after all, appointed by Zhao.

'And what of the USS *San Antonio*?' the admiral asked. 'I urge you to allow an increase in opposition to these criminal acts of incursion.'

The general secretary took a deep breath through his nose but said nothing.

'Zhao Zhuxi,' Admiral Qian said, using the title that had meant 'chairman' in Mao's day but was now usually translated as 'president' by the media. It was a matter of semantics that amounted to little consequence; the sentiment in the Chinese mind had changed little. 'I know you have kept a hands-off policy, but I do not see how we can help but concern ourselves with this escalation. Jack Ryan is exactly what he accuses us to be – a hegemon. He presumes to dictate Chinese national policy from halfway around the globe.'

General Ma gave a somber nod, as did Premier Cao. Again, Foreign Minister Li did not outwardly agree with the admiral. It was not lost on Colonel Huang, however, that neither did he offer support to President Zhao. He merely sat in his padded chair and smiled a benign smile that Huang suspected was as cancerous as any politician's in all of China. But Zhao considered Minister Li a friend, so the colonel simply watched and said nothing. Politicians of any stripe made him feel as though he'd downed a mouthful of spoiled milk. He preferred black-and-white realities to the intrigue of party politics – though the duties of protecting the paramount leader put the colonel and his men afoul of politicians on a daily, if not an hourly, basis.

General Secretary Zhao, on the other hand, thrived on the brinksmanship. He was obviously skilled at it, having gained the attention of Deng Xiaoping and his faction of princelings within the Standing Committee of the Politburo. He'd followed in Deng's footsteps as mayor of Chongqing in the early nineties, and like his predecessor, Zhao was an economic reformer. He was not, however, so quick to order crackdowns like Tiananmen – a propensity that some feared made him appear weak to the Western world.

Zhao leaned forward in his chair, eyes narrowing. 'Admiral, China is powerful enough that we need not rise every time America dangles a baited hook. There are other ways of achieving our aims than by the rattling of sabers.'

Huang braced himself as Admiral Qian nearly came out of his chair.

'With respect, Zhao Zhuxi,' Qian said. 'The Americans would sing a different song if we do more than rattle those sabers. Ryan made China look the fool under President Wei. The people of our country are weary of the bullying will of a nation on the other side of the world.'

Zhao cocked his head to one side. 'Do you insinuate that China looks the fool under my leadership?'

'I do not, Zhao Zhuxi,' the admiral said, not quite backing down. 'I merely mean to advise perceptions.'

Zhao's jaw muscles flexed.

'The Americans can send their warships to our waters as much as they wish, but we have a major advantage over them.' Zhao nodded for effect. 'We are already here. Even a man as bellicose as President Ryan will not provoke anything more than a war of words unless we ourselves raise the stakes.'

Admiral Qian continued to bluster. 'As you say, Zhao Zhuxi, our ships are already here – and could easily demonstrate our true strength to the Americans – and the people of China.'

'Oh,' Zhao said. 'China is far from weak, gentlemen. We do, however, have a severe problem with greed and corruption. I prefer we focus on getting our own house in order for the time being – and I expect each of you to do just that.'

'Even so,' Admiral Qian said. 'The container ship –'

The paramount leader raised his hand once more, this time signaling it was time to move on. The admiral, unaccustomed to taking such orders, seemed to swell even more than usual with unspoken words. Had Huang been less of a professional, he would have laughed out loud.

'I assure you,' Zhao said, 'if the Americans had anything to do with sinking the *Orion*, I will take decisive action.'

The white phone on Zhao's desk buzzed, but he did not answer it, apparently expecting the signal. He stood, grimacing a little at the effort.

The others in the room rose with him, which is what one did for the most powerful man in China, even if they did not agree with him.

'Gentlemen,' Zhao said. 'You must excuse me.' The men began to file out the door next to Huang, but the chairman spoke again. 'Foreign Minister Li,' he said.

Li paused at the threshold, close enough that Huang got a noseful of his strong cologne.

'Would you be so kind as to remain a moment?'

Li Zhengsheng turned and gave a slight bow toward the man who had appointed him. 'Of course, General Secretary.'

Zhao motioned to a chair and then turned toward a door that led to his private restroom, to the right of his desk.

'Please excuse me for a moment,' he said. 'This meeting was agonizingly long.'

Huang took a step away from the wall, but Zhao waved him off.

'You may go now, Colonel,' Zhao said.

Huang paused, waiting, as if hoping Zhao might change his mind.

The paramount leader gave a forced smile, obviously in severe discomfort. 'I will be fine, Huang,' he said. 'Minister Li is like a brother to me.'

'Very well, sir,' Colonel Huang said. 'I will remain outside the door. Please call if you need me.'

Colonel Huang closed the office door behind him, certain that he'd just left the man whom he was charged with protecting in the room with an extremely deadly snake.

The general secretary finished in his private restroom two agonizing minutes later. When he returned to his office, he found a small, skeletal man seated beside the foreign minister in front of his desk. The new arrival's thinning gray hair revealed a strong crop of liver spots on a high forehead. He wore a white lab coat and black tie. His shirt pocket was stuffed with an array of expensive fountain pens, the way a military man might wear his medals.

'Dr Hou.' Zhao regarded the man with a curt nod.

Both Hou and Foreign Minister Li stood and remained standing until Zhao was seated.

'Zhao Zhuxi,' the doctor said in a voice much too deep for his small stature. 'Your secretary showed me in. I hope you do not mind.'

'Not at all,' Zhao said. 'I trust that you read my notes and now you have some good news for me.'

Dr Hou was one of three staff doctors serving within

the walls of the Zhongnanhai. He was old enough to be Zhao's father – possibly even his grandfather – and dispensed advice with great pomposity, as if he were Confucius himself. The other two doctors were attending some medical training in Nanjing until the following day. Zhao found himself in dire straits or he never would have summoned this man.

The doctor lifted his nose toward the ceiling and fluttered his eyelashes as if he were explaining something very simple to a small child. 'I read your description of the ailment. General fatigue, pain, and difficulty in passing water, slight fever. Tell me, does it feel as if you are sitting on a stone?'

Zhao nodded. 'You might say that,' he said.

The doctor took a bottle of pills from the pocket of his lab coat and pushed them across the desk. 'No doubt the general secretary is suffering from an acutely aggravated prostate. I would prescribe two of these capsules three times a day. The pills are quite large, so be certain to take them with plenty of fluids. I also suggest a marked increase in the frequency of physical congress between the general secretary and Madame Zhao.'

Zhao took the pill bottle and rolled it around in his palm. 'Swallowing a large pill will be an easy task when compared to the remainder of your prescription.' The notion of explaining to his wife that the doctor ordered them to have more sex would have been comical had he not been in so much pain. 'What is in the capsules? Antibiotics?'

The doctor shook his head. '*Yin yang huo,*' he said.

'Horny goat weed?' the foreign minister repeated.

'And saw palmetto,' the doctor added. 'A very effective remedy when combined with the increased –'

'Thank you, Doctor,' Zhao said.

Foreign Minister Li looked away, as if biting his tongue.

All three men were silent for a long moment and then the doctor said, 'Was there anything else, General Secretary?'

Zhao shook his head. 'No,' he said. 'That will be all. I appreciate your diagnosis.'

The doctor shut the door as he left.

'I am all for Eastern medicine, Comrade Zhao,' the foreign minister said, offering a friendly smile, 'but I will see to it that my doctor prescribes you some antibiotics.'

'I would appreciate that,' Zhao said. 'This is a perfect example of how we must move forward. Herbs have their place, but there are times when one needs actual medicine.'

'If I may be so bold as to ask a question,' Li said.

'Of course,' Zhao said, swallowing two capsules of horny goat weed to hedge his bets.

'Do you think there is any chance the Americans are behind the sinking of the *Orion*?'

Zhao sighed. 'It is possible. But to what end?'

'True,' Li said. 'Truthfully, though, I would not put anything past Jack Ryan. He is, I believe, a man with much guile.'

'I do not think it is guile,' Zhao said. 'It is determination. And that is sometimes more dangerous.'

'Again you are right,' Li said.

'There is something else on your mind, my friend?'

'You are an astute observer, Zhao Zhuxi,' Li said.

'Tell me.'

'I hesitate to bring it up, but I am concerned about your push against the wealthy of the party.'

Zhao waved that off. 'I am not interested in wealth. You yourself are one of the wealthiest men I know. I am prosecuting corruption.'

'You know best, of course. I will see to your antibiotics. I hope your health improves quickly.' He gave a sly wink. 'In the meantime, I must remind my wife of her conjugal responsibility to my health.'

Zhao gave a polite chuckle, letting the bawdy comment slide. He preferred to keep things on a loftier level when dealing with members of his cabinet. 'I understand you are hosting a dinner party tomorrow.'

Li shook his head and shrugged. 'Nothing special. General Ma will attend, as well as General Xu and a few other minor guests. Such periodic functions allow me to keep a finger on the pulse of Beijing.'

'General Xu of the Central Security Bureau?'

The foreign minister nodded. 'Yes.'

'Be wary of that one,' Zhao said. 'He gives me cause for concern.'

'How so?'

Zhao narrowed his eyes, studying the man across his desk. 'He has . . . how shall I put this? A bad smell. I intend to make changes in that organization in the near future. The Central Security Bureau is, after all, tasked with your protection. I don't want to see it turned into a personality cult. You should be watchful.'

'I appreciate your concern, Zhao Zhuxi, and I will be careful.'

'See that you do, my friend,' Zhao said. 'I am very rarely wrong about my sense for a person's character.'

The foreign minister gave him a passive smile. 'That is interesting to note, Mr Chairman.'

General Ma Xiannian exited the great hall that housed the general secretary's office and turned left to make his way along one of the many wide pathways inside the high walls of the Zhongnanhai. His office was on the far side of the lake known as the Middle Sea, and he had to walk across a bridge to reach it. His status was such that he could have taken a cart, but the weather was dry and warm, and in any case, the walk allowed him to burn off some of his contempt for the young upstart who was now in charge of the party.

Deng Wenyuan, secretary of the Central Committee for Discipline Inspection, met the general before he reached the bridge. It was a well-known fact in the intelligence world that people stopped to chat on bridges, making them perfect spots in which to hide listening devices. People who wanted to speak openly avoided them, as well as any of the many benches that graced the parklike setting.

Secretary Deng was impeccably dressed in a dark business suit tailored especially for him in London on a recent junket. The CCDI oversaw the Propaganda and Organization Department, and as such had the power to sway and even direct public opinion.

The two men exchanged greetings, bowing slightly to each other. They kept their tone civil and their faces passive. Because they were senior members of the party, there was no doubt that passers-by would pay them close attention, even while pretending not to do so.

'And?' Secretary Deng asked.

'It went as you might expect,' Ma said, keeping his words vague. He was thinking *Pitiful, disastrous, unconscionable*, but he said, 'Disappointing.'

'Something must be done,' Deng said.

'And it is,' Ma said. 'Even as we speak.'

'Something drastic?'

General Ma smiled. 'Something final.'

10

Jack Ryan, Jr, parked the maroon Dodge Avenger across a side street from a weathered brick building in a sad parking lot tucked in off Harry Hines Boulevard. He and Chavez had purchased the car with cash from a dealership in East Dallas, on the off chance that someone had seen the rattle-can Taurus. Ryan now wore a shaggy wig with bleached-blond surfer tips pulled snuggly over his dark hair, just covering his ears. It was an expensive piece of equipment that looked ridiculously real and, he hoped, made him look a little less like the son of the President of the United States.

A large sign above the windowless building bore the red-neon outline of a busty woman bending over and peeking around her own thigh.

Ryan nodded toward the sign and mused. '*Chicas Peligrosas*,' he read.

Ding Chavez translated from the passenger seat of the Dodge. 'Dangerous girls.'

Ryan rolled his eyes. 'Even I could figure that one out.'

Chavez held a two-foot Yagi directional Wi-Fi antenna out his open window toward the front door of the Dangerous Girls strip club. The simple device resembled a miniature ladder made of a single aluminum bar with short aluminum cross-sections running along its length. Chavez fiddled for a few moments with the connected laptop, scrolling through a string of twelve-digit Bluetooth addresses, searching for Eddie Feng's phone.

'Our tango's in there, all right,' he said over the net, and then shot a glance at Ryan. 'Don't beat yourself up because you're not multilingual, *'mano*. You're a damned savant when it comes to analysis.'

'Thanks for that,' Ryan said. 'But I've decided I'm going to start working on my Russian.'

Chavez shut his computer and set it and the Yagi antenna on the floorboard at his feet. He opened the door and grinned. 'We all got our individual strengths. You can't help it if yours is staring at spreadsheets.'

Ryan laughed as he followed Chavez toward the double front doors of Chicas Peligrosas.

'You know I'm joking, right?' Chavez said.

Ryan patted Chavez on the back. 'I learned a long time ago, if you're not giving me shit, then something is terribly wrong.'

'Jack knows you love him,' Clark said over the net. 'How about you guys go get us some intel on Eddie Feng?'

'Copy that,' Chavez said.

Gavin Biery had a GPS proximity notification on Eddie Feng's phone, allowing the team to grab a few hours of much-needed sleep after he stopped moving for the night. But Feng was apparently a man on a mission. He was up and at 'em again just after noon.

Now Midas Jankowski and Dom Caruso were in the truck half a block away. Adara Sherman was going it alone today, another block down Harry Hines Boulevard to the south. The daylight hour made climbing onto a rooftop problematic, so John Clark sat behind the wheel of a primer-gray Pontiac Firebird around the corner in the parking lot of a Pep Boys auto-supply store. He did not have physical eyes-on like he'd had the night before, but each team member's location was transmitted via a small GPS tracker to his iPad, giving him a Common Operating Picture of everyone involved, as a color-coded icon representing each one moved around a digital map of the vicinity.

Successful surveillance operations took several teams to do them correctly – and safely. Especially if the subject decided to run SDRs – surveillance detection routes – which Eddie Feng did not. In fact, he'd committed the OPSEC fail from hell by never looking behind him and seemed completely blind to the possibility that someone might want to follow him. Ryan couldn't figure out if the man was stupid or merely bad at tradecraft.

Clark decided Ryan and Chavez would go into Chicas Peligrosas and get an eyeball on Feng, note the lay of the land inside. They would rotate out with Midas and Dom if Feng stayed too long. Midas's years working with the unit in Central and South America had made him conversant with Spanish. Dom spoke Italian, which allowed him to grab the gist of Spanish conversations going on around him.

Adara spoke passable Spanish as well, but while females were not unheard of as patrons of strip clubs, her blond hair and athletic build were sure to draw unwanted attention from the very people they were there to watch.

As team leader, Clark took his job of oversight seriously – even with a goofball like Eddie Feng. 'Everyone stay alert,' he said. 'Don't let the daylight lull you.'

'Roger that, Mr C,' Ding said to his father-in-law.

'Here we go,' Ryan mumbled as they approached the door.

'You're too young to be tired of looking at naked girls,' Chavez said.

'Not naked girls per se,' Ryan said. 'Just the kind that hang out in places like this.'

'I hear you there, *'mano*,' Chavez said.

The odor of an old carpet stewed in cheap booze and stale cigarettes hit Ryan in the face as soon as he opened the door.

'Well, this sucks,' he said under his breath as soon as he stepped across the threshold. He'd fully expected to see a handful of triad or cartel types, but was startled to find one of the largest Hispanic men he'd ever seen sitting beside a magnetometer, presumably to check IDs. Pushing seven feet tall, the big guy had to weigh in at a good 350 pounds. Much of his bulk was fat, but Jack had learned from experience that heavy guys built up a considerable amount of muscle just hauling their own weight around. This one eclipsed the small stool he was sitting on, completely blocking the entry. A tattoo of what looked like a female version of Death stuck up from the collar of his T-shirt. He hadn't shaved or showered in a long time, and Ryan was surprised they hadn't gotten wind of him outside. He half expected 'Fee fi fo fum' to be the first words out of the guy's mouth.

Instead, the big man grunted and asked, '*¿Armas?*' giving Ryan, and then Chavez, the evil-eye once-over. Guns?

Ryan hunched his shoulders, slouching some to look

less threatening than his six-foot-one frame would normally indicate. There was a time to be intimidating, and this was not it. Bouncers paid a hell of a lot more attention to tough guys than they did to nervous pushovers with bleached tips. Both men were indeed strapped, each carrying a Smith & Wesson M&P Shield nine-millimeter. The small, single-stack pistols were virtually invisible under the men's shirts, but even so, guns could be explained away. Dopers carried guns. Hell, half the people in Texas did. The wire neck-loop mics and the rest of the comms package, however, would likely earn them each a hole in the head.

Jack assumed the dozen Asian and Hispanic men in the place were armed, but management evidently wanted to double-check any new faces. Chavez started to say something in Spanish, but Jack noticed just in time that the cord at the base of the magnetometer was unplugged from the wall. He gave his partner a quick elbow in the ribs.

'No *armas*,' Ryan said, eyes on the dancers as if he was enthralled – trying his best for a lecherous-college-boy look. 'We're all about the girls, not the guns.' He peeled a couple twenty-dollar bills off a roll from his pocket and gave the big guy an embarrassed grin. 'To tell you the truth, this is my first time in a titty bar. Do we pay the cover charge to you or what?'

The twenties looked like Monopoly money in the big guy's massive hands as he snatched them away. He lifted his chin and grunted toward a trio of skinny Asian girls swaying on the stage. 'They'll dance better if you give them a little cash, but hands off the merchandise unless you work out an extra arrangement with me or Manolo – the bald guy in the white shirt at the end of the stage.'

'Got it.' Ryan gave a compliant nod and gulped for effect, his eyes wide and seemingly transfixed on the poor gyrating women. A dozen low tables ran in front of the stage, some occupied by small groups of Hispanic or Asian men. Triad or cartel according to their significant ink, each stuck with his own ethnicity. Two rosy-cheeked white guys in City of Dallas municipal worker coveralls occupied the nearest table. Ryan counted sixteen patrons in all, counting Manolo and the Asian man with the ridiculous fauxhawk sitting at the table beside him.

That one had to be Eddie Feng.

The North Texas Crimes Against Children Task Force was housed in a nondescript hangar leased by the Federal Bureau of Investigation on the northeast side of Dallas Love Field Airport. The three agents that made up the ICAC – or the Internet portion of the Crimes Against Children Task Force – worked at a bank of computers in a windowless area with their backs to the far wall. These two women and one burly man – all parents themselves – spent much of their workday posing as children, engaged in online conversation with some of the sickest minds on the planet. It was a target-rich environment – with the National Center for Missing and Exploited Children estimating 75,000 would-be traders in child pornography online at any given time.

The ICAC workstations were purposely situated with their backs to the walls, giving them some semblance of security and allowing them to look up and view a glimpse of the semi-normal life of their brothers- and sisters-in-arms in the bullpen just a few yards away.

The CAC Task Force Commander, FBI Special Agent Kelsey Callahan, didn't believe in separate offices. If her team was going to wade through the river of shit that the perverts they hunted caused, they should do it together as a unified group. She did, however, put her desk at the head of the open bullpen so she'd have direct access to the whiteboard behind her.

No straitlaced Betty Bureau Blue Suit, Special Agent Callahan wore a Neiman Marcus silk blouse in subtle pink and stonewashed jeans over hips that she wished were a smidge smaller, but that were still small enough so as to make the .40-caliber Glock 23 in the holster on her belt look huge. Her instructors at Quantico had called her curly copper ponytail a 'murder handle.' She considered chopping it off for the academy, but she'd had long hair since high school – and besides, she needed to cling to every last vestige of femininity in this overly masculine profession. Callahan resolved early on to unleash nine kinds of hell on anyone who got close enough to even touch her hair – and went on to prove that resolve to an exuberant defensive tactics instructor who thought he'd teach her the error of her thinking and grabbed her from behind. She'd dislocated her own shoulder but ruptured the instructor's testicle. Her injuries saw her recycled into the next class of NATs – New Agent Trainees – but the badass reputation that followed her into her career was worth repeating three weeks of training. The reputation of being what Texas Department of Public Safety sergeant Derrick Bourke called 'a half a bubble off plumb' only added to her success leading the North Texas CAC Task Force.

Sergeant Bourke's desk was to the immediate right of Callahan's, facing the bullpen, but the forty-year-old trooper and father of three now stood beside her, looking over her shoulder at the files on the screen of the stand-alone laptop at her desk.

It was Sergeant Bourke who had brought her the USB drive, retrieved the night before by a trooper posted to Mansfield. Department of Public Safety computer gurus had run all manner of diagnostics to check the drive for viruses. FBI techs had double- and triple-checked it for remote access Trojans, ransomware, and other viruses. Even after the device had been pronounced free from malware, FBI higher-ups still directed it only be inserted into a computer with the modem disabled and not attached to any network.

Bourke leaned in, his hand on Callahan's desk. 'Looks like some kind of spreadsheet,' he said. 'Accounting records maybe . . . and encrypted notes.'

The FBI agent scrolled upward, nodding. 'Not encrypted,' she said. 'Coded. We can open them. We just can't tell what they mean. I see the word "coronet" a lot. Mean anything to you?'

'Nope.'

Callahan mused as she scrolled, as much to herself as to Bourke. 'I'm not finding anything to give us a location of this Eddie Feng bastard. After what Blanca Limón told me about him, I really, really want to find this guy.' She leaned back in her chair and looked up at the sergeant. 'I'll let the organized-crime squads figure out the rest of the

trash on this thumb drive. What I do need is to have a little chat with the guy who pays for sex with a little girl as
young as Blanca. According to her, there's another girl, a
friend of hers named' – Callahan looked at the printed
FBI 302 beside her laptop – 'Magdalena Rojas. The guy
your trooper killed dropped Magdalena at some creepy
mansion in the country. She is at this very moment being
made to do God knows what. If we find this Eddie Feng
and squeeze him a little, maybe, just maybe, we can find
her.' Callahan took a breath, as if she was coming up for
air. Bourke, who was used to her passion, stood by and
listened.

Callahan glanced back down at the 302. 'Your trooper
made the traffic stop south of Mansfield. Blanca says a
pimp named Parrot took her and Magdalena to work
a party with a bunch of other girls south of Dallas last
night. Eddie Feng was there. He gives us the address of
that party and we'll have a search line between there and
the Mansfield traffic stop.'

'That's still a lot of open ground,' Bourke said.

Callahan scrolled through the columns of numbers,
looking for anything that might give her an address. 'It's
all we've got right now. Maybe we'll get lucky and Feng
will know where the mansion is, the sick bastard.'

Two desks away, FBI Special Agent John Olson pitched
his cell phone onto a stack of paperwork and slumped in
his chair, rubbing his eyes.

Callahan looked up at him. 'I sincerely hope you're
about to tell me Fort Worth PD has Parrot Villanueva in
custody.'

Olson shook his head. 'I wish. His apartment's empty

and he's in the wind. We have an APB out for him, but unless he gets jammed up over a broken taillight or something . . .'

Callahan stood and used the flat of her hand to pound on her Vietnam War-era metal desk. The noise echoed off the high ceiling of the spacious hangar. She did this at least twice a week, and everyone on her team knew what it meant. A new turd had floated to the surface of their little world, and he was now their priority. Six police officers from four different municipalities and two sheriff's departments, three Texas Department of Public Safety investigators, three special agents from Immigration and Customs Enforcement, and three from the FBI Dallas Field Office all peered around their computers, ready to receive marching orders. Some were relatively new, others had been on the task force for a couple years. But all the CAC Task Force members had so much experience rescuing kids that they'd accumulated a deep and abiding hatred for the men and women they hunted. It was controlled hatred, hatred that Callahan made sure they kept within the bounds of the law, but it was hatred nonetheless. Callahan banging on her desk was like the horn to a foxhound. Every member of the team sat poised, twitching to channel their hatred into the hunt.

'Okay, listen up! There's a thirteen-year-old girl out there named Magdalena Rojas who needs our help. Right now, our best chance at finding her is a worthless little creeper named Eddie Feng.' She threw the last name like an expletive. 'Not sure if it's Edward or Eddie. He speaks English, but judging from the scant information we have, he may be Chinese.'

Joe Rice, a detective working off a federal grant from the Waxahachie Police Department, raised his pen. He was in his fifties, with thinning blond hair and a drooping mustache he'd probably not shaved since his first days in the police academy thirty years before. A new grandfather and a deacon in the Waxahachie First Baptist Church, he was the reason Callahan didn't curse as much as she would have liked to.

'Do we got a photo of Eddie Feng?'

'We will as soon as you get me one, Joe,' Callahan said.

She'd conducted the interview with Blanca Limón, so she had a general physical description. 'Our only witness is another thirteen-year-old girl named Blanca who was being forced to turn tricks with Magdalena. Blanca describes Feng as being in his mid-thirties, around five-feet-eight, slender build, with glasses. She says he downs energy drinks like they're going out of style . . . and he's sporting a fauxhawk.'

'Of course he is,' Olson said, still rubbing his eyes.

'I've got him on Facebook,' an African American detective named Jermaine Armstrong said. The Dallas PD detective was a dedicated gym rat and wore the sleeves of his gunmetal T-shirt rolled up over biceps the size of cantaloupes. He also possessed the uncanny ability to sell anything to anyone – especially online. He turned his laptop around to show Eddie Feng's profile pic, complete with a can of Red Bull and the fauxhawk. Once Callahan had seen it, Armstrong turned the computer back and began to peck at the keys again. Callahan hit an icon on her desktop and pulled up an image of the detective's screen on the whiteboard behind her.

Armstrong peered over the top of his computer. 'Our little friend Sugar just sent him a friend request. According to Messenger, he's online right now. He should be getting back to her shortly if he likes what he sees.'

'Sugar' was the name of a computer-generated image of a twelve-year-old girl who could have been a Hispanic or Filipina. The avatar allowed law enforcement to pose and talk to men under her identity without using the image of an actual human child. Sugar was dressed innocently enough in a pair of pink shorts and simple white T-shirt. Sadly, that innocence was the hook for a great many men.

Eddie Feng accepted Sugar's friend request almost instantly, which was not surprising, since he'd chosen to pay for the services of little Blanca Limón. Detective Armstrong, burly man that he was, was a genius at writing under the guise of a preteen girl.

Bored, he typed. What RU up 2?

Feng's words marched across the screen. Do I know you?

Megan sez U R kool.

I guess Megan knows, Feng said. Where's she at now?

Armstrong typed, Texas stupid. He finished it with a squinty emoticon with its tongue sticking out.

Feng came back almost instantly. RU in Texas 2?

Armstrong/Sugar sent a blue thumbs-up.

Cool, Feng said.

Armstrong cast the net. Wanta trade pics? C if you like what U C? I'm bored shitless.

You shouldn't curse, Feng said.

Sorry, Daddy, Detective Armstrong typed, setting the hook.

Feng was silent for two solid minutes. No words, no flashing dots to show he was typing.

Finally, I guess appeared in the dialogue box.

I'll text them 2 U, Armstrong/Sugar said.

just attach pics to message.

Nape, Armstrong replied, purposely misspelling a few words, FB alredy warned me bout that. My mom could find out.

That's ok, Feng typed.

Callahan held her breath while the dots pulsed in the dialogue box. He was still making up his mind.

Then his cell number appeared.

Sitting at the desk beside Armstrong, Joe Rice entered the cellular number in his computer. He put an index finger to his head and pulled an imaginary trigger at Eddie Feng's stupidity.

Feng's dialogue box pulsed again. Then: What's your contact info?

Armstrong typed the number to one of the office burner smartphones – so called not because it was a prepaid, but because the disgusting photos that came across the devices rendered them unsuitable for anything but burning in a very hot fire once they'd been utilized as evidence for the prosecution. As soon as he entered the number, Armstrong typed POS – parent over shoulder – and logged out.

Joe Rice looked up from his computer and raised both fists high in the air. 'He shoots, he scores, the crowd goes wild.'

'Talk to me, Joe,' Callahan said.

'Eddie Feng's phone is pinging a tower off Harry Hines Boulevard near the LBJ Expressway. Google Maps shows two strip clubs in that quadrant. One of them is closed until six, but a place called Chicas Peligrosas opens at noon. It's not far from here.'

Callahan stood again and grabbed her jacket, glaring across the squad room. 'Why aren't y'all already in your cars?'

Less than ten minutes after Special Agent Kelsey Callahan slapped the flat of her hand on the top of her desk, fourteen members of the North Texas Crimes Against Children Task Force followed her out the hangar door en route to Chicas Peligrosas. Considering the story Blanca Limón told her about Eddie Feng and his friends, Callahan thought she might just arrest everyone in the place. Even if they weren't involved with Feng, odds are they'd be sitting around watching a bunch of kids take their clothes off. It would do them good to cool their heels in Dallas County lockup until a judge cut them loose. They might beat the rap, but they wouldn't be able to beat the ride.

11

Less than six miles from the Dallas Area CAC Task Force hangar, Jack Ryan, Jr, slouched at his wobbly table and tried to figure out how he could unsee the sad scene unfolding amid the pulsing lights and throbbing music on the raised stage less than ten feet away. He ordered a second bottle of Corona from a sullen Hispanic waitress. Unlike the girls on the stage, who wore nothing but tiny G-strings and sweaty layers of body glitter, the waitress got to wear a tube top. Unfortunately, it was so small it wouldn't have covered a roll of breath mints, let alone her full figure. Not that any strip club was an upstanding establishment, but there were strip clubs and there were strip clubs. These girls looked awfully young and it made Jack feel dirty to be within a hundred feet of them. He did his best impersonation of a happy-go-lucky frat boy, but a sticky film of unknown residue on the table's surface made him wish he'd worn long sleeves. The slightly sour smell of the place melded with the pulsing bass note from the speakers behind the stage like some kind of enhanced interrogation measure, making it difficult to think.

Ryan faced the dancers but scanned the rest of the club with his peripheral vision – a respite from focusing on the poor girls on stage doing their level best to look sexy. He knew Chavez was doing the same, taking the left half of the club – including a couple tables of triad types and Fee

Fi Fo Fum, who remained by the front door. Jack looked predominantly at the area to his right. The strobe lights of the stage left the area extra-dark, but he could just make out the curtained booths in the shadows along the back wall – where the special 'dance' arrangements were taken care of. At the far end of the stage, Eddie Feng sat next to an equally sleazy-looking Tres Equis guy and tapped away on his iPad in between slugs of Red Bull.

Feng was the polar opposite of the giant at the front door. His skin was pasty and pale, appearing to glow pulsing strobes. As with many of the people Ryan had followed over the years, there was nothing formidable about the man at all. In fact, calling him wormy was a disservice to actual worms.

In addition to working on the iPad, Feng scribbled notes in a spiral notebook on the table in front of him. Ryan didn't know exactly what this guy was up to, but he knew he wanted to get a look at that spiral notebook as well as the iPad.

Ryan nursed his beer, casting enough looks at the dark-eyed dancing girls so as not to appear out of place. He leaned sideways toward Chavez and spoke under his breath, hoping the mic on his neck loop would pick up his whisper and broadcast it to the rest of the team.

'Our friend has a tablet computer I'd like to get my hands on.'

'Due time,' Clark said. 'Does it seem like he's being protected? Guarded by the cartel or triad?'

Ryan fought the urge to shake his head at the question coming from his earpiece. 'No,' he said, still gawking at the stage and tilting his head as if speaking to Chavez.

'There's a Hispanic guy at his table chatting him up, but everyone appears to be guarding the girls.'

'He's right,' Chavez mumbled. 'I'd lay odds that there's enough firepower in here to hold off a small army.'

'Good enough,' Clark said. 'Keep eyes-on for another half-hour. Sing out if it looks like you're starting to get stale.'

Adara's voice came across the radio, calm but direct. 'That small army you mentioned,' she said. 'I've got eight plainclothes officers coming your way from a half a block south. I'm betting they're Feds, and not trained counter-intel types, either. They're too overt-covert.'

Jack nodded to himself, as if in time with the bass beat from the speakers. He knew exactly what Adara meant. Men and women who'd spent long careers carrying large and heavy firearms on their belts often tended to walk holding their arms slightly away from their bodies – even when they transitioned to a smaller, more concealable weapon for different duty. It took practice and concentration to overcome the effect of being a beat cop or even a suit-wearing detective. Simply wearing plain clothes did not make one covert.

Dom broke squelch on the radio. 'Six more of the same moving in from the north. There's a redhead leading the pack. She's Bureau, no doubt about it. I saw her belt badge when she got out of her car. I'm guessing this is some kind of task force.'

Clark's voice was tight, agitated. 'Ding, Ryan, haul ass out the back. I don't want you caught up in some whore-house raid.'

'Copy that,' Chavez said, nodding toward the dark hallway

at the rear of the building. 'You lead the way, *'mano*,' he said to Ryan. 'I'll be right behind you.'

Jack was already on his feet, slouching between the row of tables and the stage toward the back door, as if he was looking for the restroom. He wasn't the sort to run from a fight, but his getting caught in a place like this would cost his father a great deal of political capital. Not to mention the fact that the resulting media attention would severely damage Jack's ability to continue working in a covert capacity.

Even so, he turned to Chavez as they reached the end of the stage, stopping in his tracks. 'What about Fee Fi Fo Fum?'

Chavez groaned, having already reached the same conclusion. 'He's gonna hurt somebody.'

The two men had worked together long enough that they generally knew what the other was thinking in any tactical situation. Neither wanted to leave approaching law enforcement to stumble into the strip club blind and come face-to-face with the armed behemoth. The task force agents would eventually gain the upper hand, but one of them was bound to get injured – and possibly even killed – in the process.

Ryan and Chavez each took a twenty-dollar bill from their pockets and stepped up to the stage. The two tired-looking girls turned, lowering their gyrating bodies to allow the men to stuff the money into their G-strings. The girl nearest Jack looked even younger up close. She had to be in her teens, probably the reason the cops were here. Throwing a quick look over his shoulder to make sure the giant by the door was watching, Jack gave an exuberant catcalling whistle, then put both hands flat on the stage as if to climb up and dance with the girl. Though not unheard-of behavior in a titty bar, it was exactly what Fee Fi Fo Fum had warned them not to do. They had not paid for the privilege.

The giant sprang from his stool by the door with surprising dexterity. '¡Pendejo!' he roared above the throbbing music, lumbering toward Ryan. His bullish neck was arched and his head down, as if he intended to bowl Ryan over.

Extremely big men may have doled out countless beatdowns, but they rarely had much real experience with anyone fighting back. Unfortunately for the bouncer, both Chavez and Ryan had plenty.

Ryan yanked a wad of assorted bills from his pocket and pitched them onto the stage, hoping the investment would keep the girls busy doing something besides kicking him in the head. Chavez stepped deftly aside as the giant chugged by, giving him a stout two-handed shove from behind and causing him to go faster than his legs could carry him. Jack caught the man mid-stumble, grabbing him by the shaggy hair with both hands and directing his forehead toward the lip of the stage. Inertia and gravity did the rest. The resulting collision of bone against wood cracked like a rifle shot. Fee Fi Fo Fum piled up on the filthy carpet at the base of the stage, moaning, both hands on his gashed forehead, trying to stanch the flow of blood.

Chavez gave Ryan's arm a tug. 'Haul ass!' he said, without looking back.

The nearest cartel guys sat at their table and blinked. It was inconceivable that anyone could knock out the big bouncer. Everything had happened so fast, it took them a moment to process what this white kid with the frosted hair and dark beard had done.

Ryan turned to run but came face-to-face with Eddie Feng, who was now on his feet, clutching his tablet computer in crossed arms. A commotion at the front drew the Taiwanese man's attention toward the door. Ryan took that moment to dip into his pocket and then reach under the edge of Feng's table. A strong adhesive held the GSM slap mic in place – leaving Ryan free to run down the hallway and out the back door, joining Chavez in the alley at the same moment law enforcement poured in the front door.

Fourteen members of the Crimes Against Children Task Force button-hooked through the double doors two at a time, moving quickly as they came in to make room for the person behind them. They hadn't knocked or announced, so they'd seen no reason to cover the back door. With their sidearms drawn, they divided areas of responsibility as they scanned for danger. Chicas was a cartel joint, so it was a given that there would be guns inside. Joe Rice, the Waxahachie detective, had suggested they call Dallas PD SWAT. Callahan had demurred, though she knew it was probably the smarter call. She wanted to take Eddie Feng herself and right damn now, too, before he had a chance to contact even one more child online. She wasn't about to screw around waiting for a bunch of SWAT guys to convene and scratch their asses while they drew up a plan.

With her FBI badge hanging from a chain on her neck, Kelsey Callahan pointed her pistol at the Sun Yee On triad turd nearest her and gave a shrill whistle to get everyone's attention. On cue, Special Agent Olson cut the music and turned on what lights there were – which still didn't brighten things up much. A dead quiet fell over the club.

The triad and cartel pukes just blinked, sizing up the task force like dogs consider a piece of meat. They were starting to get twitchy.

'Eddie Feng!' Callahan shouted, staring down a skinny Chinese gangbanger beside the stage. She lowered her voice slightly in an effort to defuse the situation. 'I only want Eddie Feng.'

The triad guy's shoulders relaxed a notch. He tipped his head sideways toward a man with a fauxhawk holding a computer tablet and a can of Red Bull. The bleeding gigantor lay at his feet.

Two CAC Task Force officers moved in on Feng. One took the tablet while the other spun him none too gently and put on the cuffs. Callahan continued to scan the shabby club. 'Nice and calm,' she said, her voice steady and remarkably controlled considering how fast her heart was beating. She had to concentrate to focus on the threats and not the poor kids standing topless on stage. 'Hands!' she said. '¡Manos! Let's see hands.'

Ninety seconds later, seventeen fuming members of Sun Yee On and Tres Equis sat on the floor in front of the stage, hands flex-cuffed behind their backs. The big guy slouched at the end of the line, blood still oozing from a nasty cut above his brow. One of the agents stood guard over nineteen confiscated handguns – now cleared and stacked along with knives and assorted other weapons, from chains to bicycle locks.

Callahan sat Eddie Feng back down at his table while two female CAC officers got the dancers some clothes and took them outside to interview in the cars, away from the accusing eyes of their pimps. Two agents secured the front and rear doors while the rest either pulled guard duty or stood in front of the guys lined up at the base of the stage, running them through Dallas PD dispatch for wants and warrants.

Callahan tapped Feng's tablet, handing it off to Olson. 'Let's get this bagged before somebody wipes it.'

Olson reached in his jacket and pulled out a black nylon sleeve, into which he slid Eddie Feng's computer. Often called a Faraday bag, the forensic evidence sleeve shielded the device from sending or receiving signals that might shut it down, remotely wipe the information, or inform a third party that it had been compromised. FBI techs would be able to take a better look once they got the device back to a shielded room.

Feng slumped at the table, hands behind his back, his dark eyes casting around the place like a cornered animal. He glanced at the RF shielding bag and then up at Olson. 'There's no need for that. Hell, it's barely even encrypted.' He leaned forward, chest against the table, as if to confide in Olson. 'We need to go somewhere else to talk.'

'And we will,' Callahan said.

Feng looked over his shoulder at the line of triad and cartel members. Every one of them was now staring daggers at the man.

'Seriously,' Feng said. 'We should go.'

Ordinarily, Callahan would have agreed. But now the bad blood that had suddenly sprung up between Feng and the rest of the men made her think a few more minutes might rattle the guy's cage in a productive way. Her team had the inside of the club secured, and marked DPD cruisers were already rolling up to the front and rear doors. She didn't have to worry about the outer perimeter. Sticking around was safe enough, and even if it didn't turn out to be incredibly productive, it did Callahan's heart good to see this little prick squirm.

'You have the wrong man,' Feng whispered in accented English. 'I'm one of the good guys.'

'You seriously need to shut up,' Callahan snapped. Feng was the type who would talk, but she wanted to get the tap flowing good and strong of his own accord before she read him his Miranda warning. Often, the best way to do that with people like him was to tell them to be quiet.

An Asian man with a buzz cut and full-sleeve tattoos craned his neck from his position at the base of the stage. He began to shout maniacally in Chinese, eyes wild, spittle flying from his drawn lips. Feng went pale, shrinking sideways in his chair to put even a few more inches between himself and the screaming triad soldier. A task force officer gave the tattooed man a shove with the toe of his boot. Instead of going quiet, the man rolled on his side, scrambling to his feet. He continued to scream in Chinese as he rushed toward Feng. Arms behind his back, the screaming triad puke fell flat on his face when Armstrong simply stomped on his foot.

Feng suddenly stood, nearly knocking over the table, but Callahan shoved him back down. He seemed awfully frail, and it wasn't very difficult.

She nodded to Armstrong and then the screaming triad

guy. 'Get him out of here, Jermaine.' She looked at the rest of her team. 'Tase the next shitbag that so much as twitches without my permission.'

Olson held up the bagged computer, unfazed by the commotion. 'Is this going to be more of the same stuff?'

Feng's face fell. 'Same stuff as what?'

Olson shrugged, leaning back to rub his eyes. 'Record of payment, maybe? Most of it is in code. "Coronet" gets mentioned a half a dozen times or so –'

'Shhh,' Feng said, nearly apoplectic now. 'Don't discuss that in here.'

Callahan looked over Olson's shoulder. They would need to get back to the office to concentrate on the data, but this was big stuff. She already knew the triads were running underage girls, but if they'd linked up with an offshoot of the Sinaloa Cartel, that took this ballgame into a whole new league. The information on this guy's iPad could nail down a major human-trafficking ring.

'I'm begging you,' Feng whined. 'Just get me out of here.'

'You're in an awfully big hurry to go to jail,' Callahan said. 'Having sex with a minor is a pretty big deal here in Texas, Ed. Even the guys on the inside don't take kindly to child rapists.'

'What are you talking about?'

Callahan decided to play a portion of her hand. 'We have a thumb drive that came from you.'

Feng's face went slack. 'How?'

'We'll get to that,' she said.

'Can we get to it somewhere else, Officer . . .?'

'Special agent,' she corrected. 'Callahan, FBI.'

'Okay, Special Agent Callahan,' Feng said, chewing on

his trembling bottom lip. He'd become wooden, his words barely audible. 'There's more going on than you realize. Take me somewhere safe. I promise I'll tell you everything I know.'

Ryan and Chavez moved their rented Dodge to a cracked asphalt parking lot behind an abandoned warehouse three blocks from Chicas Peligrosas. John Clark and the others had scattered to various locations in the area. The GSM mic broadcast on a cell signal, so there was no need for them to congregate any closer and risk being caught by responding officers.

Chavez gave Ryan a nod during a lull in the conversation. 'I guess this Feng character is a big deal after all. Sorry I doubted you, Jack.'

Ryan raised an eyebrow, grinning. 'Wait,' he said. 'You doubted me?'

Feng started talking again. It sounded like he was about to break down in tears.

'. . . *Seriously,*' he said. '*You have to promise to keep me safe.*'

'*I can do that,*' Agent Callahan said. '*But why should I?*'

Chavez grimaced and mouthed, 'Heartless. I like her.'

Feng insisted he be taken somewhere else before he would talk. Callahan continued to play hardass, reminding him of the trouble he was in for sanctioning child prostitution.

Clark's voice came over the radio, sounding strained and fatigued. 'Dom,' he said, 'I assume you have your FBI credentials.'

'I don't leave home without 'em, boss,' Caruso said.

Officially on special 'unspecified duty' away from his

assigned field office, Dominic Caruso maintained his commission as a special agent with the Federal Bureau of Investigation. This often made him the only member of The Campus who could legally carry a weapon in all fifty states and US territories – not that any of them let a little thing like that stop them from packing. Many of the things they did overseas were, in point of fact, against the law. It was the way of counterintelligence work. The fact that one's government sanctioned an action in no way made that action legal in another country, no matter how moral or right it might be.

Clark continued. 'The human trafficking is bad enough, but there's more going on here than that. Eddie Feng is a piece of shit, but he knows something – as evidenced by Jack's earlier discovery about the Beijing subway bombing. We need to find out what that something is. Dom, I'll get Gerry to pull a few strings with the Bureau so you can insinuate yourself into Special Agent Callahan's investigation. Stick with her and find out what she knows. The rest of us will back off a bit and do more research into the unholy union between the Sun Yee On triad and the Tres Equis men.'

'Copy that,' Caruso said. 'I'll follow at a discreet distance when they come out, and then introduce myself to Special Agent Callahan in an hour or so.'

'That should give me enough time,' Clark said. 'I'll let you know.'

Over the radio, Feng's voice changed from whining to demanding. *'If you don't get me out of here, I'm going to have to ask for a lawyer.'*

'You do that,' Callahan said. *'We'll see then what kind of protection you get.'*

'*Look.*' Feng was sobbing again. '*I was bluffing about a lawyer. Just put me in solitary. These animals would kill me five minutes after I go into general population. I swear, I'll give you everything I've got.*'

The voice of a male agent came across now. '*Including whatever code you're using?*'

'*Yes.*' Sniff, sniff.

'*And what all the numbers mean in your data?*'

'*Yes!*'

'*And who they correspond to?*'

'*If I know.*'

'*How about Coronet?*' the male voice asked. '*Who or what is that?*'

'*What is wrong with you people?*' Feng spoke so quietly now that the GSM mic barely picked up his words. '*I said I'd tell you, but you have to get me out of here.*'

'*So tell,*' Callahan said. '*Show some good faith.*'

'*Okay,*' Feng whispered. '*This guy, Coronet. I think he's some kind of spy.*'

The man with La Santa Muerte tattooed on his neck sat down the street from Chicas Peligrosas in his 1994 S-10 pickup. He ground his teeth, discolored from years of smoking hand-rolled cigarettes. The man's name was Javier Goya, but everyone called him Moco. At twenty-nine, he'd spent more than a third of his life behind bars – and he'd decided after he got out the last time, he wasn't going back. His leg bounced on the floorboard, rocking the little truck and drawing a look from Gusano, the man who sat beside him.

'You got the need, the need for weed,' Gusano said.

'Shut up, *cabrón*,' Moco said, knowing his partner was right. Gusano had once eaten a worm on a bet, earning his name – and Moco thought him just about as smart as one of the slimy creatures.

Moco pounded his fist against the steering wheel, causing dust to rain down from the headliner of the S-10 pickup. He had to be the luckiest son of a bitch in the world.

The tat – a skulled female figure with scythe and beckoning bony fingers – was a prison job he'd gotten while incarcerated in Huntsville's Eastham Unit. The guy running the block had suggested the design – as long as Moco was ready for what went along with it – and sent him to another guy who worked in the kitchen. This other guy was a crazy old Mexican artist from Reynosa who used ink from the soot of burned baby oil mixed with pages from the Bible.

That ink must have been some potent shit, because La Santa Muerte had protected Moco well over the years – if you didn't count the nickel he did in Darrington for selling a tiny bit of black-tar heroin to an undercover cop in Bridgeport, Texas. The state was serious about punishing drug crimes. But nobody shanked him while he was inside, and that was saying something in a place as bloody as Darrington.

La Santa Muerte was sure as hell looking out for him today. At first he'd been pissed that his truck had broken down, but if the alternator had not gone out he and Gusano would have been inside Chicas Peligrosas when the Feds showed up – which meant they would have tried to put him back inside, which in turn meant he would have shot it out and very likely ended up dead. But that hadn't happened, thanks to La Santa Muerte.

Now he watched as his friends were frog-marched one by one out the front door of the strip club, hands cuffed behind their backs, and stuffed into waiting cop cars. A tall Hispanic and a pissed-looking redhead, both wearing FBI raid jackets, came out last, flanking that asshole Eddie Feng. Moco had never trusted that guy. He was always snooping around, paying good money for girls who weren't worth a dime bag, and asking questions about things that were none of his business. One way or another he was behind this.

Moco used his cell phone to snap photos of as many of the cops as he could, paying special attention to the ones in the FBI jackets. The curly-haired bitch was in charge. He could tell by the way she carried herself, all haughty and nose in the air. Goya hated girls like that – and so did his boss. Oh, yeah, the *patrón* would be most interested in this one. Moco grinned at the thought of what they'd do to her.

The boss had some very special methods to deal with bitches who got in the way of his operation.

12

The man known as Coronet sat on the flimsy plastic chair on Roxas Avenue. He would have liked to put his back against something more substantial than a wooden utility pole, but it was the best he could do. He was working, after all, and in his line of work, danger was a given.

Davao City, Philippines, was familiar to security experts and foreign policy wonks because of its crime – and the mayor's brutal crackdown to curb it. Attention spans being what they were, interest waned until someone set off a bomb in Davao's Roxas Night Market, killing fifteen and wounding seventy. The radical Islamic terror group Abu Sayyaf, based in the southern Philippine islands of Jolo and Basilan, had claimed, and then denied, responsibility. There had been arrests, but none of those arrested had been affiliated more than tangentially with Abu Sayyaf. Coronet made it a priority to find out who was behind the bombing. In his business, bombers who did not get themselves captured were good people to have on the payroll.

Coronet himself had never been arrested – though he'd done plenty to deserve incarceration, and in some countries, something a little more permanent.

He'd been identified as a likely candidate for intelligence work when he was nineteen years old and flunking out of National Chiao Tung University in Hsinchu. NCTU was considered one of the top schools in Taiwan, and just getting in was an accomplishment. He'd majored in business management with a minor in foreign languages – and proved a brilliant, if extremely lazy, student. His near perfect memory allowed him to score top marks on every test. But he couldn't be bothered with any essays or projects. His professors, especially the females, were smitten by his charm. None of them wanted him to fail, which allowed him to hang on far longer than he should have – and long enough for an agent of mainland China to make contact.

Over drinks one night, an English professor named Wang promised that if Coronet would commit himself and finish his studies, there would be a job for him that would be more exciting than he could possibly imagine. There was great adventure to be had for a man who could go places without being noticed. According to the professor, Coronet's medium complexion and innocuous Asian face gave him an ambiguous ethnicity, allowing him to blend in with one group or another in most parts of the world. In addition to being brilliant, the younger man's inconspicuous looks, medium stature, and a combination of fearlessness and brains put him in the Goldilocks Zone for work as an intelligence officer.

Looking back, Professor Wang had known all the right words to say to hook the naive young man who'd eventually become Coronet, and whip him into a frenzy.

Goldilocks Zone indeed.

He was thirty-two now, and he worked hard to stay 'just right' for his job. So far he'd retained the thick black hair that he kept neatly trimmed and just long enough to part on the side. His slim, athletic build looked especially good in his lightweight blue European blazer and khaki linen slacks. Some might say that he was overdressed for a visit to the night market, where T-shirts and flip-flops were de rigueur. His mentor in the business warned him that he'd grown up watching too much James Bond – but Coronet held firm to the notion that while one could be under-dressed, it rarely hurt to dress well. Apart from the Mandarin of his native Taiwan, Coronet spoke Cantonese, English, and Malay. He did not, however, speak Tagalog, and it was a thorn in his paw that he could not understand most of the people in the crowd around him. He'd not survived the last seven years in his present employment by being oblivious to his surroundings. Meetings with men who cut off other men's heads as a matter of course required a heightened sense of awareness.

A sea of people chattered in Tagalog and English amid the smells of grilling meat and burned sugar, munching on skewers of fried chicken intestine, or, if they'd braved the insanely long queue, a cone of Mang Danny's ice cream. Coronet used the varied composition of the crowd to his advantage. To tourists, he looked like a local. To locals, he was a dandy tourist. To roaming police – whose presence had increased tenfold since the bombing – he was too well dressed to be a militant.

His vantage point by the utility pole gave him a direct view across Roxas Avenue, where a girl in a pink T-shirt sold lemonade and other colorful drinks. The man Coronet had come to meet had never seen him before, so he sat, eating his grilled chicken kebab, and did not worry that he sat just fifty feet away from his dead drop.

He'd worked in places far more pleasant than the Philippines. The humidity was stifling and the native tongue harsh against his ear. Trash sometimes obscured the broken concrctc. Homclcss children begged for food when they saw his nice clothes. Many of the smells caused him to gag outright.

And he loved every minute of it.

There was something invigorating about a city where leftist Sparrow units, police death squads, and radical Islamic terrorists roamed the filthy streets. A public outcry and government crackdowns had pushed the violence underground, but just barely. Murders happened in the jungle instead of on city streets. Graves were dug deeper. Mouths kept shut. But the same killers were still out there. Coronet was sure of that.

He was, in fact, counting on it.

Five minutes before his contact was due to arrive, a HiLux pickup truck backed into a stall a dozen feet down from where Coronet chewed on his kebab. The sudden smell was nauseating, and he felt sure he must have stepped in something. A quick scan of the area revealed the awful odor – as if someone had vomited up a dinner of onions and turpentine – was coming from the pile of spiky, melon-sized durian in the back of the HiLux. Nothing to be done about it now. The NFC was already in place, and this observation point was too good to abandon, so he tried to ignore the noxious smell and focused on his mission.

He'd placed the NFC sticker almost three hours before, just after the girl had set up her lemonade stand. Roughly an inch square, the drab, off-white adhesive paper blended perfectly with the plastic folding table on which the lemonade girl set up her wares. The glare from a string of overhead lights provided plenty of shadows in the night, rendering the small sticker invisible to all but the most discerning eye. Coronet considered putting the NFC tag under the counter, but the memory of the bombing was still fresh in everyone's mind. Applying it would have drawn no notice, but his contact would have certainly garnered plenty of attention when he came along and attempted to read it by putting his mobile phone under the counter. No, better to keep movements normal, ordinary. A mobile phone set flat on the plastic table would read the NFC in an instant and raise concerns with no one.

Coronet loved the tradecraft even more than he loved the exotic travel. Dead drops, social engineering, disguises – he reveled in them all. He did SDRs – surveillance detection routes – even when there was no need to do so, though the longer he stayed in the business the more necessary they became. On the road, he kept to a strict regimen of push-ups and sit-ups, every morning in his hotel room. At home, he was in the gym five days a week, doing a 'fight gone bad' workout or on the mat sparring with one of the many white-collar boxers who lived in his area. He'd studied kung fu from the time he was a small boy, but migrated to the harsher styles of hapkido and American boxing. Unlike James Bond, he shied away from rich food and too much booze. He limited himself to the occasional girl, always young, and always paid for.

Like Bond, he enjoyed working alone, but he was smart enough to know when he needed help. He had a small crew of operators who worked for him, all of them young and, like him, in it for the excitement and money over any misguided idealism. Ideals were whimsical. Policies shifted and regimes toppled, leaving operators too closely aligned with any one side out in the cold.

Coronet wasn't particularly enamored of communist China. He could just as easily have been spying for his native Taiwan or even the United States. As a matter of fact, the ChiComs paid shit. But in order to be a provocateur for the West, one had to live in the East. That's where the work was. Even with China's burgeoning middle class and new social freedoms, it was still rife with the problems of a communist state. It was one thing to visit Beijing for a quick meeting or zip in and out of Kashgar to chat up some enraged Uyghur separatists. Coronet sure as hell didn't want to live there on anything close to a permanent basis. He wanted his Internet browser free from the Great Firewall and his indiscretions overlooked, thank you very much. He'd had a gutful of communist overwatch during his six months in Suzhou while he attended satellite classes run by the Institute of Cadre Management – the Ministry of State Security's spy school.

He'd endured five separate polygraph examinations and countless hours of interrogation – some of it bordering on torture – all while trying to attend a school that his handler had invited him to. Other MSS methods were more insidious. Once a pretty girl had approached him in a bar and offhandedly remarked how stupid it was that there were people in the government who held fast to the Two Whatevers Policy – the political statement that 'we will resolutely uphold whatever policy decisions Chairman Mao made, and unswervingly follow whatever instructions

Chairman Mao gave.' Coronet had read enough concerning modern Chinese foreign policy to know that not even everyone in the politburo still believed in this archaic notion. He was, however, bright enough to know that no matter how handsome he was, attractive women did not approach strangers in bars and discuss politics, especially in China.

The girl was in her mid-twenties, older than he preferred, so he'd called her an idiot and moved to another table.

The next day he was subjected to a three-hour interview in a very cold room with a woman who said she was a psychologist. Her job, she explained, was to make the final decision as to his devotion to the state. He pointed out that it was a member of MSS who had recruited him, but the woman had just sat there, blinking at him behind her thick round glasses and smiling a bloated smile as if she had indigestion.

In the end, she gave him a passing grade and provided instructions on where to report. Had he failed, he was told later, he would have been an unwitting class project for those already in the program and would have ended up at the bottom of Taihu Lake.

Once admitted to intelligence training, he'd studied evasive driving, shooting, surveillance, advanced communications, killing – which his lead instructor had called by the ominous 'methods for final application of lethality.' It was all great fun for a college boy, but in the end, he'd grown exhausted at the constant government scrutiny. There were certain proclivities in which he liked to indulge, practices that would get him thrown in prison in a place like China. He narrowly avoided being booted when he found and removed cameras and listening devices from his dormitory room. Tradecraft, it seemed, was to be practiced outside the walls of the facility, not in it.

No, Coronet preferred to live in his flat near LAX, where his neighbors thought he was a simple businessman who traveled to China every year to buy greeting cards for his small company – and generally left him to his own devices. There was no way he wanted to live in China full-time. So he threw in with the East and enjoyed the comforts of his new enemy, the West. Life was good and he didn't give a damn which side he worked for, so long as he could afford good clothes and sleep in his Egyptian cotton sheets at least a few nights each month.

But just because he didn't care to live full-time in a communist country didn't mean he hadn't listened in class. He took tradecraft, OPSEC, and PERSEC seriously. That was all part of what made the job exciting. It was a rare event that he met a contact at the first prearranged location. He preferred a rolling meet, sending the contact hustling from place to place, much like he would if he were collecting a ransom. Sometimes he just wanted to avoid the local gendarmerie, or get a preview of the contact's state of mind. More often than not, dangerous people ran countersurveillance teams, at least one man or woman to watch their backs. Putting a contact through the trouble of going from spot to spot made these allies easier to identify while allowing Coronet to follow at a safe distance, unseen. It was the opposite of running a surveillance detection route – sending people to designated locations they did not know about until the last minute in order to ferret out any of their friends who might be following and providing cover.

Dazid Ishmael arrived right on time, wearing a black Coca-Cola T-shirt and baggy shorts. Instead of flip-flops like most of the people here, he wore sneakers – a good choice for a ranking member of Abu Sayyaf. Wanted by the Philippine National Police, he had Red Notices filed with Interpol by national law enforcement in both Indonesia and Malaysia. He'd shaved off his trademark beard, and now looked more like a kid than a murderer, Coronet thought, but the dead and dismembered bodies he left in his wake proved his abilities many times over.

Coronet watched as Dazid placed his mobile phone on the table, nudging the device around as he ordered a lemonade. Coronet imagined the phone reading and then registering the tag, instantly downloading the location for the next meet. The man slipped the phone back into the pocket of his shorts and shot a glance over his shoulder while he waited for his cup. Coronet glanced away, not wanting to seem overly interested – though there wasn't much chance of him being seen at all, across the street and in the dark.

The Near Field Communication tag made for the perfect dead drop. Working on the same principle as a touch key for a hotel room or a subway pass, the inconspicuous NFC tags contained nothing but a simple set of GPS coordinates, with the latitude and longitude transposed. Dazid would know to reverse the numbers before attempting to go to the next location. The time he'd spend transposing the two numbers also worked to Coronet's advantage, keeping the man on site for a few extra moments. Dazid knew the dangers and took the security measures in his stride. The incredible sum of money Coronet's handler had authorized may have had something to do with his casygoing temperament.

At first, Coronet noticed no one but Dazid. But when the bomber finished up with his mobile phone and headed southeast on Roxas Avenue, a man who looked suspiciously like an off-duty policeman did a double take. He was standing at a food stall with his chubby wife, a small boy of two or three clinging to his leg. The policeman obviously thought he'd seen someone important, but could not be sure in the darkness. His eyes locked intently on Dazid, and he leaned in quickly to whisper something to his wife, peeled his little boy off his leg, and then walked into the darkness to investigate.

It was an extremely foolish thing for him to do.

Coronet had two choices. He could disappear and let Dazid be arrested, or he could act as the wanted man's countersurveillance. He looked at his watch and realized he truly had only one choice. There was no time to develop another asset. Groaning within himself, he got to his feet. He grabbed a paring knife from the stall next to him while the owner was busy fanning away the smoke. It was a small blade, not quite four inches long, but he'd watched the man cut chicken and knew it to be razor-sharp, perfect for his purposes.

Coronet dropped the knife into the pocket of his jacket for the moment and fell in behind the policeman. He remained hidden in the crowd, closing the distance slowly so as not to arouse suspicion. As he walked, he took a slender canvas bag from his other pocket. Veering off the path slightly so he was along the edge of the canal, he scooped up a handful of gravel, which he poured into the mouth of the canvas tube. He repeated this procedure three times on the move, filling the tube until he had a makeshift cosh, or bludgeon, weighing a little over a pound. An American would have called it a sock full of rocks; it would make a formidable stunning weapon in the hands of someone who knew how to apply it.

Closing the distance now, Coronet held the cosh in his left hand and the blade in his right. Bludgeoning was a gross motor skill. The bladework needed to be more precise, ensuring he could evade the inevitable spray of blood.

Unfortunately for the hapless policeman, Coronet already knew where he was going. Dazid's destination was the Talk and Text café down the street. It was the location of the next NFC tag. He'd guessed correctly that the policeman would want to keep his distance and would likely remain across the street near the canal while he summoned backup. Considering the army of law enforcement at the night market, it would not take long for help to arrive. Coronet would have to act without hesitation. Which was fine. He'd done this before and knew the entire process would not take long.

Coronet moved quickly, hopping the guardrail that ran adjacent to the canal and moving into the shadow of the trees at the same moment the policeman stepped over the rail, still focused on Dazid Ishmael.

Padding up quickly but quietly, he struck as the policeman raised the mobile, utilizing the canvas bludgeon in the same manner OSS commandos employed brass knuckles to stun opponents in advance of a dagger attack during

World War Two. The canvas-and-gravel cosh impacted the man's left temple with a sickening thud, causing him to drop his phone and stumble forward a half-step. This put one leg slightly in front of the other, opening a gap for Coronet. His blade flicked back and forth quickly inside the man's legs just above the knees, slicing at least one, and probably both, of his femoral arteries. Coronet struck him again before his stunned brain could work out what had happened. The policeman stumbled sideways, weakening quickly. Coronet gave him a solid shove, careful not to soil himself with the man's blood, pushing him into the canal. The canvas cosh and the paring knife followed him in.

Coronet cried for help at the same moment the man splashed, pointing into the shadows as bystanders rushed to help. Instead of moving closer with the crowd, he melted backward, letting the press of people swallow him up and hide his movements until he was across the street in front of the Talk and Text, where passers-by were just realizing something was going on at the canal.

Taking one of the NFC stickers out of his pocket, he held it up by way of identification as he approached Dazid Ishmael.

The terrorist looked up at him, confused. Then his hand dropped into the pocket of his shorts.

Coronet raised both hands. 'You had company,' he whispered. 'Off-duty PNP.'

'Okay,' Dazid said, still suspicious. 'Did you bring the money?'

Coronet nodded at the NFC tag between his fingers. 'Half the account number is right here. My associate has the remainder of the number.'

'Wise.'

Dazid glanced toward the back of the café.

Coronet shook his head. 'There was only one policeman and he did not make a call. We should go out the front as if nothing is wrong.'

And with that, Coronet made contact with one of the most dangerous terrorists in the Philippines.

The provocateur glanced at the date on his Rolex. He would not read about the Abu Sayyaf operation for several days, but his previous assignment would be in the papers by tomorrow morning.

13

Jack Ryan didn't exactly hate the concept of a photo op. He was not, however, in love with the *photo* portion of the op. Even before he'd been dragged by the scruff of his neck into the presidency, Ryan had long believed that a chief reason the commander in chief went gray or bald was the constant stress of being 'on.' Photos with the President, whoever he — or she — happened to be, hung on walls and sat on mantels for decades. Ryan was self-aware enough to realize he was the personification of the stereotypical corduroy-wearing history professor. Still, he was comfortable in his own skin, and if kids from Mrs Palmer's eighth-grade national champion Project Citizen team didn't like that he had a slight cowlick, well, there wasn't much he could do about that.

Besides, this was a team of middle-school kids who'd excelled at civics. He couldn't think of a better group to admit into the Oval Office for a meet-and-greet. They were intelligent and far more relaxed than Ryan had been the first time he'd come to the White House. Five-minute photo ops gave just enough time for the scheduling staff to usher in the students, Ryan to shake each hand and repeat back their names, and then maneuver everyone into place for a photo with him in front of or behind the Resolute desk. Staffers were already stepping forward to lead out the group as the photographer lowered his camera. Today Ryan caused the poor staffer from scheduling to screw up his face as if he'd been shot, when he interrupted the flow by asking Mrs Palmer a question. Ryan gave him the 'presidential eye,' which was an unspoken order to realign priorities with the boss, and then turned back to Mrs Palmer. He was about to ask a follow-up question when Arnie van Damm stuck his head in. The look on his face said Ryan's own priorities were about to shift as well.

Ryan's gut churned by the time the last student left and van Damm shut the door. The chief of staff had been around the block enough times that there was very little that bothered him. Most bad news came with a knowing pat on the back and a confident reminder that things would 'get better.' Not today. Today he was stricken, which meant someone had died.

Ryan eyed his friend.

'What is it?'

'Corporal Wesley Farnsworth of Shreveport, Louisiana, was killed in action three hours ago forty kilometers south of N'Djamena, Chad.'

Ryan took a seat in front of the fireplace, motioning for van Damm to do the same. It didn't matter how many of these notifications he received, his first assumption was always that something had happened to Jack Junior. The revelation that it had not filled him with instant relief – and shame for feeling that way.

He shook his head. 'Africa.' Then closed his eyes and gave a resigned nod. 'Africa.'

Van Damm sighed. 'Bravo Company, 3rd Battalion of the 7th Infantry, rotated into N'Djamena a month ago to assist Chadian forces in furtherance of the Trans-Saharan Counterterrorism Partnership.'

'Boko Haram, then,' Ryan said.

The chief of staff rubbed a hand over his bald head. 'It looks that way, Jack. Burgess is on his way over right now to give you a more thorough briefing, but for now, it sounds as though Farnsworth was leading one of three fire teams training members of the Chadian Army in reconnaissance and patrol tactics. Thirty Boko Haram attacked an oil-drilling operation outside Koudjiwai, just south of our guys' position.'

'A Chinese oil platform?' Much of southwestern Chad was designated a Chinese Oil Exploration Zone.

'That's correct,' van Damm said. 'Australian security personnel at the drill site were seriously outgunned and put an emergency call into the Chadian authorities for assistance at the first sign of an attack.' The CoS shrugged. 'Men were dying, the government asked for help, and our guys were close. Exigent circumstances.'

Ryan took a deep breath, seething.

Van Damm shook his head. 'Damn shame,' he said. 'One of ours died protecting Chinese –'

'Stop it!' Ryan pointed a finger at his chief of staff. 'It's a damn shame that Corporal Farnsworth died. Period. I do not give a shit about the ethnicity of the lives he was trying to save.'

'Of course, you're right, Mr President,' van Damm said. 'I don't mean to minimize this young man's death in any way.'

Ryan turned in his chair, looking toward the windows and the Rose Garden. 'I know you don't,' he said, already moving on. 'To what end, Arnie? Why does Boko Haram attack an oil platform? Crude oil is worthless as fuel and impossible to transport if you need to move quickly, as they would have to do after something like this. Why not hit a refinery? At least there's something there they can use. Was it payday or something?'

Van Damm shook his head. 'I'm afraid there is an answer to that question, Jack, but you're not going to like it. The platoon sergeant overseeing the fire teams swears that our soldiers were lured in.'

Ryan turned to face his friend, sitting up straighter.

'Lured in?'

'He says the Boko Haram forces were strong enough to completely overwhelm the much smaller security team at the drill site but only engaged with enough force to make them call for support.'

'Who knew our soldiers were nearby?'

Van Damm let out a deep breath. 'OPSEC is fine on our end, but the Chadian Army colonel likes to give interviews about the cooperative efforts.'

'So Boko Haram would know we were going to be there.'

'Virtually everyone with a radio knew the Chadian Army was going to be training in that area. It's not uncommon to let the tribal chiefs know in advance. We've warned them, but it still happens. It doesn't take much to figure out that if we're in country, our guys will be with the army when they train.'

'So it was a setup?'

Van Damm nodded. 'The platoon sergeant feels sure American personnel were the real target. His CO believes him enough to kick the sentiment up the chain of command.'

China again, Ryan thought, but he didn't have to say it.

14

Magdalena Rojas pulled her small knees to her bony chest and held her hands over her ears. She clenched her eyes shut, took small breaths, trying to block out the stench of fear and death. There were other girls in the room. Six of them. There had been nine when Magdalena arrived, each chained by the ankle to a metal eyebolt fixed to a five-gallon bucket filled with concrete. The buckets allowed the girls to move around, dragging them from the thin mattresses at one end of the windowless room to the other, where there were more five-gallon buckets to use as toilets. Magdalena's ankles had been so small, Lupe had been afraid she'd slip out of the regular leg irons. In a fit of red-faced frustration, the cruel woman had smacked her across the buttocks with Ratón, the bull-penis whip, and stormed out. She returned a few moments later with a pair of handcuffs. They were too tight, but Lupe locked them down anyway, hooking the free side to the leg irons and the bucket of concrete. Magdalena's foot began to turn purple and swell before the woman left the room.

Four of those original girls were gone – dragged through the big red door at the other end of the wide room. Lupe brought in a new girl a short time later – through the normal-sized door. Girls never came in through the red one, they only went out.

The new girl was tall, with broad shoulders, and had

many freckles on her nose. Magdalena thought she must have been new because her blond hair was still full and shiny. Apart from hope, healthy hair was always the first thing to go. The other five girls sat in one form of stupor or another, but the new one caught Magdalena's eye and wanted to talk as soon as Lupe left. She sat with her back to the wall, knees up, wearing the same kind of thin black gown that they all wore – and nothing else.

She tugged at the chain around her ankle, sliding it back and forth over the lip of the plastic bucket as if in dismay at her situation.

'My name . . . Teodora,' she said in accented English.

'Magdalena.' She attempted a smile, but under the circumstances managed nothing but a passive look.

The blond girl gave a thoughtful nod. 'In my country . . . I know girl with same name.'

Magdalena looked away. She felt sorry for this chatty thing who obviously had not been around enough for her hope to be crushed completely. 'Where is your country?'

'Montenegro,' Teodora said, sniffing back a tear. 'It is very long from here.' She stared at Magdalena. 'Do you know Montenegro?'

Magdalena admitted that she did not.

'I was to have work as nanny.' The girl's shoulders began to shake. Her breath came in ragged, gasping sobs. 'Now . . . I am . . . pris . . . on . . . er.'

'I know.' Magdalena reached to touch the girl's arm. Everything had been stripped away from her as well, but she could still offer kindness – if only for a moment. 'If we do what they say, they might not hurt us as bad.'

It was a lie but, Magdalena hoped, a comforting one.

The blond girl turned to look at her, still sobbing. 'The man who . . . who . . . had me before . . . I come here, he tell me they make us girls to fight sometimes.'

Magdalena shivered. She'd heard no mention of fighting. She'd never been in a fight in her life, not even with her sisters.

Teodora cleared her throat. Her hair hung down over her face like a curtain. 'He say we fight to death. For the cameras.'

Magdalena's words caught hard in her chest.

'I can't . . .' She shook her head. 'I do not think that is true.'

Teodora coughed, clearing her throat. 'The man say it is true.' She sniffed back the tears and sat up straighter as she composed herself. Blue eyes played up and down Magdalena. 'If is true, I hope I fight you. You are small. You no problem for me to break.'

Magdalena withdrew her hand and dragged her bucket across the room. She would learn, someday, that letting down her guard brought nothing but pain.

Pain, in one form or another, had been a constant companion since her father had died and her mother had told her to 'open her kitchen.' At first the hurt had been in her heart. She'd never been her mother's favorite. This she knew. But even in a culture where daughters often opened their kitchens to help the family, it should have been her choice. Her father had once beaten a boy who had just looked at her. He would never have suggested she do such things. Her mother, on the other hand, had said she might even learn to enjoy her work. That was a joke. She'd learned to endure the searing pain, the ache of the illnesses that were a foregone conclusion when you slept with upward of twenty different men a week. The act itself was painful enough, but the men were all so much bigger than her that it was nearly always brutal – even when the men pretended they were being nice. Her back and shoulders suffered wrenching injuries she would surely carry for the rest of her life. But even that pain she'd learned to push to the back of her mind.

She'd thought her life was bad in Costa Rica. It had taken her several days to realize that her own mother had sold her to the man named Dorian. At that point, a numbness had crept over her that left her feeling like a cardboard cutout of her former self. A spark of something inside her kept her acting the way men wanted her to act. It was just enough to keep the men who owned her from killing her – for a time, at least. If a girl gave up completely in this business, she was thrown away in short order. Men wanted a doll, but they wanted a live doll, not one who just lay there. There was a fine line between acting spirited and showing belligerence. Parrot's belt taught his girls exactly where that line was. Some girls never learned. Parrot was more than happy to keep teaching them, sometimes beating them to within an inch of their lives. But at least he knew when to stop.

Before Parrot, Magdalena had seen girls bleed to death – or get infections so they passed out and then never woke up. Some girls got too much dope in their systems and had such bad fits they cracked their teeth. Parrot was always pissed when that happened. Girls were like cows to him. He didn't get paid when one of them died or ruined her teeth.

Yes, Magdalena had seen a lot of horrible things in her thirteen years – sights that would have probably killed another girl her age. But the babbling cries of despair that washed under the big red door said this was far, far worse.

And then, as if thinking about it made it so, the red door creaked open and Lupe walked in, shutting it quickly behind her. The horrible woman wore her customary tube top and cutoff jeans that were so short the pockets hung down past the frayed fabric. A ring of dark purple bruises encircled her neck, testifying to the fact that even a bottom bitch was not immune to the brutality of the man who ran her life. The tattoo of a grim reaper covered the inside of her left thigh. The flesh of her right was adorned with the skeletal figure of La Santa Muerte, a patron saint of narco traffickers, and, Magdalena had discovered, traffickers in human cargo as well.

Brandishing the whip back and forth with the whistling flourish of a swordfighter, Lupe took a moment to look from shattered girl to shattered girl. Everyone cringed at the noise. Each of them had felt the sting of the awful rawhide whip. Teodora began to wail, leaning forward to cover her face. Lupe struck her hard across the back, warning her to shut up. At length, the woman's black eyes settled on Magdalena. She skulked across the room, towering above the trembling girl while she prodded her with Ratón.

Lupe cocked her head to one side, a show of counterfeit pity. Magdalena could smell the seething contempt as the woman stood over her. 'Come, little one.' She hooked a finger toward the big, red door. 'It is your turn.'

15

Dr Ann Miller perched on the edge of a smooth leather chair and shot a glance at the clunky digital watch that dwarfed her slender arm. The black plastic monstrosity was waterproof and practical in the woods, but it looked incredibly out of place among the three women and one man working at their desks in the smallish White House office. The guy was young – probably still in college and rumpled in appearance – but the women were dressed to the nines in stylish blouses and elegant if sparse jewelry – not a clunky watch among them. Compared to them, Miller may as well have been wearing a bathrobe. Her Kühl khaki slacks and oversized buffalo-plaid wool shirt were perfect for a canoe trip on the Shenandoah – but now she just looked ridiculous.

Hired by the Central Intelligence Agency for her uncanny ability to recognize and recall patterns, Miller didn't work at Langley or even Liberty Crossing, home of the director of national intelligence and the National Counterterrorism Center. Her office was in a satellite location, hiding in plain sight. The other tenants of the nondescript building just off Twelfth Street in Crystal City certainly guessed she was with some government agency – probably because they were from some other government agency. That's the way it was in the shadow of the Pentagon. It was better than Langley, though. Her office had easy access to the Crystal City underground, where she and her other mathematician buddies could walk when the weather got crummy – and far enough away from all the bosses that she could dress down on Friday, something she was seriously regretting at the moment.

Miller had a doctorate in applied mathematics from Duke and was certainly smart enough to realize that the information she'd found regarding payments made by a Hong Kong investment firm through an Australian mining company to a bank in Central Africa with accounts linked to Boko Haram would eventually garner her a meeting with some muckety-muck in the intelligence community. Gears in DC turned slowly, especially after lunch on a Friday, so she didn't expect to hear anything until Monday at the absolute earliest.

She'd kicked the information up her chain of command via a secure e-mail, then eaten a yogurt and some blueberries at her desk while she continued with her work. She'd just turned off her computer to call it a day when her desk phone rang. Her supervisor, a nervous sort who was always fretting about his career, said she was needed for a briefing and a car would meet her downstairs. She was not to bring any files. A copy of her e-mail had already been sent over. Miller was not one to try to get out of work, but it was five o'clock on a Friday. She mentioned the Shenandoah canoe trip she had planned with her boyfriend, hoping the fact of her casual Friday dress might postpone the meeting until Monday. The supervisor told her not to worry, though it was clear from the audible gulp on the other end of the line that he was worried enough for them both. He hung up before she could ask him just who it was she was supposed to brief.

Miller took the time to scrape the last few spoonfuls of yogurt out of the cup, figuring it would take her ride a few minutes to get there. She was surprised when she saw a black Crown Victoria waiting curbside along Crystal Drive. Must be some super-important muckety-muck, she'd thought. The bigwigs didn't usually stay this late when a weekend was looming. Just her luck that she got a workaholic to look at her information. Probably an assistant to some assistant team leader at Langley or Liberty Crossing. When the Crown Victoria turned off the Jeff Davis Highway to head east across the 395 bridge toward DC proper, Miller asked the driver where they were going.

The answer made her teeth ache.

She'd been ushered in through the East Gate and met by a man she recognized from television as the White House chief of staff. Mr van Damm saw to it that she was given a visitor's badge bearing the large letter A signifying that she had an appointment, and then ushered her into the President's secretaries' suite, between the Oval and the Cabinet Room.

The situation would have been laughable, really, if it hadn't been so terrifying as to turn her entire digestive tract into molten lava. She'd never met a mathematician who'd been summoned on short notice to the White House. It was an honor, but Miller only wished she'd taken the time to change into something that made her look a little less like Paul Bunyan's Mini-Me.

The secretary who was seated nearest the door to the Oval Office must have noted her discomfort because she offered a motherly smile. 'Everyone who comes here gets nervous, Dr Miller,' she said. 'Even the generals.'

'Thank you,' Miller said, licking lips that had not been nearly so chapped a half-hour before.

The secretary leaned in, keeping up the perfect smile. 'The President really is a kind man,' she said. 'You are here because you're an expert. Tell him what you know – but don't be afraid to tell him what you think.'

Miller was thinking that she didn't know if the President was kind or not, but he sure hired kind people – and then the high muckety himself opened the door to the Cabinet Room.

'Thanks for coming, Dr Miller,' President Ryan said, smiling and motioning her into the room with a wave of his hand. 'I understand you've found something interesting.'

She couldn't help but notice that he looked very tired.

Ryan leaned back in his chair after the mathematician left the room and looked at the four folders on the mahogany table in front of him. The problem with time bombs – political or otherwise – was that they seemed so benign until the moment they blew up in your face.

'And we're certain LKI Telephone is linked to the Zhongnanhai?'

Mary Pat Foley tapped a closed fountain pen against her legal pad. 'The Hong Kong firm Marshall, Phillips, and Symonds is definitely a PRC front. We haven't linked President Zhao personally, but he would certainly be aware of it. That's what piqued Dr Miller's interest in the first place. CTA – Cromwell Telecom Alliance – appears to be nothing but a shell.'

Ryan reached under his reading glasses to rub his eyes

with a thumb and forefinger. His suit jacket hung over the back of his chair. His tie was loose, top button undone, and his sleeves were rolled up to his forearms – signs that he considered this a meeting where everyone would get down in the analytical weeds.

The actual 'head' of the table was on the east side, with the President's back to the Rose Garden windows and the wings of the long oval extending on either side.

The room was virtually empty today, with just six other people in attendance – Ryan preferred to think of it as a strategy session rather than a meeting. The Oval Office would have been more comfortable, but the Cabinet Room gave everyone space to spread out their paperwork – and Ryan knew that the DNI liked to doodle with her fountain pen when she put on her analytical hat. The location also afforded him the opportunity to leave the others to their work rather than disrupt a fruitful discussion by kicking them out of the Oval.

SecState Scott Adler sat in his usual Cabinet Room spot to Ryan's right. Arnie van Damm occupied the chair to his left. SecDef Bob Burgess and CIA director Jay Canfield sat across the table with Foley.

Supervisory Special Agent Gary Montgomery stood just inside the door by the wall. Customarily, Ryan asked the Secret Service to give him space inside the Oval and the Situation Room, but it was not uncommon for an agent to be within 'lunging distance' during other meetings in the White House.

Ryan pondered the information for a moment, tossing it around with what he'd learned from Dr Miller.

He asked, 'How hard was this to find?'

Mary Pat looked up, fountain pen poised above the pad. 'Sir?'

'Dr Miller said she found this connection easily,' Ryan said. 'But she's obviously downplaying her intelligence.'

'True,' Canfield said. 'She's one of our brightest.'

'If it was too easy, I'd worry the information was worthless.' Ryan looked up at the ceiling and groaned. 'We need to handle this quietly. Mary Pat, how well do you know the director general of ONA?'

'Rodney Henderson,' Foley said. 'He's new. But our interactions have been positive.'

Australia's Office of National Assessments was often considered a combination of the ODNI and the Department of State's Bureau of Intelligence and Research. ONA's director general could tap into intelligence data from the Australian Secret Intelligence Service, its domestic intelligence counterparts, the Australian Security Intelligence Organisation, other members of the intelligence community, and, to a lesser extent, the Australian Federal Police.

'Very well,' Ryan said. 'Reach out to Mr Henderson and let him know we're interested in this Cromwell Telecom.'

Burgess's right hand formed a clenched fist on the table, an outward expression of his desire to hit China hard. 'This makes a damn good case that Zhao is responsible for orchestrating the attack in Chad.'

Ryan nodded. 'It's thin,' he said. 'But it does look that way at first blush. I'll be interested to see what Director Foley finds out about that telecom.'

The President turned toward van Damm before Burgess could convince him to kick President Zhao in the nuts the next time they met – which, admittedly, would not take much at the moment.

'Let's switch gears and talk about the *Orion* for a minute,' Ryan said. 'Any more evidence that there was a bomb on the ship?'

The chief of staff looked at his notes. 'Nothing concrete. The ship is sitting in six hundred feet of water. The Navy intends to send a mini-ROV down tomorrow when the seas calm. That should give us a preliminary look at the hull until they get a larger submersible on scene.'

'Update on injuries?' Ryan asked.

'Ten dead,' van Damm said. 'The remaining crew members suffering from various injuries, badly shaken, but alive.'

'Butcher's bill would have been a lot higher but for the response of the Coast Guard,' Ryan said.

Jay Canfield looked up from his copy of the latest Coast Guard situation report. 'A Filipino seaman who was in the engine room during the explosions reported an object the size of a car melting through the roof. He describes it as a huge ball of intensely white flame.'

'That makes sense,' Burgess said, also reading. 'The poor guy is blind now. A magnesium fire would account for the Welder's Fever. He's suffering from chills and gastrointestinal distress.'

Mary Pat whistled low under her breath. 'Magnesium would burn hot enough to melt right through the deck of a ship?'

'It would indeed,' Ryan said. 'I read just the other day about a firefighter near the eastern shore of Maryland who had half his body burned when he responded to a car fire.

The heat of the magnesium breaks up the water molecules and releases hydrogen – not good stuff to have around an open flame. My dad used to warn me about that when he was trying to teach me to hold on to my blue-collar roots.'

'That's exactly what it sounds like, Mr President,' Burgess said. 'Chinese ship, Chinese oil rig, Chinese money . . . That's no coincidence, sir.'

'I know what it's not, Bob,' Ryan said. 'So let's have some theories on what it is.'

Ryan stood and rolled down his shirtsleeves, grabbing his coat but not bothering to put it on. 'I know it's Friday, but I'd like some ideas on my desk by tomorrow morning.'

Special Agent Montgomery opened the door and followed the President out of the Cabinet Room and into the Oval just long enough for Ryan to grab his briefcase. He wasn't done for the day by a long shot, but things happened fast around here and he didn't like to be too far from his notes. Montgomery opened the door to the Rose Garden and Ryan stepped out, hanging a left toward the residence. He looked over his shoulder at the hulking form of his lead agent.

'Walk up here beside me so I can talk to you,' Ryan said.

'I'd prefer to stay back a step, Mr President,' Montgomery said.

'Of course,' Ryan said. He'd been under protection one way or another for decades, first from John Clark and Domingo Chavez in the CIA, and now the Secret Service. Even so, he'd never get completely used to someone following him around like this.

Jim Langford, another agent on the day shift, joined

them before they reached the residence elevator. Only then did Montgomery move forward as Ryan had requested.

'What can I do for you, Mr President?'

'I'd be interested in your opinion.'

Montgomery looked mildly pleased. 'On what, sir?'

'On what?' Ryan frowned. 'You were there in the meeting. China, the recent events in the news. Whether I should invoke the Ryan Doctrine and . . . You get the picture. Some people under protection may figure the Secret Service is wallpaper, but you hear things. You have ideas. I can see it in your eyes.'

Special Agent Langford stared at the elevator buttons, unwilling to catch the eye of his boss or his boss's boss.

Montgomery gave a sly smile. 'I'm just a knuckle dragger, Mr President. You have some supremely intelligent people in your cabinet.'

'Cut the shit, Gary,' Ryan said. 'You guys are worthy of a lot more than "trust and confidence." There's at least one of you in half the meetings I attend. You can't tell me you agents don't sit around down there below the Oval Office in W16 and talk about how you would handle things if our roles were reversed.'

Montgomery nodded slowly, exchanging a look with Special Agent Langford as all three men stepped on the elevator.

'What?' Ryan asked. 'You're thinking if the roles were reversed, I couldn't protect you?'

Montgomery shook his head. 'Not at all, Mr President. I was just thinking that I've been doing this job for nineteen years and no one I've protected has ever asked my opinion about anything other than their own security.'

Ryan gave him an isn't-it-obvious shrug. 'You're a smart guy,' he said. 'I'm always interested in the opinion of smart people.'

'That's kind of you, boss,' Montgomery said as the elevator door opened. 'But it doesn't mean I'm going to go easy on you in the gym.'

16

Kelsey Callahan pushed her chair away from the table, if only to put more distance between herself and the slimy little shit on the other side. Unlike the dark concrete-and-steel rooms depicted by Hollywood, the interrogation room at the Dallas federal building was carpeted and well lit. The table was veneer rather than real wood, purchased off a list of approved vendors by the General Services Administration. In this instance, the table and four chairs that surrounded it came from prison industries at the Federal Correctional Institution in Sheridan, Oregon. The taxpayers saved a little money, federal prisoners made a little money, and Callahan's ass hurt from sitting in a piece-of-crap chair that threw her back into a helpless and uncomfortable knees-up position.

Trooper Sergeant Derrick Bourke sat next to her at the table. If the angle of his chair bothered him, he kept it to himself.

Eddie Feng was handcuffed in front and chained to a steel ring lag-bolted to the concrete floor underneath the institutional carpet. Callahan's line of questions had seen his ashen pallor go nearly purple. Saliva foamed at the corners of his lips and his left eye twitched as if he were sending messages in Morse code.

'I am telling you,' Feng said for the tenth time. 'I didn't sleep with that girl.'

Callahan rolled her eyes. 'But you already admitted that you did.'

Feng threw his head back, rattling his cuffs beneath the table. 'How long do you really think anybody spends with one of those kids? Fifteen, twenty minutes, tops. I paid Parrot for two hours, just to keep her away from the other guys at the party.'

'How gentlemanly of you to keep her for yourself.'

'I told you we didn't do anything!'

Callahan gave a little shrug. She had the upper hand now. 'That's not what Blanca says.'

'Well, she's lying.' Feng wagged his head. 'And anyway, she told me her name was Magdalena.'

Callahan sat up straighter in spite of the chair. 'Magdalena?'

'Whatever her name is. She's just a kid, you know. I felt sorry for her.' Feng's eyes flicked to the mirrored wall. 'Who's back there? Who's watching us?'

'Don't you worry about that,' Bourke said.

Callahan banged on the table to get Feng's attention. 'Tell me about this USB drive.'

'I lost the damn thing . . .' He looked up, coming to a sudden realization. 'If you have it, Magdalena . . . or Blanca, must have stolen it. She did, didn't she? After what I did for her . . .'

Callahan just looked at him.

Feng continued to study the one-way mirror. 'Could I get some coffee or something?'

Callahan shot a sideways glance at Bourke. 'He makes a lot of demands for a kiddie diddler.'

Feng's head snapped around. 'Stop calling me that!'

'What do you prefer?' Bourke said. 'Pedophile?'

'I'd prefer you called me Eddie,' he said. 'I'm a reporter for *True Word Daily*. Just look it up online.' He was pleading now. 'Seriously, guys. I'm in the middle of a very important story and had to appear to engage in certain behaviors in order to get them to trust me enough to get access to the right people. It was my *legend*. You know, a legend, like if you were going undercover.'

'I know what a legend is, Eddie,' Callahan said. This guy was convincing. He'd even managed to get the snot flowing, a sign his tears were probably real. But he was looking at some serious jail time, so he was obviously going to be distraught. It didn't mean he was telling anything close to the truth about his involvement with Blanca Limón. Men who assaulted kids were very often the weepiest sad sacks on the planet.

Callahan pantomimed drinking motions toward the mirror. If it took a little coffee to get this bird to start singing, so be it. More often than not, there was a great deal of smiling and nodding right before she stuck it in and broke it off.

'Okay, Eddie,' she said. 'I'll get you something to drink, but you have to tell us a few things. For starters, I need you to give me the location of the party you were at when you met Blanca. She was with another girl, and that girl is still missing. I'm worried something happened to her.'

'Sure.' Eddie nodded quickly, seemingly eager to help. 'I'm not sure of the address, but it's in South Dallas. Anyway, she's not there. These parties are transient. They bring the girls in vans and cars and then take them away afterward. Blanca and the others all got carted off by a guy they called Reggie right before I left.'

Callahan shot a look at Bourke. Feng's description of the guy who had Blanca matched up, anyway.

'I don't know,' Eddie continued. 'If she's not with Reggie, I'd say Matarife has her.'

Sergeant Bourke looked up from his notebook. 'Matarife?'

'That would be my guess,' Feng said. He was already working on the map, both hands moving with the pen across the yellow legal pad since they were cuffed together.

Bourke shot a sideways glance at Callahan. 'Matarife means "slaughterer."'

Callahan rubbed her eyes with the heels of her hands. This whole thing made her bones tired. There was a reason agents timed out of Crimes Against Children task forces. Her supervisor had warned her after her last emotional outburst that she was definitely coming to the end of her shelf life with the CAC.

Feng kept at his drawing, hunched over the legal pad. 'I've never met him, but I hear Matarife is into some pretty nasty stuff.'

'Be more specific,' Bourke said.

Eddie shrugged. 'I am actually onto something else for my story, so all this stuff with the girls was just extra. Believe me, once I got what I needed, I was going to make some calls and get the girls out of there.'

'Must have been really important,' Bourke said, 'for you to leave them in slavery while you got your precious story.'

'You have no idea.' Feng hung his head. 'But I understand how it looks . . . how it is. I should have called someone.'

'Yes, you should have, Eddie,' Callahan said. 'But you can make a difference now. Let's get back to what you know about Matarife.'

'All I heard was whispers. Rumor is he leads some kind of blood cult, but I think that's just a story to scare the shit out of the competition. I haven't put it together yet, but he's somehow linked to a guy they call Coronet. That's who I'm looking to find, Coronet. I suspect he works with a contact in mainland China. Sun Yee On triad, Tres Equis, Coronet — and the PRC. They're all connected. I just haven't put it all together yet.'

'Well, shit,' Callahan said. This was starting to spin out of her control. If it got too big, then Violent Crimes or one of the counterintel squads would muscle her out. 'So tell me, Eddie. How do we find Matarife?'

Feng looked up from his map, which was incredibly detailed considering that he was drawing it with his hands cuffed. 'He's supposed to have a big house out in the country.'

Callahan pounded the table again. 'Where is this big house?'

Feng shrugged. 'Still working on that,' he said. 'I haven't managed to get myself invited out there. Until you arrested me, though, my next stop was a mid-level guy named Naldo Cantu who owns a string of massage parlors in South Dallas. He's a real piece of work, just brutal to his girls. He keeps them strung out to keep them under control. Burns them with cigars for entertainment . . .' Feng shook his head, as if to clear away the image. 'I know he pays a fee to operate in Matarife's area. He'd have to know how to get in touch with the guy in order to pay him. Cantu will have some girls on hand. He always does. Could be this friend of Blanca's is with him. I can tell you where he lives.'

'You can?' Callahan said, surprised at a glimmer of positive news.

'Sure,' Feng said.

Callahan patted her hand on the table. 'Hurry up, then,' she said. 'I'm not done with you yet, but if you know where Naldo Cantu is holding girls, I want to act on it right damn now.'

'Good,' Feng said. 'Because there are probably some other things you need to know –'

An electronic buzzer sounded at the door, nearly sending Feng out of his skin. There was a heavy metallic click and Tim Dixon, one of the supervisory agents, entered. He had a tall Starbucks cup in his hand with steam coming off the top – which meant it couldn't be for Feng. Prisoners got lukewarm coffee at best – in case they decided to try to weaponize their drink.

Feng dropped the pen on the table and rattled his cuffs. 'What's going on? Who is this? Is he one of the guys watching me?'

Callahan snapped her fingers to shush him, then looked up at Dixon, afraid of what his presence meant. Interruptions like this usually meant a lawyer had shown up.

The news turned out to be even worse.

Dixon leaned in to whisper in her ear. 'There's an agent named Caruso here to see you. Apparently, he's out of WFO.'

'Okay.' Callahan shrugged. 'What does somebody from the Washington Field Office want with me?'

'He knows you have Feng in custody,' Dixon said.

Callahan gasped. 'We just scooped him up two hours ago.'

Dixon gave her a knowing nod. 'Fancy that. And get this, the Old Man got a call from the office of the director about five minutes before this guy slithered in here, telling us to show one Special Agent Dominic Caruso all possible courtesy. He didn't say it, but I'm thinking he's gotta be counterintel. You have to admit, Kelsey, this whole case has a CI stink to it.'

Dixon had surely read Callahan's 302 summarizing the interview with Blanca Limón, and now there was Eddie Feng's reference to the People's Republic of China. All this talk of spies and geopolitical competition brought spooks swarming around like blowflies to putrid meat.

Callahan wallowed up out of the prison-industries chair, knocking it over and hoping she smashed it in the process.

'What the hell, Tim? You know this is all wrong. We're saving kids here, not working on spy shit. All possible courtesy my ass!'

Dixon sipped his coffee. 'He's standing right outside the window.'

'I don't care where he is.' Callahan yanked open the door. 'I will not hand over this investigation to a bunch of Washington counterintel weenies.'

She nearly ran headlong into a dark-haired man wearing faded jeans and a face full of stubble over a passive smile.

He gave her a wink that made her want to punch

him in the nose, then said, 'I think I can help you with that last part.'

The contract security officers in the lobby of the fortress-like Dallas field office had checked Caruso's credentials and assumed he was armed. The magnetometer beeped when he walked through, which was not surprising to the guards. He wasn't local, but he was an agent, so everyone assumed he would be armed. They did not, however, know that he wore a wire neck loop and microphone connected to the small radio hidden under the tail of his loose shirt and tucked inside the waistband of his jeans. The tiny earpieces Campus operatives wore were designed to blend in, but he'd removed his to be on the safe side. FBI agents were trained to be highly observant, and wearing an obvious wire into the lion's den was sure to earn him a case of the third degree from the Old Man – the notoriously territorial and protective special agent in charge of the Dallas office. This left Caruso blind to any communication coming from other Campus members but still able to feed pertinent information to them through the mic just out of sight below his collar. He knew it wasn't quite sensitive enough to pick up everything that was being said around him, so he strategically repeated the important stuff while trying not to sound like too much of an idiot.

'Seriously,' he said, shaking Callahan's hand as they stood in the hall outside the interrogation room. 'You and I have the same goals here.'

Callahan took a step back and folded her arms, giving him an up-and-down once-over. She was attractive, in an

I'll-kick-your-ass sort of way. Her stylish blouse was unbuttoned one button farther than she probably realized. At first glance, her ponytail gave her a look of innocence, but one look from her green eyes warned that she was anything but.

At length, she held out her hand and snapped her fingers. 'Let's see your creds.'

'They checked them downstairs.'

Callahan scoffed. She reminded Caruso of his mother checking his hands for dampness to make sure he'd actually washed them before dinner. 'Well, I want to check them again.'

He passed the black leather case to her and shot a glance at Tim Dixon while he waited.

'Don't look at me for aid and comfort,' the supervisor said. 'She just happened to ask you before I did.'

Callahan studied the ID card and the badge, obviously disappointed that they weren't fake. 'How did you find out about Feng so quickly?' Her lip curled up in disgust. 'You must have had him under surveillance, and if that's the case, why in the *hell* didn't you step in and rescue the kids? Could there possibly be anything more important than that?'

Caruso took a deep breath. 'First of all, I can't speak to how I knew. But I can promise you that if I'd seen any children in danger, they would have become my highest priority. I would have gotten them out in a heartbeat.'

Callahan looked at him for a long moment and then handed him back his credentials. 'I believe you on that one tiny count, Dominic Caruso. But that doesn't mean I'm all giddy about having you attached to my hip. And anyway, if you are what I believe you to be, I fully expect you to lie to me at least a dozen times a day.' She turned back to the interrogation room, pausing with her hand on the door. Her eyes softened a notch. 'Listen, I know what you're doing is probably super-duper important in the great scheme of the geopolitical chess game. But the work my team is doing here isn't a game in any sense of the word. We estimate that there are more slaves in the world today than at any other time in recorded history – and many of them are just kids, being forced to do unspeakable things, sometimes in a rented box truck at some peach orchard servicing a line of migrant workers waiting their turn, sometimes on a webcam. Some piece of trash gets arrested for child porn and their defense attorney boohoos to the judge and says, "Oh, Your Honor, my client is just a collector. He would never touch an actual child." Well, I say people who collect baseball cards eventually go to a game. People tell me that in adults, at least, prostitution is a victimless crime. Maybe one case in a million they might possibly have a point. But you try and have sex ten or fifteen times a day and see how you feel. Johns are rapists – they just pay somebody for the experience.'

Caruso raised both hands in surrender. 'I'm not arguing with you. Really, I am on your side.'

'I just wanted you to know why I'm so bitchy right from the get-go,' Callahan said. 'There is so much inertia in this ocean of evil shit that I have to push back or I'll drown, you know. Anyway, I haven't quite figured out Eddie Feng's angle yet. But he's about to tell us where we can find a guy one step up the ladder in what looks like a major human-trafficking ring. Supposedly there's some connection to a Chinese guy that goes by the handle of Coronet. That mean anything to you?'

'Coronet?' Caruso said, repeating it so Clark and the others could hear. 'I'm interested to hear where we can find a link to him. Mind if I come along?'

'Do I have a choice?'

Caruso grinned. 'Not really.'

17

John Clark's voice crackled over the radio immediately after Caruso repeated Naldo Cantu's address. 'We've got about twenty minutes if we're lucky with traffic,' Clark said. 'Everyone jump. I want to see what kind of intel we can grab before they get there.'

'Copy that,' Ryan said. The rest of the team confirmed they'd heard the transmission and were immediately en route.

Interstate 35 was a stone's throw away from the FBI field office, around which he and the others were strategically parked so as to be close enough to pick up Caruso's transmissions. His signal was garbled but readable. I-35 ran directly from Dallas to Red Oak, roughly eighteen miles away, which meant Ryan and the rest of The Campus could reach their objective in a relatively short time – as long as the evening traffic didn't snarl. But the same held true for Special Agent Callahan and her task force. It would take a few minutes for the raid team to hit the head and gear up. Judging from the tone of her voice, this lady didn't seem like the kind to mess around. She wouldn't be far behind.

'You gonna try and get there sometime today or what, Jack?' Ding asked from the passenger seat.

Ryan accelerated south on the freeway. Traffic was heavy but moving, and going close to the speed limit.

Midas spoke next. He was behind the wheel in the car with Clark now, and his impatience at the traffic was evident in his voice. 'They'll be able to use lights and sirens to get through this shit. Caruso sure as hell better stall.'

Adara defended her boyfriend. 'Dom will do what he can,' she said. 'He'll definitely let us know when they're on the road.'

Ryan sped past a highway patrolman doing ninety. Mercifully, the trooper had already pulled over another vehicle.

It was dark and beginning to sprinkle by the time Ryan took the exit to Farm Road 644. Midweek traffic was light on the farm-to-market road, even at rush hour, and he poured on the speed, feeling the Avenger's engine open up with a throaty roar. He'd been nearest to the interstate when Dom gave the address, so he felt certain Midas's and Adara's vehicles were somewhere behind him.

'Watch these wet roads, *'mano*,' Chavez said as Ryan drifted around a corner, a mile away from their target residence now, according to the GPS on his phone.

'Nag, nag, nag,' Ryan said, and punched the gas.

Chavez flipped him off and hung on to the side handle.

A minute later Ryan slowed, driving past a white frame house set back off the road about five hundred feet. Barbed-wire fencing, meant to keep in cattle, ran in front of the property and a heavy gate made of rusted drilling pipe blocked the entry. The porch light was visible through the trees. Ryan took the first left past the target address. He was surprised to find Clark's pickup truck already parked in the tall Johnson grass along the gravel road. He and Midas were nowhere to be seen.

'How the hell did you get here first?' Ryan said into his mic.

'Superior navigation, kid,' Clark said.

'Position?' Ryan asked.

'You guys are late,' Midas said. 'We're already moving up to the house.'

Clark suddenly gasped over the radio, whispering, 'Midas, get up here. Everyone else stand by.'

John Clark had seen great evil in his life. He was no stranger to misery. He'd experienced unspeakable sadness and unbearable pain – in Vietnam, Eastern Europe, and hot spots around the world – but the worst of it, the incident that gutted him, had happened right here in the good old USA. Admiral James Greer had known the whole story, but he'd taken the secrets with him when he passed away. Sandy knew most of it, and she'd probably guessed the rest, though they never talked about it. Clark was able to suppress the memories for the most part – Pam Madden's brutal murder and the vengeance he'd meted out against the pimps and drug dealers who'd done it. He dreamed of her sometimes still, not in a longing way as someone might pine for a lost love, but because he was so incredibly sorry that he'd not been there to save her. He was a former SEAL when they'd met, already entrenched in the ways of warfare and mayhem, but it was Pam's death that pushed him into the instrument that he'd become. Knowing her, watching her turn her life around, and then seeing that life snuffed out, had changed him forever – and left a mark on his soul that could not be erased.

His hands shook with pent-up rage when he peered through the window into Naldo Cantu's house and saw the girls. There were three of them curled into fetal positions and chained by their ankles to filthy mattresses on metal army cots. Two wore short baby-doll nightgowns; another wore nothing but a gray T-shirt and bore obvious track marks. She'd been there a while. All three of the girls had ugly burns on their arms and legs. An overturned garbage can beside one of the cots revealed several used condoms, some syringes, and a wad of candy wrappers – probably all the girls had had to eat. He could make out two Hispanic men lounging on the couch in the adjacent room watching television and drinking beer. He didn't have a view of the entire room, so there was a possibility of more men inside.

Memories of Pamela Madden and the men Clark had killed coursed through his veins. He fought the urge to rush in and shoot these men in the face. He didn't care how many there were.

Caruso's voice in his ear startled him – not an easy thing to do to John Clark.

'I'm not very familiar with Dallas. Any guess on our ETA?'

Callahan gave a muffled response that Clark couldn't hear. There was the sound of car doors slamming, then Dom said, 'I hear you . . . traffic like this we'll be lucky to get there in twenty-five.'

Clark nodded at this new information. The girls would be safe soon enough, but he wanted to get his pound of flesh. Prison was too cushy for men like these. Clark backed away from the window and into the live oaks that surrounded the house. Midas met him there.

'How do you want to do this?' the former Delta soldier asked. 'Drag them out and beat the hell out of them until they talk . . . then beat them some more after they talk?'

'You got a look inside?'

Midas gave a somber nod. 'Through the living room window,' he said. 'I counted three males, two on the couch, one in a recliner. Two handguns on the coffee table, but no long guns that I saw. I could only see one female through the open door from my vantage point, but she looked in pretty bad shape.'

'She is,' Clark said. 'I counted three girls. Not sure about the other rooms.' He shook his head to clear it, willing himself to calm down and think. Rage would only blind him. In situations like this, he needed to be calculating and calm. He didn't completely rule out killing an enemy inside the United States, but he'd try to avoid it if possible. These men had crucial intelligence. If he had to wait and let Caruso get it, then –

The sound of a screen door slamming pulled him out of his thoughts. There was laughter, and then someone said, *'Cerveza . . .'*

Gravel crunched. A car door slammed.

Midas smiled in the darkness. 'Somebody's going on a beer run!'

Clark spoke in a hoarse whisper, giving orders as he moved back toward the fence. 'Jack, move to the east end of the road. Adara, you set up to the west.' Clark checked his watch. 'Whichever way this guy turns, let him get down the road far enough they can't see him from the house, then box him in. Cautious but quick. Keep in mind, we have about eighteen minutes to do what we need to do before we have to exfil.'

Ninety seconds later, Ryan pulled the Dodge in front of a blue Subaru WRX and stepped on the brakes. The driver, a skinny Hispanic male, attempted to go around him, but Ryan put his foot on the gas and nosed the Dodge into the much lighter vehicle, shoving it back into Adara's waiting pickup truck. The skinny kid's eyes flew wide and he raised his hands as Ryan, Chavez, and Adara bailed out of their vehicles. All of them wore black balaclavas and pointed their pistols at his face.

'Damn it,' Sherman said as she yanked open the door while Chavez and Ryan covered her. 'I was hoping you'd fight.'

They had him bagged and gagged and trussed in the back of Adara's pickup by the time Midas and Clark rolled up with their lights off. Clark lowered his window and motioned for everyone to follow him back around the corner, just in case Special Agent Callahan and her crew showed up sooner than they thought they would.

The skinny kid said his name was Flaco. He started slinging snot and sobbing the moment Clark dragged him out of the truck and ripped the bag off his head. Clark shoved him into the ditch on the side of the road. He knelt there, pleading for his life. The sharp odor of urine filled the night air. It wasn't surprising. If John Clark threw him in a ditch and pointed a gun at him, Ryan was pretty sure he'd lose control of his bladder, too.

Clark wore a balaclava as well, but there was enough hatred burning out of his eyes to make his intentions clear.

He gave Flaco a brutal kick to the ribs, knocking him over, and then stepped on his neck.

'Okay, asshole,' Clark said. 'You have exactly one chance to stop me from turning your head into bits of skull and goo. Answer my questions as I ask them to you. Don't pause. Don't beg for mercy. Just answer the questions. Do. You. Understand?' Clark bore down with the boot at each word, grinding the man's face into the ground and muffling his reply.

'Yeeesss,' he said, sounding like a deflating tire.

'Who's the top guy? Cantu?'

It turned out to be harder to get the tattooed gangbanger to shut up than it had been to get his car stopped.

'Cantu is boss of the girls around here,' Flaco said. 'But Zambrano is the top guy in Texas. Everybody who runs girls gotta pay him.'

'Zambrano?' Clark said. 'Same name as the Cubs pitcher?'

'Same name,' Flaco said. 'Different dude. This one's from Mexico.'

'Where is he?'

Flaco shook his head. 'He's everywhere, man. He moves all the time.'

Clark nodded. 'How about Matarife?'

'That dude's evil as shit, man,' Flaco said.

'Where is he?'

'I don't know.'

Clark bore down again.

'Seriously, man,' Flaco whined. 'I never been to his house. I been places where he does his stuff, though, and it's pretty damn sick.'

'Who would know where to find him?'

'On my mother,' Flaco said, 'I got no idea.'

Clark looked at his watch. 'There's a Chinese guy been hanging around. What's his name?'

'Eddie.'

'Another Chinese guy.'

Flaco began to hyperventilate. 'Man, since the triad moved in, there's like a hundred Chinese guys hanging around. I'm not tryin' to lie to you, man. I swear it. I'm just not sure who you mean.'

'Coronet?'

'Okay, okay,' Flaco said. 'I only heard him called that once, but I know who you're talking about now. Sharp dresser. Likes his girls fresh and young. That dude's weird. Acts like he's James Bond or somethin', but I heard he just sold Christmas cards. His name's Chen. Vinnie Chen . . . or Vincent, I think. Hey! He would know where Matarife is.'

'That doesn't help,' Clark said. 'Describe Vincent Chen.'

'Dude, I can do you one better,' Flaco said. 'I got his picture on my phone.'

Clark nodded and Ryan retrieved the cell from Flaco's hip pocket. Fortunately, he'd been facedown when he wet his pants, sparing the phone and Ryan's hand.

'Password?' Ryan said.

'Eleven-eleven,' Flaco said.

'Want me to do it?' Ryan said, thumb hovering over the touchscreen. 'He could have a distress signal pre-programmed.'

Clark scoffed. 'Does this look like a guy who plans that far ahead?'

'Right,' Ryan said, and punched in the number. He opened the photos and, after scrolling through some seriously gut-churning pictures of girls that would be enough to put Flaco away for a very long time, he found a photo of a nattily dressed Asian man. Rather than leave a virtual trail by sending the image anywhere, Jack used his phone to take a photo of the screen.

'How about his phone number?' Clark asked.

'It's in my contacts,' Flaco said. 'But he was here a day and a half ago. He dumps his phones every few days and gets a new one.'

'Every few days?'

'See what I mean?' the gangbanger said. 'Weird shit for a Christmas card salesman.'

'Where is Chen now?' Clark prodded.

'No idea,' Flaco said.

'Who gets the girls for Cantu?'

Ryan shot a glance at Chavez. This was outside the scope of their mission. They had what they needed on Coronet.

Caruso's voice came across the radio again.

'Want me to let everyone know we're less than ten out?'

Callahan's muffled voice followed. *'They're all behind us,'* she said. *'Pretty sure they know already.'*

Chavez twirled his index finger in the air, reminding everyone that they needed to hurry.

Flaco nodded, unaware of the conversation going on in their earpieces.

'A guy named Parrot.'

Chavez raised both palms to the sky. 'Seriously, boss. We need to haul ass.'

Clark nodded. 'Okay.' He pressed down on Flaco's neck with his boot one last time before stepping back. 'Dump his body by the gate.'

'Wait, wait, wait,' Flaco pleaded. 'You don't have to kill me.'

'We never had this conversation,' Clark said.

Flaco's head wagged so hard it looked like it might roll off his skinny neck. 'Never, man. I swear it.'

Clark hooked a thumb toward the Dodge without another word.

Ryan and Chavez dumped the sobbing gangbanger alongside the road, bound hand and foot and gagged with a piece of tape so he couldn't warn his buds about the approaching parade of vehicles coming down FM 644.

Ryan kept his lights off and his foot off the brake until they were well over a mile away. He smiled to himself when he heard Callahan's voice gasp.

18

Special Agent Callahan put two Ellis County ambulances on call when she was two minutes out from Naldo Cantu's farmhouse. The headlights of her Bureau-issued Expedition played on the grassy ditch as she came around a slight curve in the road. She nodded toward Caruso. 'Jump on the radio and tell Ellis County where we are. I don't want them to – Oh, shit!'

Callahan yanked the wheel hard left, narrowly missing a slender Hispanic man kneeling in the middle of the gravel road, just in front of the gate. His arms were fully sleeved with tattoos and his hands were taped behind his back. A pillowcase had been pulled over his head.

Sergeant Bourke and Special Agent John Olson were in the car behind her. Bourke had turned his lights off earlier on the approach, and narrowly avoided rear-ending the Expedition.

Callahan reached for the radio in Caruso's hand, snatching it away.

'Listen up,' she said, at the same time she pressed the gas to drive around the hooded man.

Ellis County Sheriff's Office came back. 'Unit calling?'

'Damn it!' Callahan said. 'Disregard, Ellis County.' She pressed the button on her radio, flipping it back to the encrypted frequency. Leading a task force made up of many different agencies made secure communication problematic. Instead of 10-codes or other unique signal language, she employed plain talk and relied on encryption.

'Listen up!' she said again when she was back on the secure channel. The Expedition bounced across the rutted field as she drove around the bound man. 'Caution as you come to the gate! Hispanic male, tied and hooded. Olson, you and Winston peel off and scoop him up. You're gonna have to stay back and babysit. The rest of you haul ass to the house with me. I'm sure they already hear us coming.' She tossed the mic to Caruso. 'Now you can call Ellis County with our location.' She wheeled around to the far side of the house, out of the line of fire from the front door. 'Leave it on the open channel this time, just in case we're walking into a whirlwind of shit.'

Naldo Cantu and his cousin Reuben were so engrossed in *Dancing with the Stars* that they had not heard the approaching vehicles. Flaco, who blew a .14 on the PBT, had left the door unlocked when he'd gone for beer, so Jermaine Armstrong didn't even get to use his ram.

Now Caruso stood in the yard, just outside the pool of light from the yellow porch bulb. A Rock River Arms LAR-15 with a collapsible stock hung from a single-point sling around his neck. Pistols were well and good, but he always felt better when he had a long gun in situations like this, so he'd borrowed one from the field office. He pressed a cell phone to his ear.

John Clark filled him in on the roadside interrogation of Flaco.

'Wish I could have been there, boss,' Caruso said. He refrained from using names, just in case any member of the task force had better-than-average hearing. 'Things went off without a hitch here. Two in custody plus the one bagged at the gate.'

'The girls?' Clark asked.

Caruso took a deep breath. 'One of them is in pretty bad shape. Veins were so collapsed from all the dope they've been giving her, medics had to use an IO gun to get fluids started.'

Dom winced just thinking about the drill-like device that shot a fifteen-gauge needle directly into the poor kid's femur. She was so stoned from whatever these assholes had been shooting into her that she didn't feel it, but the heavy *thunk* of metal puncturing the large bone made Caruso gag. There was a reason he'd gone into law enforcement instead of medicine.

'Anyway,' Dom continued. 'She's on her way to the hospital. Callahan had two Child Protective Services officers follow us out and hang back until we made entry. They're with the other two girls now. Sounds like all three of them are from Mexico. How about you? Did you get anything good?'

Clark grunted. 'Some. Coronet's last name is possibly Chen. We also got a cell number he's likely to ditch in the next day or two. I've already got Gavin working on it. These guys are the tip of the iceberg with this human-trafficking ring. It's worth our time to talk to a few more. They may have more information on Chen and what he's up to.'

'Copy that,' Caruso said. 'You know that thumb drive we heard Feng mention on the GSM bug?'

'What about it?'

'Some kid – a girl he was sleeping with – swiped it from him, if you can believe that.'

'Where's this drive now?' Clark asked.

'The girl gave it to the troopers, who passed it on to the FBI. Special Agent Callahan has it now. I didn't hear all the interrogation, but somehow Feng got his hands on a bunch of data related to Coronet/Chen. She believes it has information about human-trafficking payouts et cetera. I haven't seen it, but the way she talks, it's coded.'

Clark was silent for a long moment. 'Dom,' he finally said, 'we need to get the information on that thumb drive to Gavin.'

'So put in a request,' Caruso said. 'It's national security-related. Gerry can get someone to back-channel the director. He'll order Callahan to turn it over.'

'That'll take too long,' Clark said. 'I need it tonight.'

'Are you kidding me?' This whole conversation made Caruso's stomach ache. 'You want me to steal it from the FBI?'

He could almost hear Clark smile on the other end of the line.

'Now you're tracking,' Clark said.

'The task force isn't even located at the field office. I don't have a code to get in the building.'

'Ah,' Clark said. 'But you've got Gavin.'

'Seriously?' Caruso shook his head and looked skyward. He dropped his voice even lower. 'Hell, forget prison, Callahan will just murder me. Due respect, boss, but –'

Caruso stopped talking and waved at Callahan, who was now marching across the shabby lawn, apparently on the hunt for him.

'She already trusts you,' Clark said. 'I can hear it in her voice.'

Callahan stopped directly in front of him and folded her arms tight across her chest. Her eyes were narrowed, head tilted back so she was looking down her nose. The explain-yourself-mister stance made him feel like a seventh-grader whose mother had just figured out how to search the browser history on his phone.

'Are your friends responsible for that kidnapping?'

'No,' Caruso lied, giving her what he hoped was a sufficiently indignant smirk. He chose the more direct 'no' because Callahan would have taken anything else for the dodge that it was. *Why would you ask that?* or *I'm not going to justify your question* were obvious attempts to obfuscate. A quick and direct denial was always best – making sure not to overreact. *Did you sleep with that other woman?* was at one end of the spectrum while *Did you eat the last of the cereal?* was at the other. *Did your friends kidnap that guy?* fell somewhere in the middle for the appropriate amount of indignation.

Still, lying about anything was a slippery game when played with trained interrogators, so he decided it was better to change the subject.

'Good job tonight,' he said.

Callahan nodded. It was obvious that she still didn't believe him, but she unfolded her arms. That was something. 'Still no Magdalena, though,' she said. 'I don't know why, but I thought we might find her here, too.'

'You saved three kids,' Caruso said. 'That's cause for celebration. Cut yourself a little slack.'

Callahan said, 'Don't get me wrong. I'm happy about that.' She sighed, choosing her words carefully. 'Hey, I need to talk to Flaco, but the other two have already lawyered up. Want to get a drink after?'

'So you can interrogate me, too?'

'No,' she said, mimicking Caruso's previous indignant smirk.

The radio in Callahan's hand broke squelch. 'Ellis County Fire to any unit at the Cantu residence.'

The fire department ran the ambulance, two of which had just driven away carrying the formerly imprisoned girls.

'Special Agent Callahan, go ahead.'

'Thought you guys might want to know there was a guy parked at the end of the lane when we drove out of there. He pulled a bootlegger's turn when he saw us coming and beat feet.'

'Did you get a plate number?' Callahan asked.

'Sorry,' the ambulance driver said. 'He made a right before we could catch up to him. We had to turn toward the hospital. I do have a description, though. A small dark blue pickup. I'm guessing a Chevy S-10.'

19

Coronet had no intention of telling Dazid Ishmael that his real name was Vincent Chen. The Abu Sayyaf commander didn't concern himself with such trivialities anyway, and didn't really care so long as he got paid.

Both men had chosen unforgiving professions, and they had not survived as long as they had by having lax OPSEC.

They'd elected to postpone their talk and parted company shortly after Coronet killed the off-duty PNP officer. Each man had spent the entire night running surveillance detection routes. Chen had no idea exactly what Dazid Ishmael had done. The fact that he was one of the most wanted men in the Philippines and was still alive was testament enough to the man's skill at tradecraft.

For Chen's part, he'd utilized a series of taxis and cover locations for his SDRs, spending enough time at each location to allow his team to observe and see if he'd grown any sort of tail. There'd been a scare shortly after midnight when a Davao City police truck parked across the street from the adult cinema Chen had chosen as a cover stop. A short time later, a young woman in short shorts and a halter top arrived in a taxi and got in the police truck. The two sped away into the night.

Chen held to the notion that two people could keep a secret, so long as one of them was dead. At the same time, there were large portions of his job that required the efforts of more than one man. He needed assistance, but he needed it from people he could trust. Of course, his handlers within the PRC knew this. In the beginning, he'd been part of several teams, learning from some of the best Beijing had to offer on operations from Taiwan to Los Angeles. Eventually, he'd been selected to work on his own and ordered to stop reporting to his regular handler in Beijing. His new handler, a man he knew only as Kevin, was a moderately high-ranking member of either the Chinese military or some facet of the country's murky intelligence apparatus. Chen didn't know exactly which organization or branch, and he didn't care, so long as the missions and the money kept coming his way.

In the beginning, Kevin had told him to submit eight names of operatives with whom he'd worked before to be part of his team. *Trust* was an often bandied word but a seldom felt emotion in the intelligence business. Those who engaged in such work were trained to be untrustworthy, and so expected the same behavior from others. Vincent Chen knew full well at least half the men and women assigned to work with him were sent to spy on him. It was the way the PRC did things – give someone a job, assign two people to make certain that job was completed under the guidelines of the party, and then assign at least one other to watch the watchers. At some point, all involved knew they were watching and being watched. With the right incentives – in the form of money and actual rather than forced camaraderie – all the internal spying became a laughable house of cards.

It took almost two years – and the unfortunate deaths

of four less loyal members of his team – before Chen felt he'd weeded and pruned his operational cadre into a group of three men and one woman he could trust – or, at least, on whom he could depend ninety five percent of the time. Each of these four wanted the money he paid them, and each of them had some sort of weakness that he could exploit if the need arose – gambling debts, an adulterous affair with a ranking party member's wife. In Chen's experience, everyone on earth had something of a tender white underbelly. Eventually, he'd picked up a handful of other operatives he used around the world who worked on a contract basis.

Over the past several years, the sheer size of Chen's payments had led him to realize he'd become an operative for some faction of the PRC government that most of the party knew nothing about. He began earning large 'bonuses' at the completion of each assignment. As team leader, he made sure almost five hundred thousand US dollars a year flowed into the offshore accounts belonging to each of the other members of his cadre. One hundred thousand of that was distributed by Chen himself from the bonuses he received. A yearly income of half a million US dollars appeared to be a magic number. Any less and the danger a competing entity might lure a person away became exponentially greater. Too much more than half a million and one began to feel financially independent. It became easier to sock away a little here and there, making the dream of disappearing to some remote corner of the world too much of a reality. Chen's handlers had not seemed to snap to this reality. Expensive cars, fresh young women, constant business-class travel, and five-star hotels were all enormously expensive, but the sensitivity of his missions and the sheer genius with which he pulled them off had made him a very rich man.

And the rest of his team had been handpicked because they were much like him. Sure, he had leverage. But more than threat of exposure or even the money, the members of Coronet's team preferred their new lives to their old ones. They were all in their mid-thirties, fit, and adventurous. Vincent Chen had worked insidiously to make certain that the men and women who worked for him were thoroughly and completely addicted to the excesses of their jobs and the frequent massive adrenaline spikes. He'd turned them into junkies. Their habit kept them loyal to him, because nowhere else could they find anything remotely close to the life of working with Coronet.

Vincent Chen himself was an addict, and he knew it. He had enough money in various offshore accounts that he could have easily retired and lived the seventy years in modest comfort without ever working another day.

But like the members of his team, *modest* was not something he ever wanted to experience again.

After hours of movement and a generous cooling-off period from the time of the PNP officer's death, Amanda, one of the female members of his team, made contact via mobile phone and reported that neither she, nor any of the others, had seen anything remotely resembling a tail. The Abu Sayyaf countersurveillance team, such as it was, reported the same. Both Dazid and Chen deemed the situation as safe as possible — though it was never completely so — and met at a small beachside café in Panabo, northeast of Davao City, for a breakfast of coffee, dried milkfish, and *pandesal,* the small bread rolls Chen found to be one of the best things about the Philippines.

Dazid was remarkably forthcoming for a wanted man.

'This operation you suggest,' the Abu Sayyaf commander said, chewing an unsightly mouthful of bread and salted fish. 'It will require zealots.'

'This is true,' Chen said. He dabbed his mouth with a napkin in an effort to get the other man to do the same. It didn't work and he gave up. 'I did not suppose that would be a problem.'

Dazid grinned, showing a severe lack of dental care. 'My men possess plenty of zeal. But they would prefer to escape any action with their lives intact.'

'I see,' Chen said. 'Perhaps I have wasted your time, then.'

'Not at all,' Dazid said. 'There is no shortage of religious martyrs in Malaysia – so long as their families are well compensated.'

'And you would see to it that they receive the compensation?'

Dazid grinned again, nearly losing a mouthful of fish. He ate and spoke with gusto. 'Such would be my great honor.'

Chen considered the man for a long moment. He knew the man's honor was tied to the large sum of cash coming his way. More mercenary than religious extremist, Dazid Ishmael was, however, exactly what Chen needed. A zealot might veer off and attack a more attractive target for his cause. A mercenary would complete the task he'd been paid for – so as to make himself employable in the future.

Finally, Chen said, 'Excellent. Then we may move forward?'

'By all means,' Dazid said. 'You are paying me well. I will provide the weapons, transport, and the men . . .' He paused, sitting back as if to chew his cud while staring at the sea.

Chen let him think, prodding only after he'd washed down a last bite of *pandesal* with the dregs of his coffee. 'There is something else, my friend?'

Dazid snapped out of his trance and turned to look directly at Chen. 'As I told you, the martyrs will be no problem. They are intelligent enough, and they are, no doubt, willing to die. I must admit, though, that I have serious doubts about their ability to get close enough to an American warship to do any damage.'

Chen gave the man a soft smile, a smile that said he was absolutely sure of himself – and of his plan. 'My group will be in close communication,' he said. 'If your men do what my people say, exactly when they say it, I assure you that will not be an issue. The American Navy will come to them.'

20

'I'm . . . I'm not even supposed to be here,' Eddie Feng stammered, his back against the cinder-block wall of Dallas County's Lew Sterrett jail. Individual cells ran around the edge of the open dayroom and down the corridors that radiated out like the spokes of a wheel. Time for lights-out was fast approaching, but for now, the prisoners in this pod sat in small knots of congruent color and race around the open bay. Some watched a small television in a cage on the wall. Some played cards. Some, Feng imagined, plotted to kill him. There was a control room at the far end, staffed by two DSOs who faced in opposite directions, dividing their time between a set of far too many monitors and the dayroom of a different pod. Feng doubted they would see a triple homicide if it went down right in front of them. The place smelled like farts and Lysol, but it didn't matter, he was so scared he could hardly breathe anyway. The African American detention services officer standing beside him was nice enough. She was about the same size as Feng, with hair buzzed as short as humanly possible but that could still be called hair, and an oval face that said she would have been attractive out of the formless green uniform. The tag on her chest identified her as Officer Lincoln. Feng thought she'd smiled at him once while he was standing on the red line at the book-in counter, but the more he talked to her now, the more he thought maybe she just had indigestion.

'I'm not kidding,' Feng yammered on. 'I really should be in solitary. I'm helping out the FBI on some high-level stuff.'

The DSO rolled her eyes, then scanned the crowded dayroom full of inmates. She kept her voice low, just loud enough for him to hear. 'Why don't you speak up a little bit? I'm sure there are a lot of nice citizens in here who never met a real live rat before.'

Feng gulped, pulling his arms, turtle-like, inside the top of his orange jail scrubs in an effort to chase away the chill. For some reason, they kept this place like a damned refrigerator.

'Right,' he said. 'I've just never been in jail before.' He shrugged, armless, and inched closer to Officer Lincoln like a frightened child looking to make friends with the teacher at recess.

Lincoln gave him a glare. Her voice boomed. 'Back off, inmate!'

A husky DSO with a blond porn-star mustache glanced up. Lincoln shook her head and raised a hand to let him know she had the situation under control. He went back to watching the inmates as they lined up at the pay phones.

Feng took a step back, grimacing at her sudden out-burst. She gave a slow nod. 'You're welcome,' she said.

'What?'

She continued to look out at the dayroom. 'I just gave you some undeserved street cred in here, inmate. These animals think you popped off to me, and they'll give you a little space for a minute. People in here smell fear. Know what I'm sayin'?'

'Got it,' Feng said. 'Thank you. Would you mind making a call to the FBI for me? Tell them something's messed up?'

Officer Lincoln turned now and gave him a disgusted stare. 'Seriously, inmate. You really need to back off.'

Across the dayroom, DSO Tony Chang stepped out of the control room and made his way across the open floor. A couple other correctional officers rolled their eyes, but the inmates moved out of his way. He spent a lot of time in the gym and was proud that his girlfriend had taken up the sides of his size-seventeen uniform shirt so it formed a tight V from his lats down to his thirty-two-inch waist. The inmates needed to see they weren't the only ones who could do pull-ups. Reaching the 2 East Corridor, Chang gave a quiet nod to an Asian inmate lined up at the bank of pay phones. The young man at the phones, who had a Sun Yee On triangle tattooed on his neck, was a recent initiate, and Chang knew he was eager to prove his devotion to the brotherhood.

Chang had been the one to handle Eddie Feng's booking. A simple tick in the wrong computer box saw to it that he didn't end up in solitary like the FBI requested. Chang tried to get the guy thrown in with the triad brothers who'd been arrested at Chicas, but they'd all been put on lockdown, so it was all up to him.

On cue, the tattooed man spun in line and punched the nearest inmate in the throat. This man, who happened to be a short but extremely muscular member of La Eme, staggered backward just long enough to catch his breath. The Mexican Mafia soldier recovered quickly and rushed the lighter Asian who had dared to disrespect him, driving him into the concrete wall. Four other triad members, unaware of any arrangement with Officer Chang, jumped to the defense of their embattled brother, piling on in a flurry of fists and elbows and teeth. Their presence drew more La Eme foot soldiers into the fight.

Ethnic and rival gang tensions boiled just below the surface of these men, incarcerated nose-to-nose with people who they'd just as soon see dead on the street. In prison, gang members might be segregated. County jails did what they could, but space was at more of a premium.

Alarms began to sound, echoing off the concrete-and-steel enclosure. Inmates not involved in the fight reluctantly stepped away from the free entertainment as the bored-sounding intercom announcement that accompanied the alarms ordered them to their cells.

Seconds later, heavy boots slapped the tile floor as detention officers poured into the dayroom from various points around the jail. Officer Chang stayed where he was, glancing up at the control room. The two officers inside stood up so they could see over their screens.

Inmates filed by, returning to their assigned cells. When Eddie Feng shuffled past, arms tucked inside the sleeves of his scrubs, Officer Chang fell in behind and followed him to his cell.

'Hold up,' Chang said, pulling Feng aside to give the other inmates time to move to their own cells and get out of earshot. 'Aren't you supposed to be in solitary?'

Feng's mouth fell open. 'Finally!' he said. 'Somebody's got their shit together. Thank you. Seriously, man, thank you.'

Klaxons still raged, not quite drowning out the free-for-all that had broken out in the dayroom.

'Come on,' Chang said, motioning down the now empty corridor toward the heavy steel door. 'Roll up your stuff. I was just coming to look for you.'

Feng's two cellmates would be involved in the fight, so it would just be Chang and the inmate.

The inmate was so happy about moving to solitary he was humming when he walked into the cell and didn't see Chang place the small rubber wedge that would keep the door from closing all the way. All Feng's personal belongings had been taken, either by the FBI or at booking. He'd been issued a wool blanket and a stubby pink toothbrush made of flexible rubber. It wasn't much, but when nothing is all you have, even a toothbrush that looks like a kid's toy is a treasure worth guarding.

Chang took the small syringe from his shirt pocket and stepped forward, jamming the needle into the back of Feng's thigh at the same moment the singing idiot decided to turn around and thank him again. Feng jerked away, swiping at Chang with one hand and throwing the pitiful toothbrush with the other. The syringe went flying and landed in the stainless-steel sink/toilet combination. Unfortunately, Chang had been in mid-push and the contents of the syringe that hadn't gone into Feng's leg ended up on the floor.

Chang grabbed Feng by the throat and drove him backward into the lower bunk, fingers squeezing tight to keep him from crying out. With the syringe gone, he had no way of knowing how much fentanyl had made it into Feng's muscle. Three milligrams would be enough to kill a normal-sized man – and Feng was a runt. Even so, Chang had intended to give him half again that much, just to be on the safe side.

The DSO was making a decent side living selling fentanyl in the jail. The markup was incredible, with a five-hundred-dollar investment bringing him as much as ten grand. He could have made more out on the street. These inmates weren't exactly rolling in cash – and he sure as shit wasn't going to take Cup O' Noodles or honey buns in trade. Still, ten grand was ten grand. The fentanyl came in from China, where it was manufactured in legal labs – and then stashed in the little desiccant packs of silica in pairs of running shoes he ordered online. It was almost too easy – and he got to keep the running shoes.

Everybody knew the fentanyl was coming inside – the inmates called it Murder 8. When it didn't kill them, it made them lethargic and easy to deal with – unlike the spice and other toxic shit that was being smuggled in. Chang sometimes felt that he was providing a service of calm for his fellow DSOs.

Feng had been so flighty at booking that no one would question it if he died of an overdose. Chang had the stuff on hand already. A call from a contact said the Sun Yee On brothers needed a favor – and there would be an extra twenty G's in it for him.

It would have been so easy if the dumb bastard hadn't turned around.

Chang held him against the bed with his body weight, one hand on his neck, the other flat across his mouth.

Finally, he felt the man go limp. Seconds later, he gave a series of gurgling croaks. If Chang had injected enough, Feng should have stopped breathing – but he didn't. His pupils constricted to tiny black dots. His lips turned blue and his breathing was labored, but his stupid lungs still pumped away.

The syringe lay on the ground at Chang's feet in a puddle of liquid. He thought about picking it up and trying to inject any remaining drops, but the syringe was wet. He felt in his pocket for nitrile gloves and came up with only one. That wasn't going to work. Fentanyl was potent stuff and could be absorbed through the skin.

Chang let the man drop face-first onto the lower bunk, stifling the urge to bash his head against the wall or simply choke the life out of him. Either would leave far too much physical evidence – but if it came to that, he'd do what he had to do and work out the rest later. He couldn't leave Feng like this. If the drug wore off without killing him, Chang would end up in jail himself – and correctional officers didn't do well on the inside.

Alarms still sounded up and down the corridor, but the riot would be quelled at any moment. Whatever Chang did, he had to do it quickly. An army of detention officers would have descended on the dayroom by now. His Sun Yee On brothers had done what they could, but they could keep the diversion going for only so long. Chang pulled the feed to the camera in this cell just before the fight broke out, leaving the control room no time to notice the gray screen among the dozens they already had to watch.

He scanned the tiny space, racking his brain for some

sort of plan. Then he looked down at Feng and realized the answer was right there in front of him.

Jail administrators went to great lengths to keep inmates from harming themselves, but if someone was determined to die, they found a way. Chang had seen some ingenious methods over his four years as a correctional officer. One guy had even stuffed enough toilet paper down his own throat that it was impossible to get out. It was interesting to watch, but Chang didn't have time for that now. This needed to be much quicker. Fortunately, prisoners had developed several methods to bring about their own deaths that were relatively quick, and, at least as important, could be applied right under the noses of their guards.

Chang slowly released his grip on the near catatonic Feng.

'Lucky bastard,' he whispered. 'On the outside, they'd kill you with an ax.'

Chang rolled the lolling man onto his belly. He stepped back long enough to grab the cuffs of Feng's inmate-uniform trousers and pull them off in one quick motion. Feng's head was turned sideways, and Chang could see a flash of panic in his eyes as he pulled away the man's pants. Immobile and exposed, there was absolutely nothing Feng could do.

Chang chuckled as he ripped the scrub pants with his teeth, tearing them lengthwise from cuff to cuff before twisting the orange cloth into a makeshift rope.

'Don't worry,' he said. 'It's gonna be a hell of a lot worse than you think.'

Working quickly, he tied a fixed loop in one end and a slip knot in the other. Crouching over the bunk, Chang slipped the larger loop around Feng's neck so the knot was in the back of his head. Then, grabbing Feng's foot, Chang bent it up and over Feng's back, pulling the knee upward until he was able to loop the slip knot over Feng's foot, arching his back as though he were hog-tied. Dead weight from Feng's own paralyzed leg pulled the noose tight, putting pressure against the already bulging carotid arteries in the side of his neck.

The noose did the trick of stopping blood to Feng's brain, but it wasn't quite tight enough to compress his airway. Gagging noises escaped his open mouth and his face rapidly took on the hue of an eggplant. His eyes fluttered. Chang relaxed a notch. Finally. It wouldn't be long now.

Chang spun on his heel and scooped up the rubber chock he'd left in the cell door to keep him from getting locked inside. He took one last look at the choking man. When he turned around, Officer Pankita Lincoln blocked his path.

Her eyes looked right through him. 'What the hell?'

Chang feigned a smile. He was big enough that he could run right over this puny bitch if he wanted to.

'Inmate troubles,' he said – and threw what he thought was a pretty damned good left hook.

Unfortunately for him, Pankita Lincoln's father had taught her how to box.

Chang's eyes and then his shoulder telegraphed his intention to throw the hook a mile away. She faded backward, just enough to let the hook slip by. Pepper spray in hand, she gave him a full blast directly in the face before driving her knee into his groin in a repeated, rapid-fire attack.

Chang roared in pain. His eyes slammed shut and he staggered back, instinctively trying to put more distance between himself and the searing burn. Defensive-tactics instructors taught their students to use the fingers of the non-dominant hand to hold open one eye – but DT class was nothing like real life. There was no getting ready, no time to prepare. This whole thing had gone to shit.

Flailing blindly, Chang forced his eyes into a grimacing squint. His lungs rebelled, convulsing each time he tried to draw the smallest breath. Mucous membranes kicked into overtime, sending strings of snot draining from his nose. If he could just get hold of her, he could shut her up for good, maybe even make it look like she'd killed Feng – at least long enough for him to get away.

Pankita Lincoln had other ideas.

21

Dominic Caruso thought Flaco's interview seemed to be going well when they first sat down in an interview room at the Dallas FBI field office. Flaco's nostrils flared and his upper lip twitched, rabbitlike, as if he were trying to keep on a pair of nonexistent glasses. He was obviously terrified – not a bad emotion for someone from whom Caruso wanted information. He spent more time staring at the one-way glass than he did making eye contact with the two investigators.

Then Callahan made the mistake of asking who had kidnapped him. The skinny gangbanger just sat there staring at her, blinking stupidly, head shaking like it might explode at any moment. In the end, he muttered something about a lawyer and refused to say another word. Dom suspected his reticence to talk might have had something to do with the application of particular boot to the side of his neck. John Clark was in his late sixties, maybe a little old for this kind of hands-on work, but there was a brooding air of vengeance about the man that gave even Caruso the willies.

Joe Rice and a blond Dallas PD detective named Shirley Winston took Flaco to jail, leaving Callahan to deal with Caruso. It was not lost on Caruso that both of the task force officers looked at him like a member of an invading army.

Kelsey Callahan rubbed her eyes with a thumb and forefinger. 'Want to see where I work?'

'Sure,' Caruso said, wondering how much of the conversation the mic on his neck loop was picking up. Adara was open-minded, but she would not like this at all.

'Good.' Callahan gave a contemplative nod. ''Cause I need to drop by the hangar before you buy me that drink.' She leaned back against the table, looking him up and down, obviously flirting.

Caruso gave her his best smile. 'I thought you were buying me the drink.'

She sighed. 'I know I owe you one. I mean . . . hell, I hear the words coming out of my mouth and I'm like, "That's not me."' She gave a nervous chuckle. 'Did you know that I make every boyfriend let me run a diagnostic on his computer and phone? That kind of trust is a real turn-on, let me tell you. But I can't help it if I know the stats. I can walk down the street anywhere in the US and the odds are I'm passing some pervert with child porn on his computer every couple minutes.' She breathed out hard, puffing her cheeks as if trying to keep from crying. 'This job, it can turn you into a real bitch, you know.'

Caruso shook his head and said softly, '*A carne di lupo, zanne di cane.*'

Callahan raised an eyebrow, waiting for him to explain.

'Literally it means something about wolf meat and dog fangs, but figuratively it says you have to *be* rough to fight rough things. Kelsey, your investigations pit you against some of the sickest people on the planet. You're entitled to be a little pissy once in a while.'

'Fight rough with rough.' Callahan closed her eyes to think for a moment. 'I like that . . . I like it a lot.'

The hangar near Love Field Airport was less than fifteen minutes away from the FBI field office via the West Northwest Highway, called Loop 12 by locals. Caruso followed in his rental car, parking beside Callahan. He groaned within himself as he noted the position of three exterior security cameras. If they went to a remote server, then he was screwed. Government agents didn't like being under surveillance any more than regular citizens. The difference was, they could do something about it, so there weren't likely to be any cameras inside the building.

Callahan used a proximity card to get through the front door. Once inside, she deactivated an alarm with a simple key pad. She didn't try to hide it, and Caruso memorized the five-digit code.

She flipped on the lights and said, 'Behold! The office of misfit toys.'

'Nice,' Caruso said, surveying the bullpen arrangements of all the desks in the cavernous hangar. 'You're in charge here, right?'

'I guess.'

'Then where's your office?'

'No office,' she said. 'I'd miss too much. I sit at that desk there, below the whiteboard.' She explained the makeup of the task force, the agencies involved, and ran down a list of their recent arrest and rescue statistics.

'Those are impressive numbers,' Caruso said.

Callahan scoffed. 'You want numbers? In 2008 there

were over 57,000 kids reported missing in Texas alone. In that same year, the Highway Patrol made 2,891,441 traffic stops. How many kids do you think they recovered?'

'No idea.'

'Zip,' she said. 'Nada. Zero. So they developed a program called Interdiction for the Protection of Children, which lines out a set of behaviors law enforcement should look for in trafficked children and the traffickers themselves.'

'So it's working?'

Callahan closed her eyes. 'Fifty-four kids were rescued last year. Better than zero, but we still have a long way to go. Human trafficking is a thirty-five-billion-dollar-a-year gig. There are places in the world – hell, there are places right here in this state, where women and kids are sold and traded like horses. And we're barely making a dent.'

Caruso was thinking, *You haven't met John Clark*, but he said, 'And you still don't think you're doing enough?'

'Honestly, I'm overcome with guilt for standing here talking to you now instead of trying to save another one.' She ran a hand through her hair, redoing the scrunchie that kept her ponytail in place. 'Anyway, sorry about bringing you down. I'm sort of used to having to make my case all the time.'

'No worries,' Caruso said. 'It's good to see someone so dedicated who's not completely burned out.'

'Who said I'm not burned out?' She took his hand and turned toward the back wall, behind her desk. 'Come on. There's something I need to show you.'

Caruso pulled his hand away as gently as he could. 'I'm in a relationship,' he said.

Callahan gave him an honest laugh, continuing to walk toward her desk.

'I figured,' she said. 'Men who can quote Italian proverbs don't stay unattached for long.' She sat at her desk, found a pair of reading glasses, and then bent to spin the dial on a gray metal safe under her side table. She hit the combination on the first try, and turned a handle before pulling open the heavy drawer with a loud *thunk*. 'To be honest,' she said, looking up at him, 'I'd intended to bring you here and engage in my own little version of a honey trap. You know, try and trick you into admitting what it is you're really up to. But I guess I already know. When Flaco decided not to talk, I realized we had nothing to go on but the thin stuff Eddie Feng is giving us, and that's likely just to save his own skin. He's hiding more information, I know it, but in the meantime, I'm open to whatever help you guys at the Counterintelligence Division can give us.' She took a small yellow envelope from the safe and handed it to Caruso. He could see from the outline it was a USB drive.

Callahan took a deep breath. 'I'm not an idiot, Caruso. Headquarters drops you in here on top of me, and then one of my arrests shows up duct-taped and hooded with a muddy boot print on his face.' She nodded to the envelope. 'I don't know who you are exactly, but I think you should take a look at this. There's obviously something on it that I'm not seeing.'

Caruso opened the envelope and dumped the USB drive into his palm. 'Not saying your theory about me holds any water, but we are on the same side, I promise you that. I wouldn't mind having a look at this. It's been checked for malware?'

She nodded. 'FBI techs assure me it's virus-free. You'll need to sign for it. And I do want it ba –'

Callahan's cell phone began to chime, cutting her off in midsentence. She looked at the caller ID, then shook her head. 'It's Joe Rice,' she said. 'One of the detectives who booked Flaco into jail. I've gotta take this.'

Callahan's mouth fell open five seconds after she pressed the phone to her ear. 'You have got to be shitting me,' she said with a gasp. '. . . Okay . . . I'll be right there.'

She ended the call and stood up.

'What is it?' Caruso asked.

'Apparently,' Callahan said, 'somebody thinks Eddie Feng has information that is too important to let him live.'

'Is he dead?'

'Not quite,' Callahan said. She reached behind her desk and grabbed a black 5.11 daypack, which presumably she used instead of a purse. 'Listen, Feng is in the hospital now, surrounded by a protective detail of very jumpy FBI agents. I'm going to try and get some kind of information out of the detention officer who attacked him. Sounds like he got a snootful of pepper spray, so maybe he's been tenderized a bit. You go on and do what you need to do with that thumb drive.' Tears welled in Callahan's green eyes. She sniffed and wiped them away. 'I know there are hundreds, even thousands, more kids out there. I've never even met her, hell, I barely even know what she looks like, but for whatever reason, it feels important that we find Magdalena Rojas. I'm good with using your sketchy counterintel methods if it helps us find Matarife and rescue this kid.' She stopped at the door, finger poised above the pad to arm the security system. 'Tell me how you say that Italian proverb again.'

'*A carne di lupo, zanne di cane.*'

Callahan looked at him and nodded. 'Hell yeah,' she said. 'That.'

Forty-five minutes later, Caruso sat with the rest of The Campus's operators in Clark's room at the Omni Hotel in downtown Dallas. Caruso and Adara leaned forward on the loveseat, shoulder to shoulder. Jack slouched in an overstuffed chair, and Midas leaned back in the office chair he'd swiveled around from the desk. Both men leaned as far back as their respective seats allowed, staring at the ceiling. Chavez sat on the floor, his back to the couch. Clark perched on the end of his bed. The team was used to such meetings in cramped hotel rooms and were all too tired to care about the furniture – or lack of it.

Caruso's cell phone lay faceup on the coffee table with Gavin Biery on speaker. The Campus IT wizard sounded congested, like he had a cold – which was surely a function of the fact that it was nearly two in the morning in DC.

Biery coughed. 'I found a guy named Donny Lao with an Australian passport who looks a hell of a lot like the photo you sent of Vincent Chen, who happens to have a passport issued by the ROC.'

'I'm betting Donny Lao's not really Australian,' Ryan said, stating the obvious.

'Ya think?' Biery's eye roll was almost audible over the phone. 'Vincent Chen has school records in Taiwan and the US. Sounds sinister, I know, but he owns a greeting-card company that has him taking trips between his home base in LA and China several times a year. I've sent everything I've found to you.'

'How did you come to find this Donny Lao?' Jack asked. His brain was exhausted, but not asleep . . . yet.

Biery chuckled. 'The United States required friendly nations to add biometric data to their passport photos over a decade ago. Once I had Vincent Chen's photo, it was a matter of stepping behind the firewalls of those nations and running a comparison program. Australia is part of the Five Eyes, so much of their information is available through CIA and NSA data links.'

'Still, must have taken hours.' Jack yawned. Now he was falling asleep.

'Not really,' Biery went on. 'I wrote some code that worked on it while I did other things. I had two hits within the first half-hour. Looks like your man Chen has bona fide passports issued from Canada and Australia – under the names of Todd Lee and Donny Lao, respectively. He was never discovered because, up to now, no one was looking for Vincent Chen – just another face among millions.'

'That's good work,' Clark said.

'Thank you,' Biery said. 'Also, Mr Lao happens to be booked tomorrow on the three-thirty p.m. Delta flight from DFW to Buenos Aires . . . well, technically this afternoon at three-thirty.'

Chavez gave a low groan. 'You couldn't have led with that? I might actually be able to close my eyes for a couple hours.'

'Don't want to hear it,' Gavin said. 'I'm passing you off to Lisanne. She's got some information for you about flight –'

'Hold on,' Clark said. 'What about the thumb drive? I need you to take a look at it ASAP.'

Biery heaved a sigh. 'So who's willing to risk a potential infection of their laptop to scnd it to me?'

'I'll do it.' Caruso raised his hand, despite the fact that it was a voice call. 'The agent I got it from assured me this thing's been checked by FBI computer techs.'

'Have I taught you guys nothing?' Biery snapped. 'Do not even get that drive close to anyone's machine until I get there.'

Chavez's head snapped up. 'Wait, what? You're coming here?'

'Gerry approved it. This USB is obviously important to you, but I'm not letting it near one of my machines until I run some of my own diagnostics. FBI techs ... Please! Anyway, we're at the hangar now – already on the plane – just waiting for the pilots to get here. Here's Lisanne. I'm going to get some sleep since Jack's not here to hog the couch.'

Lisanne Robertson was the new Adara Sherman – director of transportation for The Campus. Gerry Hendley had recruited the energetic former Marine after she pulled him over for speeding on the Jeff Davis Highway. Her Lebanese mother had raised her to be fluent in Arabic – she had two tours in Iraq under her belt by the time she was twenty-seven. After separating from the military, she'd spent four years with the City of Alexandria Police Department. Both jobs gave her the chops she needed to transform from uniformed flight attendant to effectively become a one-person Phoenix Raven unit, pulling secur-ity on the Hendley Associates Gulfstream when it was parked at less secure airfields — which seemed to happen all the time.

'Hey, guys,' Lisanne said in her usual chipper voice. Dom could imagine her blue-black hair bouncing as she spoke. 'We're estimating wheels-up out of Reagan in an hour with an ETA into Dallas Love Field of four thirty-five a.m., Central Time.'

A collective groan ran around the room.

Clark shot a glance at Dom. 'You're staying in Texas with me,' he said. 'The rest of you will get to Buenos Aires well ahead of Chen and set up a reception. Follow him and see what he's up to. There's still a hell of a lot to find out about him and his operation on this end.'

22

Ba Meiling braced, her small chin tucked, narrow shoulders pinned, along with six other servants in the slate-tiled entry of Foreign Minister Li's home. Dressed in black slacks and crisp white shirts, they stood with hands folded and eyes locked to the front. Minister Li did not like to be gawked at. The butler, Mr Fan, stood beside Meiling under the harsh light of the crystal chandelier. Beads of perspiration coursed down the side of the man's ashen face. A recent addition to the household, Mr Fan had been brought in shortly after Minister Li had seen an episode of *Downton Abbey*. It was a whispered joke among the staff that the minister was a Chinese man who owned a German car and lived in an Italian villa with an English butler – or at least a Chinese butler he dressed up like an English one. Mr Fan should have been in bed but was too frightened of the foreign minister to admit that he was gravely ill.

The Li home was located northeast of Beijing, outside the 5 Ring Road. It was just far enough to escape the worst of the enormous cloud of yellow haze that choked those unfortunate enough to live in the city. The thirty-kilometer distance between home and office gave Li's driver plenty of time to alert the staff, providing them a chance to convene for his arrival.

The thud of the big BMW sedan's door caused Meiling

to jump. Silence crept over the entry. No one breathed – which was good, because all the air seemed to have left the room.

Meiling willed her employer to hurry. These inspections were worse than a mere annoyance; they kept her from doing her job. She was an accomplished chef, a graduate of the Culinary Institute in Hong Kong, but the foreign minister disliked the term *chef*. He was the only chief in any area of his home, and that included the kitchen. Meiling and her assistant, a young woman named Yubi, should have been prepping for the dinner party, but when the foreign minister arrived, all else was put on hold – the immutable laws of science and cooking notwithstanding.

The front door flew open as if blown by an evil wind, and Foreign Minister Li strode in. He stepped out of his shoes so easily that Meiling wondered how he'd kept them on all day, and into a pair of slippers that were waiting directly in his path. Meiling had seen the minister on the television news, where he appeared to be so temperate and even-keeled. In his own home, even one step out of his desired routine to slip a toe into a slipper could send him into a spitting rage.

Slippers slapping the tile floor, Li removed his suit jacket. He dropped it as he walked, certain that Mr Fan would be there to catch it. The poor man was so sick he nearly toppled over in the process. If Li noticed his butler was ill, he made no mention of it. One of the two girls Li called hostesses handed him a Gibson martini with three cocktail onions, while the other exchanged his day glasses for a pair of less flattering readers and four evening newspapers.

Meiling watched the way the minister looked at the two younger women. Had either of them been able to cook, she would have been sacked. Their skin was alabaster, while she was darker. A tiny mole above her upper lip stood out in stark contrast to their flawless oval faces. An American college student had once called the mole a beauty mark, but Foreign Minister Li looked as if his stomach was upset each time he saw her. Meiling dismissed it as the will of the gods. Minister Li doted on his wife, but everyone knew the hostesses had not been hired for their ability to mix a perfect Gibson martini.

Minister Li paused at the bottom of the stairs, taking a sip of his drink. The staff, even the hostesses, who surely had his ear – and more – held their collective breath.

Li peered directly at Meiling. 'Add two more to the guest list. Minister Ip and is lovely wife will join us.'

Meiling teetered in place. She grabbed at her assistant's shoulder for support as soon as Li turned to continue up the stairs. Two more guests! That was impossible, the worst of all catastrophes. The chef wasn't worried about the food. It was to be a British feast, and, as with all feasts, there would be far too much roast lamb and too many side dishes for anyone to eat. But Mrs Ip was going to pose a problem.

Yubi's mouth hung half open, like she was about to be sick to her stomach. Meiling understood the feeling. 'Do you have enough for Mrs Ip?' the assistant chef asked.

Meiling closed her eyes and took a series of calming breaths, attempting to steady herself. It did not work. 'I do not,' she said.

'The minister will kill you.'

'He will not kill me,' Meiling said, doubting herself even as she said the words.

'But he will say we should have been better prepared.' Yubi's slight body shook with tension, causing her black bangs to shimmer in the light of the chandelier. 'What if he blames me as well?'

Meiling thought through her limited options. She found it difficult to breathe, let alone think. At length, she turned toward the kitchen. 'First we will prepare the batter for the Yorkshire puddings. It will need time to chill.'

The familiar act of breaking eggs and the comforting smell of sifted flour served to calm Meiling's spirit. An idea began to rise in her mind like the bubbles in the whisked batter. 'I will speak to Madame Li,' she said at length. If that didn't work, there would be nothing to do but accept her fate. She would be fired, but the likelihood that the minister would actually kill her was remote.

Wasn't it?

The guests began to arrive three hours later. Meiling listened intently from her post in the kitchen, counting to herself as the butler, Mr Fan, announced the names as each couple entered. Deng Wenyuan and Madame Deng, secretary of the Central Committee for Discipline Inspection and his wife; General Ma Xiannian and Madame Ma, vice chairman of Central Military Commission and his wife; Deputy Party Secretary Ip Keqiang of the State Council for Deepening Reforms and his wife, Madame Ip. Meiling's heart sank with the arrival of Madame Xu and Lieutenant General Xu Jinlong, director of the Central Security Bureau. She wished the wives no ill will, but hoped one of them might somehow fall sick at the last minute. Even the odor of roast lamb, a smell she usually found intoxicating, did nothing for Meiling's nerves. She stood by as if awaiting the gallows while the foreign minister and his guests inhaled her perfect bacon-and-leek quiche appetizer. She hardly heard Madame Li's praise at the first expertly stacked bite of pink lamb, mint sauce, and delicate Yorkshire pudding. Table talk was light, with Madame Li deftly steering everyone away from politics. Meiling grew more anxious with every bite of food the guests ate, bringing them closer to the end of the meal – and she to her fate. Dessert service saw her hoping to be swallowed up by the draperies.

Minister Li tapped on his crystal glass with his silver spoon, making certain he had everyone's attention.

'I have prepared a small surprise for our lovely wives,' he said, as if he had prepared the white ramekins himself. Each of the guests had their own crème brûlée, but the ramekins for the women were marked with a small flower of burnt sugar on the crust. It had taken Meiling an hour to prepare the delicate blossoms.

Madame Ip, the birdlike woman who shouldn't have even been there, tapped on the crust of her dessert, hitting it several times with the tiny spoon as if she didn't quite have the strength to break through the caramelized sugar. She squealed when she finally cracked it, and, forgetting about the creamy custard, used the spoon to dig around in the dessert like it was a playground sandbox, until she found the diamond bracelet.

It was a mystery where the foreign minister got his money, but each of the bracelets cost 11,000 yuan – more than $1,500 US Meiling knew; she'd purchased them all at an expensive shop in Shunyi where Minister Li had an account. He took great pleasure in showing off to his friends at his frequent dinner parties by having her bake pieces of expensive jewelry into the desserts meant for each wife. The women would fawn over their husbands, proud of them for associating with such a powerful and generous man. The husbands, in turn, would scrape and bow to the minister for making them look so good in front of their wives.

Minister Li would always smile benevolently and help his own wife put on her bracelet. She always received jewelry as well.

Except tonight, that was not the case.

Meiling had planned on only four guests and there were not enough bracelets to go around. Madame Li had graciously given her bracelet to Madame Ip, telling Meiling not to fret. But the minister's eyes had gone positively black the moment he saw his wife had been left out. Madame Ip had only made it worse when she sucked the custard off her new trinket and then held it up to Madame Li, saying, 'Such a shame you don't get one, too, my dear.'

Minister Li turned to give Meiling a saccharine smile. 'We will retire to my study,' he said. 'Please see to some brandied pears.'

'Yes, Mr Foreign Minister,' she said, backing away.

'And Meiling,' he said, the smile fading from his lips. 'Bring in the fruit yourself.'

The Ips excused themselves shortly after dinner, citing a previous engagement, but Meiling suspected they'd been told it was time for them to leave. Only three men were ever invited into Minister Li's private study.

The crystal goblets of brandied pears rattled and clinked on the lacquer tray in Meiling's shaking hands. She took small breaths, afraid she'd cough from the pall of cigar smoke that filled the study.

'Thank you,' the minister said. 'Please leave at once.'

'Of course, sir,' Meiling said. Perhaps he had forgiven her for not being prepared. 'Will there be anything else?'

Minister Li cocked his head, puffing on the awful cigar. 'You misunderstand me, child,' he said. 'I mean leave my house. Your services will no longer be needed.'

Tears welled and then fell from Meiling's eyes. 'But sir, there was no –'

Li held up his hand. 'I have made it very clear that I value preparedness over excuses.' His eyes crept up and down. At length, he nodded, as if reaching a conclusion. He looked beside the door at a terrifying man with dark eyes and the bulge of a gun under his suit jacket – then back at the weeping Meiling. 'Lieutenant General Xu's driver will take you. If that is all right, General.'

Xu gave the man an almost imperceptible nod. 'Go ahead, Long Yun.'

General Ma Xiannian took a series of puffs from his Cuban cigar and held it to one side, studying the glowing coal. 'Killing the young woman seems harsh, even for you. It seems a terrible waste of a good cook. To forget to include your wife's bracelet is . . .'

The foreign minister waved away the notion. 'That was my fault,' he said. 'But it was not the primary concern. She was not at all surprised that Ip and his bitch wife were not asked to stay after dinner. It would not have been long before she said something to someone about the meetings of our new Gang of Four.'

They never uttered the phrase outside the security of their little group. The men had come to think of themselves as a faction that wanted only the best for China but who would surely be misunderstood if they were to be discovered. The original Gang of Four had been led by Chairman Mao's wife, Jiang Qing. After Mao's death, and absent his protection, the former actress was accused with three others as counterrevolutionary and blamed by the government for virtually every evil of the Cultural Revolution.

The foreign minister loosened his red silk tie. There was no reason to stand on ceremony now. He was among friends – friends who would stand beside him in front of a firing squad if they were ever discovered – even by members of the party who essentially agreed with them.

Secretary Deng spoke next. 'Public approval for Zhao is waning, as you predicted,' he said. 'But his supporters in the politburo appear steadfast. I have even heard it said that he has the brains to hold the same progressive economic policies as disgraced President Wei, but the balls to implement them.'

'That may be true,' General Ma said. 'But I know more than a few in the party who find themselves gravely concerned with Zhao's misguided corruption probes. It is as if he is completely blind to the origin of his support.'

'Blindness is among the least of his disturbing qualities,' Deng said.

'He is quite intelligent,' Li said. 'We should not under-estimate him. General Xu, I believe –'

A metallic chime sounded at the study door, cutting him off. The foreign minister raised his hand to quiet everyone. A moment later, Madame Li appeared with her arm around the shoulders of a handsome boy in his early teens.

'*Qin'ai*,' she said. The term was akin to 'dear' or 'dar-ling.' 'Our son has had a long day and would like to say good night to his father.'

Li put the cigar in the ashtray beside his chair and took the boy's hand, holding it in his. 'Good night, my son. Rest well.'

The other men in the room looked away, embarrassed by this uncustomary outpouring of emotion from the leader they'd respected for his cruelty and cunning.

'I will leave you men to talk your treason,' Madame Li said, smiling as she escorted the boy out.

Secretary Deng winced before the door was shut and they were alone. 'Does she know?'

Li took up his cigar again, then picked a fleck of tobacco off his lip. 'Of course not. It is merely something she says. *Women chatter about the household and men talk treason.*'

'Well,' Deng said, 'it is a dangerous term.'

Li's eyes narrowed. 'Any disrespectful talk of my wife would be dangerous. Of that you may be quite sure.'

General Ma held up his hand. Had it really fallen to the military man to try and make peace? He decided to change the subject rather than appeal to either man's decency. 'It is such a shame that Chinese interests must be harmed in order to attain our goals.'

Li snatched up his cigar, took a few puffs, then snubbed it out in the ashtray. The veins in the side of his neck bulged with tension.

'Make no mistake,' he said. 'Chinese interests are not our only targets. Before we are finished, President Ryan will be ready to fly Air Force One to Beijing and shoot the fool Zhao himself.'

The foreign minister sat for a moment, composing himself before turning to General Xu. 'Your man Huang, Zhao's chief bodyguard. Will he bend?'

'The colonel?' Xu shook his head. 'From what I have seen, he is endowed with a set of iron principles that will prove quite troublesome.'

'I assume you have considered a remedy,' the foreign minister said. 'Principles are to be lauded, so long as they align with ours. One man with the wrong ideals . . . Do I need to spell it out?'

Xu puffed on his cigar until the coal glowed red, illuminating his face.

'I can assure you, Mr Foreign Minister,' the general said. 'Colonel Huang will not be a problem.'

23

Four hours after the call from Gavin Biery, Ding Chavez slouched in an uncomfortable fake-leather chair in the lounge of an FBO off Lemmon Avenue. He munched stale popcorn for breakfast and thumbed absentmindedly through an aviation magazine while he tried to stay awake enough to remain aware of his surroundings. He never understood why every fixed-base operator he'd ever seen had a popcorn machine, but they did, and he'd learned to take advantage of the fact when there was nothing else salty to eat.

Chavez was dressed for travel in a pair of gray sweatpants and a pullover hoodie. The sweats made him look like Rocky Balboa getting ready for a training run, but they were comfortable – and he'd sleep better. Lord knew he needed sleep. He had plenty of training for lack of it, having been screamed at by drill sergeants in the Army, SAS operators in Hereford, instructors at Camp Peary – hell, even his own father-in-law. Sometimes you just had to suck it up and deal with it. He was pushing fifty years old, but he kept telling himself that if Clark could keep going, so could he. That wasn't really a fair comparison, because Clark was a machine. Fortunately, Mr C was getting older and now possessed only the grit and stamina of two normal men. But Chavez still worried about him. Clark had taken the idea of captive girls hard – and seemed to focus on it now even more than the mission at hand. Feng had said Matarife was connected to Chen – but they had Chen located now. There seemed little reason not to let Special Agent Callahan and her CAC Task Force handle the search for Matarife. They would sure be able to use Dom and John for the eventualities that would come up in Argentina. When Chavez had asked about it, Clark just raised a gray eyebrow and looked at him. Anyone who spoke the language of John Clark realized this unspoken action translated as 'Step the hell back!'

Chavez, being exhausted and generally absent a filter anyway, unwisely pressed the issue. This only served to earn him an earful of all the reasons why Clark did not have to explain himself to the likes of Domingo Chavez, someone who was still 'shitting yellow' when Clark was up to his chin in brown water in the godforsaken jungles of Southeast Asia. Ding was no stranger to harsh language, even from his wife's dad, but the rest of Clark's tirade would have melted the ears off a lesser man. Still, Ding couldn't help but love the guy. They'd been through too much together.

Chavez pitched the magazine back on the glass coffee table. There was nothing he could do about it, anyway.

The whine of the approaching Hendley Associates Gulfstream was a welcome sound. It meant forward progress in this operation. More important in the near term at least, the flight to Argentina would give the team a few uninterrupted hours of much-needed rest.

Chavez hadn't gone to sleep, staying up instead to scour the Internet for possible events that might be important enough to take Vincent Chen to South America. A simple meeting could have occurred anywhere. No, Buenos Aires was a hell of a long way away. Something was happening there that required Chen to make the journey. Four cups of coffee and three hours deep into his search, Chavez stumbled over an obscure three-line post on the Liniers cattle auction website that mentioned a meeting between Argentina's minister of agriculture and his counterparts from several other countries, including Thailand, Japan – and China. Beef exportation, among other things, would be discussed. According to the website, the Chinese foreign minister deemed the meeting important enough that he would also make an appearance.

The connection was slim, but it was all Chavez could find.

The team members would make it to Ministro Pistarini International Airport outside Buenos Aires proper, a full day ahead of Chen, giving them time to sort out customs and immigration details and get accustomed to their rental vehicles before setting up to follow Chen in the ungodly traffic. Their early arrival also allowed them to secure their weapons from the hidden bulkhead compartments aboard the Gulfstream. Argentina was an emerging country, but the extremely rich and the desperately poor lived literally across the street from each other in Buenos Aires, making the place sometimes feel like a powder keg set dangerously close to the campfire.

Chavez watched through the FBO's picture windows as the Gulfstream 550 turned off the taxiway. He couldn't help imagining the soft leather seat on board that was calling his name. He tossed the rest of the popcorn in the trash and grabbed his soft-sided bag.

Outside in the predawn darkness the airplane came to a stop and the door yawned open. Gavin Biery held on to the rail as he made his way carefully down the jet stairs. The Hendley IT wizard tugged a huge black duffel down behind him, letting it thunk against one step at a time as he descended, like it was a dead body. Still fifty pounds heavier than he wanted to be, Gavin liked to point out that this was a hell of a lot better than the seventy pounds overweight that he used to be. A cool Texas wind tousled what was left of his graying hair. He dropped the duffel at the door and headed straight for the restroom.

Chester 'Country' Hicks, the first officer of the Gulf-stream, came in to hit the head as well, while Helen Reid, the pilot in command, stayed outside with her airplane to oversee the refueling for a quick turn-and-burn.

Lisanne Robertson came in next, pulling a large black plastic Pelican case that contained Biery's technical gear. She offered to help load luggage, but everyone refused, so she took care of the fuel bill with the FBO using her Hendley Associates company credit card. As director of transportation, Robertson not only took care of the logistical minutiae but, when the plane landed, transitioned to security. She wore a white uniform blouse – neat and crisp – and a knee-length navy blue skirt. The skirt didn't appear to be tactical, but it gave the appearance that the jet was staffed by a pretty hostess. As sexist as it might sound, a friendly smile and a pair of nice legs went a long way toward drawing any attention from the airplane's actual mission.

That said, there was a lot more to Lisanne Robertson than her looks. She was not officially a Campus operator, but Clark believed in a unified-team concept. Because her duties pulling security for the Gulfstream might very well see everyone, including her, going to guns at the same moment, she needed to spend at least some time training with them. In the weeks since she'd been recruited, the former Marine had demonstrated not just her poise but also her skill with a variety of weapons on the range, and her ability to kick some serious ass in the mat room. She even wore the navy blue uniform skirt during defensive tactics drills, drawing a gun or blade from a holster on the spandex shorts underneath. It was good training for the guys as well. Watching an attractive young woman hike up her skirt to do battle – though they knew full well she was wearing shorts underneath – had a tendency to slow them down a fraction of a second too long. Everyone but Adara got 'cut' several times by Lisanne's chalk blade.

The world travel and enhanced training notwithstanding, other former Marines turned cops might blanch at handling all the housekeeping stuff, but Lisanne seemed to realize that she was an integral part of something much bigger than herself. And it didn't hurt that Adara Sherman, the last person to hold the job of transportation director, was now a full-fledged operator, hopping a plane to Argentina to hunt bad guys.

Clark followed the team out into the crisp air of early morning. He pulled Chavez aside on the tarmac, just before he boarded the Gulfstream.

'Be careful, son,' he said, grabbing Chavez by one hand and pulling him in for a backslapping brotherhood hug.

Ding grinned. 'You too, Mr C.'

This was about as close as John Clark would ever get to an apology.

Jack, Midas, Adara, and Chavez trudged up the air stairs looking like workers arriving at a gulag factory. The Hendley Associates Gulfstream was well appointed, with a reasonably stocked galley, good coffee, and a bar with the team's favorite beverages – but none of that mattered at this point. Ryan made his way to the back and stowed his bag before collapsing face-first into the leather couch. The others took positions in the plush seats, reclining and closing their eyes before the two pilots and Lisanne Robertson even made it back aboard to secure the door.

Hicks gave the safety briefing to an airplane full of closed eyelids – warning everyone of possible turbulence on their departure from Dallas.

'We're looking at a fifty-three-hundred-mile flight,' the first officer said. 'Depending on winds aloft, we anticipate eleven hours and thirty-six minutes in the air.'

Chavez, who was seated in the front, nearest the cockpit, opened one eye. He was so exhausted his skin felt like it had been buffed with a belt sander, but as team leader, it was his responsibility to pay attention to the details.

'That's a long-ass trip. Will we have to stop and refuel?'

'Negative,' Hicks said. 'We should be good. We're well under gross with you guys and full fuel. That gives us a range of better than sixty-six hundred miles.'

'Outstanding,' Chavez muttered. He closed his eyes and pondered the eleven wonderful hours to recharge his depleted internal batteries – but the thought of the long flight made him open them again. 'What about you guys?' he said. 'You've just flown three hours to get here. That puts you in the air . . .' Chavez shook his head, lack of sleep robbing him of the ability to do even simple math. After several seconds, he finally said, 'Nearly fifteen hours. Don't you have an eight-hour limit?'

Hicks turned and put a finger to his lips. 'Shhh,' he said. 'Don't tell anyone.' He smiled. 'Seriously, we've thought of that. The autopilot does the heavy lifting, but we'll take turns napping as needed. We've got Provigil up here if it comes down to that.'

Provigil, or modafinil, was a 'go pill' medication the Air Force sometimes issued pilots to help them stay alert during critical missions. Hendley Associates pilots rarely used it, but they kept the medication available for times like this.

Chavez started to dream even as he nodded. Unfortunately, he rolled toward his right side and his sidearm dug into his waist. 'Well, shit,' he grumbled, pushing the button on his armrest to bring his seat upright.

The Gulfstream rumbled along the taxiway. Lisanne smiled, strapped into the aft-facing seat in front of him.

Chavez coughed, clearing his throat. Sometimes it sucked to be the only working brain in the group. 'Heads up!' he said in his best team-leader bark. It came out more like a yawn, but wary eyes flicked open in any case. Jack turned and glared at him, cheek pressed against the leather upholstery of the couch cushion.

'Everybody secure your weapons in the bulkhead storage,' Chavez said. 'We're business folks out for a scouting trip to Argentina. If for some reason we have an unplanned landing in some other country, I don't want us stumbling around trying to hide our guns at the last 'minute.' He was about to get to his feet, but Lisanne stood and stopped him.

'I'll take care of it,' she said, giving a serene but serious look. 'Not sure any of you should be handling weapons at this point.'

Chavez passed her his M&P Shield. 'Many thanks . . .'

Sidearms were stowed, and Robertson returned to her seat. The Gulfstream began its takeoff roll at five twenty-seven a.m., departing to the southeast and climbing 2,700 feet per minute.

Helen Reid flew the airplane while Hicks worked the radios and tended to other duties on the takeoff checklist.

'Positive rate,' Hicks said, looking at the altimeter just a few moments after they left the tarmac. 'Gear coming up.'

The landing gear settled into the airplane's fuselage with an audible thud, but Ding Chavez didn't hear a thing.

It was almost six a.m. by the time Caruso and Clark made it back to the Omni Hotel with Gavin Biery in tow. They helped him get his duffel and the big Pelican case full of computer gear up to his room, which was directly across from Caruso's. Biery had slept on the flight and promised to get right to work on the USB drive.

Biery ordered breakfast from room service and kicked the others out almost immediately. Dom walked toward his own room, but Clark turned at Biery's door, passing a folded scrap of paper and whispering some sort of instructions. The computer guru listened, rubbing his unshaven face. He mumbled a couple questions and then shut the door, still looking at the paper as he did.

'What was that about, boss?' Caruso asked, keeping his voice low.

'Better you don't know,' Clark said. 'For now, anyway.'

'You say so.' Caruso shrugged. 'Okay, what's the plan?'

'You link back up with Special Agent Callahan,' Clark said. 'See what else she found out from Eddie Feng. Maybe his near-death experience has shaken loose something of value.'

'Copy that,' Caruso said, looking at his watch, wishing for – and knowing he wouldn't get – a few more hours of sleep. 'What are you going to do?'

'I think I'll go for a drive,' Clark said.

Caruso narrowed his eyes. He knew that look. 'Need help with anything?'

'Nope,' Clark said.

The elevator chimed and both men turned out of habit to check for threats. Caruso shot a glance at Clark when Kelsey Callahan stepped into the hallway holding two paper cups of coffee. Shoulder-length hair hung loose around her shoulders, still wet and darker red from a morning shower.

'Hey, Dom,' she said, offering him one of the coffees. 'You never gave me your cell number, so I decided to drop by and let you know I was getting an early start.' She raised an eyebrow, looking at Clark. 'Want to introduce me to your friend?'

Clark extended his hand. 'John,' he said.

'John . . . ?' She grinned, trying to coax out the rest of his name.

'That's right.'

'I have two names,' she said. 'Kelsey Callahan, FBI.'

248

'That sounds like three names,' Clark said, smiling. 'Dom's told me about you.' He turned to Caruso. 'Listen, it was good to talk to you. We'll catch up later.' He turned to go, speaking over his shoulder as he walked away. 'Nice to have met you, Kelsey Callahan, FBI.'

Callahan watched Clark disappear into an elevator before turning back to Dom.

'I don't remember telling you where I'm staying,' Caruso said. The look of surprise was evident on his face. 'You must have some friends in pretty high places to find that out.'

Callahan smirked. 'Do you even remember who we work for? And anyway, you're the one with friends in high places, getting dropped on me like this. Is John one of them?'

'He's a normal low-places friend,' Caruso said.

'Well, your friend looks like he bites the heads off baby birds for lunch.'

'Nah,' Caruso said. 'He's harmless. He's just got one of those . . . resting bird-eating faces.'

Callahan took a sip of her coffee. 'I thought we were past all that.'

'What's the news on Eddie Feng?' Caruso asked, hoping to steer the subject away from John Clark. 'Did he pull through?'

Callahan sighed. 'Seems one of the corrections officers gave him a near lethal dose of the same stuff that killed Prince.'

'Fentanyl?' Caruso said.

'Yep. Looks like he put up a fight, but the detention officer still got enough injected to knock him out.

Murderous bastard decided to do the rest of the job with a dead-leg hanging. He hog-tied Feng and ran a noose from his neck to his ankle, hoping to let the weight of his own leg cut off the circulation to his brain and kill him. Lucky for Feng, another DSO showed up and cut him loose. Paramedics gave him enough Narcan to revive a horse, but he's in pretty bad shape from the noose.'

'That's rough,' Dom said. 'So what's next?'

'Sure you don't want to tell me anything else about your friend John?'

Caruso shook his head. 'Nope.'

'Whatever,' Callahan said. 'I told you last night. I don't care what you counterintelligence guys do so long as we find Magdalena Rojas.' She took another swig of her coffee and then nodded to his door. 'Grab your stuff. We have bad guys to catch.'

24

Special Agent in Charge Gary Montgomery relaxed as much as anyone could in the small gym inside the White House residence. He stood in front of a Universal machine, doing wimpy sets of triceps extensions and attempted not to look too creepy while watching to make sure President Ryan didn't fall off the treadmill and break something. The Secret Service customarily waited in the hallway while the President did his workout. The fact that Montgomery was present in the gym at all complicated things. If the President were to drop a weight on his toe or simply trip over his own two feet, it would be viewed by Montgomery's superiors as something he should have prevented. So far this morning, President Ryan had been walking on the treadmill while he read from a stack of briefing folders he'd brought with him. He was an athletic guy and this was a task he did all the time, but it drove the agent crazy because of the fall hazard. No doubt the boss was coming up with the questions he posed every morning. So far, Montgomery had gotten him trained to engage in philosophical debates only after they were within the relatively safe walls of the White House.

As the SAIC of President Ryan's Secret Service detail, Montgomery was supposed to be within arm's reach – but that close proximity forced him to walk a fine line between close enough and too close.

The President asked good questions, and considered the answers as if they'd come from somebody important – no matter who was giving them. Jack Ryan was a nice guy – the kind of man Montgomery liked to have beer with – and therein was the problem. Both of Montgomery's predecessors had warned him that this president was impossible not to like. It was, they warned, going to be monumentally difficult not to come off as aloof by constantly saying 'I'd rather not, sir.' But the hard truth was that to protect another human being you just couldn't be their buddy. You could be civil, politely answer questions, but the moment you let your guard down and started to look inward, to sit around and bullshit with your new pal, something important slips by and your new best friend gets assassinated.

Relationship creep was insidious, especially with someone who has an easygoing personality like President Ryan. At some point, Montgomery would have to sit down and give the 'Mr President, we can't be friends' talk. To have that talk too soon would be presumptuous. Too late could prove disastrous.

Montgomery consoled himself by admitting that this was a good problem to have. Sometimes agents just plain didn't like who they protected. Montgomery had worked on Kealty's detail when he was vice president. Now, that guy was a real asshat. But Montgomery had done his job without question. In protecting any President or other dignitary under the purview of the Secret Service, he and hundreds of agents like him were protecting not only the person but the system of governance – and the good name of the Service itself.

Ryan just made it easy – in some respects, anyway.

The President stepped off the treadmill and tossed the briefing folder on the weight bench before climbing aboard a Schwinn Airdyne bicycle. There were two of the machines, presumably so Dr Ryan could exercise next to her husband.

The boss was circumspect this morning, looking forward, staring a thousand yards away while he moved the upright handlebars back and forth in time with the pedals. The big fan where the front wheel should have been began to whir, gaining speed. Rather than ask a question at first, he gestured at the second bike with a little toss of his head.

Montgomery looped the towel over his shoulders and climbed onto the stationary bike beside the President of the United States. He was by no means a newcomer to this world, but even he had to pinch himself once in a while.

Ryan began to pedal faster now that he had apparent competition. 'So,' he said, canting his head slightly as he looked at Montgomery. 'I'm not going to read some exposé about how I relied on the Secret Service to tape up my injured foot for plantar fasciitis instead of going to a doctor, am I?'

Montgomery gave a slight bow. 'The code word is "Mum," Mr President.'

'Good to hear,' Ryan said. 'So, tell me, Gary, how does the security situation look in Tokyo?'

Montgomery didn't want to upset the boss with the intricacies of protection. It could make a person as conscientious as Jack Ryan overly worrisome if he took the time to sit down and think about all the moving parts that went into protecting him. Two versions of the presidential Cadillac limo known as The Beast, Air Force One, a spare in the event the primary had mechanical problems, the communications aircraft, three Sikorsky Sea King helicopters from HMX-1, three dozen Secret Service vehicles – and the C-17s and C-5s to transport them. That didn't even touch on all the hundred or so agents, and more firearms than anyone admitted to the Japanese. Trips like the G20 required three separate advances to make certain the routes were checked, hospitals were located and scouted, deconfliction meetings with local police and the protective details of other countries were complete, and at least three floors of hotel – one below and one above the President's suite – were procured and the staff cleared and credentialed. Equally important, parking for the Secret Service armada had to be arranged well in advance.

President Ryan had enough to think about without burdening him with the monstrosity that was his protective detail. So Montgomery merely smiled at the question and said, 'Stellar, Mr President.'

Ryan gave him a thoughtful nod, then chuckled. 'Are you sure that's not what you say when you have something to hide? You sound like Jack Junior when he was in high school and I asked him about his English classes. A lot of unanswered questions packed into your few words.'

'Seriously, sir,' Montgomery said. 'It's all set up.'

'Very well,' Ryan said, looking forward, unconvinced. He pedaled for a time in silence, then turned, half leaning on the upright handlebars as he spoke. 'Tell me your impression of President Zhao.'

The agent thought about that for a minute. Ryan wanted honest answers, but he didn't want flippancy.

'I'd say he's an old-school communist. Hard-line enough to keep the support of most of the party's old guard. He talks a lot about making some progressive changes, but I'm not sure he'll do much more than talk. He hasn't figured you out yet, and that keeps him honest . . .' Montgomery paused, pedaling away on his bike. 'At least I'd thought it kept him honest, until this business with the money trail through the Australian telecom.'

'Yeah,' Ryan said. 'That is strange. If Zhao is responsible, he'll answer for it. But considering what happened to the last couple Chinese leaders who tested our resolve, it's a dangerous thing to make assumptions – and even more dangerous to cling to them. I'm not saying Zhao would hesitate to kick us in the teeth if he thought it would be good for China, but he didn't strike me as the haphazard type. With Bitcoin and other cryptocurrency mechanisms for hiding one's money matters, he has his people run payments through a shell corporation in one of our Five Eyes partners?'

Montgomery opened his mouth to speak and then thought better of it.

'Knock it off, Gary,' Ryan said. 'Stop holding back. You had another thought.'

'Well,' Montgomery said, 'I don't know if it means anything, but my counterpart running Zhao's protective detail is a CSB colonel named Huang. We've run across each other a time or two over the years on various protective operations involving the US and the PRC. He's got a stick up his ass to be sure, but he's a heck of a capable guy. Doesn't smile very much, but neither do I when I'm working. There's something about him that I think speaks to Zhao's character.'

Ryan had stopped pedaling now and sat looking at the agent. 'How's that?'

'Well, a good protective agent will always protect the office, no matter who's sitting in the chair. But Colonel Huang is protecting the man.'

'And you can tell this how?' Ryan asked.

'There's a certain look in the eye of someone protecting a man whom he respects.'

'And you believe this speaks to what kind of man Zhao is?'

'I do,' Montgomery said. 'That said, even despots have friends. I'll keep an eye on the colonel, just to get a pulse for what kind of human being he is. If he's what I believe he is, that says something. I get the feeling this guy would walk through fire to protect Zhao Chengzhi, even if he was not the paramount leader of China.'

Montgomery glanced at his watch and grimaced at the time. The workout had gone longer than he'd planned. That was the problem with operating so close to the President. A smart, observant guy like Ryan noticed when the routine changed.

'Mr President,' he said, 'I must ask to be excused. Special Agent Gallagher will be in charge for a few hours.'

'Everything okay?'

Montgomery smiled. 'Everything's fine, sir,' he said. 'I'm going out to Beltsville to observe some AOP scenarios leading up to the G20.'

'Attack on the principal,' Ryan mused. 'Who's going to try and kill me this time?'

'Keep this to yourself,' Montgomery said. 'But it's the Chinese.'

'What are my odds?' Ryan peered over his reading glasses. 'And you'd better not say stellar.'

25

A waitress who was far too chipper for six o'clock in the morning had just brought John Clark a plate of eggs and wheat toast when his cell began to buzz on the table beside his plate. He accepted the call and put the phone to his ear, using his fork to fiddle with his eggs as he listened.

'Hey, Gavin,' he said.

'Smokinggun.txt!' Gavin Biery said, his voice jubilant.

Clark took a bite of eggs. He wasn't hungry, but he knew he would need the energy. 'I have no idea what that means.'

'Right,' Biery said. 'It's a white-hat-hacker term for the digital clue that breaks a case wide open. I'm always looking for this very thing when I search for hidden malware or forensic evidence.'

Clark trapped his phone between his ear and his shoulder while he used both hands to butter his toast. 'Okay . . .'

Biery took a deep breath, as was his custom when he prepared to launch into a lengthy explanation. 'The dark web isn't what I'd call surf-friendly, but GRAMS lets you search some of the sites.'

'GRAMS?'

'Think of it as the Google of the darknet,' Biery said. 'Anyway, I did some snooping for the name Matarife, figuring anyone who went by a moniker like "the Slaughterer" probably has an ego the size of the Death Star. There are billions of sites on the surface web, so this kind of guy can hide in plain sight. The darknet is smaller. Users rely on anonymity, but they stand out more once you focus on them. Took me a couple hops from one sick site to another, but I eventually stumbled onto your guy.' Biery exhaled hard. 'I gotta tell you, John, there's a reason they call it the dark web. This Matarife makes snuff videos – stuff you can't unsee. Prevailing chatter is that they're the real deal. The computer script alone about made me puke. I thought I might be able to grab metadata from some of the photos but didn't have any luck.'

Clark closed his eyes, willing himself not to interrupt. The crescendo of Gavin Biery's voice said he was moving toward something big.

'But you know what? People aren't suddenly born on the darknet. At some point, somewhere back in time, they had a presence on the surface web. That's how they found that Silk Road guy, an old post on Reddit advertising his site. So I did a search on the only slightly less perverted visible portion of the Web. Turns out a user calling himself Matarife 13 had a long convo on an S-and-M chatroom three years ago where he posted some photos. He was running decent OPSEC even back then, using a VPN and an anonymizer program to scrub the metadata –'

'What?' Clark said, biting his tongue.

'He used a virtual private network and a program to wipe the digital fingerprint off any photos he uploaded – except he didn't. Matarife chose a sloppy anonymizer that left behind EXIF data on a couple of his posted photographs.'

'And that means?'

'It means, John,' Gavin said, 'that you need to get a

pen, because I'm about to give you the GPS coordinates to this filthy piece of shit's house.'

Outside the United States, crime bosses employ sizable armies to guard against the almost inevitable attack from rival gangs. Like something from a Hollywood action flick, cold-blooded men wearing dark sunglasses and tight black T-shirts patrol remote hacienda grounds with MP5s, AK-47s, and even the occasional Hi-Point SMG. These residences have high walls, rimmed with broken glass to discourage intruders. They're often fortified with electric fences and vicious dogs.

Farther north of the border, cartels contend less with marauding competition and more with teams of raiding law enforcement. They're still heavily armed, but these US-based operations put more trust in CCTV cameras, often purchased from their local Walmart. Sometimes they rely on nothing but a good standoff from any neighbors and acres of grain sorghum to act as a buffer.

If Ernie Pacheco – Matarife's real name – had known that John Clark was creeping through the sorghum field behind his ranch north of Alvarado, Texas, he would have opted for a lot more than three strands of sagging barbed wire.

The team of Campus operators had originally flown to Dallas on a commercial flight. Clark had declared his Wilson Combat .45 in his checked baggage but brought little more with him on this trip than the communication and surveillance equipment needed to watch Eddie Feng. He had none of the gear he would have normally used to execute an early-morning assault of a rural compound.

John Clark was a dyed-in-the-wool .45 guy. He'd used the 1911 weapon system to great effect in Vietnam and the many – way too many – years that followed. He'd eventually transitioned to a SIG P220 – still in .45 – but a brutal injury to his shooting hand had caused Clark to reevaluate his choice of sidearm. Long and painful months of rehab had finally returned his ability to shoot the trusty SIG Sauer, though at first with only his middle finger. He'd finally regained dominion over the tendons in his index finger – but the shorter single-action pull of the 1911 made accurate shooting a hell of a lot easier. Plus, it was the excuse he needed to buy a new gun and revert to the firearm system that was so ingrained in his muscle memory. The Wilson Combat Professional felt like he was reuniting with an old friend.

Still, he'd regained proficiency with a variety of weapons. Necessities of the mission and common sense made him grab a Glock 19, a spare fifteen-round magazine, and a Gemtech GM-9 suppressor from the Gulfstream before the others departed for Argentina. He wanted to have a little deeper pockets when it came to ammo loadout. The argument of .45 versus nine-millimeter went out the window when you were out of bullets. Even so, he didn't abandon the Wilson in favor of the Glock. He carried them both. He was a firm believer in 'Two is one and one is none,' and the .45 remained his primary weapon in the Askins Avenger holster at three o'clock, while the Glock rested comfortably over his right kidney in a Comp-Tac holster inside the waistband of his pants.

Along with the pistols, Clark carried a Benchmade AFCK folding knife, a small roll of Gorilla tape, and a pocket Streamlight flashlight. It wasn't much, but he'd done more with less. His rules of engagement made the job a little easier.

If anyone fought back, he intended to kill them.

From the looks of the waist-high Johnson grass and dry stalks of grain sorghum, little else but mourning doves and rattlesnakes had spent much time in the fields behind Matarife's house in years.

Clark stayed low as he moved, crawling when the stalks were short, stooping in a fast duckwalk when the plants gave him better cover. Earth-tone 5.11 slacks and a black sweatshirt helped him blend well into the long morning shadows. The field was damp from recent rains, but the day promised to be a hot one for September and the ground was already beginning to steam. The humidity and muggy odor of wet earth, not to mention the fire ants and the high probability of coming nose-to-nose with a pit viper, brought back so many memories that Clark found it nostalgic . . . almost.

Ding Chavez hadn't exactly been wrong in his earlier assessment. John knew full well he risked becoming far too focused on the human-trafficking aspects of this op. The sight of the girls at Naldo Cantu's, covered with track marks and surrounded by used condoms, brought back memories he'd suppressed for decades, memories that made him who – and what – he'd become. Just looking at the poor drugged kids made him feel like his teeth might shatter. He was nearing seventy years old. Still a tough old bird, no doubt, but *old* was fast eclipsing *tough* as the operative word.

For as long as he could remember, something inside

Clark had pushed him to check out danger, to go and see, to help. Some accused him of being addicted to violence. If he was honest with himself, there had been a time when he relished a good fight. When there was going to be violence on his watch, he certainly didn't want to miss it. But the fight wasn't the main thing. His wife, Sandy, had summed up his sentiment best when she caught him coming back in from his private range early one morning on their Emmetsburg, Virginia, farm.

'John,' she'd said, sipping her morning coffee and looking even more beautiful than she had the day he'd met her. 'Don't worry, sweetheart. You'll still be relevant.'

It was at once the kindest and most pitiful thing anyone had ever said to him.

Maybe that was it. Relevance.

His workouts were less intense now, his runs slower. His hair was thinning . . . no, it was just plain thin. Even worse, each passing year saw him get a little more emotional. Hell, he got choked up when his grandson caught a pop fly at a baseball game. And all that blubbering just served to piss him off. He abhorred the idea of going soft.

But a guy past his use-by date wouldn't be inching through a dry sorghum field behind a murderous bastard's house. Pound for pound and year for year, he could still hold his own against most threats. He was the personification of the sentiment 'Never underestimate an old man in a dangerous profession.' Like Jack London, he wanted to go out on his own terms, 'as ashes instead of dust.'

And so Clark fought the clock by fighting bad men, whenever and wherever he found them.

The sorghum was thick enough now that he had to drop back down and belly-crawl. The tops of the plants rattled and hissed when they brushed together, brittle and heavy with grain. He moved as quickly as possible, taking care not to disturb the stalks any more than necessary. Only a trained observer would be able to see the ripple of his approach by watching the tops of the plants.

Clark heard the distant splash of someone taking a morning swim in a pool. He estimated the house to be less than a hundred meters away now. Crawling, he tapped the Wilson Combat with his elbow, habitually making sure it was still in the holster where he'd left it. Ahead, the plants began to thin and Clark found himself entering a small clearing. A mound of fresh earth, roughly two feet high and at least eight feet wide, blocked his path. Beyond the dirt pile, at the far edge of the clearing, rutted tracks ran between the grain rows toward the house.

Clark dropped flat, his chest to the damp earth, scanning the edge of the clearing. He turned his head as he looked, knowing from experience he could miss important elements of danger if he moved only his eyes. Searching inch by inch, foot by foot, he searched for anything out of the ordinary – game cameras, tripwires, fishhooks strung at eye level.

Just inches from his nose, half an earthworm hung from a ball of roots and sod, exposed to the air, cut in two by whatever tool had been used to turn the clods. The worm was still moist, telling Clark the dig was recent, probably during the hours of darkness. Small piles of tiny white pellets were visible here and there among the clods of rich black soil. At first glance he took the white stuff for fertilizer, but he inched forward, getting a closer look. He rolled one of the gray BBs between a thumb and forefinger – he moved forward immediately, scuttling around the edge of the piled dirt, dreading but knowing what he would find. He fought the urge to vomit as he came to the lip of a hole dug in the middle of the clearing, eight by eight feet square and four or five feet deep. At the bottom of the pit, from beneath a layer of dirt and pellets of kitty litter, the pale fingers of a delicate hand reached toward the sky.

26

Mamat bin Ahmad sat on an overturned wooden crate with his back to the trunk of a tall coconut palm, gazing out to sea, when the satellite phone in his lap gave a startling chirp. He and his men were on the southern shores of the Indonesian island of Buru, within easy pouncing distance of any passing pleasure craft – if one would only pass. The window for their operation was small. He'd already received an earlier call informing him that the USS *Rogue* had passed Timor-Leste hours before. The American *Cyclone*-class patrol ship was steaming north from a recent stop at HMAS *Coonawarra*, the Australian naval base in Darwin, where it would join the Philippine and Malaysian military vessels in a joint anti-piracy patrol of the Sulu Sea.

Mamat had been expecting the second call and kept the satellite phone's plastic antenna extended and oriented toward the sky. Even so, the sudden noise made him jump and he very nearly dropped the device in the sand. All his men were jumpy – it was understandable, considering their mission – but they needed leadership and, mercifully, did not seem to notice his fumbling.

Mamat was a young man, not yet twenty-five years old. Had he been a happier sort, his intensely white teeth would have shone through a broad smile. But since his father had died, his family had known nothing but poverty. His older sister had run off with a Dirty Joe – one of the older American or European men who came to Southeast Asia looking for a wife. His mother cleaned hotel rooms for wealthy tourists in the Indonesian city of Manado – but she was perpetually sick. Mamat's father had fully expected his son to follow his path. Men in his family had fished for generations. Mamat learned about boats and became a better-than-average sailor, but the tenets of Jemaah Islamiyah lured him away while he was in his teens. JI provided stability – and, even more important, a cause higher than living hand-to-mouth as a simple fisherman. Mamat's parents were both devout Muslims, observing a strict Ramadan or meticulously making up missed days when illness made fasting impossible. But even they saw things in moderation.

Moderation bored Mamat almost as much as fishing did. The leaders of Jemaah Islamiyah taught him that the one path lay in complete devotion – a religious zeal that allowed no room for moderation or compromise. Yes, Mamat knew boats, but his true skills lay in other areas. Recent interactions with members of Abu Sayyaf had made him witness to enough bloodshed that a surprise chirp should not have startled him – but it did, because this was no ordinary call.

He did not recognize the number. The men who would call this phone rarely used the same phone more than a few times. Still, he knew Dazid Ishmael would be on the other end of the line. He could almost feel the man's uncanny energy coming through the handset.

Mamat had seen Ishmael behead four different Abu Sayyaf captives, each time with an American Ka-Bar knife. The commander's resolve and devotion against the infidels was nothing short of amazing. He'd begun to think of Ishmael as a father figure and prayed for the moment he might prove himself.

That moment had come with this satellite phone call.

'Are you ready?' the commander asked.

Mamat looked at the six men sitting in the shade on either side of him along the deserted length of beach. Some stared out at the water; others sipped fruit juice as they pondered their coming fate.

'We are all ready,' Mamat said.

'Very well,' Ishmael said. 'AIS shows that a likely vessel departed Ambon four hours ago, sailing southwest. Her present bearing leads me to believe that she is trying to reach Wakatobi.'

Mamat nodded. The Wakatobi reserve was a popular yachting destination. Rich infidel tourists had sailed past his father's fishing boat many times.

Ishmael provided the AIS identifier. 'Can you intercept?'

Mamat logged in to the satellite connection on his tablet computer and pulled up a marine traffic tracker. He found the vessel immediately. A simple click gave him a complete description of the vessel and its call sign, along with direction of travel, speed, and previous track. It amazed the young man how much information a modern sailor made available to anyone who knew to look for it — all in the name of safety.

'We are less than fifteen kilometers away.'

'That will work,' Ishmael said.

'The tracker does not show the US Navy vessel,' Mamat said. 'I am unsure of its whereabouts. What if it has passed?'

'Have you seen it sail by your position?'

The Indonesian man shook his head despite being on the phone. 'I have not.'

'I anticipate it will pass to your west,' Ishmael said. 'But it should be near enough. You must proceed quickly, within the hour. Understood?'

'Understood,' Mamat said.

'Go with God,' the Abu Sayyaf commander said before breaking the connection.

Mamat folded the antenna and shoved the satellite phone into a waterproof bag at his feet. Shouldering the bag, he walked toward the long wooden runabout bobbing in the green water. His men followed him unbidden. They needed no one to tell them it was time to go.

Awang, a man five years older than Mamat, waded into the sea at the stern of the nineteen-foot open boat, checking the single 250-horse Honda outboard motor. Speed was of the essence, and Mamat would have preferred two such motors, but two big motors on a wooden skiff was considered evidence of piracy. The AK-47s and RPGs secreted under the orange tarps on board would be enough to confirm suspicions if they were boarded by Indonesian authorities. Awang had gone so far as to rub mud over the Honda's cowling to make it match the sorry state of the wooden fishing skiff.

Mamat and the other six pushed the boat deeper into the lagoon before climbing over the gunwales and taking up their respective seats. Most of the men were in their late teens and early twenties. Osman, the de facto second-in-command – because Awang refused to accept the position – sat on a wooden bench beside Mamat.

Hydraulics whined as Awang lowered the Honda into the water. The motor started with a burbling growl, and a moment later the skiff arced gracefully over the emerald-green waters of the lagoon. Awang sat at the helm, Mamat's tablet on his knee for navigation.

He looked up at Mamat. '*Lucky Strike*?'

'That is correct,' Mamat said.

Awang frowned. 'A sailing vessel seems a poor target.'

Osman turned and looked at him, shaking his head but saying nothing. Awang was trustworthy enough, but his periodic indiscretions with alcohol made him a leaky vessel when it came to important information. The rest of the men had kept the true nature of the mission from him. It didn't matter. His job was to drive the skiff.

Mamat smiled. 'Do not worry, my friend. *Lucky Strike* is not our target. She is the bait.'

Karla Downs sat with her feet up on the cockpit bench, her back against a dazzlingly blue cushion that matched *Lucky Strike*'s hull paint. Glancing down, she noticed a bit of errant sunscreen and rubbed it into her chest. They were sailing west on a close reach, and the huge sails provided welcome shade from the evening sun. A steamy breeze caressed her body, which had never been so tan. The smell of salt water and coconut oil swirled across the fiberglass deck.

She had to be the second-luckiest woman on the planet. Her husband, Tony, had remained relatively faithful over the course of their twenty-eight years of marriage, neither of her boys was in jail, and she had rich friends. Karla was remarkably fit for fifty-two, with manicured nails and stylishly dyed red hair. A cosmopolitan ponytail kept her hair off her shoulders in the heat and humidity. Round Hollywood-starlet glasses and a liberal coating of SPF 30 protected her from the intensity of the Southeast Asia sun. Her olive-green swimsuit swooped high on her hips and low on her bust. It made her feel half naked at first, but she wore it anyway, because Tony liked it.

Things had gotten a little stale in the boudoir department over the past several years. She'd hoped the bodacious swimsuit might give a yank to Tony's old starter rope, but she needn't have worried. Maybe it was the roll of the waves or just the idea of sailing the open ocean, but Karla wasn't going to second-guess it. Usually not even the type to kiss her in public, Tony didn't seem to care about the thin walls on the Whites' forty-two-foot sailboat. Judy had been winking at her every morning at breakfast from the time they'd left Darwin. Kenneth never said anything, preferring to fuss with his boat and take sightings with his sextant at odd hours of the day. Everyone else on the boat might consider this a vacation. To Kenneth White, sailing was serious business.

The Downses had known Kenneth and Judy since they'd started White's Energy Exploration in the Houston, Texas, suburb of Katy two decades before. They leased a small strip-mall office, and Judy answered the phones while Kenneth spent his time at the drill sites. They'd sold their little company the year before for a tidy sum *The Katy Times* described as 'the mid-millions' and sailed off to explore the world.

Unfortunately for Karla, drilling-rig-parts salesmen didn't get rich like oil company owners. But the Whites were generous to a fault and kept up the friendship no matter how wealthy they got. They'd even invited Karla and Tony along on a three-week sail from Darwin to Singapore on their new Texas-built Valiant yacht.

Karla had never been much of a traveler, but the Spice Islands were nothing short of jaw-dropping. They'd sailed for days across open water, passing in the shadow of huge container ships or seeing nothing at all but horizon for days. They'd stopped in places with mythical names such as Saumlaki, Banda, and Ambon, and met dozens of fascinating and wonderful people. There had been a few glares and some poverty, but yachts like *Lucky Strike* brought tourist dollars, so the unsightly portions of the area were mostly hidden from the view of travelers, allowing Karla to pretend that this was the paradise of the guidebooks.

Kenneth and Judy were excellent hosts and take-your-time sailors, loving the journey even more than the destination. Green pinnacles rose in a thousand tiny islands from an emerald sea. People smiled broad smiles and fed them dishes Karla had never conceived, much less tasted, from rich curries to the gluelike *papeda*, made from the starch of a sago palm and meant to be slurped from the bowl. The crew of the little sailboat had eaten their weight in delicious grilled fish, all of it either offered at feasts onshore or purchased from passing skiffs from which people called out 'Hey, mister!' even when one of the women happened to be at the wheel.

Karla closed her eyes and took in a breath of the moist air. No, 'lucky' didn't even begin to describe her condition. She could not imagine returning to her old life in Houston.

Judy poked her head out of the hatch from below, where she'd been working on dinner. Karla had volunteered to help, but the Valiant had a one-butt galley, meant for bracing in the open ocean, and was not suited for two women cooking together.

'Spaghetti's on,' Judy said. She was pixie of a thing, with dark hair that, as far as Karla knew, had never seen a drop of dye. She wore a yellow wraparound sundress and a smile just as bright. The wind-vane autopilot kept the boat on the correct heading, so Karla was alone in the cockpit. 'Mind yelling at the boys?' Judy asked before ducking back below.

Karla sat up on her elbows and craned her neck without moving the rest of her body. The pace of the past week had endowed all her movements with a delicious laziness.

Both Kenneth and Tony stood up front, staring over the right side of the boat. Kenneth would have called it starboard, but Karla had an awful time keeping all the sailing terms straight in her head. At first she thought Kenneth was shooting another sight with his sextant, but a closer look revealed both men were looking through binoculars. Tony had a way of rolling his foot sideways when he was focused on anything important. The way he held it now caused Karla to sit up a little straighter.

The whine of an approaching boat motor pulled Karla to her feet. She'd just started forward when both men turned. Tony motioned for her to stay where she was as he made his way around the mast. They were coming to her.

The look of worry on her husband's face was unmistakable. She folded her arms across her chest, hugging herself. 'What's wrong?'

'I'm not sure,' he said.

Kenneth stuck his head below and barked at his wife.

'Get the shotgun,' he said. 'Keep it down below, but be ready to hand it to me.'

Judy appeared at the hatch. She started to say something, but he hushed her with a look that she must have seen before, because she rolled her lips until they turned white.

'What is it?' Karla asked again.

Kenneth ignored her, bending instead to open the locker under the starboard cockpit bench. He took out an orange plastic case that Karla knew contained the flare gun. From another case, this one stored deeper in the locker, he retrieved a black metal cylinder, which he dropped into the open chamber of the flare gun. Into this he loaded a single round of .38-caliber ammunition. To Karla's horror, he put the makeshift pistol into Tony's hands.

'Keep this out of sight,' Kenneth said. 'But if you have to use it, just thumb the hammer back, aim for center mass, and pull the trigger.'

Tony licked his lips and nodded. He stuffed the flare gun down the back of his shorts and pulled his T-shirt over it.

Karla gave an emphatic shake of her head. She could see the fishing boat bearing down on them now, less than a hundred yards away.

'What the hell?' She cast her eyes around the cockpit for the colorful sarong she used as a wrap when they were near any of the locals. She'd been warned that some of the more devout might find her swimsuit off-putting, or even downright evil. She pulled the strip of cotton around her and tied it behind her neck as she continued to plead for an explanation.

'What do you think they want?'

Tony stepped between her and the approaching boat. 'Probably just to trade us some fish,' he said.

'Then why the guns?'

Kenneth shot a glance down the companionway. Judy gave him a curt nod to let him know the shotgun was where he wanted it. They'd obviously been over this drill before.

'Because *they* have guns,' Kenneth said. 'Lots of guns.'

Karla's mouth fell open. 'I thought we were staying south of pirate waters!' She gasped, her chest so tight she could hardly breathe. 'You promised we'd be fine if we stayed away from the Philippines!'

The men in the approaching boat were yelling now, ordering them in broken English to lower their sails and come to a stop.

Tony grabbed her hand and clutched it tight.

'It's not Kenny's fault,' he whispered.

'I count seven of them,' Kenneth said out of the corner of his mouth. He waved, giving a forced smile as the fishing boat motored up alongside the sailboat, matching her speed of around six knots. Outrunning the skiff was unthinkable, even as loaded down as it was.

The men on the fishing boat screamed all at once, waving their guns in the air. There were no pleasant shouts of 'Hey, mister!'

One of the pirates, a boy who couldn't have been more than fifteen, raised a rifle and pointed it at Karla. Tony's hand dropped for the flare gun at his waist, but he didn't know guns. He was a parts salesman. As far as Karla knew, her husband hadn't fired a gun in years. He fumbled with his T-shirt, causing the boy to swing the rifle his way – and loose a rattling barrage of shots that stitched up the side of the boat and into Tony Downs's chest.

Karla screamed as her husband pitched forward, toppling over the side to splash into the sea. *Lucky Strike* quickly left Tony's body behind, bobbing in the blue-green water that only moments before had been so incredibly beautiful.

Kenneth roared, reaching for the shotgun, and earned two bullets in the spine for his effort. He fell as he turned. The shotgun slipped from his hands, sliding along the deck to drop over the side with a sickening plop. It disappeared instantly beneath the surface. Judy, now armed with a large kitchen knife in the shadows, motioned Karla belowdecks – as if there could be any refuge from these men on the tiny boat.

Karla stood frozen as a man in a blue T-shirt and oil-stained khaki pants grabbed an upright metal stanchion and hauled himself over the lifelines, jumping deftly from the fishing boat to the *Lucky Strike*. The man released the sheets to let the sails pop and flap in the wind. The boat slowed immediately.

Others from the skiff began to pour onto the boat. All of them were young, with the wispy facial hair of boys trying in vain to be men. But they all carried guns and wore hateful looks, both of which they aimed at Karla Downs. She rushed past the man in the blue T-shirt in an effort to get down below with Judy. If she was going to die – or worse – she didn't want to do it alone. A sweating young man reached to grab her, but the man in the blue T-shirt pushed his hand away, shaking his head, and the boy let her go unmolested.

She had to leap over Kenneth's body to get down the companionway. She would have fallen, had Judy not been there to catch her. The poor woman had to look at her husband's lifeless eyes staring down at her from above – and still, she somehow kept her composure.

Karla gulped, trying to catch her breath.

'What . . . ? I mean why . . . ?' Her eyes were transfixed on the stern, where her husband of nearly thirty years had fallen dead into the sea.

Judy blinked at her friend, fighting back tears. 'I am so, so sorry.'

'What do they want?'

The small brunette squared her shoulders and sighed. A tear rolled down her stricken face. 'Ransom, I imagine,' she said.

Out on the deck a young Jemaah Islamiyah recruit stood to the side of the hatch, a battered AK-47 held to his chest. This was his first operation, and he chewed on chapped lips, a bundle of frayed nerves.

'What if they have another firearm down there?'

Mamat gave a slow shake of his head. Dusk was falling rapidly, but he welcomed the darkness. It would only make their job easier. 'They would have shot by now.'

'Shall I bring the women back on deck?'

Mamat closed his eyes and listened, the dead man at his feet, his back to the cabin. 'In time,' he said. 'For now, they are doing exactly what we need them to do.'

Stooping slightly and craning his neck, he was just able to hear a shaky female voice below as she whispered on the cabin radio.

'Mayday! Mayday! This is sailing vessel Lucky Strike. *We are under attack from pirates! I say again, we are under attack from pirates . . .'*

The woman repeated her call for help. Her shattered voice grew more shrill with every word.

At length, the words Mamat had hoped for crackled over the radio in a barrage of static.

'Lucky Strike, *this is United States Naval Vessel* Rogue . . .'

27

Clark had a vague idea of what Magdalena Rojas looked like from Caruso's description, but he'd never seen a photograph of the child. Some girl was dead at the bottom of this grave, and he suddenly needed to know if it was Magdalena. Belly down, he slid feet-first over the edge, bringing a small trickle of dirt sliding after him into the pit. Dropping to his knees, he used a flat rock the size of his hand to scoop away the loose dirt around the raised arm. It did not take him long to work his way down the arm to expose the pale gray flesh of a female shoulder. Her neck lay at an odd angle, encircled with a thin line of blood from some ligature that had been used to strangle her. Long purple bruises crisscrossed the portions of ashen skin exposed by the dirt. The dead did not bruise. This one had been beaten, and beaten badly, before she died.

Clark closed his eyes, remembering another girl, similarly murdered so long ago. Pam Madden's death had come during a brutal rape – and, if Biery's suspicions about Matarife's snuff videos were true, this girl had suffered the same fate before she was dumped unceremoniously into a pit in the middle of a grain field.

Clark took a deep breath, bracing himself lest the memories overwhelm him, allowing the anger just enough of a foothold to focus his actions into a white-hot beam of fury. A lock of dirty-blond hair clung to the dead girl's broken neck. Clark touched it to make sure it wasn't a wig, then, out of pity, brushed away the loose soil and smoothed it into place. He blinked away a tear, then rolled onto his back, looking skyward, barely able to see the surrounding sorghum stalks from the bottom of the grave.

Knowing what he did about technology, he was sure some Keyhole satellite was up there, watching him, tough-as-nails John Clark, as he grew weepy beside a dead girl he'd never met. He shook it off and looked at the body again. He had never met Magdalena – and she certainly had no more value than the one lying dead in this shallow grave – but he found himself relieved to find out the body wasn't hers. It was always possible that the Rojas girl was buried beneath this one, but Clark pushed that thought from his mind, chiding himself even as he did so for clinging to hope rather than cold, hard facts.

A telephone rang in the distance. A female voice muttered something Clark took for a curse but could not quite make out. Moments later, there was another splash. The call had ended and the woman was back in the pool. A tractor fired up and the female voice yelled something in Spanish. Then the tone of the engine changed as the tractor was shifted into gear and the putt-chug sound began to grow louder.

Someone was making another run to the grave.

Clark scrambled to his feet, peeking over the lip of dirt to see the top of a man's head as the tractor rolled steadily toward him. The higher angle of the driver's vantage point would put him in full view if he tried to climb out now. He dropped immediately, rolling onto his back, staying tight against the dirt wall nearest the house and pulling a layer of clods on top of him to help him stay hidden as long as possible.

With the tractor getting closer by the second, he drew the Glock 19 and hastily screwed the Gemtech suppressor onto its threaded barrel. 'Press checks are free,' he muttered under his breath as he slid the slide back a scant quarter-inch to assure himself that there was a round in the chamber. He hadn't lived to be an old man by taking things for granted.

The suppressed Glock wouldn't exactly be silent, but Clark had taken steps to close the gap between *kaboom* and a mouse fart. A slightly-heavier-than-stock recoil spring would slow down the action just enough to channel most of the escaping gasses down the suppressor instead of out the chamber. Subsonic ammunition would go a long way toward dampening the noise.

Stalks of grain rustled against the side of the chugging tractor as it broke into the clearing. The thought occurred to Clark that it might be a backhoe or some other kind of small 'dozer that could simply cover him up with dirt before he could crawl out. But the engine sounded smaller, like the little tractor he kept on his own farm. The tractor stopped. Above, and out of the line of sight, the driver switched it off. Clark could hear the man groan, as if overweight, when he climbed down from the tractor. Plastic sheeting rustled. Clark tensed as dirt rained over the edge. He was close. Very close. Any moment he would look over the edge, as people did when they neared a deep hole. Clark heard another sound that he couldn't quite make out. He'd just decided it was probably a shovel blade being driven into the dirt, followed by the scrape and subsequent ignition of a match.

The smell of cigarette smoke drifted down into the pit. Clark listened as the man unzipped his trousers and – smoking and singing a *narcocorrido,* or narco ballad, called 'Cuerno de Chivo' – relieved himself less than ten feet away. The song's title literally meant 'horn of the goat,' but that was a euphemism for an AK-47 rifle. Singing around the cigarette clenched in his lips, the man did up his zipper while he droned on about blowing the heads off his enemies with the horn of a goat.

Clark took a deep, relaxing breath. Pissing beside the grave of a dead girl, happily singing about bloody murder – two strikes against this guy being an innocent bystander.

More grunting and groans came from above, and then a heavy thud as the man dragged something into the dirt from the back of a trailer or cart. He sang with gusto about the joys of killing and then dumped another young woman into the hole. Clark ignored the falling body, focusing on the edge, waiting.

Clark fired twice when the man looked over to admire his handiwork. The nine-millimeter rounds took the man low, angling up through a distended belly to tear through his diaphragm, blow out a lung, and then bisect his heart from bottom to top before lodging in the back fat near his left shoulder blade. Blinking stupidly, he tried to swallow but could muster only a ragged cough. The cigarette dropped from his lips, followed by a stream of frothy blood that cascaded down his chin like something from a Quentin Tarantino movie. A half-second later his knees buckled and he toppled over the edge, landing on top of the other bodies with a heavy thud.

The dirt walls of the grave had absorbed much of the noise the Gemtech didn't suppress. Clark doubted anyone at the house had heard a thing. Even so, he stayed focused on the lip of the hole above for a full minute, just in case the fat Mexican had any friends he hadn't heard.

He took a moment to check the new female body. Another young woman, perhaps fifteen or sixteen. This one had dark hair, but like the first girl, she looked larger than the description of Magdalena. This one, too, had been strangled before she'd been dumped naked into this dirt hole. Clark choked back the hatred in his gut. The dead man faced him, eyes glazed, mouth open and full of dirt and blood. This fat singer of grisly ballads was an evil bastard to be sure, but he was a gravedigger, a gofer, not a ringleader.

Clark was not one to keep count of the people he killed – the dead took care of that for him. He'd told himself early on when coming to grips with his chosen path in life that if killing ever became commonplace, it would be time to step away. That never happened – though he had to admit that, emotionally, some people were easier to kill than others.

Satisfied that it was safe to climb out of the grave, Clark left the Gemtech attached to the Glock and stowed it on his belt in a small leather scabbard called a Yaqui slide. It was open at the bottom to accommodate the suppressor. It seemed cruel to leave the girls exposed to the heat of the coming day, but he didn't have time to do anything about it. Instead, he scooped up the two spent casings he'd fired and dropped them into his pocket before climbing out of the hole.

Matarife was smart enough to keep the brush and weeds mowed short in a full fifty-meter swath around his house, but there were a few old pickup trucks that provided just enough cover and concealment that, if Clark moved quickly, he could cross from the edge of the field to a brick pool house without being spotted.

He smiled despite the situation, and kept to the tall Johnson grass while he skirted the property. Long years of just this sort of action had taught him to keep a wary eye for signs of dogs – old chew toys, piles of crap, bones. Fortunately, Matarife didn't have this added layer of security.

The home itself bordered on palatial, belying the junked vehicles beside it. Heavy draperies covered four gabled windows on the upper floor. A three-car garage stuck off toward the old trucks, forming a natural barrier between the pool house of matching red brick and the road. Groomed redbud trees alternated with black lampposts on a huge circular drive out front. Clark knew from an earlier drive-by that the iron gate over the cattle guard out front was secured with a chain and padlock. That was good. People put too much faith in locks, and too much faith made them lax.

Leapfrogging from vehicle to vehicle, Clark took less than two minutes to make it to a four-foot chain-link fence surrounding the backyard and pool. The sun was high now, adding dazzle to the surface of the blue water, and, to Clark's way of thinking, illuminating far too much of the nude woman who sipped a drink on a floating chair while reading a magazine. Dark hair was piled high on

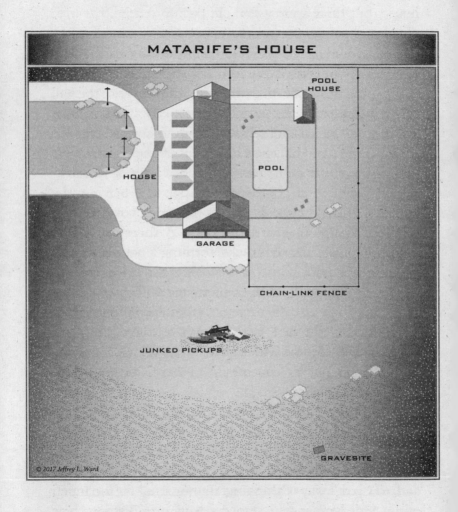

MATARIFE'S HOUSE

POOL
HOUSE

HOUSE

POOL

GARAGE

CHAIN-LINK FENCE

JUNKED PICKUPS

© 2017 Jeffrey L. Ward

GRAVESITE

her head. A pair of oversized sunglasses hid her eyes. Clark guessed her to be in her mid-thirties, but the bruises and scars on her fleshy body said those years had been hard ones. It was impossible to feel sorry for her, though. She was sipping fruity drinks in a pool while at least two girls lay dead in the dirt less than a hundred meters away. A black SMG lay poolside, just outside her reach, on a folded pink towel. Clark couldn't be sure from this distance and angle, but the gun looked like a CZ Scorpion machine pistol. The woman was serious about her protection. Beside the pistol was an empty glass that resembled the full one in the woman's hand and what looked to be a brown walking cane or a riding quirt. That would explain the whip marks on the dead girls.

Clark stayed in the shadows, watching the larger house for another five minutes. There was no good way to approach the house alone. He knew he should wait for Caruso, but there were kids' lives at stake, and he didn't have the patience or the time to wait.

Removing the suppressed Glock, he laid it in the grass at his feet and drew the .45. A single shot would wake anyone who happened to be in the house – and, he hoped, bring them outside – but was not likely to cause much concern to the neighbors. It was difficult to pinpoint the location of a lone report.

The unsuppressed round slammed into the CZ Scorpion, spinning it sideways and puffing the towel beneath it. The woman dropped the magazine on her lap and looked back and forth, unable to make sense of what had happened. Predictably, her first glance was toward the gravesite in the sorghum field.

Clark had already picked up the Glock. He set a suppressed round between her feet, causing the inflatable chair to burst beneath the weight of her fleshy body. Floundering, the naked woman untangled herself from the deflated plastic and attempted to swim toward her Scorpion SMG. Clark sent a second suppressed round zinging off the concrete lip of the pool, stopping her momentum. She spun in the water, looking for the shooter.

Clark's eyes flicked toward the house. Still nothing. But it was early, and digging graves was hard work. And Matarife might be sleeping in. Clark decided to wait a little longer.

The woman treaded water now, looking toward the back field again. She obviously had some demons.

'Who is there?' she asked, a little on the gruff side for a nude person being shot at. She followed up with the same demand in Spanish, more tentative this time. '¿Quién es?'

Clark let the Glock speak for him, sending another round slamming into the CZ, this one shattering the plastic magazine. Even if it was still operable, he'd just turned the SMG into a single-shot.

'Tell me who is there!' the woman screamed. The sound of the suppressed Glock was about as loud as an energetic hand clap, but Clark was close enough that she'd zeroed in on the pool house.

It had been a good three minutes and there was still no sign of anyone at the back door. Her boyfriend didn't care about her, or he was too deep of a sleeper to worry about, or he was gone. Not once had this woman looked toward the house, which led Clark to believe it was the latter.

The woman started toward the gun again.

Clark put a round into the water beside her. 'Keep going,' he barked. 'Makes my job a lot easier.'

She swished bronze arms in the water, swimming away from the splash of the shot. 'Who are you?' She turned, treading water again. 'Did Zambrano send you?'

'Suppose he did?' Clark said.

'Ernie left already,' she said. 'He has the girl and the money with him.'

'I see,' Clark said. He let her stew awhile, then said, 'And suppose Zambrano didn't send me?'

The woman shook her head. 'You are not police,' she said. 'Police would let me put some clothes on.'

'Lady,' Clark said, 'the last thing I want to do is sit here and look at your fat ass.'

The words seemed to bother her worse than the shooting.

'Who, then?'

Clark decided to drop a bomb and see how she reacted. 'I think you may know something about my little girl.'

The woman gave a tremulous shake of her head – but she couldn't help another glance at the sorghum field. 'I don't know –'

'Cut the shit!' Clark barked. 'Who else is in the house?'

'No one.'

Clark put another round into the water, half hoping it would hit her. It didn't, but it had the desired effect.

She held up both hands, kicking with her legs, barely keeping her head above water. 'Who is your girl?'

'Magdalena,' Clark said, gambling again.

The woman sputtered. 'You lie.' It would have been a scoff, had she not been working so hard. 'She comes from

Parrot, who got her from Dorian. I know all about her. She has no friends in the States. Anyway, she is gone.'

'Where?'

'Why should I tell you?' The woman said. 'You will only kill me.'

Clark gave an honest chuckle. 'I'm a half a breath from killing you anyway. Let's try this. What's your name?'

'Lupe,' the woman said, coughing from a mouth full of water.

'And you work for Matarife?'

'If you can call it that,' Lupe spat. 'I am his prisoner, like all the other girls.'

'Is that right?' Clark nodded despite the fact that the woman could not see him. 'You sure as hell look like a prisoner, sitting around in the pool drinking fruity umbrella drinks.'

'I am . . . how do you say it, the girl in charge,' Lupe said. 'His bottom bitch.'

'I can believe that last part,' Clark said. 'Okay, Lupe. Tell me again where Matarife . . . Ernie is.'

'He has gone to deliver your girl, Magdalena.'

'Deliver her to who?'

'Zambrano,' she said. 'Can you believe it? The man can buy any girl he wants and he picked that little whore.'

'Where is Zambrano?'

Lupe laughed hysterically. 'They do not tell me those things.' She pointed to a ring of purple bruises on her neck. 'I told you. I am a prisoner myself.'

Clark groaned. 'Ernie's cell number, then.'

'He calls me,' she said. 'Not the other way around. He is a very careful man.'

'Let's say you needed to tell him something important,' Clark said. 'Where would you start?'

'He will come back home, eventually. Probably not for a few days, though. I like it when he is away.'

'I'm sure,' Clark said. 'Who would know where to find him?'

Lupe raised her hands again. Grinning stupidly, thinking she'd use her body since it had served her in the past, she kicked upward, bringing her breasts above the surface. 'Search me, *señor*.'

Clark sent another round zipping into the pool, inches away. The smile bled from her face.

'Last time I ask,' Clark said. 'How do I find Zambrano?'

She spat into the water, then wiped a hand across her face. 'I am telling you I do not know,' she said.

'Then you're no good to me —'

'Wait,' the woman said. She was accustomed to being threatened but smart enough to hear the hard edge of resolve in Clark's voice. 'Dorian. Dorian would know how to reach him. They do business sometimes.'

'Dorian?'

'He gets girls from South America . . . and other places. People trust him because he looks handsome and kind, like a model from a magazine.'

She gave him the location of a hotel in Fort Worth that Dorian frequented, then described him. Clark committed it to memory, deciding on his next move. He needed to find out what she knew about Vincent Chen, but he wanted to check inside first.

'Who else is in the house?'

Lupe pushed a lock of wet hair from her face, black

eyes casting back and forth for any avenue of escape, a cornered she-wolf – except wolves had souls. 'There are two girls,' she said. 'Matarife's prisoners. Take them. They are yours.'

Clark slipped the Glock in the belt scabbard long enough to climb the fence behind the pool house, drawing it again as soon as his feet hit the grass.

The day was heating up and a steady breeze blew the odor of chlorine into his face. He motioned with the Glock for the woman to get out of the pool. She had several scars, at least two of them bullet wounds in her torso. It was difficult to tell where the bruises ended and tattoos began, and still, there was a nasty defiance about the woman that made it hard to feel sorry for her.

Focused on the gun barrel, she didn't really look at him until she'd hauled herself up the aluminum ladder and stood naked and dripping on the concrete deck. She rolled her eyes when she saw him.

'You are old . . .'

'I am,' Clark said. He nodded to the folded terry-cloth robe beside what looked like a rawhide quirt. It was exactly the right size to have caused the bruises on the dead girls.

Clark ordered the woman to kick the robe to him. He prodded it with his toe and kicked it back to her once he felt sure it didn't contain any weapons.

'Here,' Clark said, then nodded toward the house. 'Put that on and we'll go have a talk with those girls.'

She reached to pick up the robe, but instead of putting it on, she threw it in Clark's face, shrieking and clawing as she launched herself toward him.

Even Clark, who prided himself on situational aware-ness, was caught off guard. The sheer insanity of the move made it effective, and the naked, spitting woman was able to knock the pistol out of the way a fraction of a second before he could get off an accurate shot. Flying at him like a crazed banshee, Lupe tied him up in wet arms and legs. Her teeth sank deep into his shoulder, causing him to stagger toward the pool. He tried desperately to peel her away, bashing at the side of her head with his free hand – but she seemed impervious to his blows. She was short in stature, but Lupe was not a light woman, probably only a few pounds lighter than Clark. And she possessed the strength of a cornered animal who knew she had to kill or be killed.

Clark regained his footing but realized she was trying to pull him into the pool. No doubt she believed she would be able to take care of the old man once and for all in the deep water.

He decided to give her what she wanted.

The pool was just three short steps away. Clark took a couple deep breaths as they toppled over, grabbing the fleshy woman around the ribs and squeezing out as much air as he could an instant before they hit the water in a tangled knot of furious bottom bitch and gray-haired former SEAL.

Lupe ramped up her assault with a vengeance, disen-gaging just enough to get a hand up to claw at Clark's face when they went under. He turned his head in time to avoid her nails, trapping her hand and giving her a vicious head-butt. Blood trailed from her nose. Bubbles erupted in a muffled scream of rage.

Clark had fought underwater before, in training – and in the cold grip of real-world situations. The water was his home.

Kicking downward, he drove the writhing woman to the bottom of the pool, hearing the high-pitched whine as his ears equalized to the increased pressure. Another furious shriek escaped Lupe's lips. This one was smaller than the last, producing only a tiny blossom of bubbles. She gave a halfhearted twist in a last-ditch effort to get away – and then fell limp in his arms.

Clark counted down another twenty seconds – long enough to make sure she wasn't pretending. He had at least another minute in him when he let his natural buoyancy carry them upward, taking an easy breath when he broke the surface. He glanced toward the house, making sure no one was waiting to give him a nasty reception, and then rolled onto his back, hauling the unconscious woman in a modified rescue tow to the side.

Lupe regained consciousness the moment they reached the edge, animating with a fury as if under some voodoo spell. She ducked her chin, sinking her teeth into his forearm, surely aiming for bone. Clark's shoulder caught hard against the concrete edge of the pool, sending even more pain through his body.

'Enough!' he roared. Images of the dead girls in the field, strangled and whipped, mixed in his mind with awful memories of Pam Madden's tortured face in the morgue. He reached for a gun – either one, it didn't matter. His hand closed around the grip of the Glock and he brought it around quickly, ending Lupe's reign of cruelty with a point-blank shot to her neck.

Breathing hard now, as much from pain as exertion, Clark pushed the woman away and pressed himself up to the pool deck. He leaned forward, one hand on a knee, the other trailing the Glock by his side.

'I am old.' He coughed, clearing his throat. 'But an old SEAL still loves the water . . .'

Any death was tragic, and watching Lupe's body float facedown in the pool, Clark felt a certain amount of remorse about killing her. But ten minutes later, after he'd freed the two cowering teenagers chained to five-gallon buckets of concrete – and then walked through a tall red door to watch even a few seconds of the horrific videos – he wanted to go outside and shoot her again.

28

Electrician's mate Petty Officer 2nd Class Raymond Cooper sat wedged against the bulkhead on the long booth seat. The USS *Rogue*, a *Cyclone*-class patrol ship, or PC, was not a huge vessel at fifty-five meters, but what she lacked in size she made up for in personality. Her crew of twenty-eight, including four officers, had multiple jobs. The lack of real estate on board made each space pull double – or even triple – duty as well. Meals were eaten, briefings given, and movies watched in the padded booths just around the corner from the one-oven galley.

Finished with chow, Petty Officer Cooper – Coop to his peers – pored over an open notebook, using the space to study for his next systems exam. The five sailors sitting in the booth around him were all coming off duty and lingered for a few minutes before hitting the rack for a few precious hours of sleep.

'You're pissed because you believed the stories about the tennis balls,' a petty officer 3rd Class named Goldberg said, wagging a spoon full of chocolate pudding at the sailor across the table.

In truth, most of the newer men on the *Rogue* were more than a little upset about the lack of female attention they'd suffered in the Port of Darwin. They'd all heard stories from older hands about Australian girls who would scribble their phone numbers on tennis balls, then line up on the docks and throw the balls at arriving Navy ships.

As exciting as the prospect was of willing women lining the docks in order to spend the evening with an American sailor, Australian girls turned out to be pretty much like girls everywhere. Some of them were gorgeous and some were not. Much to the heartbreak of the sailors of the USS *Rogue*, the gorgeous ones didn't have to hunt the docks for men – and nobody showed up to throw so much as a glance.

Coop looked up from his studies. 'Don't listen to him, Peavy,' he said. 'Goldie's as disappoint –'

The XO's voice came across the intercom on the bulkhead above the table.

'Set, Counter Piracy Condition Bravo. Set, Counter Piracy Condition Bravo.'

All the men in the booth felt the telltale shift in power as *Rogue* picked up speed.

The teasing around the table stopped, and the sailors slid out of the booth, each moving to his predetermined battle station. They might have been new to the port call in Darwin, but they'd all spent time on this tour conducting counterpiracy ops, training with the Malacca Straits Patrol. Condition Bravo meant a pirate vessel had been reported. They were in hunting mode.

The intercom squawked again.

'Petty Officer Cooper, report to the foredeck.'

The other men made a hole, allowing Cooper to hustle forward. None of them had to ask why.

Six minutes later, Lieutenant Commander Jimmy Akana, the skipper of the USS *Rogue*, stepped out of the bridge and made his way forward, to where Petty Officer Cooper was busy with the contents of two large OD green Pelican cases. What looked like an oversized model airplane sat on the deck beside Cooper as he busied himself with a boxy viewfinder.

The sun was well below the horizon and the apparent wind from *Rogue*'s thirty-two knots caused a stiff breeze across the deck.

'Let's get that bird in the air,' the skipper said.

'Aye, aye, sir.' Cooper gave a nod to a petty officer 2nd Class named Rich Davies. 'Ready to launch.'

The cook aboard *Rogue*, Davies was responsible for feeding the twenty-eight-man crew, but like every other pair of hands on board, he pitched in where he was needed. A *Cyclone*-class patrol ship was not a lazy sailor's vessel.

'Ready to launch,' Davies repeated. He picked up the bird from the deck next to him and held it above his head like a javelin, facing into the wind.

The 'bird' was an AeroVironment RQ-20 Puma unmanned aerial vehicle – commonly called a drone. Weighing in at thirteen pounds with a wingspan of nine feet, two inches, the RQ-20 carried a sensor suite known as Mantis i45, boasting powerful cameras capable of daylight, low-light, and night visibility.

The aircraft control system itself was a series of buttons and a joystick. But Cooper told the aircraft only where to go; the computer did the flying. Cooper had already programmed in *Lucky Strike*'s GPS coordinates, confirmed by the sailboat's AIS signal after the numbers were given with the distress call. A Pocket DDL – digital data link – made it possible for Lieutenant Commander Akana, or anyone else with the access to the coded gateway, to view the images the Puma sent back.

The small but powerful electric motor whirred on the RQ-20's nose. Cooper gave the signal to launch, and Davies used both hands to throw the Puma into the wind. The UAV turned sideways, pushed aside momentarily by the breeze. It recovered quickly and began to pull away at once from the slower ship, gaining altitude as it sped above the waves toward SV *Lucky Strike*.

The sailboat lay ten miles away, just outside the nine-mile control range of the drone, but *Rogue* was right behind her, cutting the waves at a respectable thirty-three knots.

Cooper looked up from the controller hood.

'She's making a steady fifty miles an hour, Skipper,' the petty officer said. 'Twelve minutes to target.'

AeroVironment reported a top speed of fifty-two miles an hour, but Cooper had been known to coax out an extra two if the winds were right. Unfortunately, today, the breeze was directly on her nose.

The skipper looked at his watch. 'Very well.'

He glanced down at the tablet computer in his hands. The Mantis i45's low-light camera was sending back nothing but ghostly green-black images of waves two hundred feet below. The RQ-20 Puma would arrive on station a scant four minutes ahead of the ship, providing Akana with the equivalent of an extremely serviceable pair of flying binoculars.

In addition to putting the UAV in the air, Counter Piracy Condition Bravo set *Rogue*'s VBSS team in motion.

The crew was already gearing up and readying the launch of the seven-meter rigid-hull inflatable boat. Visit, board, search, and seizure teams were made up of sailors from virtually all ratings. Those selected were trained at one of the Navy's Security Reaction Force and VBSS schools.

Larger ships had multiple larger teams, but *Rogue*'s smaller crew necessitated a five-man team commanded by a lieutenant, plus the boatswain's mate acting as coxswain, driving the boat. Each VBSS team member carried at least fifty pounds of gear, including a Kevlar helmet with NVGs, radio headset, body armor in a tactical vest that doubled as a life preserver, flexible restraints, pepper spray, a Beretta M9 pistol, and an MK18 rifle. One member of the team traded the carbine for a Mossberg twelve-gauge in anticipation of the need to breach locked hatches.

Five minutes from target, Lieutenant Junior Grade Steven Gitlin, the ship's communications officer, ordered his team into the twenty-four-foot RHIB. Petty Officer 2nd Class Marty White, the VBSS team's usual coxswain, had sprained his ankle while on liberty in Darwin, so Chief Boatswain's Mate Bobby Rose was at the helm of the rigid hulled inflatable boat. Two minutes later, the ship's hydraulic aft doors opened, jerk lines were pulled, and the RHIB slid down the aft ramp into the frothy black sea. The 248-horsepower Steyr diesel burbled in the water, and the chief boatswain's mate, called 'Boats' by the crew, brought the inflatable up along *Rogue*'s starboard side. Gitlin looked at his watch.

Four minutes out. The first images from the Puma would just be streaming in.

*

The seas swelled in long, rolling trains, but there was hardly any chop, and it was a simple matter for Awang to bring the fishing vessel alongside *Lucky Strike* and tie off to fore and aft cleats. Rubber bumpers squealed and squeaked as Jemaah Islamiyah men moved steadily back and forth, moving quickly to load a dozen twenty-five-pound canvas bags from the skiff to the sailboat.

The women cowered below decks, clutching pitiful kitchen knives and wailing uncontrollably. Their flimsy, whorish clothing made it easier for Mamat not to pity them. Those who would act less than human deserved to be treated like dogs.

It was an easy matter to swat the knives out of the way and drag both women topside. Awang suggested they rape the women to teach them a lesson in piety. Mamat looked at his watch and shook his head. There was no time for that.

The smaller woman with dark hair remained stoic as the boy dragged her forward and tied her to the bow rail. The redhead spat and fought as they lashed her to the mast. Mamat had to club her in the face to shut her up. One hand he tied at her waist, the other Mamat fixed to a thin length of cord that ran up to a pulley above her head and then down again, leading into the cabin. Though the woman's arm was free, Mamat could raise or lower the hand by taking up or releasing the tension on the line.

As planned, the boy remained on the sailboat with Mamat and the infidel women – and the RPGs. Awang and the other men climbed back aboard the fishing skiff, the bow of which was packed with three pounds of ammonium nitrate and fuel-oil explosive – half the load they'd brought with them.

Mamat gave a solemn nod to the men and then followed the boy below. The ship would be here in minutes. For this to work, he needed to be out of sight.

A fishing skiff appears to be moving away from the sailboat, sir,' Petty Officer Cooper said, his eyes glued to the hooded viewfinder. He'd issued the Puma a command to loiter two hundred feet above *Lucky Strike*. 'I count two females on the sailboat's deck.'

'Let's get a closer look,' the skipper said. 'Zoom in. It may give us some indication of these pirates' state of mind if they didn't kill their hostages.'

'Aye, aye, sir,' Cooper said, increasing the magnification by seven.

'They're still alive,' Akana mused, studying the images streaming to his tablet. 'They're bound in place and gagged, but one appears to have gotten a hand free. Looks as though she's waving.'

'I see it too, Skipper,' Cooper said.

A sudden gust of wind blew the Puma off for a moment, disrupting the image. The bird reacquired quickly, but Akana was already giving orders.

'Bring us up to a hundred fifty meters off the stern.'

The XO nodded and relayed the order to the helmsman.

Akana got on the radio with the team. 'Lieutenant Gitlin, this is *Rogue*. Pirate vessel appears to be bugging out. The Puma shows two survivors on the sailboat's deck. Head on a swivel, Steve. Something feels wrong about this.'

Chief Rose kept the RHIB tucked in beside *Rogue*, using her as cover and concealment as they approached, veering off to speed forward only after the larger vessel hove to, a hundred fifty meters off *Lucky Strike*'s stern rail.

'Pirate vessel . . . departing . . . to the northwest.' Gitlin's voice came in stops and starts as the RHIB bounced across waves. 'I count four . . . scratch that, five skinnies on board.' *Skinnies* was the term sailors used for pirates off the coast of Somalia. Some, including Gitlin, who'd worked Task Force 151, used it for pirates no matter where they were. 'Sailboat's dark,' he added. 'Just the two females so far.'

Chief Petty Officer Bill Knight stood to the right of the coxswain's post. 'I concur,' he said. At thirty-eight, the Alabama native had more time in the Navy than all the men on the team – and Gitlin trusted his opinion implicitly.

'Skipper's right, though,' the chief continued, peering through a pair of marine binoculars. 'Somethin' about this whole thing gives me a case of the creepin' red ass.'

The two chiefs stood side by side, Rose driving, Knight watching out for the safety of his men. Neither was more than five feet from Gitlin, but they all spoke into the small boom mics on their comms gear to be heard over the roar of motor, wind, and waves.

'Boats,' Gitlin said, addressing Rose. 'Take us by for a closer look.'

Chief Rose pushed the throttle all the way forward, standing off fifty meters and racing the RHIB up the starboard side of the sailboat. Once he came abeam the bow, he stood the RHIB on its side in a tight U-turn and pointed it back behind the sailboat again to swing around her stern and then jet up the port side, all the while

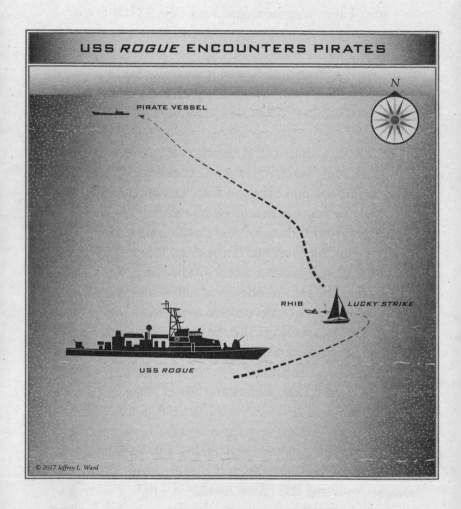

USS *ROGUE* ENCOUNTERS PIRATES

N

PIRATE VESSEL

RHIB LUCKY STRIKE

USS *ROGUE*

© 2017 Jeffrey L. Ward

holding a fifty-meter standoff. The maneuver was known as a 'horseshoe,' and it allowed the VBSS team a good look at the target vessel from a distance while traveling at a high rate of speed.

'*Rogue*, Gitlin,' the lieutenant said.

Commander Akana's unflappable voice came back across the radio.

'Go ahead, Steve.'

'Any more intel from the Puma, skipper?'

'Pirate vessel is still moving away to the northeast,' Akana said. 'Approximately eight knots. Boarding the sailboat is your call.'

'Aye, sir,' Gitlin said. The woman tied to the mast continued to wave at him. 'We plan to board.'

'Very well,' Akana said.

'Boats,' Gitlin said. 'Bring us up on the port side, slowly. Chief Knight, Cartwright, Ridgeway, cover the approach.'

'Aye, aye, sir,' Knight said, then muttered under his breath as he aimed in with his carbine. 'Yep, creepin' red ass, all right . . .'

The bobbing sailboat was a green hulk against the black sea through the NVGs. Something was off about the woman at the mast. She was mechanical, puppetlike.

Rose eased back on the throttle.

Thirty feet out, Gitlin looked toward Peavy on the bow hook. 'Ready with —'

Chief Knight's voice crackled across the radio. 'Movement on the bow!' he barked. 'She's standing up . . . waving us off. Repeat, waving off!'

The woman was indeed standing. She'd ripped away her gag and screamed something unintelligible at the

303

approaching RHIB. When they kept coming, she held her arms up in a raised X, the universal sign for NO!

'Boats!' Gitlin barked. 'Get us out of here!'

The muffled rattle of rifle fire erupted from inside the cabin of the sailboat. Bright flashes illuminated the portholes. The woman at the mast slumped as bullets shredded the deck beneath her.

The woman at the bow screamed, diving over the lifelines.

'Return fire!' Gitlin shouted above the noise. He turned to face aft with the rest of the team as Chief Rose shoved the throttle forward, pointing the RHIB directly at *Lucky Strike*'s bow.

The woman in the water went under once, then bobbed to the surface. Only the top of her head and her flailing arms were visible in Gitlin's NVGs. Knight leaned over the side while Gitlin grabbed his rigger's belt to steady him, as if they'd planned it that way. The RHIB's pontoons were huge, nearly two feet in diameter, forcing Knight to lean well out over the water in order to grab the woman when they sped past. Top-heavy from the extra fifty pounds of gear, he would have slithered over the slick tube into the drink had Gitlin's weight not provided a counterbalance.

'Got her!' Knight yelled above the hiss of spray and the roaring motor. Both men fell backward in unison, hauling the sputtering woman over the pontoon and into the chief's lap, Knight clutching a handful of her hair and the back of her swimsuit.

The two men farthest aft in the RHIB opened up in earnest with their rifles, strafing the side of the sailboat.

A green head peeked around the corner from the cabin hatch, followed by a bright flash. Gitlin had never seen a rocket-propelled grenade coming directly at him, but his instincts said that's what this was.

'RPG!' he screamed. 'Cover! Cover! Cover!'

Rose jerked the RHIB hard to port. They were so close that it wouldn't have made much difference, but thankfully, the shooter had rushed the trigger under the fusillade of oncoming gunfire. The rocket-propelled grenade hit the waves well to the left, skipping along the surface to explode well in front of the inflatable, throwing up a plume of spray.

When Gitlin looked back, Ridgeway was slumped, chin to his chest, weapon dangling from his single-point sling, arms hanging to the deck.

Chief Knight, ever aware of the men in his charge, pushed the woman away so her back rested against the side of the pontoon. He slid to the back of the speeding RHIB on both knees, lifting Ridgeway's head. A moment later, he turned and gave Gitlin the harrowed look that all good leaders dread.

'Pirate vessel returning,' Gitlin heard over his radio. 'Nineteen knots and accelerating.'

The traffic was followed by the rhythmic thump of the Mk 28 chain gun, firing from *Rogue*'s foredeck. There hadn't been time to tell them about the RPG, but they'd obviously seen it. Twenty-five-millimeter high-explosive tracer rounds creased the night air, chewing the fishing skiff into kindling. An instant later a bright flash blossomed up from where the pirate vessel had been. Gitlin and his men jerked their heads away, temporarily blinded in their NVGs.

'Holy shit!' Peavy yelled from his station on the bow of the RHIB. 'That's a hell of an explosion for a twenty-footer.'

'Chief Rose,' Gitlin said, willing his voice to stay calm – and the sailboat not to explode until they'd moved farther away from the RHIB – 'put some distance between us and that sailboat!'

Belowdecks on *Lucky Strike*, Mamat dragged himself forward with his good arm. The other was shot away, the elbow joint exposed in a sickening mess of meat and bone. Both legs had taken rounds. He didn't know how bad, but the pain was nearly unbearable. He was certain to pass out if he chanced a look at the wounds. The sound of the Navy boat's departure was a knife to his heart. He cursed himself for his mistake. He'd held off detonating the explosive, waiting for the sailors to tie up alongside in order to inflict maximum damage.

None of the Jemaah Islamiyah planners or their Abu Sayyaf financiers had thought it would be possible to get anywhere near the larger ship. The ammonium nitrate in the fishing vessel had been put in place on the off chance the captain of the USS *Rogue* had been lax or inexperienced. He turned out to be neither. But the deaths of six sailors in the inflatable would have been a mighty blow to the Great Satan – if Mamat had not been so stupid.

He should never have allowed the boy to tie the woman at the bow. She'd gotten loose at the worst possible time, warning the boarding party. The boy had panicked at his mistake, shooting through the deck at the women and drawing fire from the US vessel. Mamat was struck in both knees early in the gunfight, causing him to topple sideways and drop the push-button detonator that was hardwired to the explosives. Then the foolish boy chanced a shot with the RPG and took an American bullet through the eye for his trouble. He lost the back of his skull in the process. Even as the sailors ran for their lives, rounds continued to punch holes in both the sailboat and Mamat. He must have lost consciousness for a moment because the sound of the boat motor was dying away when he came to.

At last, he was able to drag himself to the detonator and grasp it in a bloody hand. The Navy boat was gone, but it was much too late to change his mind now. Closing his eyes, Mamat bin Ahmad said a final prayer and pressed the button.

Nothing happened.

Mamat shuddered, flooded with a heady mixture of relief and shame. Then he shifted his weight, moving the wire under his chest. The movement completed the shorted connection and the cabin vaporized in a ball of orange flame.

29

Special Agent Kelsey Callahan could not recall the moment, but she'd seen photographic evidence that her father had broken down and cried when he dropped her off on her first day of kindergarten.

The elder Callahan was a well-respected heart surgeon at Providence St Patrick Hospital in Missoula. He was also a champion of strong women – forever pushing his only child to 'get out front' and 'show them how it's done.' A burly, buffalo-plaid-wearing Montana man who looked more like a logger or mountain guide when he wasn't dressed in hospital scrubs, he was also the most overprotective father Kelsey had ever heard of.

Big Ben Callahan made it clear to every boy Kelsey dated in a jovial, not-quite-joking way that he was capable not only of saving lives but also of ending them in quiet and undetectable ways.

Kelsey made the mistake of sneaking out of the house late one night during her sophomore year of high school. Somehow her father had known, and he approached the boy's pickup just as they were about to drive away. He materialized from the shadows of the tall blue spruce in their front yard – nearly causing the poor kids to pee their pants when he knocked on the passenger window. If that wasn't bad enough, when the boy rolled down the window, Big Ben Callahan leaned in across a mortified Kelsey and asked in a quietly piercing voice if he'd brought a gun with him.

'N-n-no,' the boy stammered.

'A big-ass knife?'

'Of course not!' The boy looked like he was about to cry.

'Some kind of stick or club?'

'No, sir.'

Her father had considered the answer for a moment, then said, 'You'd better bring one the next time you come to my house in the middle of the night.' Then he opened the door so Kelsey could get out and follow him back inside.

It turned out that Austin Herbert McKay had been carrying a knife that night. He was just too terrified of Ben Callahan to use it. McKay went on to sexually assault three girls around Missoula – all of them redheads – over the next few months before he was finally arrested. Ben Callahan never once rubbed the incident in her face – though he had, over the years, raised an eyebrow at her questionable taste in men. Sadly, he hadn't been around to run off her ex-husband before she'd tied the knot.

Her dad had grown misty-eyed when she graduated with honors from Hellgate High School, but he'd broken down completely when she graduated from FBI training at Quantico, admitting that the thought of her strapping on a gun every day terrified him. She reminded him of that night he'd stood under the spruce tree – and pointed out that there were a lot of bad guys in the world. He'd understood with no further explanation, returning to Missoula and his life as a cardiac surgeon while she went hunting for all the Austin Herbert McKays she could find.

Kelsey Callahan inherited her father's protective nature along with his sense of justice, but she'd gotten a penchant for expensive silk blouses, her red hair, and her defined hourglass shape from her mother. If anyone ever asked what happened to those underwear models in the Sears, Roebuck catalogs, Sue Callahan would point out that some of them married cardiac surgeons and raised promising young FBI agents. Her mom's previous career wasn't something Kelsey ever talked about in high school – she didn't relish the idea of boys knowing there were pictures of her mom in lacy bras floating around out there – especially since Kelsey looked so much like her.

Her first posting, to the Los Angeles FBI field office, had quickly hardened the starry-eyed Montana girl – and dispelled the notion that she'd be out hunting bad guys all day. When she wasn't interviewing people with foreign names who'd signed up to take flying lessons, she was helping senior agents prep evidence for court cases or sitting in a telephone closet listening to wiretaps. It took her three years to escape LA and get a spot in Dallas – where she immediately volunteered to work the Internet Crimes Against Children squad. The ICAC was not a particularly sought-after job, so she was able to take on a lot of responsibility early in her career. By five years in she was second-in-command at the CAC Task Force. Two years later she'd doubled the number of agencies involved and sent the stats through the roof. Her success came at the expense of a personal life – but she was still in her thirties and decided she could have one of those in the future. Someday. Maybe.

In a stats-driven bureaucracy like the FBI, Kelsey

Callahan became a shooting star. Her task force saved kids and made arrests at a near superhuman rate. The special agent in charge kept her in Crimes Against Children, long after she'd reached the normal time allotted to rotate out of such a soul-crushing job. There was no doubt that the sadness and grind of it all were taking their toll. It was impossible to work a job where you might find some kid's head in the freezer and not have it affect you.

Then this Dominic Caruso guy showed up. What a breath of fresh air – even if he was a spook. There was something about the easy way he carried himself, as if he'd been on a break from the byzantine politics of the FBI. Even now, as she drove them toward an interview of their second former child prostitute who'd fallen back into 'the life' after adulthood, he stayed off his phone and nodded his head in time to some tune he hummed inside his head. Her dad hummed inside his head when he was thinking – and that habit alone put Caruso up a notch in her book.

She'd been awake since before five, and the last cup of coffee sloshing around in her gut was causing her stomach to rebel. She'd caught Caruso early at his hotel room with his scary-looking friend, John the mystery man, so she figured he was probably ready for breakfast as well.

He caught her looking at him and grinned from behind a pair of extremely sexy Wiley X sunglasses. Of course this one would be spoken for.

'You doing okay?' Caruso suddenly asked.

The question caught her off guard. As the CAC Task Force commander, she was responsible for checking on the well-being of her team, but it was a rare moment when anyone, particularly a stranger, checked to see how she was holding up. The toughen-up-buttercup culture was changing, and the Bureau had programs to be sure, but FBI agents weren't exactly the type of individuals to admit weakness.

'I'm fine,' she said, her words automatic and unconvincing, even to herself. 'Why do you ask?'

'Well,' Caruso said, as though he'd thought this through while he was humming. 'You gotta see some of the worst shit imaginable.'

'Sometimes,' she said. 'But I'm not sitting around boo-hooing myself to sleep or anything.'

'I wouldn't even suggest that,' Caruso said. 'But you must be taking in more evil than some kind of sin-eater.'

'We save a lot of kids,' Callahan said. 'Makes my petty problems seem small.' Talking about herself had always made her uncomfortable. 'You hungry at all?'

Caruso nodded. 'I could eat.'

'There's an IHOP off —'

The cell phone in her pocket began to hum.

She grunted hello, then listened, her chest tightening with each word.

'What?' Caruso asked, after she'd hung up, looking over the top of the Wiley X shades.

'Somebody found Matarife's place before we did,' Callahan said. 'Johnson County got an anonymous tip. They're already on scene and the Texas Rangers are en route.'

'Barricade?' Caruso said.

'No.' Callahan shook her head. 'A homicide. Multiple, in fact.'

She pounded the flat of her hands against the center console. She wasn't in the mood to deal with the Rangers, least of all the one who she knew would show up at this scene.

They were already in South Dallas, so a quick hop over to State Highway 67 courtesy of Callahan's lights and siren took them straight down to the sleepy little town of Alvarado, which was situated along the I-35 corridor, a favorite route for traffickers of narcotics and humans.

Caruso was grateful for his sunglasses because Callahan had not stopped interrogating him with her eyes from the moment she'd gotten the call. It only got worse when she pulled around the circular drive in front of the big red-brick house and no longer had to focus on the road. Three Johnson County SO cars were parked on the grass, along with two black-and-white Texas DPS Highway Patrol sedans, an ambulance, and a blue Expedition.

'Damn it!' Callahan muttered under her breath. She'd parked behind the other cars on the front lawn so as not to disturb any possible tire-track evidence. 'He beat us here.'

'Who beat us?'

A brawny man with a white straw hat stepped around the corner of the house. He wore navy blue dress Wranglers and a starched khaki shirt. The silver *cinco peso* badge of a Texas Ranger was pinned to his left breast pocket, over a kettledrum chest. The silver horseshoe buckle caught the light of the morning sun and a 1911 pistol rested in a tooled leather holster over his hip. Caruso guessed him to be in his mid-forties. He smiled and tipped his hat when he saw Callahan, revealing a full head of curly blond hair.

'I'm guessing you know him,' Caruso said.

'You might say that,' Callahan grumbled. 'We were married once. Worst ten minutes of my life.'

The man hugged Callahan, then gave Caruso what could only be taken as a serious case of stink-eye.

'Lyle Anderson,' the Ranger said, taking Caruso's callused paw and pumping it up and down like an overgrown Bamm-Bamm Rubble on *The Flintstones*.

Caruso, not one to measure his manhood, said, 'Easy there, hoss, I shoot with those fingers.'

Ranger Anderson's face spread into a wide grin. 'You and I are gonna get along,' he said. 'Except for Kelsey, I never met an FBI agent that wasn't worthless as tits on a boar hog. But I do respect a man who says what's on his mind.'

Callahan fished a wad of blue nitrile gloves from her vest pocket and peeled them apart. She handed a pair to Caruso.

'What have we got?' she asked, nodding toward the back of the house, ready to move on.

'I've been doin' pretty well,' Anderson said. 'Thank you for asking. Good to see you, too, Kelsey.'

Callahan just stared at the Ranger, playing a game of nonverbal chicken.

Anderson finally flinched and flipped open his notebook. 'According to Johnson County,' he said, 'an anonymous male called in and advised that there were girls out here being held against their will – oh, and, by the way, a few dead bodies to boot.'

'How many girls?'

'Live ones?' the Ranger said. 'Two. I'm guessing that neither of them is over fifteen. We're still waiting for someone to get here who can say more than "put your hands on the car" in Spanish. Paramedics are giving the girls fluids now. They were both recently branded and have been on the receiving end of some pretty nasty whippings. Nothing appears to be broken.' The Ranger shuddered at some memory. 'Physically, at least.'

Caruso gave a slow shake of his head. 'You said they were branded?'

Ranger Anderson tipped back his hat with the crook of his finger and nodded. 'Looks like somebody burned "LSM" on the side of their necks. Not a very professional job, either. I'm thinking they were branded with a red-hot coat hanger or something.' He winced. 'Had to hurt like a son of a bitch.'

'LSM . . .' Caruso said, thinking out loud.

'Or maybe "4SM,"' Anderson said. 'It's sorta flowery writing, and, like I said, not very professional-looking. Damnedest thing, really. We've seen this brand more than once on dead prostitutes.'

Callahan's head snapped up. 'These girls are prisoners, not prostitutes!'

Anderson held up both hands. 'Easy-breezy,' he said. 'I didn't say they were prostitutes. I'm talking about other cases – in which I'm sure the FBI would have no interest.'

Caruso said, 'You said something about a couple bodies.'

'Caller said a couple,' Anderson said, turning and

motioning for them to follow with a flick of his hand. 'We have four so far. Three in the field and a floater in the pool around back.'

Callahan stopped in her tracks, as if steeling herself. 'Another girl?'

Anderson shook his head as he walked on. 'This one was all grown up. Pretty sure she's one of the bad guys.'

'Cause of death was drowning?' Caruso asked.

'Nope,' the Ranger said. 'She was belly-down in the pool when we got here, but the cause of death was a bullet to the throat. Punched a hole right through her spine.'

Caruso followed Anderson through the open gate in the fence. He stooped beside Callahan on the pool deck to examine the body of a Hispanic female who was laid out face up on top of a yellow body bag.

'The Johnson County deputies recognize her as Guadalupe Vargas,' the Ranger said. 'AKA Lupe or Lupita. She's been arrested a couple times for heroin and turning tricks in a massage parlor outside of Cleburne, but nobody's seen her for a year. They were all surprised she was still around.'

'Recognize the tats?' Callahan asked without looking up.

'Death?' Caruso said, scanning the woman's legs. '. . . And another death.'

'That female skeleton on her thigh is La Santa Muerte,' Ranger Anderson said. 'Patron saint of shitheads. We see it a lot around here, statues, tats, paintings on black velvet.'

'La Santa Muerte . . .' Dom said. 'LSM.'

Anderson raised an eyebrow. 'I'll be damned,' he said.

'Yes, you will,' Callahan muttered. She leaned in closer

with her cell phone, snapping a photo of an entry wound in the dead woman's neck. A sizable chunk of flesh was missing in what was likely the exit wound, exposing the glistening white of her trachea. Callahan ignored the gore and bent even closer. 'Looks like a contact shot,' she said.

Anderson stepped back, making sure he didn't block their view with his shadow. 'See that burn signature?'

'Yep,' Caruso said, feeling his gut tighten.

'Either of you two Feds think that looks like the business end of a suppressor?' Anderson asked. 'Because I sure as hell think it does.'

Callahan held up the phone. 'Why do you think I took the photo?' She looked at Caruso. 'This mean anything to you?'

Shouts came from the back field before Caruso had a chance to answer.

Anderson's phone rang. He fished it from the pocket of his Wranglers, listened for a moment, then dropped it back in.

'Johnson County says they've got at least three bodies buried under the three we already knew about. From the looks of it, one of Lupita's guys was out with his tractor, dumping bodies in a grave among the sorghum plants when some unknown person capped his worthless ass.'

'Do they recognize the dead male?' Callahan asked.

Anderson nodded. 'Fat guy named Salazar, they said. His brain's half toasted up from huffing gasoline when he was a kid. Anyway, unless you guys intend to take over the case, I'm going to have the sheriff's office order up some construction lights and ground-penetrating radar. Looks like we're gonna be here awhile.'

'Knock yourself out.' Callahan pushed to her feet. 'No sign of a guy who calls himself Matarife?'

'Nope,' Anderson said. 'That name has come up in a couple of different interviews lately, but we didn't have an ID. Anonymous caller said Matarife's real name is Ernie Pacheco. This is Pacheco's place, but he's not here.'

'What about a girl named Magdalena?' Callahan asked. 'She should speak some English.'

'Sorry, Kelsey,' Anderson said, more tender now. He'd obviously been around Callahan long enough to read that this was something extra-sensitive. 'We haven't identified the bodies out back, but neither of the girls inside call themselves Magdalena.'

'Tell me about what's inside the house,' Caruso said.

Anderson turned. 'Follow me. But I gotta warn you. It is some gruesome shit.' He nodded to the Johnson County deputy at the door, as if FBI badges weren't enough to gain Caruso and Callahan entry.

The living area of the house looked normal enough, if a little on the tattered side for such a large home. Wood paneling and oak furniture gave the place an early-1970s feel and added to the oppressive darkness of the situation. Caruso imagined this would be what Jeffrey Dahmer's place would have felt like if he could have afforded a big house. There was a big-screen television fixed to the wall above a gas fireplace. A half-bowl of salsa and the remnants of tortilla chips occupied the coffee table along with a half-dozen empty bottles of Corona. The place could have easily belonged to an upper-middle-class Texas family who had gone to bed without cleaning up after watching a ball game – except for the smell.

Caruso had never been one for incense. The sweet smell of patchouli was overpowering – but not quite strong enough to hide the outhouse odors coming from the next room.

Anderson pushed open a door off the kitchen and motioned for them to come inside.

'We found the two girls in here. They were chained to eyebolts set in five-gallon buckets of concrete. Six more buckets had no girls attached. We'll swab those for DNA.' Anderson shook his head, pointing to the far side of the room with his notebook. 'Sick bastards made the poor kids use those buckets there to go to the restroom.' He nodded to a tall door painted bright fire-engine red at the far end of the room. 'The worst part is on through there.' He stopped. 'I wouldn't blame you if you don't go in, Kelsey.'

She glared daggers at him. 'What?'

'I'm just saying, I wouldn't go back in there if I didn't have to.'

'Come on,' Callahan said.

Caruso felt himself holding his breath as he followed the others into what had once been a deep three-car garage but was now bricked off from the outside. Sound-proof foam and old mattresses covered the walls. In one corner, a high-back leather chair sat atop a rough plywood podium. A leg iron and chain were affixed to the base of the chair. There was a small HD camera mounted to a tripod set up out front, with a cable running from the camera to an open laptop computer. In the farthest corner from the chair, three cameras and three pole-mounted lights surrounded a timber bed. Clear plastic sheeting took the place of regular bed linens. Blue plastic hospital restraints hung from each post of the heavy bedframe. A stainless-steel table behind the cameras held an assortment of whips and gags.

'I've seen a lot of crazy shit in my day,' Anderson whispered. 'But I never seen anything like this.'

'I have,' Callahan said. She motioned them out of the room, and then out of the house.

'I didn't want to talk in front of that open computer,' she said once they were standing in the driveway. 'Not until Forensics gets a chance to look it over. There's too big a chance it's streaming everything we say to some other location.'

'That's why you make the big money, Kelsey,' Anderson said.

'You said you'd seen this before,' Caruso said.

'Sadly, I have,' Callahan said. She peeled off the gloves with a hooked thumb so they turned inside out and she didn't have to touch the outside of either with her fingers. 'I'm pretty convinced they were sitting the girls in that big chair and auctioning them off on video. Any girl that didn't bring in a high enough bid was then used in a snuff video.'

Caruso stifled a gasp. He shook his head, imagining John Clark's reaction when he'd seen something like this. It sure explained the dead guy at the gravesite and the woman found floating in the pool missing part of her windpipe.

Callahan cocked her head toward Anderson, something dawning on her. 'Did either of the girls give a description of the guy who saved them?'

Caruso kept his face passive.

The Ranger shrugged. 'Like I said. We're still waiting on a Spanish speaker. Why? You have an idea who it was?'

Callahan shot an accusing glance at Caruso. 'I've got a pretty good guess,' she said.

30

The Hendley Associates Gulfstream hit heavy turbulence six hours north of Buenos Aires. The movement jostled Jack Ryan, Jr, awake from a much-needed seven-hour nap. Chavez was still sawing logs in the seat across from Lisanne, but Adara and Midas sat at the small conference table in mid-cabin. They both made good use of the G550's encrypted satellite Wi-Fi.

Jack sat up from the leather couch and raised both arms above his head in what his kid sister called a 'squinty-eyed' stretch.

Midas glanced up from his computer.

'Morning, sunshine.'

Jack nodded but said nothing. He stood, steadying himself against the armrest in the bumpy air.

Lisanne unbuckled her seat belt and moved toward the galley. She whispered, so as not to disturb Chavez. 'I have a fresh pot of coffee on.'

Ryan made his way forward and put his hand on the lavatory door. Still barely conscious of the fact that he was hurtling through the air at 35,000 feet, he gave her what he was sure was a dopey grin.

'Filling up on strong coffee is second on my to-do list.'

Lisanne leaned forward, giving him a conspiratorial nod. 'It'll be waiting here for you,' she said.

Three minutes later, Ryan set his coffee cup on the

conference table and then dropped down in the aisle to pump out thirty push-ups and make sure he was fully awake.

'Any new crises while I was out?' Ryan asked when he was done and seated at the table with the others.

Adara was deep in thought, poring over some article.

Midas looked up and shook his head. 'Not that I know of. I woke up about ten minutes before y –'

'Listen to this,' Adara said, cutting him off.

Ryan moved closer. Midas lowered his computer.

'There's a shop near Recoleta Cemetery that sells lemon-cucumber-flavored ice cream.'

Midas shook his head. 'And that's big news why?'

Adara said, 'It's big news, my good sir, because I like cucumbers and I like ice cream.'

Midas chuckled. 'I'm a mint chocolate-chip man.'

'But seriously,' Adara said. 'I bring it up because I was checking the lead that Ding found regarding the visiting trade ministers. Several countries have posted agendas on their respective websites. Looks like they're all attending a dinner not far from Recoleta Cemetery, so I decided to do some research prior to our arrival.'

Ryan shook his head. 'You keep saying "Recoleta Cemetery" like we should know it.'

'Sorry,' Adara said. 'Some Navy buddies and I burned a week of leave down here one winter – summer here, I guess. Recoleta Cemetery was one of my favorite places. Evita Perón's buried there. It's beautiful but slightly spooky, with above-ground crypts like little houses. Many of them have windows where the coffins are visible.' She consulted a legal pad beside her computer on the teak conference table. 'Anyway, so far, it looks like the ministers of agriculture from Argentina, Canada, Uruguay, China, and Japan are on the guest list for the dinner. The Chinese foreign minister is also supposed to be in Argentina by tomorrow, but his staff is a little more taciturn about posting his itinerary.'

Jack gave a thoughtful nod. 'How about the US?'

'No one, as far as I can tell,' Adara said. 'I'm not sure how the beef lobby would feel about us doing anything to help Argentine exports.'

'Speaking of beef,' Midas said, 'I volunteer to post up inside the restaurant. Argentina's supposed to be hell on wheels when it comes to beefsteak. You can keep your damn cucumber ice cream, thank you very much.'

Ryan grabbed the laptop from his bag and brought up a map of the Recoleta area of Buenos Aires.

'What's the name of the place?'

'*Helado . . .*'

Midas chuckled and shook his head. 'He's talking about the venue restaurant, not your ice cream parlor.'

Adara blushed and then glanced down at her notepad again. 'Parrilla Aires Criollos.' She pronounced the double *l*'s like *y*'s, as someone from Mexico would.

'*Parizha!*' Ding Chavez corrected without opening his eyes. He coughed, licking his lips and turning slightly in his seat like he might drift off to sleep again. 'Argentines speak Castilian Spanish. *Parizha Aires Criozhos.*'

'Damn it!' Adara said. 'I knew that.'

Jack grinned. 'How long have you been awake?'

'Since lemon-cucumber ice cream,' Chavez said. He opened one eye a crack and shook his head at Sherman. 'Don't tell me that's seriously a thing.'

'Anyway,' Adara said, 'of course we'll stay glued to Vincent Chen, but I'm thinking the dinner is a likely place to gather intel. Maybe we can go there tonight and put up a listening device or two.'

'I'm on board with that,' Midas said.

Jack looked out the window at the plane's shadow drifting over a lumpy layer of clouds. 'Or maybe Chen's just interested in one of the players – not the dinner meeting.'

'That's true,' Adara said.

'Whatever the case may be,' Chavez said. 'The Chinese delegation being here is too big a coincidence.' He leaned forward, rubbing his face with both hands. 'Lisanne, you've squared away a couple rental cars?'

'I have,' Robertson said. 'They'll be waiting for you at the airport when we land.'

'Thank you,' Chavez said. 'We'll pull small arms from the bulkheads after we clear customs.'

Midas gave him a hearty thumbs-up.

'Roger that, boss.'

In the past, it had been a relatively rare occurrence for Campus members to carry firearms on a surveillance op – whether in or out of the United States. It was uncommon for intelligence officers to go armed, and Gerry Hendley thought it put them in too much jeopardy of getting jammed up by the local police. But surveillance often morphed into something more sinister, and the times that the team needed and didn't have a firearm seemed to happen with greater and greater frequency.

Chavez had taken his concerns to John Clark – who carried his 1911 ninety-nine percent of the time anyway – and

Clark took the issue to Gerry. He reasoned that the work Campus operators did was often 'extralegal,' whether on American soil or in another country. There was no reason they should not routinely be prepared to protect themselves during the course of their duties. There were times – certain operations during which a weapon would have proven more dangerous than not – but those would be the exception. Clark's recommendation, along with a review of the last dozen operations, made Hendley easy to convince.

Unless otherwise directed, Campus operators were to be armed.

Unless Otherwise Directed, or UNODIR, was a technique often used from the bottom up, where a field commander or team leader might slip an operational plan outlining his intentions into the CO's box – at the last minute and marked UNODIR. The team leader could claim due diligence, though, more often than not, the CO didn't see the ops plan until after the mission was complete. But a UNODIR order coming down from above signified much more than simply allowing Campus operators to go armed most of the time. UNODIR meant that the bosses trusted them to act independently. As former Delta commander Midas Jankowski happily noted: 'They've taken off our choke chains and let us decide who we're going to bite.'

As before, what each Campus operator carried was dictated by personal preference. Ops such as a surveillance in Argentina would require deep concealment. For that, everybody chose the Smith & Wesson M&P Shield in nine-millimeter. In the United States, Caruso and Ryan sometimes carried the same weapon in .40 caliber, but nine-millimeter ammunition was easier to come by in most parts of the world. With a total capacity of nine rounds, the pistols were easy to tuck into a Thunderwear or SmartCarry holster. Both units consisted of a small, flat, and breathable textile pouch on a Velcro belt, worn below the waist and centered low over the groin. These were not designed to be 'quick-draw' holsters, but each operator had extensive practice presenting and firing their weapons from this mode of carry. When the need arose, they could do so quickly and safely – almost as fast as they could with an inside-the-waistband or more traditional belt holster.

No one argued that diminutive M&Ps were optimum primary weapons for going offensive against man-sized targets. Every Campus operator knew from harsh experience that for that they'd use a long gun. But virtually any pistol was better than being a naked clawless bear, so they were happy to have them – along with the hard-earned trust of their superiors.

Yet trust didn't mean the lack of pre-op briefing. Ding Chavez was no micromanager – but he was a leader, and he wanted to be certain everyone on his team was on the same page.

He checked his watch again. 'We'll hit the ground about the time Chen leaves the US. That gives us roughly eleven hours to set up in our rooms and run the routes between the airport and downtown before he arrives. Our goal is to gather intel, but we don't yet know if Chen is running a countersurveillance team – or what the hell he's even up to for sure. Beyond that, street crime in

Buenos Aires isn't exactly unheard of, and we're working without a net here. We use the handguns to save our lives, but if you're mugged by some street thug, I'd much rather see you put a boot up the bastard's fourth point of contact.'

'Copy that,' Midas said. Jack and Adara nodded.

Chavez continued. 'Buenos Aires is supposed to be the most European city in South America, but I don't care to cool my heels in a European jail, either. It goes without saying, but we'll keep everything in our pants unless they're absolutely needed.'

The others, including Lisanne, exchanged glances, stifling laughter.

'Of course, boss,' Midas said.

'Righto,' Adara said.

'Shut up,' Chavez said, leaning back in his chair again. 'I'm still asleep.'

31

It was just after four p.m. when Moco Goya parked his blue Chevy S-10 pickup nine houses down from the FBI bitch's house on Buttermilk Circle. Zambrano had sent a kid to watch her, and he said she must have knocked off work early, because she was already home. The kid was born without a right hand. He was eager to get some trigger time, but Zambrano said he should be a lookout for a while. Everyone called the kid Chueco, or 'crooked' – what you called a lefty. It was weird that the kid wasn't parked out front like he was supposed to be. Lucky for him, Zambrano didn't know he'd abandoned his post. He must have gone for a Coke or something. It didn't matter. Moco didn't need him anyway. He had Gusano, the village idiot.

The Worm sat in the passenger seat, gaping at the rows and rows of fancy homes like he'd never seen a nice house before. Moco cursed himself every time he brought the slow-witted *sicario* along – until the shooting started. Idiot or not, the Worm was a killing machine. In more than a dozen hits, Moco had never seen him hesitate. It was just getting to that point that was tedious.

Gusano turned and blinked like some kind of tree sloth. '*¡Güey!* What do you think these houses cost?'

Moco just shook his head and got out of the truck. Gusano was like a little kid. If you answered one question, he would only come up with another.

The houses were big, though probably not too expensive in the great scheme of things. An FBI agent lived here, after all, and she couldn't be knocking down enough to buy one of the real McMansions that were springing up all over North Dallas. These brick monstrosities had high roofs and wooden privacy fences to keep the neighbors from snooping on one another, but they were pretty much all the same, with a rock wall here or a wood panel there to give off the illusion that the developer had used more than four different blueprints. A wide concrete walking trail ran behind the houses on this street, winding along a low creek choked with cottonwood trees and impenetrable tangles of mustang grapevines. The developer probably advertised it as a greenbelt and the homeowners got a healthy charge in their yearly association dues for the privilege of living next to a swamp that the developer couldn't build on anyway.

No, the neighborhood around Buttermilk Circle wasn't exactly wealthy, but it was rich enough that Moco and Gusano couldn't just walk around without looking like they had a reason to be there. A couple Mexicans pushing lawn mowers for a bunch of white Texans was stereotypical – but Moco wanted to blend in, not climb up the social ladder.

It was warm, but Moco had fastened the top button on his Western shirt in order to hide most of the Santa Muerte tattoo. Gusano had a similar tattoo, but it was on his back, so a T-shirt was enough to hide his.

Moco opened the dented tailgate and slid out two treated two-by-six pieces of lumber before climbing into the bed and guiding the greasy lawn mower down the makeshift ramps. He wasn't even sure the old thing would run. Gusano grabbed a Weed Eater and the red gas can that contained their guns. As slow as he was, the Worm had figured out on his own that a five-gallon fuel jug could hold two TEC-9 machine pistols, two Glocks, and a break-open shotgun with both barrels sawed down to ten inches. He'd cut the red plastic with a jigsaw and then used a piano hinge and a couple hasps to keep his new gun vault closed while he carried it. The hasps were visible, but cops wouldn't even pay attention to a fuel jug.

They'd no sooner left the truck than an old guy with a young blond wife who was way too hot for his fat gut whistled Moco over as he pushed the mower past. The fat guy wanted to know if he had time to take on a new customer. Gusano was already in killing mode and braced beside him, setting the fuel jug on the sidewalk. Moco gave a slight shake of his head, hoping the crazy assassin noticed. In any other circumstance, he would have flipped the guy off – or maybe even beat his ass for disrespecting him with a whistle. But Moco smiled instead and said he'd drop back by when he was done with his present job and set something up. The lady, who obviously had better sense than her asshole husband, kept tugging on his hand to try to get him to follow her inside. The old man finally relented, listening to his wife for a moment, and then said not to worry about it.

Moco watched them walk inside and made a mental note of the address. The couple had gotten a good long look at him. He'd have to think about coming back and tying up that loose end. Moco chuckled to himself as the blonde peeked out a crack in her door one last time to give him the eye. Yeah, he'd come back, all right. It would be fun.

Moco pushed the lawn mower up the sidewalk until they reached the FBI lady's place. Gusano read the number on the mailbox. It was mottled red brick to match the house. 'Twenty-three forty-eight.'

'This is it, then,' Moco said, feeling the tightness in his lungs that he felt before every hit.

A large ceramic frog squatted among neatly trimmed shrubs along the concrete porch. Fresh wood chips covered the manicured area under a newly planted pecan tree in the front yard. This lady cop had obviously already hired another company to take care of her yardwork. Moco felt a pang of professional jealousy, and then remembered he wasn't there to do her lawn.

He'd expected to see an unmarked cop car out front, but the driveway was empty. The curtains moved a little, and he caught a sliver of light, so she had to be home. She'd probably just put the car in the garage. He studied the house as they approached. The gate to her backyard privacy fence stood open. Moco figured FBI agents probably traveled too much to have a dog, but the open gate calmed him nonetheless.

Gusano stopped on the sidewalk before they turned to walk to the front door. 'Can I go first?'

Moco didn't want to appear too eager. The Worm might mention it later and the boss might think he was a coward. But the truth was, he didn't mind at all if Gusano was first at the door. Lady cops died just like everyone else, but this one was certain to try to shoot back. The curtains had moved, so for all Moco knew, she was sighted in on him with her finger on the trigger. Being a cop, she was probably paranoid enough to have a shotgun by the front door. Hell, Moco wasn't even a cop and he had a shotgun by his front door.

'If you really want to go first,' he said, 'I guess that's okay.'

Gusano hefted the Weed Eater in a salute of gratitude and turned to walk quickly toward the door. Moco followed, standing off to the side toward the garage, clear of the line of fire in case the lady cop decided to go all Rambo on them.

Gusano set the fuel jug on the concrete porch between them and then reached down to flip the hasps, lifting the handle to reveal the guns inside. He made sure the TEC-9s were clear of the other weapons, butts pointed up, and then rang the doorbell.

A few moments later, there was a shuffle of movement inside. The door opened a crack.

'Lawn service —' Gusano said, throwing his weight against the door at the same moment he came up with the TEC-9. A shadowy figure fell away under the assault. There was a short, yelping scream as Gusano rushed in, hitting the door with such force that it rebounded off the wall and slammed shut behind him, leaving Moco standing outside on the porch.

Three quick pops followed, muffled by the heavy door. Moco threw a quick glance over his shoulder. The sprinkler across the street still hissed. Kids still played soccer in the nearby field.

With his own gun tucked in close to his waist, shielding it from view of passers-by, Moco reached for the door handle. Gusano opened it first, sticking his head out through the crack as if he wanted to spare Moco a look inside.

'Hey,' he said. 'I think we might have a problem.'

'What?'

'*Éste es un hombre rubio*,' he said.

Moco groaned and shouldered his way into the house. Sure enough, Gusano, the Worm, had just shot a man with blond hair.

'Is anyone else in the house?'

'Right.' Gusano grimaced. 'We should check.'

Moco thought about killing the idiot right then and there – but then there wouldn't be anyone to blame when they told the boss. Instead he stepped over the dead man and the two would-be hitmen searched the rest of the house. The blond man turned out to live alone.

'Where is she?' Moco said to himself while he stood over the dead man. He knew better than to engage Gusano with an important question. All three rounds from the Worm's TEC-9 had impacted him center-chest, killing him in seconds.

There was a wallet on the kitchen counter, next to some keys and a loaded Ruger LC9 pistol. Moco hoped against hope that this was another FBI agent – maybe the lady cop's boyfriend or something. He cursed when he found an ID card from a nearby mortgage company that identified the dead man as Aaron Bennet.

Gusano just stood and stared at the man he'd killed, nodding smugly, as if he were proud of his handiwork.

Moco glanced around the living room. Every piece of art, all the furniture, the photos above the mantel, all had to do with hunting and fishing. The few photos of women were of Bennet with the Dallas Cowboys cheerleaders or family shots with his mother. No females lived in this house.

Moco scratched his head. 'I don't get it. This is the house. Twenty-three forty-eight Buttermilk Circle.'

Gusano gave a sideways look. 'This is Buttermilk Place.'

Moco's hand tightened around the butt of his pistol. His head began to shake.

'Are you shitting me? You knew we were at the wrong address?'

The Worm shrugged. 'I was wondering why we came to Buttermilk Place.'

'We need to go,' Moco said through clenched teeth. 'Did you touch anything?'

'No,' Gusano said. 'You think I'm stupid?'

Moco didn't answer. The boss was going to hack them up alive with a chainsaw. But there was nothing they could do about it now. Too many people had seen them to risk another hit right now. But Moco was sure of one thing. There was only one way he could rectify his mistake. He had to find the FBI lady and kill her.

32

Helen Reid, Hendley Associates' chief pilot, battled white-knuckle downdrafts and a torrential downpour to bring the Gulfstream 550 in for a long landing, touching down farther along Runway 29 so she could scoot out of the way of an Aerolíneas Argentinas Airbus coming in behind her on final approach. A ground controller with excellent English got her off the runway quickly and guided her to the northeast corner of Buenos Aires's Ministro Pistarini International Airport, where she parked at the General Aviation terminal.

Jack and the other Campus operators were relieved to be back on terra firma and were packed and ready to go by the time she set the parking brake. The ownership of the Hendley jet was a matter of open record, but Argentines considered their country an extremely worthwhile destination for tourist travel, so the operators would just declare the purpose of their trip was pleasure and claim it was a company getaway.

The team traveled with passports issued by the State Department with all the appropriate biometrics for their cover identities. It was one of the benefits of having friends in extremely high places. Argentina's kidnapping rates had dropped some in recent years, but the son of the President of the United States made for an awfully tempting target.

Argentine Immigration and Customs required those arriving via private aircraft to carry all luggage inside the terminal for scanning and inspection while the aircraft remained locked behind a secure fence – which made bringing in the firearms problematic. Chavez solved the issue by having the pilots report a problem with an oil-pressure gauge. This necessitated a move to the nearby maintenance hangar, where Adara and Lisanne could pop in and retrieve the handguns and comms gear. The appropriate amount of exposed leg was still one of the most useful social-engineering mechanisms in the world. The women were much less likely to be challenged considering the Latin machismo of the country. Even so, they would tuck the pistols under their clothing just to be on the safe side.

Less than twenty minutes after they touched down, the team carried their bags out the front doors of the General Aviation terminal and sprinted through the late-afternoon downpour to locate the three rental cars that were supposed to be staged outside. The plan was for Adara and Lisanne to wait with the pilots and grab the guns once the Gulfstream was towed to the maintenance hangar while Ding, Midas, and Jack took the other two cars to check into their rooms at the Hotel Panamericano downtown.

Except there was only one rental car – a tiny orange Renault Clio hatchback.

Lisanne whipped out her cell phone like it was a weapon. With her black hair plastered to her cheeks, she stood in the driving rain and set about chastising the rental car company in a mixture of Spanish, Arabic, and English for making her look bad. No plan survived first contact. Shit happened. And luckily, this screwup didn't cost the team anything but wet clothes and time. Jack couldn't help but think her handling of the situation was pretty damned impressive.

Someone at the rental car company finally owned up to the mistake and promised to deliver the two larger cars to the hotel. Chavez, Midas, and Jack would cab it to the Panamericano with the bulk of the luggage. The pilots would drop Adara and the weapons off later and then return to their hotel nearer the airport with Lisanne. Clark had been clear that he didn't want them near any kind of surveillance operation, no matter how much Lisanne offered to help – which she did. A lot. They were crossing the line by having her help retrieve the pistols and comms gear, but that couldn't be helped unless they wanted to go in naked.

Chavez and Midas rode together in one cab while Jack, who spoke only enough Spanish to order a beer, piled into another one by himself with the rest of the luggage. His cabbie was an avuncular man named Rodrigo. Rodrigo, who had sandy hair and a philosophical bent, started speaking the moment Jack's door slammed shut.

It was rush hour and the Autopista Luis Dellepiane was bumper-to-bumper and door-to-door. Drivers appeared to pay no attention to the lane markings or the rain and oozed forward in a magma flow of steaming gridlock. Periodically, a motorcycle would find a gap and roar between the slower-moving cars, splitting lanes. Sometimes they missed the side mirrors. Sometimes they did not.

In the first five miles Jack counted at least a half-dozen

billboards displaying a variety of beautiful and long-legged women in classy clothing that, as far as he could tell, advertised various clinics that removed unwanted body hair. He would have joked with Midas about it, but then he considered all the crazy crap hawked on billboards in the United States and thought better of it.

Inching toward a tollbooth, Rodrigo pulled a one-hundred-peso note from his pocket. He must have seen Jack looking from the large bill to the sign above the booth that said he was in the lane for exact change.

'No one pays attention to the signs,' Rodrigo said in a slow but earnest voice. 'The price of toll changes every week or two.' He glanced in the rearview mirror. 'Inflation in my country . . . It is . . .' He held his hand in front of his face, fingers together in the gesture used to explain something important. 'It is . . . *subir como pedo de buzo* – how do you say? It rises like the fart of a scuba diver.'

Ryan wanted to chuckle at the imagery of bubbles shooting toward the surface, but the look on Rodrigo's face said the euphemism was no laughing matter.

They continued through the tollbooth after paying, inching down the *autopista* in the heavy traffic. Rodrigo used the time to give Ryan a crash course in Argentina, enlightening him on everything from the economy – he had to pay his mortgage in US dollars – to the beauty of Iguazu Falls – Ryan and everyone else in the world simply had to see this place at least once.

In a tediously slow but earnest voice, Rodrigo went on to declare that Argentine beef was the most delicious, Argentine women were beautiful beyond all description – especially when dancing the tango – and Argentine footballers possessed a superhuman talent at the game. Ryan was an Arsenal fan, but he kept quiet about that, knowing football – soccer to Americans – was a touchy subject in many parts of the world. Argentine fans often seemed to treat the act of simply attending a match as a blood sport.

Rodrigo continued. 'God gave Argentina the most beautiful rivers in all the world. He blessed Argentina with incredible mountains and fruits that are sweet above all others. Here in Argentina, God has planted fields that yield bushels of grain and endless pampas of grass, filled with herds of fat cattle and fine horses –'

Just then the driver of the car ahead of the taxi rolled down his window and tossed a full bag of trash onto the wet roadway. A piece of sopping-wet paper flew up and stuck to the cab's windshield, forcing Rodrigo to roll down his window and reach around to remove it.

The cabbie smoothed his sandy hair with a rain-soaked hand and glanced at Jack in the rearview mirror. 'And then God messed it all up by putting the Argentines here.'

The two cabs arrived within moments of each other, dropping Ryan, Chavez, and Midas at the Panamericano on Carlos Pelligrini, a short walk from the city's famous obelisk on a small one-way street that ran adjacent to the greenbelt and the fourteen-lane-wide Avenida 9 de Julio.

Ryan retrieved the luggage from the back of the taxi and paid the seven-hundred-peso fare – around forty US dollars. Rodrigo nodded and wished him well in a droning voice that sounded as if the cabbie was certain something ominous was going to befall him.

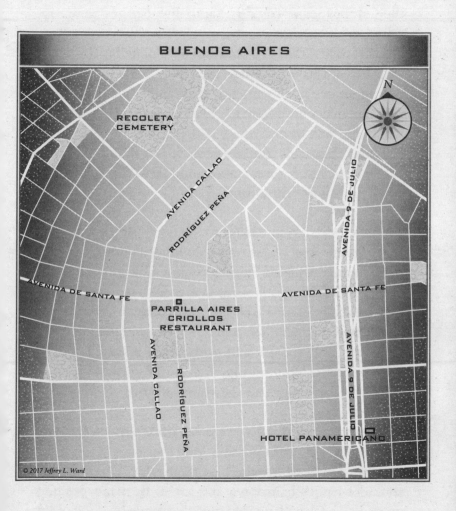

Ostensibly the Panamericano was a five-star hotel, and its limestone façade and turn-of-the-century signage looked welcoming enough after the long trip south, but it had just enough sketchy online reviews to make it unlikely the Campus team would run into anyone they were supposed to be watching.

Jack stacked the bags on a cart and looked at his watch and then at Chavez. 'What's the plan?'

'Argentines don't eat until after eight. We'll do some foot recon, but if we want to get a true picture of the place, we should wait to eat.'

Midas chuckled. 'You're just scared of Adara.'

'Well' – Chavez gave a mock shudder – 'she does spend a hell of a lot of time doing CrossFit.'

Three hours later, six blocks to the north of the hotel and seven blocks west of Avenida 9 de Julio, an attractive brunette named Amanda Salazar sat at a table at the back of the Parrilla Aires Criollos restaurant with her friend Beatriz, an equally attractive blonde. A set of rawhide *boleadoras*, a weighted throwing weapon of stone and rawhide, hung from the wall above them with other assorted gaucho paraphernalia. Multitasking, or at least multitasking skillfully, was impossible, so the young women divided their responsibilities.

Amanda's job was to laugh between sips of La Azul Malbec and bat her impossibly long eyelashes at the attentive older man who waited on their table. She wore her shoulder-length hair down and loose. Beatriz wore hers up, pulled back with unseen pins that made her look older, though at twenty-six she was actually the younger of the two.

Beatriz did her share of smiling as well, but she left flirting with the waiter to her partner. Under the table, the blonde concentrated on her work, wiggling the face off the heating vent with the tip of her toe.

Parrilla Aires Criollos was an upscale restaurant with gaucho decor, tile floors, and crisp white tablecloths. As the name implied, it served Argentine cuisine and grilled meat with a distinctly Spanish flair. The long tablecloths, aided by Amanda's entrancing laugh, helped to conceal the tedious work removing the vent cover.

Amanda and Beatriz were dressed in stylish blouses and skirts, each wearing just enough makeup and jewelry to make them attractive but not especially memorable. Classy dress was the norm in Buenos Aires, and dressing down would have garnered more attention. Each woman carried a brown leather briefcase, leading people to think they were lawyers, or perhaps some other brand of young professional women who had decided to grab some dinner before they got an early start at some of the local clubs.

Tonight, they had chosen to arrive exactly at eight p.m. The restaurant was busy enough that all eyes would not be focused on them but not so crowded that they would have trouble finding a table in the area they wanted. They'd come in for a late lunch two days earlier, locating the area where they would have to sit in order to accomplish their mission. The area near the bar, it seemed, was reserved for private functions. But if no such function was scheduled, guests were seated here when all the other tables were filled. A visit to the restrooms during their lunchtime visit took the young women near enough to locate the vent cover and devise their plan.

Either woman was capable of removing a vent or captivating the emotions of all manner of man or woman. They had met Franco, the waiter, on this previous visit. Whether he intended to or not, the man's extra attention to Amanda's water glass made it obvious that he was smitten with the beautiful brunette. He took her order first and smiled his thin smile when he gave her his suggestion for just the right pairing of wine and food. Far from being jealous, Beatriz had considered this a happy circumstance and allowed it to dictate their respective duties the following night. She would much rather deal with high explosives than the attentions of an overly attentive waiter with greasy hair.

Tonight, Amanda had caught Franco's eye across the long and narrow dining room as soon as they came through the door. He rushed forward, still carrying a tray of dirty glasses he'd just cleaned off one of the tables, greeting her effusively. She pointed out the area near the bar and begged to sit there.

Like most instances where women preplanned their dealings with men, it was all too easy.

The scouting visit on the previous evening revealed the heating vents were held in place by friction rather than screws. In theory, this should have made it easier to remove. Beatriz kicked off her shoe as soon as they sat down, going straight to work with her toe. The metal louver appeared to be glued in place at first, but she finally got it to budge a little by pushing the face back and forth rather than trying to simply hook it with her nail and pull it out. Eventually, she was able to wiggle it out. She felt the metal and surrounding boxy collar slide free from the wood panel at the same moment Franco chose to visit their table. Beatriz was just able to catch the piece of metal with her bare foot and wedge it against the wall. The waiter smiled at Amanda, paying Beatriz no attention at all, and placed a platter containing their *picada* on the table. The girls' accents gave away the fact that they were not from Argentina, and Franco felt it a duty to explain the bits of baked cheese and sliced meat people from his beloved country ate before a main meal. Beatriz balanced the grate in place, keeping her face passive while the arch of her foot began to spasm and cramp. Amanda noted her friend's discomfort and asked Franco to suggest another wine for them to try. He scurried off to find 'something just right' for the beautiful *señorita* who had chosen to return to his restaurant.

Beatriz sighed with relief when she let the grate slip to the floor and come to rest on top of her foot. Franco was a waiter and therefore not trained in the art of espionage or tradecraft – but surely any man with his pudgy physique and halting demeanor would suspect that two attractive women he'd only just met might have ulterior motives.

One of them might, perhaps, be trying to distract him while her friend placed a bomb inside the wall of his restaurant.

Beatriz gave a whispered scoff, shaking her head at Amanda. 'Hope. It is every man's demise.'

Amanda raised her eyebrows, the facial equivalent of a shrug. 'And the downfall of most women,' she said.

The bomb itself was small, made from military-grade RDX. A key component of C-4 was cyclotrimethylen-etrinitramine. The name was a mouthful, so the British developers simply called it Research Department eXplosive. This particular batch of RDX was manufactured at a munitions plant outside Islamabad. Pakistani operatives were fond of the stuff and had used it to great effect in bombings against India and the West. Motor oil or some other carbon-based product was often mixed with the explosive to mask the material's origin. Amanda and Beatriz left it plain. They wanted investigators to know the RDX came from Pakistan. Their briefcase device contained half a kilo of the plasticized material, a bit of PETN, and a blasting cap with a detonator attached to an arming device and then a mobile phone – also from Pakistan.

As the two women talked, Beatriz used her foot to lift and push her briefcase into the space behind the vent cover. It took only a moment, and stooping slightly, she was able to replace the cover before Franco returned with a bottle of Schroeder Merlot from Patagonia.

To his shame, Amanda said she preferred the earlier Malbec, and he slunk away with the open bottle.

Fairly giddy with the success of this portion of their mission, the women dug into the contents of the *picada*. Beatriz absentmindedly twirled a lock of blond hair over her ear as she began to peruse the menus, getting down to the business of deciding what to have for dinner. It turned out that placing a bomb was very good for one's appetite.

Neither woman noticed the tall, bearded man with the fit-looking blonde. The well-dressed couple stopped just inside the front door, both scanning the now crowded restaurant as if looking for just the perfect table.

33

Moco almost hit his head on the roof of his S-10 pickup when his mobile phone began to buzz in the front pocket of his jeans. He nearly ran a fat woman in a green minivan off the road. She flipped him off, which would have normally caused him to chase her down, if only to scare her for disrespecting him. Instead, he took a deep breath and imagined the woman's head sitting on a fence post. Maybe later. That calmed him down some. The phone buzzed again, but Moco let it. He was terrified that it might be Zambrano, checking on the status of the hit. The *sicario* had felt like he was about to throw up ever since Gusano wasted the wrong dude. Not because he felt any remorse at Aaron Bennet's death, but because he knew that Zambrano would very literally set him on fire if they didn't kill the FBI bitch today. This Callahan *puta* had her federal fingers all over the boss's North Texas operation – and Zambrano had made it clear. He wanted those fingers floating in a jar of tequila on his mantel by the time he went to bed – pretty nail polish and all.

The danger of being stopped with the guns inside the plastic gas jug post-shooting scared the shit out of Moco. He'd never wanted a joint so bad in his life. Gusano just sat in the passenger seat of the S-10 and listened to his playlist. Nothing ever bothered him. Stupid bastard.

Special Agent Kelsey Callahan lived alone, but Moco

fully expected her to be armed. She was sure to put up a fight, so he couldn't very well get rid of all the guns if he wanted to get the job done. Still, he left the kid watching her house and did a quick run over to Lake Lavon to dump the TEC-9 so there wouldn't be any ballistics to match the bullets in Aaron Bennet's chest. There was a metric shit-ton of work to do if they were going to find their way around Gusano's mistake. Moco had started saying it that way in his head right after the shooting, throwing the blame to the Worm by calling it 'Gusano's mistake.' Maybe the boss would believe it if he said it enough times.

Moco leaned back from the steering wheel to dig out the phone in the middle of the fourth ring. It was Chueco, the kid who was sitting on Callahan's house.

'Some guy just drove up and went to her door,' Chueco said. 'Tall, dark beard. Looks like a tough dude. She let him in, so I guess she knows him.'

Moco mulled over this new information. A new guy would add a wrinkle to the problem, but it might even help. If he was a boyfriend, maybe his presence would mess with Callahan's mind, make her easier to take. He had a sudden thought.

'Is this guy a cop?'

'I don't know about him,' Chueco said. 'But about five minutes after he got here, a bunch of cops showed up on the next street over. There must be a dozen marked cars. Must be something bad.'

The kid had no idea.

'Sit tight,' Moco said. 'We'll be parked at the 7-Eleven up the street. Let us know when the cops clear out – or if Callahan leaves.'

'She left already,' Chueco said.

Moco stomped on the gas. There was always the risk of getting pulled over, but he figured every cop within fifteen miles was already at Buttermilk Place.

'What do you mean gone? Did the guy go with her?'

'He did,' the kid said. 'They got in her car and followed another cop over to the commotion on the next street. Want me to get closer and see what's going on?'

'No!' Moco snapped, maybe a little too quickly.

Gusano looked over at him, wires hanging from his ears, head bobbing to his tunes.

'Just stay where you can see her car,' Moco said. 'Call me when she moves again.'

'*'Tá bueno*, bye.' Chueco ended the call now that he had his assignment.

Moco eased off the accelerator, feeling an unseen hand tighten around his gut. This was all coming down too fast for him to process. Damn, he really needed some weed.

Special Agent Kelsey Callahan stood over the body of the man she'd never met and clenched her fists until she was afraid her nails might tear through the blue nitrile gloves. Two crime scene technicians from the Garland, Texas, police department busied themselves placing yellow plastic markers on the floor, enumerating the location of three spent shell casings and several boot prints on the polished slate floor around the entry. A uniformed officer photographed the interior of the house while a handful of other officers combed the yard and interviewed the neighbors for any clue as to who had murdered Aaron Bennet.

One of the uniforms, a sergeant named Morris, had served on the Crimes Against Children Task Force for a couple years and knew Callahan lived nearby. He'd snapped to the similar address and taken it upon himself to inform her of the homicide – much to the chagrin of Detective Fran Little, who made it extremely clear that she didn't want the Feeble Eyes getting their Fed gunk on her homicide case.

Detective Little hitched up the thighs of her 5.11 khakis and squatted on the other side of the body with a digital camera. 'You know this guy?' she asked without looking up.

'Never met him,' Callahan said. 'It's obvious what happened, though.'

The detective stood, pushing a lock of straw-colored hair off her forehead with the back of her gloved hand. 'And how's that?'

Callahan bit her tongue to keep from saying what she really wanted to say. 'I guess there's a chance this guy has gambling debts or a jilted lover, but there's a more obvious answer. This is 2348 Buttermilk Place. I live at 2348 Buttermilk Circle.'

Detective Little raised both eyebrows, like Callahan was some kid she was trying to humor. 'I'd rather look at the evidence in total, if you don't mind.'

'I'm pointing out all the evidence,' Callahan said. 'If you don't –'

'Better check yourself,' Detective Little said. 'It sounds like you're about to give me an ultimatum, and I don't respond well to those.'

Callahan closed her eyes and took a slow breath. 'I was going to say, "If you don't see it, I can spell it out for you."'

Detective Little scoffed. 'Well, ain't that just downright neighborly of you. Makes me feel a lot better.'

'The only motive to kill Aaron Bennet is that he happens to live at an address similar to mine.'

Caruso touched Callahan on the elbow to guide her gently away. The shrinks at Quantico taught that this was one of the most unthreatening places to touch most people, but apparently Callahan was not most people. She jerked away and glared as though she might punch him in the face.

'Look,' Detective Little said. 'We will get around to checking with any people who want you dead. I can imagine that list will be a long one. But if I'm not doin' my job in the order you deem fit, well, I got plenty of more important things to do than stand around here and argue. Be my guest if you want to take over. I'll have my guys out of here so fast your head will spin, lady.'

Callahan turned as if to walk away, then wheeled. 'You listen, Fran. I'm not trying to piss on your leg. I'm merely pointing out that the person who killed this guy was really after me. When you snap to that fact, give me a call.'

Moco needed weed so bad. But he couldn't chance it with so many cops swarming all over the place. Luckily, there was enough hash oil hidden in the door panel of his truck for two dabs. Making the hash oil was tricky business, requiring him to boil off the liquid butane he used to extract it from the buds. High heat and butane didn't go well together, so the process took forever. When he was finished, he had an amber, honeylike substance packed with THC.

Moco liked to put a little dab of the sticky stuff on the end of a nail and smoke it. The buzz helped him think straight. Problem was, that would be almost as noticeable as smoking a joint – and he didn't want to go there. Dabs tasted like shit if you ate them straight, but he had a plan. A lighter, a metal spoon, and a little bit of coconut oil he kept in the glovebox would help the dab slide down quickly – even if it didn't do much about the taste.

He wedged the spoon in the crack of the center console to hold it, and then added a dab – about the size of a Tic Tac – with a half-teaspoon of coconut oil. He was just in the middle of mixing the concoction with the point of his pocketknife when his phone began to vibrate again.

'Hold this,' he said, passing the mixture of dab and coconut oil to Gusano, who took his earbuds out and blinked stupidly. 'Don't spill it.'

Gusano promptly stuck the spoon in his mouth and slurped down the whole thing.

Moco wanted to stab the idiot, and would have had he not needed help. He punched him in the shoulder instead.

'What?' the Worm said. 'I thought you gave it to me.'

Moco shook his head and answered the phone.

It was Chueco again. 'She's coming your way,' the kid said. 'That tough-looking dude with the beard is with her.'

'Follow her,' Moco said. He hung up and then looked across the seat at Gusano, still fuming over the stolen hash oil. He spoke through clenched teeth, hardly able to sit still. 'You son of a bitch.'

Gusano nodded at the crumpled piece of plastic wrap in Moco's lap. 'What? You got another one. I'll help you make some more after we kill the FBI lady.'

'You better,' Moco said, still glaring. He peeled back the plastic and bit off the rest of the hash oil, clenching his teeth at the bitterness. Eating it straight wouldn't give him nearly as good a high as when it was mixed with oil, but it would have to be enough.

Callahan's unmarked Expedition rolled by the 7-Eleven and Moco threw the pickup in gear. At least he was starting to get the 'dab sweats.' Maybe he'd be thinking straight enough to kill the right person this time.

34

The thing Magdalena Rojas first noticed about Ernie Pacheco was his teeth. This would have pleased him had she mentioned it, because he'd paid a lot of money for them. She remembered that her father had had a nice smile, but this man they called Matarife was different. His perfect smile was starkly mismatched to the rest of his craggy, misshapen face. She'd heard he was injured in a bar fight, but whatever the cause, his flat nose looked like it had been melted and then smeared above his lip. An asterisk-shaped scar puckered the sunken flesh under his left eye. The ear on that same side was a mass of scar tissue. He kept his dark hair pulled back in a thick man bun. He seemed to believe the style anchored him to a more youthful appearance, but Magdalena thought it just called attention to the severity of the mess that he called a face. Oddly, while all those who followed him were adorned with images of La Santa Muerte, Matarife, the self-professed leader of her cult, did not have a single tattoo on his body.

Magdalena had met the man many times, but he never paid for her, even when she'd belonged to Dorian or Parrot. He took her just the same, always pretending like it was all her idea and that she should be happy because he was saving her from the other guys. It pissed off Parrot, but he never said anything. He just chopped her when Matarife left.

He sat across from her now, naked, chewing on a bite of rare steak and gesturing at her with his knife as he spoke. He liked to eat dinner without his clothes. Magdalena didn't care. Like most things that had to do with sex that didn't cause her too much pain, she'd grown numb to it. But he hit her if she didn't giggle and raise her eyebrows up and down and pretend she was impressed. She had seen many naked men, and apart from the black hair that covered his body like a wild ape, there was nothing impressive about him.

He nudged aside a small silver cross and picked a bit of fallen meat from his matted chest hair, looking at it for a moment to see what it was before popping it between his perfect teeth.

He pointed with the steak knife again. 'I should tell you of Matarife's trip to Colombia,' he said. 'It was very dangerous.'

He boasted a great deal for someone who didn't care about impressing her. She supposed he was bragging to himself. He liked to speak of things that made him seem handsome and tough and smart. Magdalena thought he was none of these things, except perhaps tough, considering the scars on his face. Well, maybe he was a little bit smart, or else he would not have been so rich. He wasn't smart enough to take her straight to Zambrano's like he was supposed to, that was for sure. Ernie Pacheco was a cruel man, but Zambrano was crueler, and would kill him for disobedience. Probably.

He looked at her with his narrow pig eyes, the left one even narrower because of the scar. 'You not gonna eat? You haven't touched anything.'

She faked a smile. 'I am not hungry. You want another beer?' She hoped he'd eaten so much meat and drunk enough beer that he'd just fall asleep. Guys did that sometimes, so she always asked them if they wanted more.

He pushed back from the table and clapped his hands, rubbing them together like a housefly. The man bun, the strange eyes. He looked a lot like a fly, she thought.

He rubbed his hairy belly and gave a long sigh. 'Hey,' he said. 'I got an idea that will help us get in the mood.'

Magdalena groaned inside, struggling to keep up the fake smile.

He put his hand behind her back and gave her a shove. It didn't knock her over, but there was no doubt that she had no choice about going to the bedroom.

'We'll watch one of my movies,' he said, chuckling a little. He gave her another shove, harder this time. 'It'll be fun. You might even know some of the stars.'

35

Dominic Caruso accelerated Kelsey Callahan's Bureau-issued Ford Expedition down the on-ramp of the President George Bush Turnpike, heading toward Plano. He'd insisted on driving, despite Callahan's objections. She already suspected him of being complicit in the murder of a couple cartel members, though she hadn't said much about it, but the run-in with the Garland PD detective had left her leg bouncing like the needle on a sewing machine. Caruso considered talking to her about the incident but quickly decided that he was in mortal danger of getting his head bitten off.

Turf wars notwithstanding, whoever killed Aaron Bennet had come gunning for Callahan. The fact that the killer or killers went to Buttermilk Place instead of Buttermilk Circle gave Caruso a little peek into their intellect and psyche – but, in his experience, assassins hit the wrong person more than a quarter of the time. Two of the first fugitive cases during his early career – when he worked for the FBI more than just on paper – had been victims of mistaken identity. In both cases, the killers had realized the screwup and rectified it in short order.

Caruso checked the rearview mirror several times a minute as he drove, knowing that the people who wanted Callahan dead were very likely back there now. Traffic was heavy and it was getting dark, which would work to

Caruso's favor if he needed to avoid an attack but made it easy for any bad actors to blend into the sea of headlights behind him.

He took the exit toward Campbell Road, watching to see if anyone followed. Three sets of lights came off behind him. He turned left to pass back under the freeway, but instead of continuing down Campbell, he camped out at the green light, squirting through just as it turned red to make a quick left back up the frontage road to the east, paralleling the turnpike back in the direction they'd come from. No one behind him did anything crazy to follow.

Callahan turned to look at him but said nothing. She obviously knew he was working to shake off any unseen tails.

Caruso glanced across the dim interior of the Expedition. 'How long since you've had anything to eat?'

'I'm fine,' Callahan said.

Caruso decided to press the issue. 'Seriously. How long?'

She gave a dismissive shrug. 'I don't know. I had that coffee for breakfast.'

'Before that?' Caruso said. 'I've been with you since before seven this morning and I haven't seen you eat so much as a breath mint. You're starting to look a little hollow around the cheeks.'

Callahan beat her head against the headrest. 'We've known each other for what, twenty-six hours? I don't think you're allowed to call me too skinny.'

'What?' Caruso grinned. 'You've called me bastard, son of a bitch, and asshole – along with pretty much every other name in the book over that same time period.'

'I did not.'

'Not even in your brain?'

Callahan laughed out loud. 'That doesn't count.'

Caruso turned his head to look at her as he drove. 'So you admit it?'

'I admit that I may have thought one or two unflattering things about you.'

'Good,' Caruso said. 'Then I'll admit *I* am hungry. Can we please get something to eat?'

Moco pounded his hands against the steering wheel, craning his head left and right in search of the lady cop's Expedition. He cursed Gusano for eating the dab. He'd been forced to eat the rest of his hash oil plain. Without the benefit of the coconut oil, it wasn't doing a damn bit of good.

Taillights flashed and blinked in a confusing river of red. Oncoming headlights blinded him. She'd gotten away from him – and now the boss was going to set him on fire – or pump him full of so much dope he wouldn't pass out while the guys cut his feet off with a chainsaw.

This. Could. Not. Be. Happening.

The Worm sat with his nose pressed against the passenger window, head bobbing to his tunes. He held one of the Glocks in his lap, which was the only thing keeping Moco from shooting the stupid bastard in the back of the head.

Moco's mobile phone buzzed as he merged back onto the turnpike. It was the kid.

'What?'

'You want me to wait outside or follow them in?'

Moco's stomach did a flip. 'What are you talking about?'

'They're going into the restaurant,' the kid said. 'Want me to sit on her car?'

'What restaurant?' Moco shot a look at Gusano. 'Never mind. Just tell me where you're at. We'll meet you outside.'

'Texas Roadhouse,' the kid said. 'I'm on the north side of the parking lot.'

'Wait there for us.' Moco ended the call. He turned to Gusano, suddenly feeling as if he might make it through the night without getting his feet sawed off. Even his anger at the Worm began to fade. 'Get ready, my friend.'

Gusano raised an eyebrow. 'Are you certain we are going to the correct restaurant?' His tone said he was serious.

Ten minutes after he cut back under the turnpike at Brand Road, Caruso sat with his back to the wall across the booth from Callahan, watching her slather cinnamon butter on a Texas Roadhouse hot roll. She spoke with her hands as much as her voice and was imbued with such energy and fervor that her red hair bounced in time to her words. The food animated her and she appeared to forget about Detective Little and the dead bodies at Matarife's ranch.

Two hot rolls down, Callahan suddenly put both hands flat on the table and looked across at Caruso with narrow eyes. 'You know why they're trying to kill me, don't you?'

Caruso started to say something, but she cut him off.

'It's not because I've gotten into their business, if that's what you were going to say. I muck up people's illegal criminal enterprises all the time.'

'Okay.' Caruso shrugged. 'Enlighten me.'

Callahan gave a tired smile. 'It's because they don't think I'm playing by the rules.'

'But you are.' Caruso did a quick scan of the room before making eye contact to show he was listening.

'Ah,' Callahan said. 'But they don't know that. Your buddy, John – or whatever his name is – grabs Flaco and pressures information out of him, and then blows away Matarife's yard help and his girlfriend . . . naked in the swimming pool. Except your friend's pretty good at staying hidden, so they can't find him. I'm the face of the investigation, so they're coming after me.'

Caruso put his hands on the table as well, an interrogation tool called mirroring. She'd be familiar with it, but he did it anyway. 'I want you to think about something,' he said, keeping his voice low. 'Do you honestly believe that someone who calls himself "the Slaughterer" and sells human beings at online auctions or murders them on camera really gives two shits if you play by the rules? I doubt he even sees any rules.'

Callahan shrugged. 'Maybe not,' she said. 'I thought it might get you to spill something useful about your friend John . . . What was his name again? I know he's gone off the reservation – and when this is over, it'll be my job to stop him. Our job, really.'

'Nice try,' Caruso said. 'I need to hit the restroom. If the waitress comes back while I'm gone, order me a bone-in ribeye, medium rare, and broccoli.'

Callahan nodded, eyeing the last roll. 'Are you gonna eat that?'

The restrooms were to the right, but Dominic Caruso turned left, heading for the front door. There were several emergency exits, but there was only one public entrance to the restaurant, and he'd made sure he had a table that watched the door. It wasn't likely, but anyone who was bound and determined to kill Callahan might decide to come in through the kitchen. Caruso decided he'd do a quick check of the parking lot to look for anything out of the ordinary. Their waitress caught him as he was walking past a big barrel of peanuts in an alcove just inside the front door.

'Everything all right, hon?' the young woman with wide hips and a black ponytail asked.

Caruso held up the keys to the Expedition. 'I forgot something in the car,' he said. 'I think my friend could use some more hot rolls, though.'

The cowbell on the front door clanged, and Caruso saw the reflections of two men in the plate-glass window as they entered behind him. The waitress said something about getting the rolls for Callahan, but Dominic stopped listening as soon as he saw the Santa Muerte tattoo on the reflection of the man in the lead. He was short and stocky, with the brim of a tattered denim baseball cap pulled low over a flat nose. The man behind him was taller and staggered a little, like he might have had a bit too much to drink. Both wore their shirttails untucked – a convenient way to hide handguns.

Caruso kept his back to the men and his head down.

'It's a forty-five-minute wait,' the hostess told the two men, obviously hoping to persuade the shady newcomers to go somewhere else.

'That's okay,' the man with the flat nose said. 'We're meeting friends. We'll find them.'

Caruso waited for both men to walk past before holding a finger to his lips so the waitress could see. When they were out of earshot, he leaned in and said, 'I'm FBI, call nine-one-one and tell them there are federal agents on scene.'

'What –'

'Do it now!' Caruso hissed. He reached inside his shirt collar to pull out a gold FBI badge, letting it hang from a chain around his neck. Ahead of him, the men worked their way around the bar area, stopping to look at each booth as they went by. Callahan was on the other side of the restaurant, short enough that she was hidden behind a high wooden barrier. Caruso had taken the gunfighter seat, so her back was to the door. He estimated the men would be on top of her in less than a half a minute.

He rested his right hand on the .40-caliber Glock 22 in the holster under his jacket. There was no way to know how many off-duty cops were in the restaurant. He didn't want to draw the pistol too early, for fear of a blue-on-blue shooting. He took out his cell phone with his left hand, glancing down just long enough to punch in Callahan's number.

It went immediately to voice mail.

Caruso cursed under his breath.

Thirty feet ahead, the guy with the flat nose motioned to his partner, who had stopped to watch a soccer game above the bar. The taller man shrugged, swayed on his feet a little, and then the two men turned down the row of booths where Callahan sat. She was in the back corner, the one that had given Caruso the wall – which meant that they'd get to her last. But it also meant she wouldn't see them until they were almost in her lap.

Caruso took slow breaths, planning his next move. The wall beyond the two bad guys made for a decent enough backstop. But the booths on either side were packed with people. A little boy climbed in and out of the booth where his parents sat, and chased crayons that rolled across the floor. Caruso was an excellent shot, but little kids were like quicksilver in their ability to dart into the line of fire.

The two guys from Santa Muerte were five paces away now, so intently focused on what they'd figured out had to be Callahan's booth that they didn't bother to look behind them. The taller one was now in the lead.

Caruso picked up his speed, closing the distance in moments. He could sweep his jacket, draw, and fire two rounds from the Glock in a hair under one second. But the men were both armed, and stacked one in front of the other. He'd have to shoot more than twice, and those would have to be head shots.

Caruso's hand closed around the grip of his Glock when the tall guy and Flat Nose were four steps from the booth. He shouted, 'FBI!' at exactly the same moment a teenage boy to his right slid into the aisle to block his path.

The Santa Muerte soldiers spun, dragging pistols from under their shirts.

Caruso grabbed the teenager with his left hand and shoved him sideways, out of the line of fire, while he brought the Glock up. The startled kid had no idea what was going on and fought back, infuriated that Caruso would lay hands on him. He grabbed at the table in an effort to push himself up, screaming bloody murder. Caruso pulled the gun back to keep the kid from knocking it out of his hand – or accidentally eating the barrel.

36

Bonnie Porcaro had just taken a bite of her medium-rare ribeye when she heard what sounded like a very angry man in the aisle behind her booth. A petite blond woman in her mid-sixties, she had grown up in Harlingen, which was just about as close as one could get to Mexico and still be in Texas. She hadn't been back to her hometown in more than twenty years, but she still understood enough Spanish to know what a man behind her had whispered.

'Time to kill the whore.'

That just wasn't something good men said, even if they were joking. The slurred tone of his gravel voice told Bonnie this man was deadly serious.

Her husband, Mike, sat across from her. He started to say something, but she raised her hand, shushing him. They'd been married more than four decades and he knew all too well when she was serious. At the same time, Bonnie Porcaro reached beneath the table with her right hand and drew a stainless-steel Kimber K6s .357 revolver from a simple pancake holster under her vest. The vest was stylish lightweight cotton and suited a woman of her age. It also did a nice job of hiding her sidearm – which she was seldom without.

Bonnie had done her research, quizzing her nephew, who was a detective with the Dallas PD, and watching dozens of videos of different models on the Hickok45

YouTube channel. This was the first gun and holster she'd ever owned.

Bonnie wasn't a gun nut any more than a person who needed a pickup and bought one for a certain purpose was a truck fanatic. She did not concern herself with all the fancy gadgets and gizmos in the firearms culture. Still, she was practical and went to the range with her girl-friends once a month, religiously presenting the weapon the same way each time she took it out of the holster at night as her instructor had taught her. The little Kimber was plenty for her needs – and she was a heck of a shot. Her nephew told her so.

Her husband's eyes grew wide as she brought the weapon up. He didn't say anything or try to be a hero.

Bonnie had this.

She shifted her body sideways in the booth, head toward the wall, feet toward the aisle and the threat. She was aware of the booth across from her, which was thankfully empty, making her shoot/don't-shoot decision a little simpler.

Bonnie's finger tightened on the trigger as the front sight of her Kimber covered a tall and slovenly Hispanic man who was clutching a pistol that was tucked down into his waistband. He staggered, dragging his feet as if he were intoxicated. Definitely a bad guy.

A male voice to the left suddenly yelled, 'FBI!' causing her to pause her shot.

Bonnie hardly had time to blink before the redheaded woman in the next booth swung around the corner with a long pepper grinder in both hands like a baseball bat. She bashed the tall man in the face, dropping him at the same moment that a second man, this one with a flat nose, staggered by. His attention split between the FBI agent behind him and the woman who'd just bashed his friend in the face, and the flat-nosed man roared, spewing curses in Spanish as he drew a black pistol from under his shirt.

Bonnie Porcaro let the man's silhouette blur, focusing on the Kimber's front sight as she pressed the double-action-only trigger. Her instructor had told her over and over that slow was smooth and smooth was fast. The pistol barked twice. It was so loud on the range, but, oddly to Bonnie, it seemed to make no noise as it fired. She wasn't even sure it had fired, and then thought maybe she'd missed if it had. The man with the flat nose just turned his head to look at her, as though he was put out by her behavior. He started to bring his gun around, but she'd already adjusted her aim and pressed the trigger again. The Kimber's third bullet punched an almost perfect hole in the bridge of his flat nose.

He lingered there for a moment, then pitched sideways on top of his dazed friend, who'd just been smacked with the pepper grinder.

'FBI,' a man's voice said again to her left. 'Ma'am. Please put down your weapon.'

Bonnie slowly lowered the Kimber to the table before raising both empty hands above her head. She'd trained for this as well. Across the table, Mike stared at her slack-jawed, as if he wasn't quite certain who he'd been sleeping with for the last forty-four years.

Dominic Caruso secured the blond woman's revolver while he aimed his own weapon at the guy Callahan had clobbered with the pepper grinder. Callahan had her handcuffs out and was already moving in. She looked up at the blonde.

'You okay?'

'He was going to shoot you,' the woman said. Her hands were still up, but she was remarkably composed for someone who'd just blown off the back of a man's skull.

Callahan slapped the cuffs on the moaning assassin and smiled. 'You can relax, ma'am,' she said. 'Lucky for me you're a good shot.' She looked up at Caruso. 'And that you had the good sense to call my cell. I knew something was up because you'd just left. I did a quick peek over the booth and saw these rocket scientists wander in.'

Caruso scanned the restaurant, looking for any other would-be assassins. These guys tended to travel in packs. He saw no immediate threats, but what he did see was at least five more restaurant patrons with their hands either on the butt of an exposed sidearm or in a purse getting ready to draw one.

'FBI,' he said again. 'Everyone please relax and keep your firearms where they are.' He chuckled and helped Callahan to her feet. 'Texas appears to be a bad place to become an assassin.'

The blond citizen who'd saved the day gave a solemn nod, her hands just beginning to shake from the post-shooting adrenaline dump.

'You got that right, hon,' she said.

37

The alarm on Jack Ryan, Jr's cell phone began to chime at two a.m., nudging him awake with gradually increasing volume. He'd read somewhere that being jolted out of a deep sleep was a good way to suffer brain damage – and if that was the case, he and most of the people he knew were in serious trouble.

He pumped out thirty quick push-ups to clear his head and then suffered through a moment of benign panic that there was no hot water in the shower, until he remembered that the C on the faucet did not stand for *cold*. After a shower that was plenty *caliente*, he wiped the fog off the mirror and took a few moments to square away his beard with a razor and a small pair of scissors he carried for that purpose. He'd recently shaved down to a mustache – but he was glad to have the beard back. People said he looked like his dad. He didn't see it. The full beard kept others from seeing it as well.

Ryan had taken the time to lay out his clothes and gear before his nap – he shot a quick glance as the tritium hands on his watch – just four hours before.

The area recon had been interesting if only for total immersion in the European-ness of Buenos Aires.

Lisanne Robertson had dropped Adara off an hour and a half behind the others – and stayed to check personally that the rental-car company had come through on their promise. The valet in the lobby of the Panamericano Hotel assured her that there was a Peugeot 408 and a Renault Duster parked in the garage. Like just about every other rental vehicle in Argentina, both had manual transmissions, a fact that drew a twinkle from every Campus member's eye. They'd all attended numerous driving schools, and there was nothing like a stick shift to spur the last few horses out of an otherwise humdrum ride.

Lisanne had grudgingly returned to her airport hotel only after a direct order from Chavez. She'd suggested she could provide countersurveillance and force protection. It sounded like a good idea to Ryan, but Ding would have none of it.

They'd given Adara a few minutes to check in and get settled before spending the next three hours doing recon around Parrilla Aires Criollos. Any surveillance of Vincent Chen was likely to end up on foot anyway, so they opted to leave the vehicles parked and walk the few blocks between the hotel and the restaurant. It was their only lead, so they would exploit it until they found something better.

They'd walked in teams of two, going north on Avenida 9 de Julio, with Jack and Adara making up one team while Chavez and Midas brought up the rear. Ninth of July Avenue, so named for the date of Argentina's independence from Spain, was lined with a greenbelt and many parks and fountains on either side. It was touted as the widest city street in the world.

Ryan had been warned not to refer to himself as an American. People in South America took issue with citizens of the United States coopting that title for themselves. Argentines customarily took siestas in the afternoon and worked late. It was dark by the time the team had ventured out, and many businessmen and -women were just beginning to get off work. Avenida 9 de Julio was flooded with tourists at this temperate time of the South American spring. Members of the middle and upper classes tended to dress in business casual for nearly all endeavors that didn't require business dress. It had been an easy matter for Jack to pick out the T-shirt-and-Bermuda-shorts-wearing tourists in the crowds.

Argentina's high inflation made for a thriving underground currency exchange. Called *arbolitos*, or 'little trees,' for their propensity to spring up everywhere, these men and women stood at strategic points along the avenue, usually in front of stores that sold high-end merchandise, and whispered '*Cambio, cambio*' – change, change – as wealthy tourists walked by. Their jobs required *arbolitos* to carry a large amount of cash, and though it was probably lost on an average tourist, Ryan noted that there was always a second standing a few yards away, no doubt protecting the person but also – more important for the black-market investors – the money.

The Campus operators had strolled through the Recoleta district, exploring the iconic cemetery and El Gran Gomero, the enormous supposedly two-hundred-year-old rubber tree, the crown of which spanned fifty meters. Ryan found it pleasant and even refreshing to incorporate a little tourism into his recon – even if he was out for a walk with his cousin's girlfriend and not a girlfriend of his own. This line of work sucked the life out of relationships.

Eventually, he and Adara had used a visit to the inside of Parrilla Aires Criollos as an excuse to have a nice sit-down dinner. Chavez and Midas waited outside. No one thought there was much danger that they were being followed yet, but the last thing they wanted to do was huddle up together in a venue of interest to Vincent Chen. Beyond that, Ding had been to Argentina before and he knew a place that made 'killer empanadas'; it was across the street from the sprawling branches of the giant rubber tree.

The evening had ended by ten o'clock, after a zigzagging surveillance detection route back to the Panamericano. They'd talked over the plan for the coming day on the radio as they walked. Chavez was reluctant to discuss anything in the room of a foreign hotel, even in a relatively friendly country like Argentina. It was decided that they would meet at two-thirty the next morning and take a circular route back to the airport by way of the Chinese embassy at the edge of the Saavedra district in the northern part of the city.

'Don't be late,' Midas said, still a little grouchy about eating fried meat pies while Ryan got to have an Argentinian beefsteak. 'And don't be light.'

Ryan didn't intend to be late or light.

Freshly showered and shaved now, he looked at his watch again and then rubbed a dab of gel into his dark hair before brushing his teeth. For the same reason they didn't discuss logistics in foreign hotel rooms, he was careful about displaying his pistol or other gear.

He'd checked the obvious locations for bugs and hidden cameras, using a handheld device Gavin Biery had issued each Campus operator to scan for RF interference, and then looked for the telltale glint of pinhole camera lenses by taking a few flash photos of each wall with his phone and then studying them for reflections. Ryan found nothing, but since he was a good spy, that only made him more suspicious.

He used the half-open closet door to conceal most of his body while he geared up. Cameras and microphones needed electricity, and though Campus operators themselves often used battery-powered devices, when possible they tied into existing sources – especially when running a long-term or open-ended op. Ryan himself hadn't known he was coming to Argentina until the day before, so any cameras that did happen to exist would likely have been set up to catch targets of opportunity. Those units would need a power source. There was no light inside the closet, and Ryan reasoned that apart from it being a sucky place to put a device, any foreign operative worth his or her salt would place any cameras in more productive locations.

With his movements hidden by the open door, he popped the Smith & Wesson's magazine, then seated it firmly back in place. He retracted the slide a scant half-inch. He'd been the last to touch the weapon, but as Clark hammered home at least once during every tactical scenario, 'press checks were free insurance.' Reassured the pistol was loaded, Ryan held it at arm's length, acquiring the front sight with his dominant eye, the same way he did each time he picked up the weapon, even to put it away.

This was bound to be a long day, and a long day of surveillance required clothing that was comfortable. Equally important, it required clothing that did not stand out. If his clothes could be changed or altered through the day, so much the better. Ryan decided on a pair of light chinos and a pale blue button-down oxford shirt with long sleeves. The slacks were loose enough to hide his Thunderwear holster and the shirt thick enough to conceal the neck loop and mic of his communication gear. He and the other members of the team customarily carried a folding clip knife. Ryan chose a Benchmade called Big Summit Lake. It wasn't as tacti-cool as a black knife but was razor sharp and large enough to do the job. Wooden scales made it look more like a tool than a weapon. In addition to their 'people-killing' knives, they'd all opted for what Midas called 'granddad blades,' smaller folders that could be used to assist with the chores normal people used knives for – bypassing locks and cutting cordage. Ryan had learned the hard way that he'd rather be attacked by just about anything besides a knife. Conversely, he'd rather launch an attack of his own with just about anything else.

He dropped the radio the size of a pack of playing cards into the pocket of his slacks and slipped into a pair of lace-up Rockport Boat Builder high-tops before shrugging on a navy blue blazer. Last, he opened a flat plastic pill case and removed one of two beige earpieces about the size of the nail on his little finger. He replaced the small hearing-aid battery that was nearly as large as the device, not wanting to risk comms failure at an inopportune moment. Batteries never died after they finished an op, failing instead at the most critical moments. Ryan chuckled to himself as he dropped a spare battery into the inside pocket of his sport coat. James Bond and Jason Bourne made it look easy, but there was sure a lot of technical shit to worry about in this business.

Removing the chair he habitually propped against any hotel door, he did one final 'testicles, spectacles, wallet, and comb' check to make certain he had everything he needed – and then headed into the hallway, leaving the POR FAVOR, NO MOLESTAR sign hanging on the handle.

He made it to the lobby at two twenty-five a.m.,

teaming up with Midas in the blue Peugeot 408 – which, to Jack's surprise, was turbo-charged.

The streets were far from empty at three in the morning, but the traffic was light enough that Jack had no trouble keeping Chavez and Adara and their Renault in sight as they headed northwest on Avenida del Libertador. The two-car caravan worked its way through Barrio Chino and then drove west to do a quick drive-by of the Chinese embassy.

The Peugeot was far from quick off the line, especially compared to his Beemer back home, but Jack found it zippy enough to get him into trouble at intersections. Buenos Aires seemed completely devoid of four-way stops. According to the guidebook, the vehicle with the most momentum carried the right-of-way, and for a damn-the-torpedoes hard charger like Jack, that came in pretty handy.

Adara's voice came over the net as they passed the high walls of the embassy. 'Here be dragons.'

'No doubt,' Ryan said. 'But just what kind of dragons remains to be seen . . .'

They continued west, eventually hitting Avenida General Paz and taking it south until it joined the *autopista* back to Ministro Pistarini International.

Chavez went into the terminal while the others posted outside. The rain had stopped, but the early-morning air was still cool enough to be bracing.

Ding came over Ryan's earpiece less than an hour later.

'Heads up, guys,' he said. 'A blond female just met our guy and one other Asian male when they cleared customs.'

'A blonde, you say?' Adara said. 'Interesting.'

'That's affirm,' Chavez said. 'I have one more Asian

375

male in the middle of the pack behind Chen and his buddy. So far they haven't had any interaction, but that doesn't surprise me. Chen's wearing gray slacks and a black three-button. His buddy's in jeans and a white long-sleeve. Female is in dark slacks and a fawn blouse.'

Midas chuckled. 'Fawn?'

'Yes, fawn,' Chavez said. 'Like tan.'

'I see her through the window,' Midas said. 'Pretty sure that color is wheat.'

'Dumbass,' Chavez said. 'The blonde is pulling the bags. I'm right behind them. The lone Asian male is in jeans and a light blue jacket. Jack, you and Midas mark him, see what he does when we get back on the *autopista*.'

'Copy that,' Jack said. 'We'll be . . .'

Ryan paused, watching Chen and his small entourage exit the double doors from the airport. He focused on the blonde who brought up the rear.

'Does the female look familiar to anybody?'

She didn't, so Jack kept working on the connection, whatever it was, in the back of his mind. There was something about her that struck a nerve.

Adara picked up Chavez, but they lingered an extra two minutes as though they were waiting for someone else before pulling around to follow Chen and the others to the parking lot across the street and beyond a row of concrete construction barriers, where they got into a red Chevy compact.

'Got him,' Midas said a moment later. Jack and he watched the loner load his bag into a black Toyota HiLux pickup and climb into the passenger seat. The back glass was tinted, but Jack thought he could make out a female behind the wheel.

Jack counted to twenty, then fell in behind the HiLux.

Both teams stayed well back in the light traffic of early morning. Where the *autopista* crossed General Paz, the HiLux took the ramp to go north, generally backtracking the route the Campus operators had taken to reach the airport. The Chevrolet continued toward downtown.

'You want me to follow?' Jack asked, eyes over the guardrail as he watched the HiLux accelerate northwest while the Chevrolet continued northeast. 'They could be going to the Chinese embassy.'

'Negative,' Chavez said. 'Let's focus on Chen. We're not even certain they're together.'

'Copy that,' Jack said. As usual, there were never enough of them to do perfect surveillance.

They followed the Chevy east along Avenida 25 de Mayo, and then wound through the city in what were surely a series of halfhearted surveillance detection routes, only to end up at a tall set of brick apartments off Avenida Santa Fe in the San Isidro neighborhood of Acassuso, northwest of Buenos Aires proper.

Adara kept the Renault heading north on Santa Fe while the Chevy turned left down Libertad, a much smaller street, and came to a stop in front of what looked like a small school or daycare center.

Adara came over the net. 'That's interesting.'

'I agree,' Midas said. 'They wound back through town, when the General Paz would have gotten them here much quicker.'

'There is that,' Adara said. 'But the blue HiLux we saw at the airport, it's parked right around the corner.'

38

Ryan and Midas sat in the Peugeot half a block up Libertad from the apartment building while Adara and Chavez met Lisanne to grab the little Clio she and the pilots had been driving. With Chen turning up with so many confederates, the team needed a fresh set of wheels.

When they returned with the Renault, Ryan and Midas went to check out the neoclassical French mansion that was now the Palacio Duhau–Park Hyatt hotel on Avenida Alvear. The hotel also happened to be located in the swank neighborhood of Recoleta – less than eight blocks from the Parrilla Aires Criollos restaurant, where Argentina's minister of agriculture was hosting tonight's dinner. Several US intelligence agencies, including the CIA and National Security Agency, kept tabs on traveling members of foreign governments via both open-source and intercepted signals intelligence – and Gavin Biery's team at Hendley Associates kept tabs on the tabs-keepers. A quick check with the IT guru told the Campus operators the Chinese foreign minister had chosen the Hyatt for his stay in Buenos Aires.

The team was still unsure as to the purpose of Vincent Chen's visit, other than being reasonably certain it had something to do with the Chinese foreign minister. And even that didn't narrow things down very much. They knew someone had bombed a subway tunnel outside of Beijing. Eddie Feng obviously thought Chen was behind the attack. He was Taiwanese and he had a code name, so it wasn't outside the realm of possibility. They booted around the idea of sending up a warning through the State Department to contact the Chinese delegation regarding a possible threat to the foreign minister – but decided against it for a number of reasons.

First, the halls of the government in the People's Republic of China were even more byzantine than those of the United States. Given the fact that President Ryan had dropped a bomb on a Chinese office building that housed a group of hackers destroying American defense computers, trust between the two nations was less than nil. PRC bureaucrats would see treachery in any US action. They would hold the information while its credibility was verified, ensuring that this was not some ploy to make them lose face – or worse. Any pertinent intelligence regarding a plot against the foreign minister would take days to climb to the top of an actual decision maker's desk and then trickle back down to his security detail – who now formed a phalanx of armed men in dark suits around Foreign Minister Li, half a block from the spot where Jack Ryan, Jr, stood on the sidewalk.

Beyond the simple believability of the information, the team also ran the risk that someone from the foreign minister's delegation was an ROC spy and Chen, being Taiwanese, was his handler, there to collect information.

Ryan stood out of sight of the Hyatt on Rodríguez Peña street, around the corner from the concrete-and-red-brick building that housed the Argentine Ministry of Culture. Midas was farther east down Avenida Alvear, window-shopping at a small art gallery across from the hotel. His vantage point gave him an eye on the Hyatt's porte cochère and a direct line of sight to the arriving detail.

Ryan spoke into the mic on his neck loop. 'See anyone we should recognize?'

'Negative,' Midas said.

Chavez and Adara were too far across town to be in contact via the radio intercom, but Chavez had just confirmed by cell phone that there had been no sign of movement from Chen or his people. Both the HiLux and the Chevy were still parked at the apartments in Acassuso.

Ryan and Midas settled into what seemed would be a couple hours of lurking, without looking like lurkers.

The Palacio Duhau–Park Hyatt was located in an architecturally rich area of Buenos Aires that reminded Jack of Paris. But as nice as the area was, the Ministry of Culture, in front of which he now stood, was covered in graffiti. Ryan couldn't understand the Spanish, but he could tell from the sheer volume that the writing didn't tout confidence and trust in the Argentine government. Even the street around the building was covered in graffiti – though this was made with a stencil and more precise than the spray-painted scrawl on the building's walls. Ryan scuffed at the white paint with the toe of his Rockport.

'You speak Spanish, right?' he asked over the radio.

'A fair amount,' Midas said, knowing the question was meant for him, since the others were too far away.

'What does "*Esto huele mal*" mean?'

Midas chuckled. 'Where'd you see that?'

'Painted all over the street in front of the culture ministry.'

'*Escrache*,' Midas said. 'I read about that. Argentines are big on shaming elected officials that they feel have done wrong – graffiti, signage, even screaming at them on airplanes or in public places with megaphones.'

Ryan laughed. 'My dad gets a lot of that.'

'I voted for him,' Midas said. 'Anyway, "*Esto huele mal*" means "This smells bad" or "This stinks." Not sure what –'

Ryan cut him off. 'Hold on,' he said. The urgency in his voice caused Midas to fall silent.

Walking up Avenida Alvear, past the Hyatt and almost even with Ryan, was a tall brunette. He turned quickly, looking away before she had a chance to see his face. Jack had seen this woman the evening before, at the restaurant with Adara. It dawned on him that the blonde who met Chen had been with this one. Ryan hadn't been able to see more than her profile from his vantage point, but the brunette had been facing him. The two women had definitely been together. He saw no headphones or Bluetooth earpiece, but the brunette spoke to someone as she walked, perhaps, Ryan thought, utilizing the same sort of hidden microphone and neck loop he wore.

He started to follow but caught sight of an Asian woman from the corner of his eye. She was about the same age as the brunette, early thirties, with high cheekbones framed by shoulder-length hair. She stepped out of a side door of a building connected to the Hyatt, waited a beat while the brunette walked past, and then fell in behind her. She was dressed nicely in snug jeans and a loose designer T-shirt, but she bore angry pink scratches from jaw to forehead, as if she'd slid into home plate on her face. Ryan couldn't tell if her dark eyes were beautiful or terrifying, but he decided he would find out soon enough.

He gave Midas a quick brief over the radio.

'Good catch,' Midas said. 'I don't know about the Asian, but the brunette has to be in comms with Chen. She's probably letting him know the foreign minister had arrived.'

'That's my guess.' Ryan looked over his shoulder at traffic before crossing the street after the Asian, who seemed to be locked on to the brunette. 'I'm going to stick with them and see where they go.'

'Stay in range for comms,' Midas said. 'I'll reach out to Ding and bring him up to speed.'

The Asian woman took a right at the first block while the brunette went straight. Ryan knew it was stupid, but he was more than a little disappointed. Maybe she wasn't involved at all. The leggy brunette continued walking against traffic on Alvear for several blocks, past the popping flags of the Palace Hotel and two sets of *arbolitos*, touting their money exchange outside high-end shops selling Montblanc and Rolex. Any preconceived notions Jack had on this surveillance were quickly dashed. The Asian woman was nowhere in sight, and now the brunette wasn't going to her car as he'd first assumed. She turned right, as if to head back to the Retiro train station. A block later she turned left again.

'Northwest on Libertador,' Jack said, as much to make sure he still had a clear signal with Midas as to update him on the location.

'Copy that,' Midas said.

'This is weird,' Jack said, 'Asian girl has broken off.

Doesn't look to be a factor. I can't tell if this one is doing a really basic SDR or just zigzagging her way to wherever she's going. So far she hasn't even checked behind her.'

'Watch your ass,' Midas said. 'Maybe she's not alone. Your Asian woman could turn up again soon and stick a knife in your fourth point of contact.'

'That's a nice thought,' Ryan said, watching the woman trot across Avenida del Libertador. Risking one's life against ten lanes of aggressive Argentine drivers made for the perfect method to shed a tail.

Ryan tried to keep the woman in his peripheral vision as he continued up the street toward the crosswalk, willing himself to remain at a normal pace. The signal turned green just as the brunette disappeared into the trees.

No one would think twice about someone running to beat the crossing signal on such a wide street, so Ryan made up some time sprinting toward the park. He slowed when he reached the grass, staying parallel to what the brunette's route would be if she went straight after entering the trees.

The park was a fairly narrow one, and a railway yard with numerous tracks, switches, and uncoupled train cars lay directly on the other side, spilling out of Retiro Station to the south. This yard formed a natural line of demarcation between the upscale Recoleta neighborhood and the shanty town of broken brick dwellings in a warren of narrow streets known as Villa 31 – one of many such slums in Buenos Aires collectively, and appropriately, called *villas miseria*. Nearly fifteen city blocks long and more than five blocks wide at is widest point, the Villa – Argentines pronounced it *'vizha'* – was a gray swath of nothingness next to the tracks on most maps. Tourists might think it was just part of the train yard. Close enough that its residents could smell meat cooking from Recoleta restaurants if the wind was right, Villa 31 was home to many of the hardest-working people in Buenos Aires – as well as some of the city's most violent criminals.

Maids and service workers who lacked the proper references to rent an apartment in the city often paid half as much to rent a room with a communal bath and pirated electricity in a crumbling *departamento* from one of the neighborhood bosses who ran everything from rent collection to dispute enforcement inside the Villa. Villa 31 was a city within a city, but few people admitted to living there. Police braved the streets only in well-armed squads, and then only during daylight hours. If someone needed an ambulance at night, as Ding Chavez put it, 'forget about it.'

Ryan caught sight of the brunette a moment later, a hundred feet away and walking in his direction. He sat down on a bench across from a weathered older man who was throwing pistachios to a chattering flock of bright green parrots about the size of small pigeons. Ryan put his back to a gum tree but used the man's eyes and expressions to help guard his six o'clock. It wasn't an optimum setup, but human beings usually reacted in some way to danger, and Jack couldn't very well keep looking over his shoulder all the time. The birds and the man ignored him.

The brunette worked her way through the waist-high grass and weeds along the railyard fence until she found what she was looking for, a gap in the chain-link. Jack imagined the same makeshift gate was used by commuters from Villa 31 each morning and evening to and from their jobs so they didn't have to walk all the way to the other side of Retiro Station to get over the tracks. If the brunette had seen Ryan, she showed no sign of it. Instead, she turned sideways to slip through the gap, and then, checking both ways for oncoming trains, trotted across multiple sets of railroad tracks. Ryan couldn't help but think she looked like pictures he'd seen of East German refugees fleeing the no-man's-land to get over the Wall. Reaching the far side, she ducked through a second gap in the railway fence to enter the slums.

If it was difficult to follow her through the park, it would be impossible for Jack to follow her into the shanty town. Aside from the prospect that she might see him, venturing into Villa 31 without knowing someone on the inside was a good way to get yourself dead in a hurry.

Ryan gave a nod to the man feeding the parrots and headed back toward Midas. He bought a *choripán* – chorizo sausage on a bun – from a guy in the park, because he didn't know when he'd get to eat again. He'd give Midas a break when he got there.

'Lost her,' he said, eating as he walked. 'I'll explain when I . . .'

'Say again,' Midas said. 'You cut out.'

Ryan lowered his voice and dropped the barely eaten *choripán* into a trash can along the path. 'It's her,' he said. 'The Asian woman. Looks like she's picking the lock on some kind of tool shed or utility building in the park.'

'Copy,' Midas said.

Ryan swung wide, keeping to the trees and keeping the small stone building in view. He came around in time to catch a glimpse of the Asian woman's back as she pulled the door shut behind her. The building was maybe eight by eight and had no windows. It didn't look like she'd been running from anyone. Jack scratched his beard, thinking through his options. One of them, probably the smartest one, was to walk away. He'd been never been very good at that.

He listened outside the building for a half a minute. Nothing. The lock fell quickly to his granddad knife. There was nobody inside, though there was only one door, so the Asian woman had to have gone somewhere. Ryan took a small flashlight from his pocket and played it around the small space. There was a lingering smell that he couldn't put his finger on – but it wasn't good. The building looked to be storage for the lawn maintenance department, with a couple Weed Eaters and assorted rakes and shovels. A row of plastic trash cans lined a platform along the back wall. One lay on its side, presumably tipped over by the woman. Ryan entertained the idea that she could be hiding in one of the cans. But that was stupid. To what end? She hadn't even known he was following her. He peeked over the edge of each one anyway, at once relieved and disappointed to find them empty. The platform was about six inches high and made of weathered wood timbers. It was old, probably older than the building, making Ryan wonder if the place had been used as something other than storage in the past. Closer inspection revealed grass clippings sticking from under the edge of the wood, and, when Jack gave it a shove, it moved.

He pulled the overturned trash can out of the way, revealing four freshly disturbed timbers that formed a three-foot square.

'I'll be damned ...' he muttered, pushing what was essentially a trapdoor out to one side. 'She's gone underground.'

'Underground?' Midas said. 'Speak to me, brother. What's going on?'

'I'm going after her,' Ryan said. 'Don't be pissed, but I'm pretty sure we're about to lose comms.' He coughed at the rank wind that hit him in the face when he moved the boards.

'*Es huelte* something something?' he said.

Midas came across the net, confused. 'What?'

'That phrase from the graffiti I asked you about earlier,' Ryan said. 'It means "This stinks," right?'

'*Huele,*' Midas corrected. '*Esto huele mal.*'

Ryan peered down into the blackness below, pausing for a moment in hopes of picking up any sound of the Asian woman. He heard nothing but the moan of the sickening breeze as it blew upward out of the inky hole.

'It sure as hell does,' he muttered, half to himself.

39

Each Campus operator carried the same basic components for Everyday Carry – firearm, knife, flashlight, and cell phone. Some of them, like Clark, carried little else, relying on their pistol and badass experience to get the job done. Dominic Caruso, who'd been trained by the FBI, carried things like extra nylon restraints that looked like shoelaces and even flat rubber stoppers used to block interior doors when searching buildings. Ryan fell somewhere in the middle. In addition to his pistol and an extra eight-round magazine, he carried two knives, a small Streamlight ProTac flashlight, and a Zippo lighter. His cell phone would be useless for communication underground, but it did provide a backup source of lighting. Adara had issued each operator a small trauma packet containing an envelope of Celox hemostatic gauze and a SWAT-T soft rubber tourniquet. The kit was just one more thing to carry, and he'd be a happy camper if he never had to open the damn thing, but given the dark hole in the ground over which his feet now dangled, he was glad to have it.

Ryan thought seriously about ripping up a piece of his shirt and plugging his nose, the smell was so noxious.

'Talk to me, Jack,' Midas said. 'Give me a description of where you're going down.'

'I'm sending you my lat and long now.'

'Perfect,' Midas said. 'That way we'll know where to look for your body. How about you wait for me and I'll come back you up?'

'Stay put,' Ryan said. 'Somebody needs to keep an eyeball on the Chinese delegation. I'll be fine. Just going down to have a little look.'

'Copy that,' Midas said, sounding unconvinced. 'My training says to trust the guy on the ground . . . but watch yourself.'

'Will do,' Ryan said, and lowered himself into the blackness.

Ryan found a rusted iron ladder just inside the opening and hooked an arm through the top rung while he dragged the wooden cover back into place. He was hesitant to use his light, concerned that it would tip off the Asian woman that he was behind her, and he counted nine rungs before his feet splashed into something cold and oozing. The awful smell told him it probably wasn't water. Though it was only ankle deep, his Rockports were going to be good for nothing but a short trip to the nearest dumpster when he made it back above ground.

Pausing in the pitch blackness, he fought the urge to gag and strained to hear any sign of the departing woman. When he heard nothing, he drew his pistol and decided to take a chance with the flashlight. Ryan found himself completely alone at the bottom of a deep tube of red brick and mortar, approximately thirty feet in diameter. It looked like an old grain silo set in the ground. Four arched brick doorways – each about the same size as his six-foot wingspan – ran from the sides of the cavern with what was presumably sewage flowing out of the two doors to his left, and into the two to his right, toward the Río de la Plata. The bricks at the base of the arch to Jack's immediate right had telltale splash marks on one side. Closer inspection revealed hairlike moss just below the surface. The color of unripe limes, the moss swayed and billowed with the current like some kind of primordial ooze. By holding the powerful beam of the Streamlight at a low angle, Jack could see an obvious trail of discoloration in the moss, made by the weight of recent footprints. Most of the moss was undisturbed. He followed, moving slowly, pistol held back near his waist and flashlight slightly away from his body. Every few seconds he stopped and listened, but he heard nothing except the gurgle of flowing water . . . or whatever this was.

Buenos Aires was old, first settled sometime in the late 1500s. It was already a thriving city by the time the thirteen American colonies north of the equator declared their independence from England. There were tunnels under cities all over the world, the Catacombs beneath Paris; waterworks of an old wool business under Bradford, England; and abandoned sewers crisscrossing subterranean New York City. Ryan remembered from his history classes at Georgetown that Jesuit priests used a series of hidden tunnels here to move secretly between their numerous churches – both in centuries past and in more recent times of bloodshed during the 'Dirty War,' when the military junta ferreted out communist insurgents and anyone else they deemed to be a dissident. Some of the tunnels had been discovered and were now in the guidebooks. Some remained hidden. Others had been flooded by overflowing groundwater and sewer systems. This one was covered with a wooden door, obviously known to someone besides the Asian woman. Small niches, approximately a foot high and half as deep, were built into the brick walls, as if meant for statuary, leading Ryan to believe this tunnel wasn't originally intended to be a sewer.

He passed three smaller archways splitting off from the main tunnel as he sloshed along, one to the right and two more to the left. The trail of discolored moss told him to continue straight ahead. Twenty minutes after he'd first splashed down in the tunnels, Ryan came to another rusted iron ladder on the wall. The tunnel continued into the darkness, but the ladder was wet. Someone had recently climbed up.

Ryan felt like he'd been going generally east, and he suspected he was somewhere near the marina on the Río de la Plata, but it was impossible to know for sure without going up to peek out. When he stood completely still, he thought he could hear laughter.

He holstered his pistol and dropped the flashlight back into his pocket. Faint pinholes of light shone down from something at the top. Ryan hauled himself upward rung by rung, going slowly enough to let the sewage drain from his boots. He was careful not to slip. Walking through shit was one thing. Going for a swim in it was a whole other ballgame. He was reasonably certain he'd been vaccinated against hepatitis. Probably. Maybe. He began to mull over the idea of contracting cholera or jungle rot or whatever bug might swim up a person's toenails from fetid water. A bath in Clorox was starting to sound inviting by the time he wrapped one arm around the top rung and put the flat of his hand against a metal grate.

Ryan pushed up slowly, peering under the edge at a pile of steaming donkey crap inches away. He knew very little about barnyard scatology, but the donkey that had manufactured the stuff happened to be standing right above it. A quick look around said he'd not been going east at all, but north. The dirt streets and broken block buildings could be nowhere else but Villa 31 – the same place where the tall brunette had disappeared.

Frenzied Spanish voices, most male but at least one female, jerked Ryan's attention to his left. His vantage point from under the donkey cart allowed him to see little but a set of scrambling feet. They were small and wet, and sliding under the donkey cart, directly for him.

Ryan barely had time to yank his head back into the tunnel before the Asian woman shoved the metal grating aside, pulling it shut behind her as she slid feet-first into the hole – landing squarely on Ryan's knuckles where they curled around the pitted metal rung. Ryan was strong, but the impact of 120 pounds of fleeing woman knocked him off the ladder.

Customarily, Ryan would have tucked his head and rolled when falling from ten or twelve feet – but something told him he'd be better off with a broken leg than swimming in this slimy muck. The scant ten inches of water did little to break his fall, but he did his best to absorb much of the impact with bent knees. The floor of the tunnel was at a slight angle and he was just able to keep his feet, surfing on the snot-slick moss when he splashed down, wildly waving both arms in an effort to keep from falling face-first into the sewage. It was far from graceful, but it worked. He spun in time to see the shadow of the Asian woman slide to the bottom of the ladder behind him.

Floundering for just a moment, she wasted no time before sloshing off toward her original point of entry. Jack limped to go after her, but his right knee rebelled, slowing him down to a fast, hobbling limp. Lighter than Jack by nearly a hundred pounds – and a hell of a runner – the Asian woman looked over her shoulder, directly at Jack, her eyes wide.

'*Nee-ge – rō!*' she said. 'Run!'

The way she spoke was full of urgency, and he felt certain it was Japanese. Ryan heard a splash behind him and turned to face a man with a machete who'd just come down the ladder.

The wiry man stood with his mouth hanging open and the machete raised above his head. He was alone and looked almost as surprised as Jack felt.

'Friend?' Ryan said, peering at the man in the scant light from above. '*Amigo?*'

The man shook his head and grinned, realizing he was the only one with a weapon in hand. Even in the shadows – hell, especially in the shadows – Ryan could see the vacantness in the man's eyes.

'You can't reason with evil,' Clark always said. So Jack didn't try.

He could have tried to draw his pistol, but his hands were wet and slick. Even if he was able to get a shot off, the man would be on top of him in an instant with the heavy blade – making the odds too great that it would be a lose-lose endeavor. Instead, Ryan feinted right, causing the man to swing the blade across his own body. The slick footing

393

made the man's actions more exaggerated, allowing Ryan to shoot in and trap the arm against the other man's chest and drive him backward into the ladder. The snotty moss worked both ways, making it all but impossible for Ryan to keep his opponent trapped. He followed up with a quick head-butt to the bridge of the man's nose. The blow stunned him, but without proper grounding, there hadn't been enough power in it to do much damage.

'*¡Boludo!*' Machete Man grunted, struggling to escape and bring the blade back into play.

Jack wasted no effort on words, instead driving his knee into the man's unprotected groin. It worked to dislodge the blade, but unfortunately it also dislodged Ryan, and both men fell, splashing into the flowing filthy water.

Ryan's feet had grown used to the temperature, but the cold liquid hitting his knees took the breath out of him. The other man took the worst of it, landing on his back and slamming his head against the mossy stone floor. Fighting blind, Ryan straddled him, clawed for the face now, feeling and then losing a grip on his chin. Ryan heard him gurgle and then felt a sharp blow to his side. The son of a bitch had gotten a hand free and now proceeded to pummel him in the ribs. A shot went low and took him over the liver, sending waves of pain and nausea through Ryan's gut. He redoubled his efforts, sinking a thumb into the man's eye and forcing his face sideways and into the muck. The man bucked and thrashed, sputtering, trying anything to get his nose above the surface. Ryan braced himself against the slick moss with his free hand as best he could, coming up on his toes and pressing down with all the weight of his body on the other man's chest. He heard a sickening gurgle as the man aspirated a lungful of fetid sewage, and then the struggling ceased. Ryan waited a few more seconds to be sure and then pushed himself upward, chancing a quick look with his flashlight once he got to his feet.

Panting, filth dripping from his nose, he stood with a hand on one knee and vomited. Jack wiped his mouth with the sleeve over his biceps – the only relatively clean portion of his shirt. He spat and opened and shut his eyes several times to clear them, knowing this image would stay with him for a very long time. The silhouette of the other man was barely visible in the shadows as the river of sewage carried him away. That, he thought, was a hell of a way to die.

The pain in Jack's knee and ribs had subsided to a dull ache by the time he limped back to the stone building. A quick peek out the cracked door revealed only a young couple feeding some ducks and a uniformed grounds-keeper on a riding lawn mower. Ryan knew he was likely to cause an international incident – or at the very least commit aggravated assault to the noses of every Argentine he passed – if he didn't get out of his sewage-soaked clothing.

Chavez was grouchy about it, but he told Midas to break away from Foreign Minister Li's hotel and grab Jack a pair of sweats and his Brooks runners from his room at the Panamericano, along with a half-dozen bottles of water and the biggest container of hand sanitizer Midas could find – which turned out to be not nearly as big as Jack had hoped for.

Ryan rinsed off the best he could inside the stone building while Midas stood guard outside. Beyond salvation, everything from his skin out, including the Rockports, went into a dumpster. The fresh clothes and relatively disinfected feet allowed Ryan to make it back to the hotel without drawing too much attention. People who passed him smelled something amiss, but Jack looked clean and tidy. Such an awful stench couldn't be coming from him. Midas led the way and called the elevator while Jack waited by himself in a deserted corner beyond the baby-grand piano in the Panamericano's lobby until he was sure they would have the elevator to themselves.

He cleaned his gun and other equipment first. Some scrubbing and a few minutes under the blow dryer took care of the Thunderwear holster. It was made of textile, but thankfully it had been semiprotected by his slacks. The radio equipment was waterproof, so it was a fairly straightforward process to get it clean. His watchband, on the other hand, was toast. His cell phone had survived unscathed but for a cracked screen. Twenty minutes in a near scalding shower and two more bottles of hand sanitizer later, Ryan finally felt almost clean again.

He briefly considered calling his mother to see if there was some kind of prophylactic medication he should take, but there was no good way to explain his situation to her. *'Hey, Mom, I was just tromping around in some South American sewers today. Wondering if I should be worried . . .'*
He decided he'd ask Adara if he got the chance.

Ryan had to will himself to take it easy on the aftershave, knowing too much would draw as much attention as the phantom odor he hoped to conceal. Finally scrubbed and wearing a pressed button-down shirt, fresh khaki slacks, and a pair of Crockett & Jones dark brown oxfords he'd be able to run in if the need arose, he headed to meet Midas in the lobby.

The former Delta commander's nose curled as soon as Ryan walked up.

'Like my granny used to say, you got something Bab-O won't wash off!'

'Damn it!' Jack grimaced and started to turn around and head back to his hotel room. 'Seriously? You can still smell it?'

Midas's wide shoulders bounced as he chuckled, already walking toward the valet with the keys. 'You're fine,' he said. 'I think my nose hairs are still melted from when I picked you up.'

40

Midas didn't mind navigating, so Ryan slid in behind the wheel of the Peugeot. He enjoyed driving a stick. It made him feel alive, even in the stop-and-go Buenos Aires traffic. He nearly ran over an older female pedestrian at a four-way intersection – which meant he was getting the hang of driving like an Argentine. She gave him an energetic 'Up yours' gesture and called him '¡Pelotudo!' which appeared to be the go-to word for angry people in this country.

Ryan turned left on Avenida Santa Fe, working through what little they did know about the situation while he drove. The team had been over it until they were blue in the face, and there were a dozen plausible scenarios – but some vital piece of evidence that would make everything fall into place still eluded them.

Eddie Feng was a Taiwanese national. Vincent Chen was also from Taiwan, but living in the United States with a cover identity selling imported greeting cards from the People's Republic of China. So far, the only thing linking the two men was their propensity to frequent Tres Equis/ Sun Yee On triad strip clubs that exploited underage girls – a trait that should have earned them both a spot in a very dark hole but didn't explain Chen's connection to the PRC and whether he was friend or foe. The meetings between the Chinese and the other delegations had definitely brought him to Argentina.

This Japanese girl added a new twist to the mix. The guy Ryan killed from Villa 31 had apparently been after her with a machete – which by virtue of her enemies edged her into the good-guy column. Sometimes, though, the enemy of my enemy was, well, just another damn enemy. It was not too much of a leap to assume she was there because of the Japanese delegation – but ministers of agriculture rarely engendered enough intrigue to cause someone to run through a tunnel filled with sewage. And if this woman had arrived with the Japanese agricultural delegation, how did she even know about the existence of the tunnel? Jack had seen her exit the Palacio Duhau Hyatt, the same hotel where the Chinese foreign minister was staying. The Japanese had rooms at the Four Seasons, more than five blocks away. Why was she there? Why had she gotten to Villa 31 right after the brunette with known ties to Chen? She'd warned Jack to run. Why hadn't she confronted him – or, at the very least, left him to his own fate?

Ryan tapped the steering wheel in thought. He had a lot of puzzle pieces. They just seemed to be from different puzzles.

He passed the Parrilla Aires Criollos restaurant on his right, and continued for another block and a half to a parking garage just beyond the intersection with Riobamba. A chilly wind blew in from the Río de la Plata, which, at 120 miles wide, seemed more like a bay off the Atlantic than a river. Once he was parked, Ryan grabbed a dark windbreaker from the back of the Peugeot. It would cut the wind, and had the added benefit of being nighttime camouflage, should he need to move covertly when the sun went down.

The men split up after they left the vehicle, Midas loitering his way east, browsing the shops along Santa Fe while Jack went north a block on narrow, tree-lined Riobamba. Businesses occupied the bottom floor of most buildings, but judging from the many balconies above, most of the upper floors were private apartments. Ever thinking strategically, Jack noted the prevalence of concrete railings and statuary around the balconies and thought how the Secret Service would avoid this kind of street like the plague. There were just too damn many places to hide.

Pockets of old men with jaunty tamlike gaucho hats sat here and there at the many sidewalk cafés on the quiet street, sipping *yerba mate* through a silver straw in a communal gourd called a *mate* that gave the drink its name. *Mate* was a national pastime. Entire shops were devoted to *mate* mugs and straws and thermoses, as well as exotic leather carriers resembling a tall binocular case in which to store everything. The hotel valet had offered Jack a drink from his *mate* straw, instructing him to empty it before passing it back. Jack had complied, grudgingly, and found it tasted like a mixture of boiling water and hay. He preferred to get his caffeine fix from actual tea, or a good old cup of coffee. The stuff made by the Navy stewards in the White House was particularly good . . . but he didn't get by there to see his folks as much as he used to. Certainly not as much as he should.

It was a little after four p.m. when Ryan turned back to the east on Arenales, paralleling Santa Fe for several blocks so he could come in the opposite direction from Midas with the restaurant in the middle. The thought of Navy mess coffee made him wish for a cup, and he began to look for a likely shop as he walked. It would give him something to do as he whiled away the hours ... and watched.

In days gone by, arriving on station early was a double-edged sword. Get there too late and you missed important changes in personnel, local habits, and anyone from the other team who decided to set up an ambush or conduct countersurveillance. Coming in too early ran the risk of drawing unwanted attention.

Then smartphones came along and devoured the collective brain of society. Mobile phones were the single greatest thing to happen to a surveillance team in recent history – and communication had nothing to do with it. Trained observers generally relied on a set of known habits and best practices. But just as a baboon might alert the gazelle of a leopard's presence in the wild, being noticed by the local populace was a surefire way to spook a target. Since most noses had become buried in a phone screen, it was a safe bet that a person could spend a couple hours browsing local stores in a three-block operational area without drawing so much as a second look. That time more than doubled if a stop at the neighborhood coffee shop was added to the mix.

City crews had already come by and dropped off wooden barricades in front of Parrilla Aires Criollos. These ten-foot-long sawhorses leaned against a row of garbage bins, causing pedestrian traffic to split and flow around them like water around a boulder in the middle of a river. Uniformed officers began to arrive approximately an hour after Ryan and Midas came on station.

The newly formed Buenos Aires city police looked to

be playing second fiddle to the beret-wearing Grupo Alacrán, the elite Scorpion Group of the Gendarmería Nacional Argentina. Dour-looking men with H&K MP5 submachine guns and Steyr AUG assault rifles deployed from two four-door Volkswagen Amarok pickups and a white Mercedes-Benz communications van on either side of the restaurant door.

Right-wing death squads during Argentina's 'Dirty War' of the 1970s and 1980s left the population suspicious of the military – or anything that resembled it. The Army was not allowed to take part in civilian affairs, but the government got around this by describing the GNA as a 'civilian security force of a military nature.' The Scorpion Group looked about as military as they came, but then they had to be. While other squads within the Gendarmería provided Argentina with border security, Grupo Alacrán was tasked with the mission of combating terrorism and often assisted with the protection of Argentine and visiting dignitaries.

These new arrivals set up the wooden barricades quickly, forcing pedestrians to cross Avenida Santa Fe in order to go east or west rather than walk in front of the restaurant. Ryan and Midas quickly found themselves outside the perimeter, half a block from the restaurant.

The presence of men with machine guns upped the feel of the operational tempo, putting Ryan and Midas on their toes. Buenos Aires had seen more than its share of domestic terror, with a recent bombing in front of a Gendarmería building. Members of the Scorpion Group eyed people in the passing crowd as if they were food, their mean-mug looks sending people across the street as surely as the wooden barricades. A dog handler with a visage as fierce as that of his Belgian Malinois stood at parade rest to the right of the restaurant doors.

None of *these* guys were on a mobile phone.

In an effort to remain inconspicuous, Ryan and Midas had looked through the window of every shop for three blocks on either side of the restaurant up and down Avenida Santa Fe, some of them twice. Midas was able to work his way up to a vacant seventh-floor balcony above a restaurant called La Madeleine at the end of the block. Ryan claimed a vacant window seat at the McDonald's almost directly across the street from the dinner meeting venue. He was pretending to surf on his cell when Adara called. He relayed her message to Midas over the radio a moment later.

'Chen's moving.'

'About time,' Midas said. 'I stopped to gawk at that shoe store down there so many times I was about to have to break down and buy me a new pair of Pumas whether I need them or not. They coming this way?'

'She didn't know yet,' Jack said. 'Don't you get shot up there, brother. These Gendarmería guys look a little jumpy if you ask me.'

'Yes, Mom,' Midas said.

Across Santa Fe, a caravan of dark sedans, each much larger than the bulk of the vehicles in Buenos Aires, began to arrive in front of Parrilla Aires Criollos. Men in dark suits dismounted from the front to hold the doors for more important men in more expensive suits as they exited the rear seats. Uniformed Buenos Aires city police officers moved wooden barricades while Grupo Alacrán operators stood by and glared over their SMGs.

Little of this would be for the agricultural delegations. The foreign minister of China was definitely on his way.

Personal security was minimal for secretaries and ministers of agriculture, but it wasn't nonexistent. Express kidnappings – impromptu abductions of people who looked like they had money – were all too common in South America. To make matters worse, the respective countries of each of these delegations had advertised their attendance well in advance. Some governments, like Japan, sent a security man; other officials, like the Swiss minister of agriculture, were wealthy enough to hire someone on their own to watch their back.

Jack made a mental note of each delegation as it arrived. So far, he'd seen representatives from six countries: Argentina, India, Japan, Switzerland, Thailand, and the Netherlands. Each minister had at least one security man, and between three and five assistants. The Gendarmería had closed the restaurant to regular customers, but it was a relatively small space, and the private function would come close to filling at least half the seats.

Ryan looked at his watch – six twenty-three. Another hour and it would be dark. It was still far too early for most Argentines to eat dinner, but many of the visiting ministers would be more in the mood for breakfast. Seven p.m. in Buenos Aires was midnight in Amsterdam and six a.m. in Beijing – so concessions for the time differences were made in the spirit of good diplomacy. Ryan's North American stomach was on DC time. Six-thirty was just about right for dinner. He loved a good steak, but eating one every night after nine o'clock seemed like a recipe for bad dreams and blood with the consistency of 30 weight motor oil.

Ding Chavez broke squelch fifteen minutes later, crackling with static as his radio came into range: '. . . you guys copy?'

'You're coming in slurred and stupid,' Midas said. 'Go ahead, boss.' Being a retired lieutenant colonel with Delta earned Midas a great deal of latitude. He never would have said such a thing to Clark, but Chavez played by somewhat looser rules in the name of team cohesion when it came to radio decorum.

'Roger that,' Ding said. 'Chen and one of the Asian males are in the in the Chevy, heading . . . They're heading south . . . No . . . Shit . . . These streets are all turned around . . . East on Libertador . . . Turning south on Ayacucho now. Looks like we're coming to you – scratch that. He cut back toward Recoleta Cemetery . . . Pulling over at Adara's ice cream shop.'

'Copy,' Midas said. 'We're getting movement here. Gendarmería has the place buttoned down. Due respect, boss, but shouldn't we send this information to higher and maybe have someone from State contact the Argentines and warn them of a possible threat? Chen and one actor leaves three still in play somewhere.'

'I ran it by Clark,' Chavez said. 'He thinks we still have too many variables. He gave me the option, and I say we sit and see what develops, at least for the next few minutes.'

A tall Asian man with a buzz cut exited the restaurant and gave the officer with the dog a dismissive nod. The pigtail of an earpiece disappeared into the collar of his suit jacket. Ryan made out the telltale print of a pistol over his right hip. A similar bulge on his left side, this one slightly blockier, was surely a radio. The man motioned to the BA city police officers with a flick of his hand, and two of them scurried to move the barricades off the street for an imminent arrival.

Buzz Cut was the advance, on station early to see that things were safe before his boss got there.

A yelping siren drew Jack's attention to the east and he watched two Yamaha police motorcycles nose out from Rodríguez Peña a block away. Strobe lights flashed in the gathering dusk. A black Cadillac sedan stayed tight behind the bikes onto Santa Fe, followed by a shiny black Escalade, and then five more sedans. Two more bikes brought up the rear. It was nothing close to the size of his father's detail, but a seven-vehicle motorcade package with a motorcycle escort was a lot for a foreign minister, even from a country as large and controversial as the People's Republic of China. Jack had read a couple CIA briefs on Li Zhengsheng. For someone so high up in PRC government, little was known about the man, but for the fact that he appeared to dote on his wife and son – and he was apparently quite full of himself.

'The ego has landed,' Ryan said. 'Foreign Minister Li is on site.'

Ten minutes later, the Canadians and Uruguayans arrived in turn. The Gendarmería posted out front appeared to relax now that the dignitaries who'd been invited were all safely off the street.

'We've got ten digs inside,' Midas said. 'Including Foreign Minister Li. Thirty to forty staffers and a whole shitload of armed dudes, half of those from Li's detail.'

'Copy,' Chavez said.

Jack took a sip of his coffee. It wasn't White House Navy mess, but it wasn't too shabby, either. 'Any movement from Chen?'

'That's a negative,' Adara said. 'They've dismounted and gone into a café for dinner.'

'You've still just got eyes on the two?' Jack asked.

'Correct,' Chavez said. 'Chen and one of the Asian males from the airport.'

Jack pushed away from his table. 'No females?' The question was rhetorical. Chavez had already told him who he was watching – but muttering was part of Ryan's process.

'No joy,' Adara said. 'Or the second male.'

'Hmm,' Jack said. 'Both women were here last night, scoping out the restaurant at the same time we were. They would fit in with the locals, so it makes sense for Chen to send them in close while he stays back. I'm betting they're somewhere nearby. Could be they're waiting for a meet with one of the Chinese staffers. Midas, anybody look like they're waiting around with the vehicles?'

'Can't tell,' Midas said. 'I have a good eyeball on the front door, but from up here Santa Fe's a river of black sedans . . .' His voice trailed off. When he spoke again, it was in a rasping whisper. 'Jack, didn't you say that Japanese girl you followed had a big scab on her face?'

'Scratches,' Ryan said. 'Not exactly a scab. Why? You see her?'

Midas whispered, 'On the balcony two floors below me, sitting behind a rifle. The girl's runnin' a gun.'

41

Inside Parrilla Aires Criollos, Chinese foreign minister Li Zhengsheng followed his lead Central Security Bureau protection agent, Long Yun, to his assigned seat. Two other men, both as stone-faced as the colonel, were posted along the far wall, eyes scanning areas of responsibility on either side of the room. Li paid the men little heed. They weren't there to be noticed. They were there to protect him – and the good name of the party.

The long table was at the back of the restaurant with rustic earthenware settings for ten. As guest of honor, Li sat at the head, facing the door, his back to the rich mahogany bar that stood nearly four feet high. José Prieto, Argentina's minister of agriculture, sat immediately to Li's right under a set of rawhide *boleadoras* that hung from the wall along with assorted other gaucho memorabilia. A white linen tablecloth partially concealed the air-conditioning vent behind the Argentine's chair.

Most of the ministers knew one another, some of them quite well, but Anika Bos from the Netherlands was newly appointed and worked the table, introducing herself. She was a stunningly beautiful fifty-year-old woman. Most of the men had traveled without their wives, leaving them free to sample the local nightlife – and, perhaps, they seemed to think, explore a cross-border relationship with the Netherlands. A number of them maneuvered for the opportunity to buy her a drink after dinner.

Li kept his face passive but scoffed inwardly at the thought. Unfortunately for Anika Bos, the lascivious Argentine minister had made certain she was seated beside him. Drinks with anyone would not be in her cards.

Prieto tapped his knife against the side of his water glass after everyone was seated and began to welcome the attendees on behalf of his country, calling them each by name as if they were old and dear friends instead of economic rivals or potential customers for Argentine beef and grain. He jokingly apologized to the Canadian minister that the evening's discussion would have to take place in English because not everyone at the table spoke French.

Li stopped listening almost at once. He moved as if to readjust his chair, glancing at his watch, and laughed along with everyone else at another of Prieto's asinine jokes, though he had no idea what the man had said.

Five minutes past seven. He could begin whenever he chose to do so.

Li sat through the *picada* of baked cheese, cured meats, and crusty bread – not because he was hungry. He'd already eaten breakfast in his hotel room. But there would inevitably be survivors, and some of them would eventually regain their senses enough to recall things that had been out of place.

At seven-twenty he leaned back slightly in his chair to get Long's attention. The colonel nodded to the other two Chinese security men, telling them to remain in place and watch his food while he accompanied Li around the bar to the restroom. The entire restaurant had already been swept for threats, but anyone with a protective detail would see nothing out of the ordinary if Long Yun checked it again.

Once in the restroom, Long Yun made a call, making certain Amanda was ready. He spoke quickly, then nodded to his boss, keeping the woman on the line. From this point on, there could be no error in communication.

Li removed a device that looked like a mobile phone from the inside pocket of his suit jacket and entered six digits – the first half of the code needed to detonate the small shaped explosive that he knew was behind the wall vent. It would be a directed blast, not much larger than a hand grenade. There would be a great deal of noise and smoke, and those sitting directly in front of it would be cut in half. The rest of those present would have a very exciting story to tell. To that end, it was imperative that both Li's hands be visible when the device exploded. Too many things could happen to allow the bomb to be detonated at any specific prearranged time. He'd not risen to his present office by being careless. No, Long Yun would let Amanda know he was in the clear after he armed the device. She would then enter the second half of the code, detonating the device while he was standing slightly around the corner and behind the safety of the thick wooden bar, chatting amiably with the bartender.

'Sixty seconds,' Long Yun said. He dropped the phone into his pocket but kept the line open so the woman could hear if anything changed.

Li began a silent countdown in his head. The bar was close, right outside the door, so he took a moment to wash his hands. The colonel gave an approving nod at his gravitas. He liked to appear in complete control, especially in front of his security detail – two of whom were about to die, though they had no idea.

'Be sure to open your mouth, sir,' Long Yun said. 'It will help with the pressure of the blast. The temptation to look toward the device will be great –'

'I will be fine,' Li said.

With twenty seconds to go, he tossed a crumpled paper towel into the trash can and stepped out the restroom door.

It was obvious from the tone of his voice that Ding Chavez was sitting up straighter in the car.

'She's on a rifle?'

Midas still whispered. 'Affirmative. Suppressed bolt-action. Looks like a small-caliber, maybe a .22 from the size of it. She's sweeping the crowd like she's looking for someone – holy shit!'

Jack stood at the McDonald's window and watched a well-dressed woman with dark curly hair pitch headlong into the crosswalk on the north side of the street. He thought at first she'd stumbled, but it was impossible to mistake the rigid spasms of someone who'd been shot in the brain. Her nervous system short-circuited, and she lay on her side, arms suddenly stiff, as if she were sleep-walking. Her legs made obscenely grotesque pumping motions as if she were riding an invisible bicycle. A dark wig fell away, spilling tresses of blond hair onto the pavement. A moment later her muscles relaxed and she was still.

'It's her,' Ryan gasped, loud enough to draw a look

from a little kid eating an ice cream cone at the window beside him.

The Gendarmería officer at the nearest barricade also recognized a shooting victim when he saw one. He brought his MP5 to high ready and began scanning the storefronts for a threat.

The blonde's body lay half in the street. The light turned green and traffic honked, unaware. For a moment Jack thought she would be run over, but the drivers in the lead slowed down and stopped, forming a blockade, for the moment, at least. It really didn't matter. She was beyond saving.

Ryan thought of running to act as though he was rendering aid, and maybe grabbing any identification.

Midas came over the net again, still a quiet hiss. 'Jack, I can hear you thinking. Don't go out there. This shooter is still on her gun.'

'Sitrep when able,' Chavez said, surely feeling blind.

'Shooter just took out the blonde from the airport,' Midas whispered. 'Suppressed subsonic .22 and a bolt-action. I didn't hear shit and I'm twenty feet above her.'

'He's right,' Ding said. 'You stay put, Jack. I mean it.'

Ryan started to say he understood, but a familiar face drew his attention across the street. A crowd of panicked pedestrians braved the traffic to cross against the light directly toward Jack. Amid the fleeing pack, a tall woman with her hair tucked up into a baseball cap walked briskly, working to go just fast enough to stay in the middle. She carried a mobile phone in one hand, and with the other she tugged at the bill of her cap. It was the brunette Jack had watched disappear into Villa 31. A look of barely controlled panic flashed in her eyes. She'd just watched her friend die, and it was obvious she thought she was about to be next.

Only the two men of the Gendarmería nearest the dead woman realized something was amiss. The second, though highly trained, had never seen anyone in the throes of death. Too far away to see the tiny spot of blood below the woman's left ear, he thought she might be having a seizure – something she would get over – and it took him almost a full minute before he radioed his command post to request an ambulance. He was on a protective detail and did not leave his post at the door to the restaurant.

The officers in the room heard the call go out to the command post reporting a possible heart attack victim and turned their attention back inward to watch the staff. After all, this was a steak restaurant. Virtually everyone in the place had a blade.

Li Zhengsheng stood with both hands up on the bar and fumed, trying to think of something else to say. It had been well over a minute since he'd entered his half of the code – but nothing was happening. The bartender did not speak English or Chinese – the only two languages with which Li was conversant – making this an extremely uncomfortable predicament. Long Yun stood to his left, carefully positioning himself between the far wall and the foreign minister, but making certain to keep his body behind the protection of the heavy mahogany bar.

Li nodded stupidly at the bartender, forcing a smile that he was certain made him look insane. He kept his feet planted but tilted his head to the side toward the colonel. Anger knotted with the anticipation already in his gut.

'I cannot stand here forever!' he whispered. 'Something has gone wrong!'

'Abort?'

That fool, Prieto, shouted across the room as if they were at a sports match. 'Mr Foreign Minister,' he said. 'Please come and resume your seat.'

Li held up a hand, signaling that he would be a moment longer. What was the girl waiting for?

Minister Prieto stood and motioned toward Li's chair with a flourish, as if he would not take no for an answer. 'Please, *señor*. I will order you a special drink if you wish, but it is no meeting without our guest of honor.'

Li clenched his teeth, hardly able to breathe, let alone speak, he was so livid. He reached into his pocket to retrieve the device with which he could enter the abort code – at the same moment the west wall of the restaurant belched a great ball of dust and debris. The explosion was not a huge one, as explosions went. Li had seen much larger. Still, the concussion in the confines of the small restaurant was deafening.

The initial blast knocked José Prieto completely out of his Italian loafers and threw what was left of his burned and mangled body across the table. Anika Bos was killed instantly, her beautiful face slammed into her water glass. The Japanese minister of agriculture would certainly die as well from his massive head wounds, but he lingered now, trying in vain to stanch the trickle of blood and brain matter that obscured his vision.

The blast also claimed one of the two Central Security

Bureau men who'd been left to guard Li's food, a necessary sacrifice to make the story of his miraculous escape even more plausible.

Long Yun was on the radio immediately, calling the limousine forward to evacuate the foreign minister. Security personnel from all the delegations, some more professional and experienced than others, stumbled around overturned chairs and burning tables to locate their charges amid the smoke and chaos. The ministers of Uruguay and India had been seated closest to the door. They both ran from the building, abandoning any thought of a security team.

The concussion of the blast had shattered the restaurant's large front windows, startling locals who were not unaccustomed to bombings. Most fled for fear of secondary explosions, but some paused long enough to snap a few photographs of the escaping ministers, who now stood with hands on their knees, coughing and sputtering and trying to get their bearings.

A Chinese CSB agent with very short hair burst from the front door and shoved the Uruguayan minister out of the way, while Long Yun dragged the limping foreign minister through the melee and to the waiting motorcade. Foreign Minister Li Zhengsheng smiled within himself when he saw at least a dozen mobile phones aimed in his direction. With any luck, some of them had gotten it on video.

Jack watched the leggy brunette turn as soon as she crossed the street. The moment her feet hit the sidewalk she began to fiddle with her mobile phone – and the front doors blew off the restaurant. The sudden *whoof* of pressure shook the window, causing Ryan to take a half-step back. Car alarms up and down Santa Fe began to chirp and wail. The brunette walked briskly away from the blast without looking back – conspicuously ignoring the carnage going on behind her.

A moment later, members of Li's protective detail emerged from the smoke through the front door and whisked him away. Pretty damned efficient security, Jack thought.

Midas spoke again, panting now, voice hollow, like he was running down a stairwell. 'Our Japanese girl's about to *di di mau* outta here,' he said. 'Keep eyes on the brunette. I'll stick with this one.'

Ryan located her easily, moving away through a still-confused crowd without looking back. 'Got her,' he said.

Ryan all but flew out the door, against the river of people now fleeing across the street toward him. The brunette was a block ahead when he spotted her again, moving north at a fast trot.

'Brunette's coming at you, Ding,' Jack said. 'I'm half a block behind her on Callao Ave.'

He briefed Chavez and Adara on the situation as he moved, using the crowd and darkness to keep from being seen. If she had anyone running countersurveillance, Ryan knew he was screwed, but she'd detonated the bomb. He couldn't just let her walk away.

42

Ding Chavez and Adara Sherman sat at a sidewalk café nursing cold bottles of Quilmes Patagonia beer while they listened intently to the drama playing across their earpieces. They were too far away to hear the report of the blast, but they'd been able to tell something was up from the alarmed reactions of Midas and Jack. Ding stifled the human urge to ask questions and give advice. He wasn't on scene, and Jack was doing a good job of keeping him up to speed as things went down. It was best to keep his mouth shut and let the operators do what they did best – operate. And anyway, things were about to get interesting here. At eight blocks away, the brunette would be there in minutes.

Adara suddenly tipped the neck of her beer toward the Italian restaurant two businesses to the east. 'Chen's moving. Looks like he just put one cell phone in his pocket and took out a second. He's in comms with somebody.'

Chen put the second phone away and walked to the street with another Asian male. Both men looked up and down the wide sidewalk before trotting diagonally across Junín and turning left to walk briskly along the fifteen-foot brick wall surrounding the cemetery.

Chavez peeled a couple hundred-peso notes off the roll in his pocket and left them on the table. Tipping was outside the norm in Argentina. The waitress would think him an idiot *turista* for leaving the equivalent of twelve bucks for two beers that cost half that, but it was better than her chasing them down the street for leaving too little.

Chavez pushed away from the table and held up the flat of his hand, signaling for Adara to hang back while he took the first eyeball on Chen. She nodded and crossed the street directly while he took a more diagonal route to intercept Chen's trail immediately. She'd follow at a respectable distance and the two would leapfrog, so as to give a fresh face to the follow. Chavez slowed a half-step when Chen and the other man hung a right at the end of the block, still following the cemetery wall. Chavez continued across the street and then turned right himself so as not to round the corner where Chen had gone without checking it out first from a different vantage point. The two Asians were still moving steadily, not quite trotting, halfway down the block now.

'Got your right,' Adara said, letting Chavez know she'd seen the turn.

Ryan and Midas were still giving a play-by-play of their individual pursuits. Chavez waited for them to pause, then claimed the airspace.

'Listen up,' he said. 'We got a lot going on. Keep the bullshit to a minimum. Necessary traffic only. Speed, direction, and any threats. Got it?'

Ryan responded with 'North on Callao.'

'North ... Rodríguez Peña ... behind the shooter,' Midas said, still running.

'I'm right behind you, Ding,' Adara said, for Midas and Jack's benefit.

Chavez started to give his location when the two men

ahead of him broke into a run, taking another right at the end of the block.

Adara picked up her pace. 'They see you?'

'I don't think so,' Chavez said.

He called out the location, following his own orders so Jack and Midas could keep up with the common operating picture. He trotted now, again swinging wide around the corner to avoid an ambush. He made it around in time to see the second Asian scale a construction fence behind Chen. Both men scrambled up some scaffolding to the top of a construction trailer, and then bounded over the cemetery wall and out of sight.

Adara ran up behind Chavez, turning to check behind herself as she came to a stop. It was long past the time to try to stay covert if anyone was trailing them down the dark street.

'You sure they didn't see you?' Adara said again. Both she and Chavez cupped their hands over their chests, blocking the neck mics so they didn't clutter the radio net.

Chavez said, 'They never looked behind them.'

'Cemetery gates are locked up for the night,' Adara said. 'We'll have to go in the same way they did.'

Chavez rubbed his face and studied the construction trailer, his mind racing. He'd been in leadership positions in the past two decades. Hell, he'd led a team of some of the most elite operators with Rainbow. But life was so much easier when he'd been an impetuous troop and could let the bosses worry about the magnet in his ass that pulled him, without thinking, toward danger. He'd never been very good about aborting a pursuit, but he reminded himself that he had the entire team to consider.

Like a good leader, he made the decision look as though it was second nature.

'First rule of following someone blind into a dark alley?'

'Is not to follow someone blind into a dark alley,' Adara finished his mantra. It was one of many, and she knew it well. 'You gotta admit, the cemetery is a heck of a good SDR It's a maze in there. They'd know for sure if we followed them in.'

'The problem with an alley,' Ding said, toying with the beginnings of a plan, 'is that you're walking into a fatal funnel – that is, the way you're expected to walk in. We just need to find a different way than the one they used.'

'Hellooo, Midas,' Jack hailed his fellow operator, once he'd learned Chen had gone over the cemetery wall. 'What's your position?'

'Rodríguez Peñ –' he said, cutting out, still breathless.

'You're moving parallel to us,' Ryan said.

The brunette moved more quickly now, still walking, but much faster than the rest of the crowd. She touched her ear as she jigged around a bus-stop shelter, in comms with somebody. Looking right at the next intersection, she paused for a split second, then ran across the street to her left.

'She's coming toward you, Ding,' Jack said.

With his eyes on the brunette, he didn't see the oncoming Japanese woman until it was too late, and the two ran headlong into each other. The woman bounced away, falling sideways, spitting like an angry cat. Ryan was stunned from the impact but able to remain standing. He reached down to offer the woman a hand, but she slapped it away, springing to her feet, ready to run again. Midas had caught up by now and grabbed a handful of her collar, giving it a yank, lifting the sputtering woman off her feet. She'd been holding a cell phone when they collided and it now lay on the ground with a badly damaged screen.

People on the street were still stampeding away from the bomb blast around the corner, and ran by without interfering.

'Let. Me. Go.' The woman said it through a clenched jaw. Her English was accented English but very good. 'She is . . . escaping.'

Ryan turned to watch the brunette disappear into the darkness at the other end of the block, then turned back to Midas, both hands up, as if to say *What gives?*

Midas knew exactly what he meant. 'You can't hear me, can you?'

Ryan shook his head.

Midas raised his eyebrows. 'Then my radio's tits-up. I tried to tell you we were coming. Took me a half a block to realize I wasn't hearing my own voice.'

Chavez came across the net, unaware of this new development.

'We're walking toward you on south side of the cemetery,' he said. 'We're trying to find a way in that won't get our asses handed to us.'

'Copy,' Ryan said. 'Midas is with me, but his comms are down. I've lost sight of the brunette. We're having a talk with our Japanese friend.'

Chavez's dismay was apparent. 'You made contact?'

Ryan rubbed his aching ribs, injured for a second time

by a female hurtling through space. *We sure did,* he thought. He said, 'I'll explain later.'

He relayed Chavez's situation and location to Midas.

The Japanese woman reached for the shattered phone, but Midas wrenched her arm back with the hand that wasn't holding her neck. She was shorter than Jack by seven or eight inches, fit, built like a runner. Even restrained, her chin tilted upward slightly – a match to the defiant glint in her eyes.

She tried to jerk away and, when she found that was impossible, turned her glare on Jack. 'You are wasting time.'

'I'll take care of this,' Jack said, scooping up the broken phone. Close enough to study now, the scratches down the left side of her face looked like they were maybe a week old. Healing, but still pink and quite deep, probably caused by a very determined set of fingernails. 'Who are you?'

She scoffed, then mocked his tone. 'Who are *you*?'

Ryan feigned an unconcerned shrug. The truth was this woman was beginning to piss him off. He needed to get this done and catch up with the brunette. 'You might reconsider that attitude since we just saw you shoot someone in the head.'

The Japanese woman's eyes went momentarily wide, but she regained her composure quickly.

'Have it your way,' Midas said, increasing his grip on her arm until she winced. 'I guess you'd rather talk to the police.'

'*Bakayaro!*' she spat. 'You fools! I am the police.'

43

President Ryan sat in the Oval Office, waiting, mulling over what he was about to say. An eight-by-ten color photograph of a smiling sailor with rosy cheeks looked up at him. The twenty-year-old sailor sat in front of an American flag, wearing enlisted 'crackerjack' blues and a white Dixie cup hat. It was one of those boot-camp graduation portraits that proud grandpas and nervous parents keep on the mantel. Petty Officer 3rd Class Stephen Ridgeway had helped save a life – a woman under attack from pirates, no less. Parents would want to know that. Wouldn't they? Ryan would want to know, if something happened to one of his children. That was the thing about death. It was always personal. Somebody else's kid died and you immediately thought of your own, how fickle life was, how incredibly easy it was to snuff out the spark that made someone alive – no matter how brightly it burned.

Betty Martin's sure voice came over the intercom.

'Mr President, the White House operator has Randy and Lois Ridgeway on the line.'

'Thank you, Betty.' Ryan took a deep breath, attempting to settle himself. Best not to think about things like this for too long. It made the speeches sound canned. Truth was, he thought about it all the time. He couldn't help it.

'Mr and Mrs Ridgeway,' he said, 'this is Jack Ryan. I am so very sorry for your loss . . .'

The condolence call lasted four minutes. There was not much he could say, at least nothing worthwhile. The Ridgeways already knew what sort of man their son was. They didn't need the President of the United States to remind them to be proud of him. Ryan looked at Stephen Ridgeway's portrait for another full minute while he thought over his next course of action. At length, he moved it reverently to the side and centered a yellow notepad on his desk.

He pushed the intercom button.

'It's a Saturday night, Betty,' he said. 'You shouldn't even be here. Go ahead, take off.'

'Right away, Mr President.' It was what Betty Martin said when she wouldn't commit to leaving. Her husband probably sat at home sticking pins in a Jack Ryan doll for all the time she spent at the White House.

'Seriously,' Ryan pressed. 'I just have one more call to make.'

'I'll get the party on the line for you.'

'Go home,' Ryan said. 'That's an order from your commander in chief. I'll make the call myself.'

'There are protocols, Mr President,' Betty said.

'Very well.' He read back the number written on his notepad and then said, 'Now will you go home?'

'Right away, Mr President,' she said.

The Watermelon Park Campground wasn't exactly roughing it, but compared to the bustle of downtown Arlington,

Virginia, the picnic tables, drop toilets, and fire pits over-looking the Shenandoah River were a blissful wilderness. It had taken Dr Ann Miller all the way to Leesburg just to calm down the night before after her command performance at the White House. Her boyfriend was getting sick of hearing the story.

Miller wore the same red-and-black buffalo-plaid shirt that she'd worn to the meeting, but she and Eric had spent the day canoeing, so she'd traded the long pants for a pair of swimming shorts. She was strictly a yogurt-and-blueberries girl back in civilization, but she'd opted to splurge with s'mores tonight. She hunkered shoulder to shoulder with Eric, toasting marshmallows over a snapping fire. It was marvelously dark beyond the chestnut trees, just cool enough to make the heat of the fire against her bare knees feel perfect.

She teased at Eric's toasting stick with hers, pushing it out of her way.

He chuckled, letting his marshmallow catch on fire, and watched it burn. 'I guess people who get summoned to the White House should have the prime coal areas.'

'My thoughts exactly,' Ann said smugly.

'You know,' Eric said, casting a glance at the tent, 'you being in such demand by the highest officials in the land is a real turn-on . . .'

She scoffed. 'Eric Jordan, a leaf falling off one of those red oaks would turn you on.'

Eric moved his eyebrows up and down. 'Depends on where it fell. But seriously, getting called to the White House is a big friggin' deal.'

Miller's phone began to play 'The Ride of the Valkyries'

in her jacket pocket. She'd sealed it in a Ziploc bag in the event they swamped the canoe, and it took her a couple seconds to dig it out.

'Wonder who that could be?' Eric teased. 'Ten Downing Street, mayhaps?'

She waved him away and put the phone to her ear.

'Hello.'

It was a woman's voice, straight to the point.

'Dr Ann Miller?'

'This is she.'

'Dr Miller, please hold for the President of the United States.'

Miller stood at once, dropping her stick into the fire. It was stupid, she realized, but she remained there anyway. Eric looked at her like she'd lost her mind.

An instant later: 'Dr Miller, Jack Ryan here. I apologize for calling so late, but I have some things I'd like you to look over. Would you mind coming by my office tomorrow morning?'

Eric moved in closer now and pressed his ear to hers, listening.

'Of course, Mr President.'

'Very well,' Ryan said. 'I'll send a car for you.'

'No, no,' she stammered. 'I mean, that won't be necessary, sir. We're in the Shenandoah right now. My boyfriend can drop me off.'

'Shall we say nine o'clock tomorrow morning, then?'

Eric feigned a pout after she'd hung up. 'Should I be jealous?'

She laughed, draining off nervous energy. 'I don't know,' she said. 'He is pretty cool. Maybe a little.'

She picked up a camp chair and headed to the car.

'What are you doing?' Eric said.

'Going home,' she said. 'A girl can't wear flannel to the White House twice in a row.'

Ryan hung up the phone at the same moment Arnie van Damm burst in through the door from the secretaries' suite.

'What's Betty doing here on a Saturday night?' He waved his hand before Ryan could answer. 'Never mind. You need to get to a television. Something's going on in Buenos Aires.'

Ryan groaned, moving toward his private study off the Oval. Arnie never wanted him to watch TV when good news was breaking.

'Some kind of bombing,' van Damm continued.

Ryan's stomach tightened at the word. 'Any of our people?' It was always his first question.

Van Damm shook his head. 'A meeting of agricultural ministers, I guess. No US representatives were present.' The CoS scratched his bald head. 'I'm not sure why, but Foreign Minister Li was there. It's unspooling even as we speak. Unconfirmed number of dead.'

Arnie followed Ryan into the small study down a short hall off the Oval Office. He picked up the remote because God forbid Ryan should have to turn on his own television.

They stood together in silence for a time and watched live reports of shaky cell phone footage. The plate-glass windows in the front of what looked like a restaurant had been shattered. Uniformed men and women appeared to be moving in all directions. Two fire trucks were parked out front, their lights pulsing in the evening darkness, causing the video footage to flare dramatically. Ambulances rolled up on scene, motioned forward by the uniforms. The commentary was in Spanish, and an American news anchor did her best to repeat a whole lot of nothing over and over again. What else could she do? *Nothing* was precisely what everyone in the United States knew at this point.

Arnie asked, 'Shall I round up the NSC? The Principal Committee, at least?'

The Principal Committee was an abbreviated version of the National Security Council – consisting of the DNI, the chairman of the Joint Chiefs, D/CIA, and a handful of cabinet secretaries. They could convene in the Situation Room, but the number was small enough that they could meet in his office.

Ryan thought over the value of calling in even the abbreviated committee on a Saturday evening. 'No Americans are involved?'

'Not to my knowledge,' Arnie said.

'But China again . . .'

'Yep.'

Ryan watched two Argentine firefighters carry a body out of the restaurant in a bag. He shook his head. 'No,' he said. 'Let's just get Mary Pat on the line for now. I want to run a couple things by her.'

Van Damm sat down at the small desk in the cramped study and went to work getting in touch with the DNI while Ryan sat back on one of the two tufted leather chairs to watch the coverage from Buenos Aires. The news crawl along the bottom of the screen carried the BREAKING

NEWS message, but with nothing but amateur video coming in, there was little to report. The crawl repeated headlines from the last few hours, including news of Typhoon Catelyn gathering strength two hundred nautical miles east of Okinawa. He'd already been briefed on what was then Tropical Storm Catelyn when it narrowly missed the US Naval base on Guam. Now the damn thing had turned north toward Yokosuka, Japan.

'I have MP,' Arnie said. 'Want me to put her on speaker?'

Ryan shook his head. 'On second thought, go ahead and patch in Bob Burgess, too. I'd like to get a sitrep on the safety of the Seventh Fleet while we're at it.'

44

Ding Chavez stood with Jack Ryan, Jr, on the sidewalk in front of the Freddo ice cream shop, across the street from Recoleta Cemetery. Ten feet away, Midas and Adara flanked the seething Japanese woman.

'Impossible to prove,' Ding said. 'It's not like Kōanchōsa-chō carry around ID cards.'

The Kōanchōsa-chō, or Public Security Intelligence Agency, was akin to the CIA, FBI counterintelligence, and MI6, responsible for gathering intelligence and conducting counterespionage activities against both internal and external threats to the people of Japan.

'She has support and training,' Ryan said. 'It's no easy task to get a suppressed rifle into the country and then set up a sniper hide across the street from an international event. And I did see her following the brunette.'

'Tell me her name again,' Ding said.

Ryan looked at the palm of his hand where he'd written it down. 'Yukiko,' he said. 'At least that's the name she gave.'

'Well, shit,' Chavez said. He'd worked with a couple Kōanchōsa-chō guys a few years before. They'd been good intelligence officers, if a bit humorless for Ding's taste. But the IC world was not one where you could name-drop. For one thing, cover identities came and went. A real name might get nothing but a blank stare – even if you were both talking about the same person.

Chavez walked over to look the woman in the eye. 'You've put us in a bit of a pickle,' he said.

Yukiko glared. 'I could scream rape.'

'Go for it,' Chavez said. 'I doubt you want to talk to the cops any worse than we do – even if you are Kōanchōsa-chō. Hell, especially if you are.'

Her eyes flashed toward the cemetery wall. 'We waste time standing here.'

'How's that?' Chavez said.

'You are CIA?'

Chavez shook his head. 'Nice try.'

The Japanese woman stared hard at him, obviously thinking through her options. If she were truly Japanese intelligence, she'd realize she didn't have many. At length, her shoulders dropped and she heaved a long sigh. She nodded toward Jack.

'Your young friend says they went into the cemetery.'

'They did.' Chavez played along. That tidbit of information wasn't exactly a state secret. 'Probably went straight over the far side before we could get around.'

Yukiko shook her head. 'I do not believe that is true.'

Adara moved a half-step closer. 'What, then?'

'The Basilica del Pilar is at the northeast corner of the grounds. Many of the churches in Buenos Aires have underground cloisters where nuns or Jesuit priests –'

'No, no, no.' Jack cut her off. 'No more tunnels!' He said it loud enough that a passing couple turned to look at the crazy *turista*.

'As I was saying.' The Japanese woman gave a half-smile, then turned back to Chavez. 'Jesuit priests constructed tunnels under many portions of the city. Some believe they planned to build a network so vast as to connect most of the churches in Buenos Aires.'

'Okay . . .' Chavez said. 'Let's say Chen took one of these tunnels. Can you take us to the entrance?'

'Trust me,' Jack said. 'You don't want to go down there.'

Yukiko shook her head. 'There are almost five thousand burial vaults in an area covering fifty thousand square meters. There may be many entrances . . . or the way down could be beneath the church itself.'

'If there is one,' Chavez said.

The Japanese woman conceded the point. 'This is true,' she said, nodding at Jack again. 'But as your young friend will tell you, at least one of the tunnels leads to the slums on the other side of the tracks. Vincent Chen has a contact there who offers him protection, a man named Santiago Salazar. He is the father of Amanda Salazar, the Paraguayan woman you followed from the bombing. He is what you would call a neighborhood criminal boss in this *villa miseria*. I placed a listening device against the window of his home earlier today.'

'Let me guess,' Jack said. 'Right before a guy with a machete chased you back into the sewer tunnel?'

'Correct,' Yukiko said.

Adara sighed. 'Then he knows the device is there.'

'Maybe not,' Jack said. 'The guy with the machete never made it back to tell him.'

'Ah,' Adara said. 'Right.'

Ryan turned back to Yukiko. 'I watched Amanda Salazar cut through the train yard,' he said. 'Why didn't she use the tunnel if it comes up near her father's house?'

'Would you?' Yukiko said. 'If you did not have to? I

believe she suffers from ... *heijokyōfushō* ... fear of small places.'

'Claustrophobia,' Chavez said.

'Yes,' Yukiko said. 'That is the word. In any case, we should hurry. My phone was damaged when you knocked me down. My room is behind the Hyatt on Montevideo. I have another phone there, but they will reach Salazar's very soon. We must hurry if we hope to learn anything of value from the device I planted.'

Chavez raised an eyebrow. 'Sure you don't have a partner there as well?'

'Believe me,' Yukiko said, 'if I had a partner, you would be aware of that by now.'

Chavez looked at the rest of his team.

Both Midas and Adara shrugged.

'We have to do something,' Jack said.

'All right, then.' Chavez motioned up the street with his open hand, nodding to Midas and Adara. 'Feel free to shoot her if she tries anything.'

'Aye, sir,' Adara said.

Chavez turned to Ryan as the other two led the way with the Japanese woman in tow. 'Notice how she kept calling you my "young friend" like you were some kind of kid?'

Jack chuckled. 'Ding, Ding, Ding,' he whispered so Yukiko couldn't hear the name. 'She's not calling me that because I look like a kid. She's calling me that because you're old.'

'Get your ass moving, Ryan.'

President Jack Ryan rummaged through the bottom drawer of the desk in his study while Arnie van Damm took care of arranging the phone call. Ryan found the golf ball he was looking for and dropped it on the floor. Van Damm looked up at the clunk as the ball hit the carpet, and saw Ryan had kicked off his shoe.

'What?' Ryan said, rolling the ball around under his foot.

Van Damm held up both hands. 'Hey,' he said. 'This is your office. Who am I to judge?'

The phone gave an audible tone and the White House operator said, 'Both parties are on the line, Mr President.'

The director of national intelligence and the secretary of defense acknowledged that they were, indeed, there.

Ryan said, 'Are you guys watching the news?'

'Just now,' Mary Pat said. 'My deputy called me about thirty seconds before you did.'

'Same here,' Burgess said. 'They're saying Foreign Minister Li was injured but not badly. He'd be a likely target if Zhao's behind this.'

'Could be,' the DNI said. 'One thing's certain, Li will leverage the hell out of this. Surviving an assassination attempt is a great way to boost political approval ratings.'

'Don't remind me,' Ryan said. 'My numbers went up fourteen points after the bombing in Mexico City. For some reason, not dying is seen as heroic. In any case, we shouldn't discount the possibility that this bombing is related to everything else.'

'I agree,' the SecDef said. 'If you put together the *Orion* explosion, the attack on the oil rig in Chad, the USS *Rogue* incident, and these events in Argentina – all lines converge on Zhao.'

'Maybe,' Mary Pat said. 'But the woman who survived

the attack in which the *Rogue* was involved described the pirates as being Indonesian or Malaysian.'

'That is true,' Burgess said. 'But I'd put money on finding Zhao's fingerprints on the payment to any of a half-dozen terrorist groups around Indonesia – as we did with Boko Haram in Chad. He's pissed because our Freedom of Navigation ops are making him look bad, so he makes a play for one of our ships. *Rogue* wasn't broadcasting on AIS and her schedule wasn't advertised, but the fact that they were helping out as part of Malaysian anti-piracy efforts was in all the papers down there. It was no secret that she was to berth in Australia prior to returning to her task force group. The average speed of a *Cyclone*-class PC is open-source. Anyone who wanted to target her would have had to wait for her to leave and start a countdown. Enough yachties sail through that area this time of year heading for Bali or Singapore that it would be easy to grab one when *Rogue* was presumably close enough to render aid.'

'A lot of moving parts,' Mary Pat said. 'But it very nearly got the job done.'

'Not really,' Burgess said. 'We have security measures to keep bad actors from getting too close to one of our ships, but at some point the VBSS teams have to close the distance with the RHIB to do their jobs.'

'I'm glad you brought up the terrorist groups, Bob,' Ryan said. 'I've asked Dr Miller to come in tomorrow and do some focused digging. Mary Pat, I'd appreciate it if you could get with her bosses and make sure she's read into anything we have on Laskar Jihad, Jemaah Islamiyah . . . and that old East Timor independence group we looked into . . . What were they called?'

'Revolutionary Front,' the DNI said, demonstrating why she held the position she did.

'That's the one,' Ryan continued. 'We'll cast a broad net. Hell, let's get Dr Miller access to cases on the He-Man Woman Haters Club if they have a chapter in that part of the world.'

Mary Pat chuckled. 'As soon as we're done here, Mr President,' she said. 'I'll look into this Argentina thing as well.'

Ryan knew by 'looking into it' Mary Pat would bring to bear the investigative and analytical brainpower of the sixteen US intelligence agencies under her purview. For all the information silos, turf wars, and territorial fights between the various agencies, when a personal directive went out from the DNI, one could almost hear the collective mental gears turning in Washington.

'You're excused, then, Mary Pat,' Ryan said. 'And thanks for your work.'

'Thank you, Mr President,' the DNI said, and then disconnected.

'Now,' Ryan continued, 'Bob, bring me up to speed on our ships in the WestPac.'

'We've moved everyone out of the storm path,' Burgess said. 'Or at least we did. This typhoon is all over the damned place. Its westerly course has now veered sharply north, putting it on a collision course for Central Japan. The Bōsō Peninsula gives some protection to Tokyo Bay if a storm comes in from the east, but Typhoon Catelyn is heading straight up the pipe.'

'Leaving Yokosuka vulnerable,' Ryan said, picturing the geography around the American Naval facility.

'Correct,' the SecDef said. 'The storm may well yet turn west again, but Admiral Blackley ordered all vessels out to sea. They'll head north and wait out the storm in colder waters. Even if it continues that way, it'll lose steam.'

'Very well,' Ryan said. He knew Vice Admiral Blackley well and trusted the man's judgment. 'Let me know if anything develops.'

Ryan leaned back on the couch and gave a nod to van Damm, who ended the call.

The CoS drummed his fingers on the desk, eyes narrow. Arnie van Damm's mind was always moving near light speed, one or two steps ahead of most people in the room – when it came to politics, at least.

Ryan raised an eyebrow. 'What's on your mind?'

'Jack,' van Damm said. Calling him by his given name was a sure sign the CoS was about to dispense some serious advice. 'I know you, and I know you're counting on this upcoming summit to meet face-to-face with President Zhao.'

Ryan had the golf ball in his hand now, rolling it back and forth with his fingers. 'I've met him before,' he said.

'True, but that meeting was absent the present facts.' Van Damm glanced at a scratch pad on the desk. 'RSMC Tokyo clocks Typhoon Catelyn with sustained winds of a hundred five miles an hour. And she's showing rapid intensification.'

'I don't think we're supposed to call them "she" anymore.'

Van Damm rolled his eyes. 'If this genderless storm with a female name makes landfall anywhere near the

Kantō Plain, Japan might be a little busy with recovery efforts to host the G20.'

'True,' Ryan said.

'The evidence against Zhao is mounting,' van Damm said. 'And what we do have is pretty damned . . . well, damning. I know you want to meet him, shake his hand, get what you believe is a true measure of the man, but that might not be possible. Jack, you may well have to make a decision on Zhao without looking him in the eye.'

45

Yukiko's apartment was on the fourth floor of a tidy but older brick building a block and a half to the northeast of the Palacio Duhau Hyatt, where the Chinese foreign minister was staying. Buenos Aires city police and members of Foreign Minister Li's protective detail had barricaded both ends of Avenida Alvear in front of the hotel and Posadas behind, forcing the Campus operators to approach the Kōanchōsa-chō operative's room from Libertador. On the other side of Libertador was the train yard. Five hundred meters beyond that were the slums of Villa 31 and, presumably, Vincent Chen's little band of terrorists.

Chavez placed a call to John Clark as they walked, asking him to check with his contacts in the Japanese intelligence community to see if any of them could verify a Monzaki Yukiko. He was still waiting to hear back when they arrived in front of the building.

The single apartment elevator was Old World-style, with a wooden door and an accordion gate that had to be shut manually before the car would operate. There was only enough room inside for four at a time, so Chavez, Ryan, and Adara squeezed in with the Japanese woman, leaving Midas to bound up the stairs.

The car chugged upward slowly with the weight of four passengers, and the former Delta commander was leaning against a plaster-covered wall when Jack pushed open the door.

'You're staying alone,' Chavez asked again.

Yukiko held up her little finger, bending it at the knuckle. *'Yubikiri,'* she said. 'I promise.'

Midas and Adara went through the door first, clearing the room before allowing Yukiko inside.

'I guess you really weren't expecting company,' Midas said when he came back to the door. 'You're as messy as my young friend.'

Chavez's phone buzzed. He answered it, nodded a few times, and then motioned for Yukiko to hold up her right hand, thumb extended. She did, revealing a crescent scar on the web.

'Looks like it's her,' Chavez said. 'Thanks, Mr C.'

Yukiko smiled. 'Mr C? My father knew a man named John who was sometimes called that.'

Chavez winked at the others in the group. 'That's what Mr C said.'

It took more than a phone call to be completely accepted, but the fact that John Clark apparently knew her father put Monzaki Yukiko well on the road. The IC world was often a multigenerational affair, with children following parents into the business. Clearances could be somewhat easier to obtain when a relative had already been scrutinized to the nth degree during a security background check.

Free now to move as she pleased without getting shot, Yukiko wasted no time in retrieving a spare mobile phone from a bag on her dresser and dialing up what was presumably a GSM bug like the ones Campus operators often deployed.

All of them were accustomed to the boredom of monitoring a bug and took up comfortable positions around the small efficiency apartment. Yukiko sat on a cramped loveseat beside Adara, elbows on her knees. Midas and Ding took up positions in the two wood slat chairs covered with quilted pillows, while Jack sat on the edge of the hastily made bed.

The device was active, picking up the periodic clang of pots or the sound of someone belching.

'Kitchen?' Adara asked.

Yukiko nodded. 'The microphone is directly against the window. Cheap glass is very good at conducting sound. There is a large table approximately five feet from the wall. If Chen holds a meeting, there is a good chance it will be at that table.'

Jack rubbed a hand over the top of his head. 'I don't get it, Yukiko. What's the Japanese connection?'

'Please call me Yuki,' she said. 'That is a very good question. Have you heard of Chongryon?'

'Sounds Korean,' Jack said.

Chavez nodded. 'Isn't that the political arm of the DPRK in Japan?'

'Precisely that,' Yuki said. 'My organization has linked members of Chongryon to acts of espionage in Japan. Kim Soo, a Korean woman with strong ties to this group, is one of Vincent Chen's many paramours. My research leads me to believe Chen has many female contacts around the world – Amanda Salazar as a case in point. He is quite charming, but mixing work with pleasure will be his eventual downfall. I would not have been aware of Vincent Chen if he'd had better taste in women.'

Midas took a deep breath. 'This is a cruddy thing to bring up, but it impacts operational security. If we're working together now, we need to know about the blonde who was shot.'

Yuki tilted her head to the side, her face passive. 'Beatriz Campos was also from Paraguay. She is . . . was a known assassin and a terrorist, already convicted in absentia for the murder of two Japanese businessmen during a visit to Peru. My organization believes Kim Soo is complicit in a plot to disrupt the upcoming G20 Summit. I was sent here to follow her and glean any useful intelligence. Suspicions against Kim are just that, suspicions, but the evidence against Beatriz Campos is irrefutable. I had no idea she would be here, but when I found out, I simply seized the opportunity . . .'

Midas pressed the issue. 'So you carry the suppressed .22-caliber rifle around, just in case?'

'Another fair question,' the Japanese woman said. 'There must be trust if we are to work together. Were the intelligence on Kim to reach a high enough standard, I would contact my superiors with the information, and then proceed as ordered. Such orders may include the use of a rifle.' She shrugged. 'Your country has been known to put the faces of certain . . . high-value targets on playing cards.'

The group nodded.

Midas said, 'Targets, indeed.'

'High value, indeed,' Yuki said. 'Beatriz Campos was not our ace of spades. She was, however, an ace.'

Less than six hundred meters away, at the Palacio Duhau Hyatt, Chinese foreign minister Li reclined barefoot and shirtless on a blue velvet *duchesse brisée*, his legs propped on a thick pillow on the elongated footstool. The room had a distinct French neoclassical style with claw-foot furniture, wing-backed chairs, and the 'broken duchess' style of chaise longue, where Li was undergoing a thorough examination from his physician. The bespectacled Dr Ren used a pair of tweezers to pick bits of wood and gypsum wallboard from Li's shoulder.

He would not have been injured at all had the idiot Paraguayan woman not been so slow to detonate the device. Her stupidity would have infuriated him, but the minor shrapnel wounds would only enhance the story of the cowardly attempt on his life. The death of one of the members of his security detail and the injury of another should have been enough, but you played the hand you were dealt.

Li's mobile phone began to buzz across the ornate glass-topped table at the foot of the *duchesse brisée*. He shot a glance at Long Yun, who looked down at the number and then picked it up without answering.

'Madame Li,' Long said.

The foreign minister nodded and held out his hand, causing the doctor to stab him with the tweezers. Li cursed at the idiot and shoved him away, ordering him out of the room before taking the phone.

'*Wei, xingan baobei,*' he said. Hello, sweetheart. 'No, I am fine. Minor scratches, that is all. No, no, really. I am well . . . Please tell our son not to worry. He must be brave and take care of his mother . . .'

Journalists from Xinhua – reporting directly to Secretary Deng's propaganda department – would speak with

Madame Li shortly. The foreign minister knew his wife well enough to be sure that she would quote her selfless husband, who, though wounded in a foreign land, exhorted their son to 'be brave and take care of his mother.' He felt a pang of guilt at using his family so cruelly, but quickly disabused himself of the feelings. Drastic actions were necessary for the survival of the party, perhaps even for China itself.

'Yes, my dear,' he continued to console his wife, 'they are taking good care of me. I will be home very soon. Yes, my love. I must hang up now.'

He did not actually end the call first. Such an act would have proven disastrous. Even a man as powerful as the foreign minister of China knew to let his wife be the one to end the call. She finally did, and Li handed the phone off to Long Yun.

The CSB officer set it back on the table.

'Will we go forward, Mr Foreign Minister?'

'Of course,' Li said. 'Why would we not? I am fine. We have come too far to turn back now.'

Colonel Long nodded toward a flat-screen television across the room. The sound was off, but the photos showed the whirling white vortex of a typhoon on a large map that included Taiwan, Japan, and the East China Sea.

'The typhoon has turned northward,' Long said. 'It may prove problematic if it reaches Japan.'

'Nonsense,' Li said. 'The summit is still days away. Many things will occur between now and then. Now get that egg of a doctor back in here.'

Li knew all too well that there were countless things that could go wrong with his scheme – this typhoon, the unknown person who had shot Amanda's blond compatriot, even idiot servants who were dilatory in their duties. President Zhao might suddenly realize that Li was not actually his best friend. No, the man was much too dense for that. And even if Zhao did come to that conclusion, he would have to grow a pair of testicles in order to do anything about it. Perhaps by then the President of the United States would have used his famous Ryan Doctrine to put an end to Zhao and his witch hunt for anyone in the party who had exhibited a shred of financial success. And if President Ryan was himself too dense, then there was always another way.

In truth, Li had begun to think of their cause as a noble one. Just as Chairman Mao must have seen the task that had been before him. A work of the gods – or, in a world absent any gods, at least the work of destiny.

Maybe they turned in for the night,' Chavez said.

'Perhaps,' Yuki said. 'More likely they are upset about the death of Beatriz Campos.'

Jack rubbed a hand across his beard. Talk of the sewers had left him feeling like he needed another shower. 'How long will the battery last on your device?'

'The microphone is voice-activated,' she said. 'That will conserve some power, but I am afraid we have no more than thirty-six hours.'

'We'll listen in shifts, then,' Chavez said. 'Jack, you're voltold to take the first rotation.'

'Excellent,' Ryan said through a feigned smile.

'I will listen with him,' Yuki said. 'To make certain he does not drift off to sleep.'

Midas stood and raised his arms high overhead in a long, shuddering stretch. 'I call dibs on half the bed.'

Adara stuck out her bottom lip in a mock pout. 'What happened to guys taking the couch?'

'I only called half the bed,' Midas said. 'You can fight Ding for the other half.'

'I'm good on the floor,' Chavez said, dragging the cushions off his chair.

Midas fell back on the mattress, bouncing once before curling up in the sheet, apparently unfazed that Yuki had slept in it the night before. He'd surely slept in much, much worse. 'Don't try anything,' he said without opening his eyes as Adara got in beside him.

'I'll do my best to contain myself,' she said.

Chavez was already breathing deeply.

'I like your friends,' Yuki said, looking at Jack, who now sat beside her on the loveseat.

'Me too,' Ryan said. He wanted to ask her about the scratches on her face but decided against it. He was surrounded by people he trusted, and was alive after a particularly bloody day. A little mystery was a good thing.

46

John Clark was nothing if not patient. He'd seen Magdalena's auction video in the room at Matarife's ranch. It had sickened him enough to make it his mission to find the one who'd brought her to the States. The person who had used her and then quite literally sold her into slavery. According to Lupe, that person was Dorian Palmetto.

Clark had a nose for bad men like Palmetto, but even so, it took two days of watchful waiting to find him.

Lupe had given him the location of the cheap hotel where Palmetto liked to hang out and a vague physical description, but Clark still didn't know exactly what he looked like. He considered the idea of calling in a favor with an old friend from the Agency – or even getting Gavin to pull the guy's photo. In the end, though, he decided he didn't want any kind of trail, even with trusted friends. As it turned out, in addition to running a side business trafficking in human cargo, Palmetto had a real job managing an auto parts store near the Naval Air Station Joint Reserve Base in West Fort Worth. Navy C-40 Clippers and Air Force Reserve C-130s had replaced the iconic B-52 Stratofortresses of Clark's day when it had been a Strategic Air Command Base. Air Force F-16s and an occasional Navy F/A-18 Hornet roared overhead, invigorating Clark and helping rather than hindering his thinking process.

Clark was a traditionalist when it came to investigation, preferring well-worn shoe leather and telephoto lenses over computer analysis. But even he didn't have any trouble learning that there were three people named Dorian Palmetto on Facebook – and one of them had graduated from Arlington Heights High School, also in West Fort Worth. It was a dangerous endeavor to see stereotypes in the world of intelligence gathering, yet looking at the smarmy mug of Palmetto's profile picture, Clark couldn't help thinking that he would have shot this guy had he ever approached one of his daughters. Shooting him certainly wasn't outside the realm of possibility now.

According to his profile, Dorian was married with two children, both boys. His wife was a slender waif of a thing, with freckles and braids that, not incidentally, made her look like she was in junior high school. It made Clark sick to his stomach to contemplate her horrible life. It was all based on a lie and she went to sleep every night with no idea she was married to a monster – or it was a living hell. Either way, that was about to change.

Clark knew there was a way to get GPS locations from photos on Facebook. He'd heard Gavin talk about it. But again, he decided to watch and wait. He had the address of the Auto Sphere where Palmetto worked and of the Sleeptight Inn tucked in off Loop 820, where, according to Lupe, he took new girls to 'break them in.'

The chain-smoking woman with peroxide-orange hair behind the front desk hadn't given Clark a second look when he checked into the Sleeptight Inn the day before. She was evidently used to older single men in dark glasses who paid cash and kept to themselves. For a two-hundred-dollar deposit – a little over four nights' rent – she didn't make him show any ID.

Clark had stayed in worse places, though that had been many years ago – and Vietcong soldiers had been trying to kill him at the time. All the rooms in this single-floor motel faced the parking lot, and Clark's room, the last one on the short leg of the L-shaped building, gave him a decent view of all the doors but the two adjacent to his. The walls were thin enough that he could hear if anyone came or went in the next room – but no one ever did.

Palmetto's Facebook photos showed that he drove a blue Dodge Durango with damage to the right-front fender. Clark woke up to peek out the window and find the Durango parked across the lot. But by the time he got his pants on and slipped the 1911 into his holster, it was gone. It didn't matter. He'd always been patient, and years of hunting men had endowed him with even more of that particular virtue.

Now that Lupe's information was confirmed, Clark had no doubt that Palmetto would return.

Clark made it a habit to carry a couple Clif Bars in his bag, but when Palmetto still hadn't shown by late evening, the chocolate chip and peanut butter washed down with Diet Pepsi from the motel vending machine was wearing thin. He reasoned that Palmetto was a predator, and as such, he would have a territory. When he wasn't bringing in girls from South America, he'd surely be trolling for them somewhere within driving distance of home. The money in human trafficking was incredibly good. There was no doubt of that. But Palmetto's Facebook didn't show him spending money on his family or his vehicle – and he certainly wasn't blowing it on fancy hotels. No, a man like Dorian Palmetto was in it for the hunt.

A quick computer search pulled up crime statistics for the local area, noting a higher-than-average number of prostitution arrests near a bus transfer station just a few blocks away. If Palmetto wasn't at the Sleeptight Inn, he was either at home with his baby-faced wife or out trolling.

Clark stopped at a Whataburger to grab a sandwich and then ate in the rental car while he drove. The bus station turned up nothing, so he drove around the mall parking lot, thinking and looking for the Durango. He found nothing there, either, so he decided to cruise by the nearby seedy motels he'd found through the Internet. There were plenty of guys going in and out of various rooms. Hookers hardly ever worked the corners anymore. Sites like Craigslist and Backpage had taken the girls off the street – and when the adult-services ads on those sites had been taken down, more sprang up to take their place.

It was beginning to get dark when Clark finally saw a blue-gray Durango parked on the side of the road, half a block from the bus transfer station. He made a mental note of the license plate number and then slowed as he continued down the block. A tall Ken doll of a man with perfect black hair was busy chatting up a couple young girls. Clark couldn't see his face at first, but knew in an instant that this was Dorian Palmetto. Surely fresh meat to him, both girls carried small backpacks and had probably just gotten off a bus. Palmetto paid no attention to

Clark as he cruised past in one of a dozen dark sedans, focusing instead on his quarry.

Palmetto leaned in close, body-blocking both girls as they stood against the brick building next to the bus stop. The taller of the two wanted no part of it and waved him off. She went so far as to duck under his outstretched arm and walk away.

'Way to go, kid,' Clark said out loud. He fought the urge to drive up and slam the man's face against the brick wall, but consoled himself in the knowledge that that would come later.

Sadly, a much smaller girl, likely a runaway and still hardly more than a child, appeared to be interested in Palmetto's proposal. She had short purple hair and a nose ring big enough that Clark could see it from a distance. Palmetto did a lot of talking with his hands, pointing up the street, then opening both arms as if he were offering this girl the world – or, at the very least, a whole lot of money.

The driver of a dually pickup behind Clark lay on his horn, forcing him to drive on or risk drawing attention to himself. He flipped a quick U-turn as soon as he had an opening, but the Durango was already pulling away by the time he got back to the bus stop, and the girl with the purple hair was gone.

Clark hung back, sipping his Diet Pepsi and reaching into the Whataburger sack to grab the last of his french fries as he followed Palmetto and the girl back to the Sleeptight Inn. He got out of his rental car at the same time Dorian opened the door to his Durango. Clark did his best to rein in the hard look he knew he possessed, rounding his shoulders a little and even affecting a slight limp. He was just some random man who'd rented a room, too old to be any trouble. Palmetto paused anyway, giving him a quick once-over. His hand shifted nervously to his waistband, likely touching a handgun.

Nice of you to let me know where you keep it, Clark thought.

Palmetto pointed toward number 5. That figured. He'd want a room away from the office – or at least the office would want him far away so they'd have some deniability. The girl followed dutifully, cords to her earbuds trailing down the sides of her face, her head bobbing to whatever music was playing on her phone. She never even looked up at Clark, which made his next move much easier.

47

The doors at the Sleeptight Inn had seen plenty of wear from police boots, so it didn't take much effort with the flathead screwdriver Clark carried in his pocket. He'd anticipated having to make such an entry and already practiced on his own door. The key would have been slower.

Clark rolled a black balaclava over his face and pushed. The screwdriver was still in his left hand, a nine-inch leather sap in the other. Palmetto had just hit the girl hard in the back of the head. She pitched face-first into the unmade bed, perfectly framed in front of two tripod-mounted cameras. Palmetto's head snapped up at the noise behind him. Clark's sap took him across the temple, the ten ounces of lead shot impacting bone and rattling teeth with a satisfying thud. He dropped like a sack of wet sand.

Clark registered a flash of movement to his left. He turned in time to see a very large black man with long dreadlocks barreling at him from the open bathroom door fifteen feet away. Focused as he was on Palmetto, the attack caught Clark flatfooted, driving him against a wall and knocking the wind from his lungs. Clark attempted to bring the sap into play, but the man was too close, robbing the swing of any power.

The man was at least forty years younger – though with Clark's balaclava, he hadn't figured that out. What he did know was that he was a half a head taller than Clark.

Clark exhaled quickly, relaxing his paralyzed diaphragm. He couldn't do anything about the searing pain in his ribs.

'You messed up!' the man growled, stepping back to have a good look at the little man he was about to crush. 'Parrot is about to put a chop on you that you never gonna forget!'

Clark stopped listening when he heard this guy was Parrot. The name had come up too many times – always in association with a bruised or broken girl. He'd read Blanca Limón's statement, heard the stories about the brutal 'choppings' this monster used to discipline his girls and keep them in line.

With his back to the girl on the bed, Clark feinted with his right hand, drawing the much larger man's attention to the leather sap.

'Punk ass,' Parrot said, and chuckled. 'I'm gonna take your little bat an –'

Clark wasted no time on words. Bounding forward, he drove the screwdriver straight up through the bottom of the big man's jaw, shoving upward, aiming for the ceiling. The steel shaft of the screwdriver pierced Parrot's tongue and impaled the soft palate at the back of his mouth. His teeth slammed together. His eyes flew open in shock. He made a vain attempt to grab at the screwdriver, but Clark batted his hand away with the sap. Clark pressed the attack, slamming the lead-filled sap into the man's elbow as he fell.

Clark shot a quick glance toward a sound to his right and saw a black girl in her early teens peeking around the bathroom door. The fog of battle made it difficult to tell for sure, but Clark thought she had a bloody nose.

Parrot gurgled, trying to draw a breath around the screwdriver through his sinuses. Clark turned in time to see the man claw for a pistol in his waistband.

Enraged at the sight of a bleeding child, Clark bounded forward, kicking the handle of the screwdriver, driving the remainder of the shaft into the man's brain with a sickening pop. Like his life, Parrot's death was brutal, ugly, and loud, and it was over.

Clark spun, dropping the sap to the floor in favor of his .45. He needed to be sure Dorian Palmetto was still out of play. Palmetto wasn't dead — but not for lack of effort on Clark's part. He'd learned long before that knocking someone silly wasn't all that difficult so long as the possibility of killing them in the process wasn't taken off the table. Palmetto's eyes were closed and a thin trickle of blood seeped from his ear, but unlike Parrot, he was still breathing. The girl on the bed was either out cold or pretending to be.

Clark secured Palmetto's Glock in his waistband, and then, his own .45 held at low ready, inched sideways to bring the bathroom into view. Cutting the pie.

He found the black girl huddled alone on the floor beside the tub. Blood soaked through a bath towel she'd wrapped around her naked shoulders. Clark holstered the pistol and held up both hands.

'I'm a friend,' he said.

The girl hugged her knees to her chest, rocking back and forth, eyes clenched shut.

Clark shot a peek around the corner to make sure Palmetto and the girl were still out. They were, so he squatted down to be more or less on the same level as the cowering girl.

'What's your name?'

She said nothing.

'Look.' Clark took a deep breath. He was hell at being mean. Tenderness was a little more difficult, so he decided he'd just be honest, and as kind as he knew how to be. 'These men aren't going to hurt you anymore. Let's get you some clothes.'

Clark backed out of the bathroom, not wanting to pressure someone who was already shattered. A few moments later, he had both Palmetto's and the purple-haired girl's hands zip-tied behind their backs. He suspected this one was still pretending to be unconscious, but she was an unknown entity, so he decided to leave her restrained until she came to.

Technically, Clark was holding the girl against her will, but compared to the other crimes he'd committed – and those he intended to commit in the very near future – kidnapping a juvenile for her own safety seemed like a minor offense.

A quiet voice drew Clark's attention back to the bathroom door.

'Jo,' the girl said. 'My name's Jo.'

She stared, eyes locked on the screwdriver jutting like a gruesome goatee from under Parrot's chin.

'Hi, Jo,' Clark said softly. He moved quickly to cover the dead man with a sheet and then held the heavier bedspread out for the girl. The blood-soaked towel slipped off her shoulders as she took it, revealing an angry burn on her neck. A brand.

'You want to call your mom?' he asked softly.

'My mom's dead,' the girl said. Her chin quivered as she spoke.

'Your dad?'

The girl shook her head. 'Oh, *hell* no!' she said, sounding heartbreakingly like someone twice her age.

'The police, then,' Clark said.

Adrenaline from the fight began to ebb, leaving him suddenly sore and exhausted. His eyes misted over as he imagined the horrors the poor kid must have endured.

'Are you a policeman?' the girl asked.

'Not exactly.'

'The police stopped Parrot's car twice, you know,' Jo said. 'But they was always lookin' for drugs.' She closed her eyes, starting to tremble at the memory. 'Parrot, he just hug me in close to him and say in my ear, "You my drugs, Jo. You my drugs." Them cops didn't ever even notice me, I don't believe. Maybe they think I was his daughter or somethin'.'

Clark put the back of a hand to his eye, wiping away a tear, and realized he still had the black balaclava pulled over his head. 'Don't be scared.'

Jo shook her head. 'You ain't scary, mister,' she said. 'Nobody looked at me and cried in an awful long time. Nobody at all . . .'

Jo went into the bathroom and put on a pair of shorts and a loose T-shirt while Clark examined the camera and computer setup.

By the time she came out, he had Dorian sitting upright,

hands behind his back, a piece of duct tape across his mouth. On the other side of the bed, as far away as humanly possible without falling off, the purple-haired girl breathed peacefully, fear or embarrassment making her keep up the unconscious act.

'You like music?' Clark asked.

Jo nodded.

He'd pulled up some music his grandson liked on his cell phone and connected the earphones he carried for backup communication with other Campus members.

'How about . . . Imagine Dragons . . . or . . . Maroon 5?' In truth, Clark was just reading off a playlist. He had no idea what either of the bands sounded like, but if his grandson liked them, maybe the girl would, too. He imagined she hadn't gotten to make a choice about anything in some time.

Jo almost smiled.

Clark pulled the only chair in the room away from the wall.

'How about you listen to the music,' he said. 'I have some things I need to talk over with Dorian.'

Clark put the purple-haired girl's earbuds back in her ears. Hopefully, her music would blot out what was about to happen. He was beginning to fear that something might be physically wrong with her, but she opened one eye, chickenlike, and shot a quick look at him before slamming it back shut again.

Across the room, Jo slumped low in the chair, suddenly a teenager again. She looked up suddenly and took out one earbud to give Clark a quizzical look. Her voice was calm now, matter-of-fact.

'You gonna kill him, mister?'

Dorian gave a muffled cry behind the duct tape. He began shaking all over, eyes wide as saucers.

'No,' Clark said. 'We're going to use his computer to let him call the police.'

'Cool,' Jo said, and went back to her music.

Clark ripped the tape from Dorian's mouth and then walked back across the room to retrieve the screwdriver from Parrot's jaw. It came out with a sickening croak, which only added to the psy ops. Palmetto was used to being in charge – the one calling the shots over kids like Magdalena Rojas, Jo, and the girl with the purple hair. Finding himself at the mercy of a determined killer like John Clark had him completely unglued.

Dorian's chest heaved with sobs. 'You don't have to do this.'

'Oh, I know that,' Clark said, leaning in close so the girls couldn't hear. 'What I'd really like to do is put a bullet in your brain pan. And to be honest, I still might. But I need some information first.'

All the air seemed to leave the man. 'What do you want? I mean, just take the girls. They're yours, man.'

Clark didn't bother to wipe Parrot's blood off the screwdriver, but held it in plain view while he quizzed Palmetto in a harsh whisper about Matarife and Zambrano. Palmetto held nothing back, giving the location of Emilio Zambrano's ranch as well as an address west of Dallas where Matarife might be hiding out.

Clark cocked his head to one side, holding the bloody screwdriver like he hadn't decided what to do with it yet. 'So you're the one who found Magdalena?'

Palmetto nodded. At this point, he hadn't figured out exactly what Clark's game was. He decided wrong, and guessed a member of the competition. 'Everyone's always looking for a Magdalena.' His confidence was returning since Clark hadn't killed him yet. 'I gave her mother five grand. She has two other daughters, though. I'm happy to put you in touch –'

Clark pressed the business end of the screwdriver against Palmetto's thigh and leaned in, feeling the satisfying scrape as the flathead nicked his femur.

The man yowled in pain and surprise, but Clark hit him before he could form words – GI Joe smacking a Ken doll.

Clark grimaced. 'Geeze,' he said, showing mock concern. 'You're gonna want to have that looked at. I'm thinking Parrot might have had a few STDs.'

Palmetto swayed like he might pass out.

'Oh, no you don't.' Clark left the screwdriver buried in the leg, but nudged the handle toward the centerline, using it like a lever.

Palmetto's eyes lit up and he lurched, kicking his foot as if shocked.

'Felt that, did you?' Clark said. 'That's what we call your common peroneal nerve. We should stay away from that. It hurts like a son of a bitch.'

Palmetto clenched his jaw and nodded quickly.

'Where is Magdalena now?'

'Z . . . Z . . . Zambrano,' he said. 'I heard he won her at auction.'

'Isn't he the boss?'

'Yesss,' Palmetto said, biting his lip. His eyelids fluttered. 'I . . . I think he bought her as a present for Chen.'

Clark moved the screwdriver involuntarily at that, scraping bone again.

'Stoooooppp!'

Both girls looked up and then just as quickly turned away.

'Why give a present to Chen?'

'She's . . . his girlfriend.'

'Chen's male.'

'N . . . Not Vincent,' Palmetto said, hyperventilating now. 'Lily, his sister. Like I told you, she . . . she's Zambrano's partner. Brings triad money and muscle into the cartel.'

Clark withdrew the screwdriver. So Vincent Chen had a sister. This was all beginning to make sense – not complete sense, but at least the pieces were starting to fall into place. Lily Chen would possess information on her brother and his business dealings that would help Ding and the others. That was plenty enough reason to hunt her down. Clark shot a glance at the two girls, one of them branded and raped, the other having only narrowly avoided the same fate. He'd never admit it, not even to himself, but he didn't need another reason.

'Let's have the password for your computer,' he said.

Palmetto clenched his eyes shut, pressing tears through the lashes. 'It's . . . unlocked.'

'I'm working with geniuses here,' Clark said.

He used Dorian's cell phone to call the Fort Worth Police Department Vice Section and requested an e-mail address to which he could make a video confession. He'd made enough Skype calls to his wife and grandson that it was a fairly simple matter to put through a video call – even for him.

Jo and the other girl listened to their music, eyes closed.

Clark stood just off camera with the bloody screwdriver as Dorian Palmetto began to spill his guts to the female detective with the Fort Worth Police Department. He couldn't help grinning behind the black balaclava. Vengeance shouldn't feel this good. But it did.

He looked at his watch. The coppers would be tracing the computer's IP address and should be here in short order.

Time to make a call.

48

Yukiko's GSM listening device had been completely silent for the last hour and a half. Jack Ryan, Jr, leaned back in the loveseat with both hands behind his head. The Japanese woman sat beside him, gazing forward in a thousand-yard stare, deep in thought. Chavez snored softly a few feet away. Adara and Midas were sacked out on the unmade bed.

'You okay?' Jack asked. He didn't whisper; that would have woken everyone in the room. Instead, he kept his voice low and unthreatening.

Yuki nodded. 'I am. Thank you for asking.'

'Maybe we should wake one of them,' Jack said. 'Give you a break.'

'Let them sleep,' Yuki said. 'I am not tired.'

'I know what you mean.' Jack found himself wanting to talk to this woman. She smelled good. That was something he hadn't paid attention to in a long time. He paused for a beat, then asked, 'How long have you been on the job?'

'Awhile,' she said. What else could she say? Jack's answer would have been just as ambiguous, and he felt stupid for asking such a pointed question.

If she was angry, she didn't show it. 'My father was . . . on the job, as you say. I grew up not knowing what he did for some time, only that his job took him away a great deal.'

Jack could understand that, but he just gave her what he hoped was a sympathetic smile.

'I hardly knew him, really,' she continued. 'But I thought him an honorable man. My final year of university, my father took me to climb Fujisan. If you do not climb it once, they say, you are not Japanese.' She smiled. 'If you climb it twice, they say you are a fool. Anyway, halfway up the mountain, we passed a small handicapped man being harassed by two other, much larger teenagers. My father urged me to continue walking and forget about the poor soul. He said we should not get involved in other people's lives, and then recited a proverb that I will never forget: *jaku niku kyō shoku* – the weak are meat, the strong eat. I knew my father had taught me better than that, but on that day I saw the truth. He was a coward. I told him that I had never been so ashamed. But my father was not sad. He merely smiled at my anger and then turned back to confront the bullies. I had never before seen him in a physical fight, and I must say that it was quite impressive.'

'It was a test,' Ryan mused.

'Just so,' Yuki said. 'My father had given me an out with this unplanned situation. Had I been silent, I am certain he still would have gone back to assist the poor man. But he never would have let me inside, invited me to follow him in his chosen calling. That is what he called this work, a calling. It was never a job to him.'

'That's a good observation,' Ryan said.

'My father very much liked your American idea of a sheepdog, protecting the weak. I am sure he wished he would have had a son . . .'

'I doubt that,' Ryan said. 'I'd like to meet your father.'

Yuki gave a solemn nod. 'Sadly, he passed away last –'

She paused, focused on the cell phone in the center of the coffee table. An audible click said the GSM bug had activated at the other end of the line. Hushed voices rose above a hiss of static. A female spoke in broken Chinese.

'That is Kim Soo,' Yuki said, whispering though she did not need to. She leaned forward to listen intently.

Chavez and Adara sat up in their respective sleeping spots, as if programmed to rouse at the sound of static.

Amanda Salazar wailed in Spanish, vowing revenge for the death of her friend Beatriz. Chavez translated. Apparently, none of them knew who had pulled the trigger. No one had seen someone named Matías since earlier that day. He and his machete were both missing. Amanda said she had never trusted him. He certainly had something to do with Beatriz's murder. Several men began to speak at once, this time in Mandarin. Kim Soo's voice came over the phone again, louder than the rest, probably nearer the mics. From her tone, it sounded as if she was flirting with one of the men.

Jack waited for someone to translate. Yuki suddenly looked up at him. She started to speak, but Midas beat her to the punch.

'They're going to Japan,' he said.

The conversation continued for another ten minutes along with the clank of silverware and the slurp of someone eating soup. At length, the microphone turned off. The battery may have died, but it was late and it was more likely that they'd all gone to bed.

'So apparently,' Midas said, sitting up now, 'somebody wants Chen in Japan for a meeting.'

'What kind of meeting?' Ryan asked.

'That is not clear,' Yuki said. 'His statements make no sense. It is as if his operation was of his own making.'

'What operation is that?' Chavez asked.

'That I do not know,' Yuki said. 'The conversation was too broken. Chen sounds unsure of himself. This is odd behavior for someone who has exhibited nothing but extreme self-confidence up to this point.'

'I heard no mention of the bombing,' Adara said. 'It seems like that's all they would be talking about.'

'Indeed,' Yuki said.

'Amanda Salazar has to be involved with that bombing,' Ryan said. 'I watched her do something with her cell phone at the exact moment it went off. And if she is involved, then Chen is involved up to his ass.'

'That would certainly seem to be the case,' Yuki said. 'But all we know for sure is that Vincent Chen plans to return to Japan with Kim Soo.'

Ryan rubbed his eyes, suddenly feeling incredibly tired. Air Force One would be in Japan in less than forty-eight hours with his dad on board, touching down right in the middle of – Ryan didn't know what, but it wasn't good.

Yukiko was already on her feet. She pulled a bag from the closet and began to throw in her things. 'I am very sorry,' she said, 'but I must return to Japan at once.'

'How will you get back?' Jack asked. He started to offer a ride on the Gulfstream but caught the slightest head-shake from Chavez.

'My embassy has an aircraft,' Yuki said. 'I apologize abandoning you like this.' She looked at Jack and smiled.

'Perhaps we will meet again, Jack san. Under more pleasant circumstances.'

He smiled. 'I hope so,' he said.

She had little to pack and her toiletries were loaded and her suitcase zipped in under two minutes. She handed Ryan a business card – blank but for a telephone number. 'I am not so stupid as to think you will not try to find a flight to Japan. If you work for who I think you do, and you are able to get there in the next few days, please give me a call.'

She gave a slight bow and then was out the door, leaving the entire team alone in her apartment.

'Okay,' Chavez said, snapping his fingers at the rest of the team. 'She doesn't realize we have our own airplane. I would have offered her a ride, but the fact that we don't have any bona fides as government intelligence officers might have posed a problem when we landed. Better that we go in on our own as tourists. I don't plan to get in the way of the Japanese government, but I'll be damned if I'm going to just sit back and wait to see how this plays out. There's no quick way to get to Tokyo. Our asses need to be on that plane ten minutes ago.'

49

Nada. Zip. Zilch.

No, this was worse than zero.

Special Agent Callahan pounded the hood of her Ford Expedition and screamed at the night sky. A whip-poor-will answered her back from the line of cedars that grew along the fence beyond the twenty-two other police cars. The creepy bird was probably confused by all the strobing red-and-blues. Callahan had read somewhere that whip-poor-wills could sense death. This one sure knew its business.

The cartel guy tied to the tree on the side of Emilio Zambrano's ranch house had been dead a couple hours at least, but not quite long enough for the fire that killed him to burn itself out. What was left of his head glowed like the poster for the Nicolas Cage *Ghost Rider* movie. His face was unrecognizable – gone, really – but they'd be able to get one set of fingerprints. The corpse was missing a hand, probably since birth. That should help to identify him. The killer had wrapped the guy's head in what looked like a bath towel, taking care to leave the area around the mouth and nose exposed so he wouldn't suffocate and die too quickly. One of the crime scene techs said he'd seen it before. They'd doused the towel in lamp oil so it burned more slowly and lit the turban from the top to make a human candle. A slow and extremely painful way to die.

Maybe Caruso's scary friend had done this. He certainly

had the eyes for it. Callahan was pretty sure he'd whacked the woman in the swimming pool, and the dead guy by the grave. Some would call what he did a service, like taking out the garbage. But there were lines you just didn't cross. She would catch him eventually, and that was sad because he was making a difference.

Just hours before, Fort Worth PD had received a bizarre Skype confession from a guy who was obviously under duress from someone off camera. Even conservative Texas courts would throw out that confession. According to the FWPD detective, Parrot Villanueva had been stabbed to death with a screwdriver. Maybe the sobbing confessor had whacked him. Captive girls had been rescued in both those cases.

She couldn't help but believe that if the vigilante had killed the one-handed guy, Zambrano's body would have been tied to the tree along with him. No, this guy had committed some infraction against the cartel. Zambrano had murdered him for it and then vanished. Callahan would catch them both, Zambrano and Caruso's friend. Eventually.

She stared at the shadow of the smoldering corpse across the yard and smacked the Expedition's hood a final time for good measure. A couple of the Dallas County SWAT guys gave her better-luck-next-time shrugs. Her logical brain said they were only trying to assuage the guilt of her failure. But Callahan wanted to feel guilty.

Special Agent John Olson came out of the house on his cell, squinted at all the flashing lights, and then started toward Callahan when he found her. He dropped the phone back in his pocket and approached tentatively.

She gave him a hard look that he didn't deserve. 'What?'

'No ID yet on the dead guy,' he said. 'But get this. Witnesses where that guy got killed up the street from you reported seeing a Hispanic male hanging around just before the murder – and he was missing a hand.'

Callahan just nodded.

'Anyway,' Olson said, 'I thought you'd want to know.' He shot a sympathetic look to Caruso, who'd taken refuge in the shadow of a big pecan tree on the other side of the Ford. 'Okay, then. I'll leave you guys to it.' He turned and went back inside the house.

The ranch was about as close to the middle of nowhere as one could get and still be within an hour of the population centers of Dallas–Fort Worth. Rolled bales of Bermuda grass hay moldered in shaggy fields surrounding the two-story brick house, remnants of some prior year's cutting. The gate had been unlocked and open – which should have been a sign that they were all wasting their time.

SWAT breached, giving Zambrano and anyone else inside precisely zero seconds to come to the door since there was a steaming body in his backyard. EOD cleared the residence once SWAT found it was empty. FBI forensic techs were inside now, combing the place for everything from cigarette butts to pubic hair. They would find something, they always did, but that took time, and Callahan didn't have much of that. Zambrano could run a hell of a lot faster unencumbered. The girls would be the first things to go, if he hadn't killed them already. The ranch was big, and they'd have to wait until daylight to search for graves.

She'd called in the assistance of twenty-five other law enforcement officers from six different jurisdictions, including the DEA, the US Marshals, and the entire CAC Task

470

Force. Six of the responders were Dallas County SWAT. Everyone not on perimeter or helping Forensics was in the process of slipping off their armored-plate carriers or stowing long guns and ballistic shields. They all averted their eyes when they walked through the front yard, afraid they might bring down the wrath of the redheaded banshee.

This entire day had been a colossal waste of time.

Eddie Feng was still in a medically induced coma and likely suffering from permanent brain damage. Gusano, the other idiot from the steakhouse attack, was also in the hospital, chained to his bed with a leg iron. He was conscious but badly concussed. His brain hadn't been one of the brightest stars in the firmament even before Callahan had bashed him in the face with the pepper grinder. Neither man was going to be much help.

An anonymous tip came in five minutes after she'd dropped Caruso off at his hotel, pointing them to Emilio Zambrano's ranch south of Granbury. The call had led them to this failure. To make matters worse, Magdalena Rojas was nowhere to be found. She'd been here, though. Callahan could feel it.

Clark lay belly-down on the scrubby grass and loose caliche stone. He'd checked the place for fire ants and other stickers, stingers, and stinkers while he set up his hide. It looked clear, but things changed by the second when you were lying in the dark. This was Texas, and it was impossible not to think about rattlesnakes. There were certainly enough rocks and roots for them, but the night was too cool for snakes to be crawling around. At least that's what he told himself.

A wire hung from his left ear, connecting the earbud to the phone in his pocket. He expected Caruso to call him with an update any minute. Five hundred feet below, down the rocky hillside covered with yucca and scrub cedar, a new Airstream trailer sat nestled under a copse of live oaks. There was a chicken coop and a doghouse, but no sign of chickens or dogs. Clark had been watching the trailer for more than an hour. Dorian Palmetto had lawyered up the moment Fort Worth PD booted the door to his room, but he'd given Clark this address for Raul Pacheco. It made sense that Matarife might try to hide out with his father.

Clark knew he should have mentioned this location when he'd called in the information on Zambrano – but the legal hurdles of getting a warrant for one location on a tip were steep enough. He decided he'd give Callahan and Caruso the one that would save the girl while he paid a little visit to Matarife. He had a vague plan of what he would do when the Slaughterer showed up – if he showed up. It would take a little coordination and there were still some kinks to work out, but that was par. No plan survived first contact completely intact.

There was no moon, leaving the sky to the stars alone. Even under these present circumstances, Clark couldn't help but glance up. It wouldn't be such a bad life to teach the stars to his grandson – to take the time to look up. His own father had taught him the major constellations. He'd learned the navigational stars in the Navy – Polaris, Sirius, Rigel –

His phone began to buzz, the noise pushing him flatter against the ground, though there was probably no one for miles to see or hear him.

'Speak,' he whispered, kicking up a puff of dirt and dry grass with his breath.

Surprisingly, it was not Caruso but Jack Junior.

'New wrinkle,' Ryan began, and then ran down the latest developments in Buenos Aires. Clark in turn let him know about Lily Chen and her connection to the Sun Yee On triad and Zambrano's cartel. 'Makes sense why Vincent was in Texas now,' Ryan said. 'John, I'm thinking Japan might well be about to become a very dangerous place. Maybe we should contact my father and tell him not to go.'

Clark tried – and failed – to stifle a quiet chuckle. 'Your dad doesn't respond well to mights and maybes. I can't remember a single time when Jack Ryan Senior or Junior listened to me when I warned either of them not to do something because it was dangerous.' More serious now, he whispered, 'But I'll make some calls and let the Secret Service know through channels that there's a possible threat. I'm sure they'll want to talk to any of those people who were around when the bomb went off in BA. I trust your Japanese intel officer will let her superiors know. Make sure she has the aliases for Chen that Gavin found. With any luck, they'll grab him coming into the country.'

'Those are only the aliases we know about,' Jack said. 'I'm not counting on it.'

'Me either,' Clark said, peering into the darkness. 'Looks like you guys need to go to Japan. I'll clear it with Gerry.'

'Ding's on the phone with him now,' Jack said.

'Good,' Clark said. 'Don't get in the way of the Japanese, but it sounds like their interest may be with the Korean woman. You guys make Chen a priority.'

'Roger that –'

Clark's phone chirped with another incoming call. He rolled on his side to look at the caller ID. 'Anything else?'

'Nope,' Jack said.

'I have Dom on the other line,' Clark said, and ended the call with Ryan.

'Speak,' he said again.

'Can you talk?'

'Go.'

'Zambrano and Chen cleared out before we got here,' Caruso said. 'Left behind a torched body. Probably one of their crew.'

Clark groaned. 'No Magdalena Rojas?'

'Nothing, boss,' Caruso said. 'Oh, I should tell you, though, that Callahan is hell-bent on throwing your ass in jail when she catches you.'

'It's been tried before,' Clark said.

Far in the distance, a set of headlights arced through the night as a lone vehicle drove along the narrow farm-to-market road.

'Anyway,' Caruso said, 'we'll see what Forensics finds, but I'm not hopeful. All the bad guys are lawyering up as fast as we arrest them. We're running out of leads.'

The oncoming vehicle slowed and turned up the narrow two-track that led to the empty Airstream.

'Sit tight,' Clark said. 'I may have more information for you shortly.'

Caruso started to say something else, but Clark ended the call and began to work his way down the hill.

50

The man who arrived at the Airstream that was tucked back among the oak trees was at least sixty, and probably a little older. Clark was less than fifty feet away, watching from behind the doghouse, lying on his belly yet again. He looked at the photo of Ernie Pacheco that Caruso had sent him, and guessed this guy to be his father. Pacheco senior didn't even go inside the trailer. Instead, he grabbed a shovel that was leaning against the makeshift wooden porch and headed for the chicken coop. Ducking down through a small doorway, he disappeared inside with the shovel, then came out a short time later carrying not only the shovel but also a large black duffel – and got back in his truck and drove away.

Travel cash, Clark thought. All his compatriots dropping dead around him had rattled his cage. He needed money to run, and he'd sent his daddy to get it for him.

Clark jogged around the base of the hill to his rental car, reaching it about the same time he saw the lights of Pacheco Senior's pickup turn back onto the farm-to-market road. Clark stayed well back, following with his lights off and keeping his foot off the brakes until the pickup got on the highway. Traffic was light, but at least there were other cars on the road, making it far easier to tail.

He didn't have to go far. Twenty minutes after he'd left the chicken coop, the pickup pulled up in front of a white stone house in a rural neighborhood of five- and ten-acre ranchettes on the outskirts of the small community of Glen Rose, about fifty miles southwest of Fort Worth. Clark killed his lights and watched from two lots up. He wished he'd brought some NVGs, but a nearby street-light, out front of Pacheco's place, gave him just enough light to make out what was happening.

Pacheco Senior didn't seem all that thrilled about being a bagman. He cast worried glances over his shoulder when he got out of the truck, the kind of looks people used to bleed off nervous energy, but didn't really see any-thing. A shadowed figure opened the door and then stepped out on the porch.

'Hello, Ernie,' Clark whispered. He'd stopped thinking of this idiot as Matarife. It imbued him with too much worth if he had a spooky nickname.

The old man all but threw the duffel bag at him and turned to go. Ernie looked like he might follow him back to the pickup, but he raised his hands in surrender and took the bag back inside.

'Not the reunion you were hoping for,' Clark said, an idea forming in his mind.

The pickup turned back onto the main road at the same time Clark pulled down the short drive to the white stone house. He parked his rental on the far left of the driveway, making it more difficult for Ernie to see it unless he came outside. He moved quickly, hoping to take advantage of the old man's recent departure, banking on Ernie think-ing his dad had forgotten something and returned – maybe even to say good-bye.

There was no peephole, just a floor-to-ceiling window to the right of the door. Clark stayed to the left, out of the line of sight. He beat on the door with the flat of his hand, not too hard, but like someone who knew the occupant had just walked inside. Pacheco opened the door a half-second later.

Police Tasers deliver a fifty-thousand-volt shock for a five-second duration. Clark shot Pacheco with a civilian model called a Bolt that gave him a thirty-second ride. The instant he pulled the trigger, a compressed nitrogen canister propelled two barbed steel darts from the nose of the device on coils of whisker-thin wire. Deploying at an angle, one dart struck Pacheco just over his left nipple, and the other in the center of his right thigh. The device chattered as it discharged electricity. Pacheco came up on his toes, arms rigid, teeth clenched, and toppled backward on the tile entry like a felled tree, body arched on his heels and the back of his head.

Thirty seconds gave Clark plenty of time to duct-tape Pacheco's wrists behind his back, using several turns of tape to connect his hands and feet, bending his knees almost up to his buttocks and effectively hog-tying him. Next Clark stuffed a wadded paper towel into the man's mouth and then covered that with a strip of tape before dumping him into the trunk of the rental car. Two minutes later, Clark was driving north on Highway 144.

Traffic was almost nonexistent, and he reached his destination on the outskirts of Fort Worth in just under an hour. The rental car bounced as he turned off the main street into a deserted industrial park. Clark did his best to hit every pothole and bump, bringing a chorus of muffled cries from behind the backseat.

He used a pair of bolt cutters to defeat the cheap padlock and pushed open the gate, closing it behind him after he'd driven through so as not to rouse the suspicions of any roving police or security patrols – though he doubted there would be any. This area didn't have anything worth stealing.

Clark parked the rental beside a nondescript metal building, tucking it in behind row after row of bright red fifty-five-gallon rubber bins full of old oil filters and other industrial waste. Whistling to himself, he got out and slammed the door, pausing a few seconds so his passenger could anticipate – and worry about – what was going to happen next.

Clark stood off to the side as he opened the trunk. There was always a chance that Pacheco had wriggled free of his bonds. Still tied, he gazed up at Clark in the red glow of the taillights. His eyes sparkled with abject horror.

'You scared?' Clark asked.

Pacheco nodded emphatically.

Clark gave him a wink. 'Kiddo,' he said, 'you ain't seen nothin' yet.'

He hauled the terrified man out of the trunk and dragged him by his feet along the gravel. It would do him good to watch the process as it progressed.

Clark had never been here before. That would have left him at too great a risk of being recognized. He had, however, studied the place at length through the satellite images from Google Earth. He knew that the iron contraption the size of a train engine beside the tin building was an industrial incinerator. He also knew that the controls were located in a square blue box on the side of a steel chute where employees of the plant loaded refuse to be destroyed. What the Google images did not show was that a fire from the day before still glowed inside the belly of the incinerator, the thermometer on the box still reading 600 degrees.

A placard above warned that temperatures should not drop below 1,600 degrees when refuse was being burned. The company's website advertised its ability to destroy industrial and hospital waste at temperatures exceeding 1,900 degrees.

Clark studied the directions for a moment, surprised to see there was no lock or computer key code, just a simple on/off switch to start the flow of gas to the primary burners and two buttons on either side of the box that needed to be depressed simultaneously.

He turned the switch, then counted to three before pressing both buttons. On the ground at his feet, Pacheco gave a muffled cry behind the duct tape as the gas inside the chamber ignited with a hollow *whoompf!*

'Hmmm,' Clark mused, loud enough for Pacheco to hear. 'Works just like my grill at home.'

The chamber of the incinerator itself was a somewhat stubby cylindrical tank, approximately ten feet long by seven feet high. A large walk-in door was cut into the front, used for raking ash, replacing any of the foot-thick insulation, or loading refuse that was too large to fit into the rear chute. Secondary burners at the top of the chamber reached 1,200 degrees, igniting unburned gases before they could escape through a fifteen-foot chimney.

Clark waited for the reading on the control panel to reach 1,880 degrees and then lifted the heavy metal lid on the three-by-six-foot chute attached to the rear of the chamber. The rusty, coffinlike box was smeared with black oil and flecked with bits of fiberglass insulation and other trash. A trapdoor hung down in front of the firebox, telltale orange flames just visible around the edges of blackened metal. The face of a heavy steel ram was flush with the back end of the chute. A red plastic sign affixed to the box above the controls warned: *Use by unauthorized persons is prohibited.*

Clark looked down at his prisoner and smiled. 'Don't pay any attention to that. I'm authorized.'

Pacheco was no lightweight, and it took some maneuvering for Clark to get the thrashing man up over the edge. Both men were sweating, albeit for different reasons, by the time Pacheco landed inside the chute with his feet toward the fire chamber and his head against the ram. He rolled and thrashed, trying in vain to gain some kind of footing that would allow him to escape from the narrow prison. As he was wearing only gym shorts and a T-shirt, his hairy legs and arms were covered in black oil and grime in a matter of moments.

Clark leaned over the side, peering down into the greasy darkness. He caught the sudden odor of urine. That made sense. For an instant, he felt a pang of guilt, and then remembered the dead girls in the sorghum field, the snuff videos, and a child named Magdalena who was still somewhere out there, perhaps even dead already.

He clapped his hands together. 'They say this can melt bone,' he said. 'But I'd imagine they'll find a knuckle or two.'

Pacheco began to sob.

Clark pushed the red button.

Nothing happened, except for the muffled screams, thrashing – and more urine.

'Ah,' Clark said. 'The lid needs to be closed.' He reached toward the hinge and flipped a manual override that allowed the mechanism to operate with the lid open, before hitting the red button again.

This time, the heavy door at Pacheco's feet began to slide upward, metal squealing against metal. At the same time, the ram at his head pushed him toward the waiting flames. Pacheco tried to brace himself, but even if he hadn't been tied, the slippery steel box would have made that all but impossible.

Clark pushed the button again, relieved that the hydraulic ram actually stopped. It occurred to him that he should have tested it beforehand.

'Okay, Ernie,' he said. 'Here we go. I need information. You have information. It's a simple process.'

Pacheco nodded, seeing a possibility of survival for the first time.

Clark continued. 'I should tell you, I'm not a patient man. I'm looking for Magdalena Rojas. You're going to tell me where she is.'

More nodding and some muffled grunts.

Clark shrugged. 'Not good enough. I told you I wasn't patient, Ernie.' He pushed the red button again, waiting for the door to get halfway up and the ram to begin its movement before pushing it again.

'Sorry about that,' Clark said, ripping away the tape. 'Guess I do need to take this off so you can talk.'

Pacheco spat out the paper towel and let fly a string of Spanish curses, hyperventilating to the point that Clark thought he might vomit. Clark reached as if to push the button again.

'Okay! Okay!' Pacheco said. 'I dropped her at Emilio's. She was good when I saw her last. I swear on my mother's grave.'

'I've probably seen your mother's grave,' Clark mused. 'Zambrano. Where do I find him?'

Pacheco gave him directions to the ranch Caruso and Callahan had already visited.

Clark shook his head. He left his hand over the red button. 'Already tried there.'

'Hang on!' Pacheco cried. 'He's got another place out in Palo Pinto County.' He rattled off the directions.

'And if he's not there?'

'If he's not at his other place, that's where he'll be,' Pacheco said. 'Good luck getting to him, though. He's got a shitload of guards. Lily's guys. Emilio is a badass, but his woman, I ain't shittin' you, man, she's the devil. And her guys ain't much better.'

'Triad?' Clark asked. He'd been wondering where all the Sun Yee On goons were hiding.

Pacheco nodded. 'She keeps a dozen or more around all the time. Look, *amigo*, I told you what you wanted to know. Can you please untie me now? You're scaring the shit outta me. Know what I'm sayin'?'

'I'm not your *amigo*,' Clark said, his voice hoarse and pointed. 'Let's say Magdalena's not with Zambrano. Where else would I look for her?'

Pacheco snorted. 'What is it with bitchy little Magdalena? Did you bid on her? And if you did, how did you find me?' He studied Clark for a moment and then threw him a conspiratorial smile. 'You wily bastard! I knew Lupe didn't know how to make that computer anonymous. You found me with the IP address, didn't you?'

Clark nodded. 'How much did Zambrano bid?'

'Twelve grand,' Pacheco scoffed. 'Can you believe that shit? Hey, come on, let me out and I'll get you set up with somebody even better. If Magdalena's your type, I got a line on a couple young ones down in Reynosa —'

Clark slammed his fist into the red button. The trapdoor rattled upward. The fire greeted them with a terrifying roar. A cyclone of orange and yellow whorled and danced inside the glowing chamber. At the other end of the chute, the ram slid into the battery with a resounding clunk. Pacheco drew himself into a ball, flipped sideways, bent his neck, doing everything he could to brace himself. Nothing he did would stop the unrelenting steel ram from pushing him toward the flames. Now free of the gag, he loosed a shattered scream — surely the same kind of cry the countless young women he'd murdered had screamed before him.

Clark lowered the heavy door to the sound of metallic thuds and hysterical, shrieking pleas. The frenzied howls grew more intense, drowning out the hydraulic hum of the ram — and then fell silent, leaving only the roar and pop of the flames.

'The Slaughterer,' Clark said, sliding in behind the wheel of his rental car. 'What a dumbass name.'

51

The Hendley Associates Gulfstream touched down on Atlanta Hartsfield's runway 8 right at nine thirty-four a.m. Pilot in Command Helen Reid made the short taxi to Signature Aviation FBO and brought her airplane to a stop on the FBO's ramp. She hung her Lightspeed Zulu headphones over the yoke and climbed out of her seat to go check on fuel. Chavez wanted a quick turn-and-burn — and it was Reid who would make that happen. The flight from Buenos Aires to Atlanta had been just over nine hours, thanks to a decent tailwind. Unfortunately, they wouldn't be quite so lucky on the Atlanta-to-Tokyo portion of the trip. First, she'd have to take the time to grab more fuel in LA, and the winds were on the nose, adding back any time they'd gained on the trip north and then some.

Reid liked the hell out of Domingo Chavez. He was a good guy with lofty goals and a commitment to mission that was beyond laudable. But no matter how important the mission, physical laws being, well, the law, Tokyo was a lot of miles and minutes away. Reid expected total time in the air to be almost twenty-five hours. She and Hicks were talented pilots, but no one wanted to fly with a pilot who'd been awake for twenty-five hours. To that end, Reid had made a call to her boss before they left Buenos Aires. To his credit, Gerry Hendley had two G550 pilots waiting inside the FBO when they landed in Atlanta. Sonny Cobb and Rich Caudill both had thousands of hours in the Army's C37B, the military version of the G550. After the military, Cobb had flown for the US Marshals Service's Justice Prisoner and Alien Transportation Division, and Caudill for the FBI's Hostage Rescue Teams. Neither of the pilots was a stranger to Campus operations, and they often provided relief and augmentation to Reid and Hicks.

Reid gave each man a peck on the cheek and then went to hit the head inside the FBO, relieved that they'd made it to Atlanta so she didn't have to let Chavez down.

Twenty minutes later, Reid and Hicks were back aboard and snoozing in the forward seats across from Lisanne Robertson. The Signature ground crew pushed the Gulfstream back from the ramp with Cobb and Caudill in the cockpit for the Atlanta–Los Angeles leg.

In the rear of the airplane Ding had Gavin Biery on speaker.

'Any information on Chen's phone?'

'The last activity was a ping off an antenna in Buenos Aires at . . . seventeen-thirty Argentine time.'

'Shit!' Chavez said. 'I saw him use his phone after that. That means he's already dumped the phone we know about.'

'Well,' Biery said, 'for whatever reason, he's gone dark.'

'I don't like this,' Jack said, feeling an uncomfortable gnawing at his gut.

'Maybe Yuki and her team will grab him,' Adara said. 'If he uses one of the IDs Gavin found for him.'

'Maybe,' Jack said. 'But that's an awfully big if.'

'Okay, Gav,' Chavez said. 'We'll be wheels up from Atlanta in five minutes. I'll check in again when we get to LA if I haven't heard from you before then. Keep us informed if you get anything else.'

Chavez ended the call and then looked at the rest of his team. 'ETA Tokyo one p.m. local. That gives us thirteen hours to figure out how we're going to find this guy.'

Special Agent Olson was quick on the keyboard for a hunt-and-peck typist. Callahan actually used *all* her fingers, which made her fast, but Caruso was even faster. Both agents sat at the desks on either side of Callahan's, consulting small notepads as they typed. The Old Man had made it clear that Callahan and her people were to glue their asses to the chair until they'd completed their paperwork – even if it was the weekend.

Dallas was a large field office and normally the special agent in charge left the day-to-day oversight of investigations to the various squad supervisors. This case had drawn enough national attention for someone to drop Dominic Caruso on top of them. That had the Old Man feeling antsy, and when the Old Man felt antsy, he got down in the weeds. He focused his wrath on the supervisors, and they, in turn, made the lives of working agents like Callahan a living hell. She needed to be out doing interviews, finding the trafficked kids, not in the hangar doing reports.

The FBI Form 302, or record of a witness interview, got a lot of press, mostly from people who felt their words had been twisted by the time they got to court. From Callahan's point of view it wasn't an exaggeration to say that the Bureau was fueled by the damned things – and paperwork in general. New agents learned quickly to plan on three hours of paperwork for every one hour in the field. So much for the intrepid gumshoe detective. Sometimes she felt like a typist with a Glock.

The time spent on paperwork did, however, give her the opportunity to accomplish at least one little bit of actual detective work. She'd already filled Caruso's coffee mug three times, hoping that he'd get up and go to the bathroom. She'd seen him drop his cell phone into the pocket of his blazer, which now hung over the back of his chair. With any luck, the coffee would give him a morning 'push' and he'd have to spend a couple minutes in the bathroom. Olson had said two minutes would be better, but a minute might be enough.

Finally, Caruso stopped typing and pushed back from the desk.

It looked like he was going to grab his phone, but Callahan said, 'You done? We need to get on the road.'

Caruso said he had two 302s left, but that he would hurry – and scurried off to the bathroom in the back corner of the hangar.

Callahan waited for the door to close and then fished out the phone and passed it to Olson, who was waiting with a cord that he used to attach the phone to his laptop.

'We should probably get a warrant for this,' he said, working feverishly at the keyboard. 'Don't let him shoot me if he comes out.'

'It takes at least a minute to pee,' she said.

'This is some serious government-level encryption,' Olson said. 'I'll try and clone it, but the rest will take some time.'

'Can you get call logs?'

'Maybe.' Olson detached the phone and handed it back to Callahan. 'What exactly are you hoping to find?'

Twenty feet away, the toilet flushed behind the bathroom door.

Callahan dropped Caruso's phone back into his jacket and flopped back down at her desk, feeling more than a little guilty. 'Find me all the numbers he's called in the last forty-eight hours,' she said. 'Specifically during the time we were making the arrests at Naldo Cantu's place. I'm really interested in any of his contacts that go by the name John.'

Clark took a short nap parked among half a dozen class-A motorhomes in a Walmart parking lot in West Fort Worth. No one bothered him while he waited for the store to open, and he slept deeply, his activities of the past six hours notwithstanding.

Purchasing a handgun in a state where he wasn't a resident posed a problem, so he'd have to make do with the Glock 19 and the Wilson Combat .45. It was, however, no problem at all to purchase extra magazines and ammunition. He wore a baseball cap against the dozens of security cameras inside the store and made sure to keep it pulled down over his eyes as he chatted with the young man behind the sporting-goods counter. No one appeared to give a second thought to the old dude stocking up for a trip to the shooting range. He bought more ammunition along with three extra magazines for the Glock 19 and two more for the Wilson, giving him five and four respectively – and a total loadout of 109 rounds carried on his person. He threw in a bottle of brake fluid, along with a couple energy bars and a twenty-ounce bottle of water — name brand, with a heavy-duty container, not the generic stuff.

He stopped by a swimming-pool supply store for a bag of chlorine granules. The Internet was rife with people using the stuff for purposes other than intended, but Clark was just another old dude buying shock treatment for his pool. He didn't get a second look.

Loading magazines was a Zenlike experience for him, and Clark took his time, thinking through his plan as he depressed the follower and slid in each successive round. He tucked the mags in the pocket of his navy blue windbreaker and stuffed the remainder of his gear into the CamelBak hydration pack. He left the Gemtech suppressor attached to the Glock, and put that in the pack as well, wearing the Wilson on his hip for the time being. In his pocket, he carried a small flashlight, a Zippo lighter, and a heavy-duty Benchmade automatic knife called a Presidio. He was not one to consider blades very good defensive weapons. They just weren't tactical. Offensive killing was an entirely different story.

Clark spent the next ten minutes sitting in the parking lot studying Google Maps of the area around Zambrano's place, committing the various possible routes of approach to memory. He'd look at them again when he got closer, but it gave his mind something to chew on while he made the hour-and-a-half drive.

In the meantime, he pushed the speed-dial button for his wife. She answered on the first ring.

He had no news, at least none that he could share with her. Sometimes it was just comforting to hear her voice.

*

Emilio Zambrano had done Clark the great favor of building his house on a lake. People in the United States tended to feel more secure when they faced the water, as if any threat would have to work too hard to get to them from that direction.

There were several lots for sale across this arm of the reservoir, and it was a simple matter for Clark to park and pretend to be an interested customer. He would eventually work his way closer, but a pair of 18-power marine binoculars from a quarter-mile away helped him rough out the beginnings of a plan.

Zambrano had gone a step further than most and picked a site in a secluded bay, cut back approximately fifty meters from the main body of the lake. The home itself was a gray brick two-story, tucked in at the head of the bay in between two limestone ridges that were covered with cedar trees. The eastern ridge jutted out farther than the one on the west and looked like it would make a good vantage point when he did decide to move closer. A long grassy hill, as manicured as any fairway at Augusta, ran down from a raised deck on the front of the house to the water's edge. A runabout, gleaming white in the Texas sun, was tied up to a set of floating docks. To the right of the house, a swimming pool had been cut into the side of the hill along with a brick cabana that matched the house. The cabana, as well as a small utility shed partway down the hill, hid much of the pool from any boats that happened to venture too close to the property. For Clark's purposes, the outbuildings conveniently created a blind spot from above, leaving a good portion of the dock invisible from the upper portion of the property.

Clark watched long enough to count seven different men wandering the grounds. There was something going on up at the pool, but the angle was wrong so he couldn't tell what it was. He took a swig of bottled water before pouring the remainder into the dirt and replacing it with about a half-cup of brake fluid. He re-capped the bottle and put it in the CamelBak with the unopened sack of pool shock. After one final gear check, he drove to the other side of the lake.

Clark had arrived early enough in the day that he could take his time. He drove past Zambrano's nondescript steel gate and left the rental in the trees nearly a mile down the gravel road. From there he traveled cross-country, going up and over two scrubby hills before arriving at the eastern ridge overlooking Zambrano's docks. His dark blue windbreaker and khaki slacks melded perfectly with the mottled shadows of scrub cedar and caliche rock.

Clark often thought that he'd spent at least a quarter of his adult life flat on his belly peering through one kind of scope or another, watching, waiting. There was, to him, a great virtue in stillness.

His initial assessment had been correct. The ridge offered a near perfect vantage point of the house, the expansive deck and hot tub, the pool, and the docks below. He was much closer than before but, at just over a hundred meters and in the trees, was far enough away that he didn't have to worry too much about being seen. Still, years of discipline forced him to move slowly and deliberately, staying off the ridgeline to keep from silhouetting himself.

Making himself comfortable, he set the binoculars on the ground beside him and took out the notebook and pencil again, entering data in more detail now that he was close enough for a better look. His first course of business was to identify as many of Zambrano's men as he could. From the looks of things, Pacheco had been right. Security here was the Sun Yee On triad, likely employed by Lily Chen.

It wasn't like the movies – the men did not wear any kind of uniform or patrol with open firearms that might draw attention from a passing bass boat or party barge. The man farthest down by the docks was carrying a fishing rod in his left hand, though he never used it to fish. His T-shirt was a size too small for his husky frame, making the imprint of a pistol easy to see if you looked for it, but that wouldn't draw any attention in Texas, particularly out here, where water moccasins and rattlesnakes were common encounters.

Clark printed 'Muffin Top' on the top line of a new page in his notebook. In a matter of fifteen minutes, he'd written 'Pigeon' (for the man's propensity to jut his neck out when he peered back and forth to look for threats), 'Richie Rich' (because of his fancy gold watch that provided an eye-catching target), and 'Geezer,' 'Rattail,' and 'Sasquatch' – all for obvious reasons. All of them were Asian, heavily tattooed, and apart from Muffin Top, they looked to be in reasonably good condition. Clark was beginning to think he'd miscounted when the seventh man walked out from under the deck. While the others on the security team kept their weapons hidden, this one carried a short CZ Scorpion SMG on a single-point sling around a thick neck. Short and blocky, he was nearly as wide as he was tall.

Clark picked up his pencil again and scribbled another name in the notebook.

'I will call you Mini Fridge.'

52

President Jack Ryan stepped across the corridor to the Roosevelt Room, where Dr Miller was setting up shop on the long oak table. The White House never slept completely, even on the weekends, so there were still a few staffers pecking away at keyboards up and down the halls or compiling reports that had to be ready by Monday morning. Al Chadwick in the communications office came in every Sunday to watch the morning shows at his desk while his wife took the kids to church.

Ryan carried two paper cups of coffee and the Saturday edition of *The Wall Street Journal* he'd never gotten around to reading. Miller shot to her feet when she saw him, but he gave her a friendly toss of his head and set both cups on the table.

'Relax,' he said. 'You're the one giving up your weekend. Cream and sugar?'

Miller shook her head, stricken. 'I can't believe the President of the United States brought me coffee.'

'I make terrible coffee,' Ryan said. 'Lucky for you I only had to open the spigot to get this stuff.' He nodded to the three notebooks and multiple colored pencils with which the mathematician was taking notes. 'I don't want you to feel rushed, but I can reinstitute the draft if you want to recommend a few co-workers to come in and help you out . . .'

'I'll be fine, Mr President,' Miller said. 'Frankly, my process is somewhat . . . odd.'

'Odd?' Ryan said. He didn't intend to stay long, but sat down so Miller would follow suit. 'How so?'

'I don't mean to brag,' she said, 'but I was born with a near perfect photographic memory. It drives my boyfriend crazy . . .'

Ryan smiled, enjoying the young woman's forthrightness.

Dr Miller continued. 'You know those color-blind tests where you see a number or a letter among a bunch of squiggled nonsensical globs?'

Ryan nodded.

'Well, if you were to show me a bunch of globs that formed an unintelligible half of a letter or number, and then an hour – or even a day – later showed me a bunch of globs with the corresponding half of that original letter or number, my brain would recall the first image and then superimpose the two, filling in the blanks and giving me the whole picture.'

Ryan said, 'Here's to you filling in some blanks for us, then.'

'I'll do my best, sir,' Miller said.

'I'll be in the Oval Office for a few hours.' He pointed to the phone at the end of the table. 'You can push this button if you have any questions. Tell the operator who you are and she'll let me know.'

Miller stood again when he did. 'Sir, don't forget your cup of coffee.'

'Oh, no,' Ryan said. 'Those are both for you. I expect you'll need them.'

*

By four p.m., Clark had watched the triad security men make their prescribed rounds three times. They appeared to have six assigned posts, with a seventh spot behind a small utility shed down the hill between the pool and the lake. There they'd stashed a folding camp chair out of sight of the main house and used it to rest their feet during periodic smoke breaks. Muffin Top and Geezer both seemed to get winded just walking up the steep hill when they had to reach a post nearer the house. Clark noted that in the book by their respective names.

There was movement in the house, and once, someone inside called out to the nearest security man to bring something inside from a truck parked out back. Clark had yet to see anyone who might be Magdalena Rojas, or, for that matter, Emilio Zambrano or Lily Chen. They were here, though. No one had this kind of roving security just to guard an empty residence.

Then, at almost exactly five straight up, the double doors on the second floor yawned open and an Asian woman stepped out onto the deck. She wore a red one-piece swimsuit that fit her well and showed off long legs and an athletic body. Clark guessed her to be in her late thirties, maybe even forty. Her hair was short, shaved on one side, the front turned up in a high pompadour. A pair of large heart-shaped sunglasses covered much of her face. Even from a distance Clark could see a haughtiness in her walk – chin up, one arm crooked out to the side, as though she were leading an invisible dog. Two girls followed her out like attendants. Both dark, probably Hispanic, and wearing red swimsuits that matched the older woman's. The lead girl – Clark guessed her to be

Magdalena Rojas – carried a rolled towel and a container of sunblock. A somewhat taller and heavier girl followed with a round tray loaded with two tall glasses and a bowl of popcorn. Each girl wore a wide strap around her left ankle. In any other situation Clark might have thought they were decorative. He'd never understood the fashion of youth – even when he'd been young himself. But given the circumstances, the straps were more likely restraints. Neither girl looked to be older than thirteen. A well-muscled man with salt-and-pepper hair brought up the rear, pulling the doors shut behind him. Emilio Zambrano wore red board shorts and a white Hawaiian shirt, open in front to reveal a hairless chest draped in gold chains. Had it not been for the dazed looks on the faces of the girls, it would have been easy to mistake the foursome for a family out for a swim in matching suits.

The girls followed a few steps behind Lily Chen, careful as they descended the stairs from the upper deck to the pool. Richie Rich, the triad security man with the blingy watch, stepped into the cabana. The heavy bass beat of some rap song Clark didn't recognize – which wasn't saying much – began to thrum from speakers around the pool.

Clark smiled inside. 'Well, that's helpful,' he whispered.

He was gratified to see that all the security men turned to look inward at the sound of the music, when the more practical thing to do would have been to face outbound. Either the triad guys weren't very well trained, or they considered Zambrano and Chen to be more dangerous than anything that might possibly attack their position from the outside.

Clark scribbled a couple more notes in his book. A barked command from Zambrano to one of the Asian guards – Rattail, from the looks of it – caused the heavier of the two girls to drop her tray. The glasses crashed onto the concrete walk beside the pool. Lily turned slowly, lowering her big sunglasses to glare down at both cowering girls. Zambrano cuffed the tall girl in the back of her head, shouting something Clark couldn't quite make out. The girl fell, wilting from the blow, and began to pile the broken glass on the tray. Magdalena set the towel and sunscreen on the ground and stooped to help. Cursing now, Zambrano walked to the edge of the pool next to the diving board and then turned to give the girl a swift kick in the thigh. She'd apparently gotten glass in the pool.

Chen pointed at the water. The girl stood slowly, glancing at the pool, then shaking her head. Chen nodded, smiling and continuing to point at the water. The girl shook her head again. It was obvious that Chen was telling her to go retrieve any broken glass, and it was just as obvious that the girl was terrified to get into the water.

Chen grabbed the girl by the hair and dragged her in, shoving her over the side. The poor girl sputtered and kicked, but, after her initial panic, was able to stay afloat by dog-paddling. There were no markings on the edge, but the diving board said it was at least eight feet on that end.

Lily Chen continued to point, shoving the crying child away with her bare foot each time she made it to the edge. By now, Rattail, Muffin Top, and Mini Fridge had all gathered around the pool to watch the fun. Muffin Top laughed, but a glare from Lily sent him hustling back down the hill to his post at the docks.

Chen pantomimed holding her nose and diving, but the girl was too panicked to pay attention to any directions. She could barely keep her head above water. Magdalena approached with her head down, staring at the ground. She said something to Chen, who gave a flick of her hand and turned away.

Magdalena jumped in immediately, helping her friend to the edge of the pool and then turning to dive to the bottom, surfacing a moment later with the jagged bottom of a broken glass. She climbed out of the pool and set the glass on the tray, offering to carry it back inside. Instead, Lily snapped her fingers and Rattail took care of it, trotting dutifully up the steps to the deck and disappearing into the house.

Clark wrote 'pool boy' beside Rattail's name in the notebook. When he looked up, Zambrano had attached a short leash from a metal deck chair to the taller girl's ankle. There was a similar leash on another chair, probably meant for Magdalena, but she was busy rubbing sunscreen on Lily Chen's shoulders. The Chinese woman said something to Zambrano, who shrugged, and then dragged the deck chair, along with the attached girl, to the edge of the deep end. He pointed in again, as if telling her there was still more glass at the bottom from her accident, and then he kicked the chair over the edge.

The heavy chair jerked her under mid-scream.

Clark's heart leapt into his throat. His hands clawed at the dirt beside him. There was no way he'd be able to cover the distance from his hide to the pool in time to save her — even if he wouldn't have been cut down by gunfire. He could start shooting, but at nearly a hundred meters away, he'd be hard-pressed to make pistol shots effective. Shots would only send everyone running for cover, leaving the girl to drown. No, his only hope was to bank on the fact that Zambrano had likely bid a great deal of money on both girls – and would not want to kill off his investment.

Half a minute in, Zambrano gave Magdalena a nod. The skinny little Costa Rican sprang forward at once, diving in to save her friend. Zambrano stood on the edge with Mini Fridge, watching in amusement. When the chair proved too heavy even for Magdalena to keep afloat, Zambrano begrudgingly hooked his thumb at the water and the short Chinese man handed off his SMG to dive in. The taller girl gagged when Zambrano dragged her out, vomiting on the concrete pool deck.

Lily Chen could not be bothered to look up from her magazine during the entire ordeal.

Clark focused on his breathing, having to work hard to relax his jaw. His original plan had been to wait until sundown, but he wasn't about to stand by and watch something like that again. He took one last scan with the binoculars. The Sun Yee On guys had just rotated posts, so he could count on them being in roughly the same position for the next half-hour.

He carried both pistols and all his magazines on his belt, keeping the Glock mags from nine o'clock over his left hip and forward. The Wilson .45 mags he kept from nine o'clock rearward toward the small of his back, but still within reach. The Presidio was in his left pocket.

He could have solved this whole problem with a rifle. Any warfighter worth his salt knew that if you ever had to pull a handgun during a fight, you were in deep shit. But pistols were better than fists and feet. Clark had always been breakable – everyone was – though he hadn't admitted it as a younger man. He just didn't heal quite as quickly anymore. That, along with the lack of a long gun, couldn't be helped. And anyway, he'd decided to play the hand he was dealt early on in this game. He ran through the plan again in his head, drawing a circle around his sketch of the docks.

'Well, Muffin Top,' he whispered. 'Looks like you get to be first.'

It was not at all uncommon for President Ryan to work through lunch and dinner when he was focused on something. The G20 was looming and there were dozens of topics, economic and otherwise, that he needed to bone up on before he left for Japan the next morning. With Cathy out of town and no one from the scheduling office ramrodding him through endless appointments, he was able to get through half the stack. It was almost six by the time he came up for air.

'I apologize,' he said after he'd stepped out of the Oval and across the corridor into the Roosevelt Room. 'I didn't mean to abandon you.'

Dr Miller stood again. 'Al from Communications brought me a chicken wrap.'

'Good,' Ryan said, eyeing the open notebooks beside Miller's laptop. 'Anything interesting?'

'I think I'm about done,' she said.

Ryan shook his head. 'I don't want you to feel as though you have a deadline, Dr Miller. This is important, and I fully realize it takes time.'

'Frankly,' Miller said, 'I wish I could say I needed more time. This place is amazing compared to my office. Anyway, I found the initial financial ties between China and the bank in Africa the old-fashioned way – by analyzing computer data. I figured I could broaden my focus after you pointed me in the right direction. Once I had an idea of what to look for . . . I was sure all the blobs I told you about would become crystal clear as long as I did enough snooping.'

'And what did you find out?'

'Well,' Miller said, 'entities that appear to represent the government of China, and even President Zhao Cheng-zhi himself, have assets in Africa, Bali, and Paraguay. There's a Balinese company which appears to be a shell business for Zhao with ties to Jemaah Islamiyah. They're tenuous, but they are there.'

Ryan sat in a chair across the table and leaned back, thinking. 'I don't understand,' he said. 'There are so many methods to stay under the financial radar. Cryptocurren-cies, cutouts, middlemen, and offshore banking. Why would anyone conduct business this way if they wanted to hide it?'

'That's the thing, Mr President,' Dr Miller said. 'I wish I could tell you that my amazing photographic memory cracked this case for you, sir. To be honest, I might have done it a little more quickly than others could have, but any good forensic accountant would have found these connections once they knew where to look. If someone was trying to hide these transactions, they didn't do a very good job of it.'

53

Dave Holloway, skipper of the Defense Intelligence Agency's Research Vessel *Meriwether*, was a civilian now, but his time in the Navy had taught him to believe in the rule of threes.

Three bad events or circumstances, no matter how seemingly minor or unrelated, warranted a hard look at declaring a no-go.

Strike one: His crew was green. But for himself, the navigator, and the mechanic, the ten souls on board were scientists, not sailors. Only five had even minimal experience on blue water. Strike two: The maintenance records for the converted eighty-nine-foot fishing trawler left much to be desired. Oh, the boat ran, all right, and the logs showed no recent problems, but maintenance issues had a way of rearing their heads in the darkest parts of the sea. Strike three: His bosses at the Joint Functional Component Command for Intelligence, Surveillance, and Reconnaissance were in too much of a hurry. There were times to rush, but launching a boat with a new crew and poor records was not one of those times. The guys at JFCC-ISR praised his seamanship, played up the talents of his crew and the beauty of the little boat. He'd returned their cajoling with Warren Buffett's sentiment that 'no matter how great the talent or efforts, some things just take time. You can't produce a baby in one month by getting nine women pregnant.'

He wanted a month to assure himself that the boat and the crew were ready, but the folks at Anacostia gave him three days. They did not believe in the rule of threes.

At fifty-three, Holloway was a fourth-generation sailor, and as such, he knew how to follow orders. If the bosses said go, he noted his concerns in the log, and then gave a sharp 'Aye, aye, sir' before going.

The typhoon worried him at first, but it had turned northward, leaving Holloway and his little boat to their duties of gathering signals intelligence from any PRC or DPRK subs plying the waters of the East China Sea. Masquerading as a fishing research vessel, *Meriwether* ran a zigzagging surveillance run out of Naha, heading for Taipei to refuel before making the return trip back to Okinawa.

It should have been a straightforward mission, but now the storm track had changed again.

'I don't like the look of this,' his navigator, a nautical engineer named Rockie Bell, said, tapping the radar screen on the console at the helm. She was sharp, a graduate of the US Merchant Marine Academy, and one of the few real sailors on the boat.

'I know,' Holloway said. 'Damn thing's moving west again. We can duck into Keelung City on the north end of Taiwan if need be.' He nodded to the forecastle. 'I'll be out on deck a moment.'

Holloway left the pilothouse through the side door and made his way forward. Instruments were all well and good, but he preferred to look at the waves and sky for important information. He didn't particularly like what he saw.

The muggy air was clear above, but a line of black clouds to the east made him clench his teeth. The sea was already heaping up and a stiff wind blew at least thirty knots, carrying with it the heavy smell of rain and ripping foam and spray off honest eight-foot waves.

Holloway turned to walk back inside, but a sudden jolt, like an earthquake rippling along the deck, nearly threw him off his feet. He looked through the pilothouse window at Rockie, who shrugged.

A rogue wave, maybe?

Holloway felt *Meriwether* shift under him as the stern swung around, broadside to the wind. They were slowing.

Stumbling back inside on the rolling deck, Holloway glared at his navigator. 'What the hell just happened?'

'I'm trying to raise engineering now,' she said, microphone in hand. She tapped the instrument panel on the console. 'Engine temperatures are through the roof.'

The fire klaxon sounded a half-second later, followed by the voice of Don Patton, the twenty-six-year-old ship's mechanic, halting and breathless.

'Scavenge fire in the diesel . . . crankcase explosion,' Patton said.

'Steam it out,' Holloway ordered.

'I've done that, Skipper,' the mechanic said. 'Fire's under control.'

'Are you hurt?'

'A few burns,' Patton said. 'But not as bad as the diesel.'

'How long until you can get her running again?' Holloway asked.

There was a long pause as *Meriwether* swung around, broadside to the gale, at the mercy of the approaching storm.

'I'm not sure it's even –'

Holloway cut him off. He didn't want fatalistic talk.

'Give me an estimate.'

'I'll do my best, Skipper,' Patton said.

'That's all I can ask, son,' Holloway said. 'So long as you understand that we're about to get a very uncomfortable saltwater enema if this typhoon hits us while we have no power.'

'Aye, sir,' the mechanic said.

'I'll send Rockie down to see to your burns.' He nodded to the navigator, who was already grabbing the medic bag from under the console.

Holloway took a deep breath, cursing at his own stupidity.

He'd taken out a green crew on a ship he didn't quite trust. It didn't matter how much the suits back in Anacostia had wanted him to hurry. He knew better. DIA wasn't to blame for this. He couldn't even blame the previous mechanic for faulty diesel maintenance – though that was surely the cause.

The little spy ship groaned, turning again before the wind, wallowing in the middle of a vast and unfriendly ocean. There was a lot of tech on board that the Chinese navy would just love to get their grimy hands on – if the typhoon didn't sink her first.

Whatever happened, the blame rested squarely on Holloway's shoulders. He was the skipper and he'd disregarded his rule of threes.

Clark estimated it would take him less than a minute to cover the forty meters to the dock. Most people who tried to swim that far underwater ended up flailing around and wasting energy trying to go too fast for fear of running out of breath. Clark would swim at a walking pace, gliding rather than powering through, because if you fought the water, you always lost. Holding his breath wouldn't be an issue. Staying on course in the chocolate-brown lake water would be the challenge, that and timing his arrival so Muffin Top was facing the other direction.

The heavy beat of rap music was still rolling down the grassy hill when Clark made it to the bottom of the finger ridge east of Zambrano's. He kept low, on the far side of the hill and out of sight. Hours of surveillance had shown him that each of the triad sentries had his own method of patrol. Muffin Top spent a great deal of time gathering skipping stones on the shore, in between sauntering out the twenty feet or so of pier to walk back and forth a few times on the floating T where the boat was tied. The boat occupied most of the western arm, which made it more difficult to skip stones. Consequently, the chubby sentry spent a hair more time on the easternmost ten feet of floating dock — a fact that Clark intended to exploit.

He entered the water silently, wearing the CamelBak and all his gear. The slow, deliberate movements came as second nature to him, and he was up to his chin in no time without creating even the slightest splash. He ducked his head under once, wetting his hair and face while he took the time to get a feel for the rocky bottom under his boots.

In the Navy they'd almost always had a swim buddy — especially in the perilous world of the SEALs. The hazards of going it alone underwater were well documented. But the real world was a brutal place. Taking three deep breaths to saturate his lungs with oxygen, he worked his way around the point, slowly cutting the pie to bring the docks into view. Muffin Top was on the shore, his back turned, picking up stones. Anyone who hadn't done their homework might think now was the time to go, but Clark didn't need the man with his back turned now. He needed him with his back turned in forty seconds.

The chubby sentry turned with his hands full of rocks. The second his lead foot hit the pier, Clark ducked beneath the surface and began his swim.

The poor visibility that made navigation difficult also saved Clark from getting shot as he swam. Even so, he stayed as deep as possible, skimming just inches above the rocky bottom. He concentrated on keeping his strokes and kicks even, making certain to go in a straight line. Forty seconds later, he slipped under the darkness of the dock. It was relatively shallow and he was able to stand with his head above water. Long shafts of light showed through the wooden treads above Styrofoam floats.

Muffin Top hummed softly at the other end of the dock, pitching stones one by one. This was the point where things grew difficult. Sentries were human beings. Enemy or not, they were somebody's kid, somebody's brother, uncle, or husband. Some of them sang and skipped rocks. But Muffin Top wasn't just a security guard who happened to be working for the wrong guy. He was Sun Yee On triad, complicit in the slavery of at least the two girls up by the pool. He'd laughed his fat ass off when one of those girls had almost drowned. No, he could sing like Pavarotti for all Clark cared. That didn't give him a soul.

Wood creaked and swayed as Muffin Top walked to the east end of the dock. Waiting at the far end, just outside the edge, Clark brought the Glock up a fraction of a second after his face broke the surface, tipping the barrel slightly to let the water drain. The shot struck Muffin Top as he threw his first stone, straight through the bottom of his chin. The triad man teetered there for a moment, the rest of his rocks slipping from his hand, and then fell face-first toward the water. Clark rounded his shoulders, collapsing under the weight of Muffin Top's body, mitigating the splash. Ready to duck and swim, he glanced uphill and breathed a sigh of measured relief that no one came running down with guns blazing.

Clark stuffed Muffin Top's body under the edge of the dock and then, without looking back, swam past the boat to exit the water at the other end of the cove. He moved quickly, up the long finger ridge that ran along the west side of the house, opposite his earlier vantage point. He had about ten minutes until the guards shifted posts, if he was lucky.

It took him five minutes to work around to the circular driveway behind the house. He would have put a guard up here, by the vehicles, but was glad Zambrano and Chen relied on a man in the trees a hundred meters away up by the gate. Clark hadn't actually seen this one's face, just enough movement when he'd driven by to know someone was there. The gate guy was too far away to be an immediate threat, but Clark would have to remember to watch his six once the rodeo began.

Clark shrugged off the CamelBak in the relative safety of the cedar trees along the driveway. Music still thumped around the corner, muted some by the house. The sun was low, and though it was still plenty light, would soon fall behind the ridge, throwing the little valley into shade. There was a strong possibility Zambrano and Chen would go back in the house when that happened, which put more pressure on Clark. He wanted them outside to make this work.

The half-cup of chlorine granules dumped in the water bottle of brake fluid gave him about a minute and a half. He didn't bother with the lid, but left the bottle upright beneath the gas tank. The mixture did nothing at first. Clark punched a hole in the rear of the gas tank with his Benchmade, large enough that fuel began to drain into the gravel beside the water bottle. This done, he rolled out from under the truck to crawfish back into the buckbrush along the driveway, well away from what he knew was about to happen. Roughly a minute and a half in, white smoke began to pour out from the edge of the truck. An instant later, Clark heard a rush of sound like a jet engine, and then a hollow *whoompf* as the fuel tank caught fire. Richie Rich, who was posted near the end of the house, heard the noise and trotted out to investigate, earning him two shots to the face from Clark's suppressed Glock.

Pigeon poked his head around next, and met the same fate.

It would have been nice if they'd just keep offering themselves as targets, but sooner or later the others would get wise to the fact that their buddies weren't coming back. When in doubt, Clark preferred to err on the side of action. He decided to press the issue, not wanting to give the folks on the other side of the house time to figure out what was going on. He shot a quick glance toward the road. The guard out there would notice the fire soon enough, and Clark wanted to be done with the other seven by the time he got here.

He turned back around just in time to see Mini Fridge run out of the back door with a fire extinguisher. Instead of dropping the canister and going for a gun, Mini Fridge ducked his head and ran, intent on bowling Clark over. Clark brought the Glock around a fraction of a second too late, getting a shot off, but impacting the extinguisher instead of the man. Mini Fridge growled, lashing out with the aluminum cylinder, knocking the gun out of Clark's hand and into the bushes.

The short man looked at a now empty-handed Clark and laughed, moving his thick neck back and forth like a wrestler warming up. Surely the younger man was thicker and stronger than Clark. No doubt he saw only a granddad there in the driveway, soaked to the skin, no less. And in some ways, Mini Fridge was dead right. Clark was breakable – and the vagaries of age and passing time had robbed him of his once great strength, made him slower than he'd been.

He was, however, still an incredibly accurate instinctive shooter.

The Wilson Combat all but jumped into Clark's hand as soon as he'd swept the tail of the windbreaker aside. He thumbed down the safety and brought the gun upward, indexing the target as naturally as pointing a finger. Clark shot three times in quick succession, twice to the chest and once to the head, in the event Mini Fridge was wearing a ballistic vest and decided to stay in the fight.

Mini Fridge wasn't – and he didn't.

The Glock was gone, hopelessly lost along with any semblance of surprise Clark had against the rest of the bad guys. He met Sasquatch head-on as the other man came running to investigate the shots from the .45. Clark gave him two more to investigate, these up close and from the hip. He reloaded a fresh magazine into the Wilson, tucking the used one into his back pocket in case he needed the remaining three later.

By now, Zambrano and Chen were both on their feet. Neither appeared to be armed, but Zambrano lunged toward a side table for something. Clark shot him twice center mass, causing both the girls to scream and cower by their deck chairs. Lily Chen shouted something at the nearest triad goon. A glass tabletop shattered behind Clark as Geezer began to empty a pistol in his direction from the direction of the cabana. Bullets snapped off the concrete, at least one twanging off the surface of the swimming pool to ricochet into the trees. Clark returned fire, causing Geezer to retreat behind the cabana. Rattail shot then, from the other direction, catching Clark in a crossfire. The first round went wide, but the second took Clark in the calf. It felt like he'd been hit with a sledge-hammer, but he could still walk.

Clark sent another round toward Rattail to keep him honest, took a step, stumbled, and then regained his footing. He was in the open now. Geezer must have seen the wound and decided to press his attack, coming around the cabana, blazing away with his pistol. Clark shot him twice, in the shoulder and the neck, reloading a fresh mag as he spun immediately back to Rattail, hobble-walking toward the cover of a deck pillar as he kept the other man's head down with spaced shots from the Wilson. He wanted Lily Chen, but Rattail put his body in front of hers, gallantly, and stupidly, absorbing two rounds from Clark's .45. The man was tough and kept shooting long enough for Chen to shove Magdalena into the water – along with the metal deck chair that was chained to her ankle.

The child sank like a rock, dragged to the bottom by the heavy chair, obviously chosen for that purpose. Clark shot as he moved, emptying the .45 but hitting Chen at least once in the belly and knocking her to her knees as she attempted to drag the other girl into the water.

Clark dove headfirst, eyes fixed on the struggling girl at the bottom of the pool. The shot probably wouldn't kill Chen – not quickly enough, anyway. She'd surely crawl to Rattail's gun and shoot Clark while he swam down to Magdalena. But he didn't care anymore. If he did nothing, the girl would die. If Lily Chen got a gun, the girl would die. This way, at least, she wouldn't die alone.

Clark made it to the bottom of the pool with two powerful kicks. Magdalena Rojas reached for him, eyes wide, waving her arms, still struggling to pull the chair to the surface. Clark drew her close and gave her a quick rescue breath, suddenly finding his own limbs incredibly heavy. It was impossible to lift the deck chair, let alone swim to the surface with it. He considered dragging it up to the shallow end, but even that seemed a herculean task. Clark checked the leash connecting the chair to Magdalena, and found it to be a chain, not too big, but big enough he couldn't break it by pulling. A small padlock held it in place. Hopeless . . .

There was a splash behind him and he turned to find a new face, a female face, surrounded with billowing red hair, swimming toward him. Then Caruso was there, too, and Clark thought he must be dead. But if that was true, then Caruso and the redheaded FBI agent were dead as well. Then he remembered the bullet wound in his calf.

Being dead hurt like hell.

Dominic Caruso dragged Clark to the shallow end of the pool. Callahan and Olson brought up the Hispanic girl and her deck chair while two other agents saw to a wounded Lily Chen, who now lay on the pool deck, screeching as though her guts were being torn out. One could dream, Caruso thought.

Callahan helped Olson push Magdalena up on the pool deck to Trooper Sergeant Bourke and then waded into the shallows to stand beside Caruso. Water pressed the silk blouse against her skin.

Clark coughed, blinking up at Caruso, then worked his jaw back and forth.

'Shit,' he said. 'Guess I'm not dead.'

'Nope,' Caruso said.

'But you are under arrest,' Callahan said.

Caruso frowned. 'Now, hang on. This was all in self-defense and you know it.'

'Self-defense my ass,' Callahan scoffed. She wiped the water off her face and sniffed, looking down at Clark. 'I'm happy you saved these girls. Don't get me wrong. But you can't just go all John Wick and then expect to walk away.'

'Do what you have to do,' Clark said. 'I don't blame you.'

'That's special,' Callahan said. 'So you agree to being arrested. That's big of you, considering the pile of dead bodies left in your wake.' As she spoke, she helped pull Clark out of the pool and rolled up his pant leg to check the wound in his calf. There were other scars there. A lot of them, as well as a bunch on his neck. This dude had been around the block.

'I'm not admitting to anything,' Clark said, coughing again. 'But there may or may not be another one under the dock.'

'Marvelous,' Callahan said. She nodded to the bullet hole. 'Looks like a through-and-through, but it might have nicked the bone. You may have to walk with a cane.'

'That's probably not going to happen,' Clark groused. He glanced up at Caruso, eyes narrow. 'How'd you find me?'

'Not entirely sure,' Dom said, looking sideways at Callahan. 'I think somebody might have screwed with my phone.'

Clark groaned. 'I'm lucky she's better at investigating than you are at operational security. Anyway, Lily Chen will have a cell phone somewhere. And on that phone will be a number for her brother, Vincent. Our people need that number yesterday. Understand?'

Dom nodded. 'Copy that.'

'Oh, no you don't,' Callahan said. 'No one messes with that phone before my tech guys get a look at it.'

Caruso gave her a passive look. 'Afraid I'm going to have to pull rank on you there,' he said. 'I'll give it right back, though.'

Callahan waved him away. 'Whatever.' She glared down at Clark. 'Who are you?'

'John,' he said.

'John . . .?'

'John,' he said again, as he winced at the pain in his leg. '. . . better go with *Doe*.'

54

The phone beside President Jack Ryan's bed rang once, dragging him out of some dream that he could not remember. He rolled over, coughed to clear his throat, and squinted at the blurry numbers on the clock as he picked up the handset. He'd gone to bed early in anticipation of an early ride to Andrews and a seven a.m. wheels-up for Tokyo. Surely it couldn't be that time already. Nowhere near it.

One forty-five a.m.

It was an accepted – and probably true – notion among White House staff that one could not get fired for waking the President. One could only get fired for *not* waking the President. Most would have erred on the side of caution, but Arnie van Damm had a pretty good handle on when events were important enough to rouse Ryan from his 'much-needed beauty sleep.' Van Damm had witnessed so many national crises that he remained absolutely unflappable while so many others ran around with their hair on fire. Van Damm joked that he had no hair, so . . .

'Mr President,' the voice on the other end of the line said.

'Good morning, Arnie.' Ryan stretched, fought the urge to say something flippant. No one called to joke at this ungodly hour.

'Sorry to wake you,' the chief of staff said. It was van

Damm's custom to engage in a few seconds of small talk before he got to the meat of the matter, to make certain his boss was thinking with some relative coherence.

'That's fine,' Ryan said, coughing again and rolling onto his back. Out of habit, he reached out to the other side of the bed to see if the call had woken Cathy, but she was still in Nepal. 'What's up?'

'Typhoon Catelyn,' van Damm said. 'There are some developments you'll want to know about.'

'Who else is here?'

'Commander Forrestal and I,' van Damm said. 'We have an Air Force weather guesser on his way over from the Pentagon.'

'Okay,' Ryan said. He was fully awake now. 'Notify the Secret Service that I'll be heading to the Oval in' – he put on his glasses and checked the clock again – 'ten minutes.'

'Already done,' van Damm said. 'I'm standing outside your door, speaking with the agent now.'

'That's just creepy, Arnie,' Ryan said.

'I do my best, Mr President.'

Posted outside the President's bedroom door in the central hallway, Special Agent Tina Jordan lifted the small beige microphone on her surveillance kit to her lips. She hit the push-to-talk button to call the command post – and other Secret Service personnel on the White House campus.

'CROWN, CROWN, from Jordan,' she whispered. 'SWORDSMAN is on the move in ten, en route to the Oval Office.'

*

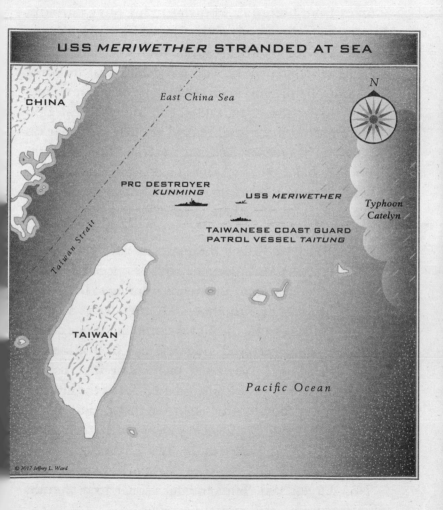

USS *MERIWETHER* STRANDED AT SEA

CHINA

East China Sea

N

PRC DESTROYER
KUNMING

USS *MERIWETHER*

*Typhoon
Catelyn*

Taiwan Strait

TAIWANESE COAST GUARD
PATROL VESSEL *TAITUNG*

TAIWAN

Pacific Ocean

© 2017 Jeffrey L. Ward

Ryan was surprised to find the secretary of defense waiting for him in the Oval Office with van Damm and Commander Robby Forrestal. All three men stood when he stepped inside.

Apart from Forrestal, who was in his Navy uniform, the men were dressed as if they'd met for a poker game instead of to discuss world events. Ryan wore faded jeans and a light bomber jacket with the Presidential seal over the USMC T-shirt he'd been sleeping in. Van Damm was dressed similarly to Ryan, sans the Presidential seal. Bob Burgess was normally well coiffed enough to appear on the cover of *Washington Life* magazine, but his thick salt-and-pepper hair now stuck out in a dozen directions.

Ryan sat in his customary spot in front of the fireplace and motioned for the others to take the couches.

'Let's have it,' he said.

Arnie glanced at Robby Forrestal and gave him a nod.

The deputy national security adviser opened a laptop and looked at the screen, apparently wanting to be certain he had the latest information. 'Mr President,' he said, 'forty-five minutes ago, the Naval communications center at Sasebo, Japan, received a distress call from Research Vessel *Meriwether*, a converted eighty-nine-foot fishing trawler with a crew of ten. She is based out of the University of Hawaii but is on loan to Kyushu University's Coastal and Ocean Engineering Department, ostensibly conducting fishing studies in the East China Sea –'

'Ah,' Ryan said. 'But she's not doing fish studies?'

'No,' Burgess said. 'She's towing a sonar array to study submarine traffic and communications.'

'Just so, sir,' Commander Forrestal said. 'RV *Meriwether*

has been seconded to the Defense Intelligence Agency for two years.'

Ryan rubbed his eyes, thinking this through. Virtually every nation with the capacity to launch a boat had some sort of spy ship. Some were overt about it, dragging sonars or flying masts to intercept foreign signal intelligence, but some were disguised. Chinese and Russian fishing vessels were often cover identities – and the United States had more than one such vessel of her own.

'Do we have open communication with the vessel?' van Damm asked.

'We do, sir,' Commander Forrestal said. 'So far, everyone aboard is fine, but *Meriwether* has lost propulsion and Typhoon Catelyn is driving her directly toward China.'

'Lost propulsion?' Ryan asked. 'What's their position?'

Forrestal turned his laptop around so Ryan could see the radar image on the screen. 'Approximately thirty kilometers northeast of Kuba-shima, one of the Senkaku Islands. This one is known as Huangwei Yu to the Chinese. At this moment, they're in waters claimed by both Japan and China, but at their present rate of speed they'll drift into undisputed Chinese territory in less than six hours. Chinese Coast Guard and fishing vessels are in and around the disputed islands almost daily when the weather allows. On a positive note, we're not tracking any right now.'

Ryan shook his head. 'How is this boat handling the storm if she doesn't have an engine?'

'Not well, I'm afraid,' the commander said. 'She is still ahead of the typhoon, but only just. *Meriwether*'s skipper, Captain Dave Holloway, reports seas in excess of thirty feet.'

Ryan exhaled slowly and leaned forward in his chair. He studied the red arrows behind a white swirl of clouds on the radar image. 'I see the storm's turned back to the west.'

'It has,' Forrestal said.

'Does anyone else find this situation odd?' Ryan asked, 'Considering *Meriwether*'s location and everything else that's been going on with China?'

Burgess nodded. Van Damm raised his eyebrows.

Forrestal said, 'The events and proximity to the PRC are extremely coincidental, but Captain Holloway doesn't believe this was sabotage. He's reporting it as a crankcase explosion caused by a fire in the scavenge space.'

'Bad maintenance, then,' Burgess said, shaking his head.

'Scavenge fire,' Ryan said. 'So it was something with the engine itself.'

'Correct, Mr President,' the commander said. 'Could have been caused by any number of things, like a buildup of carbon in the scavenge air space – basically the trunk that feeds air to the engine. The crankcase relief valve blew, and the resulting oil mist ignited inside the engine room. We're fortunate the whole ship didn't go up in flames.'

'Or not,' Burgess said. 'Still sounds like poor maintenance.'

'Captain Holloway is new to the vessel,' Forrestal said.

'Not an excuse,' Burgess said.

'But it is a reason,' Ryan said. 'Any casualties?'

'The mechanic suffered some burns,' Commander Forrestal said. 'But the skipper reports nothing life-threatening.'

'There's always some son of a bitch who didn't get the

word,' the SecDef said, obviously referring to then President Kennedy's response when he was informed of the American U-2 pilot who, navigating with all he was given – a compass and sextant – inadvertently flew from Alaska into Soviet air space. It was the height of the Cuban Missile Crisis, and the incursion very nearly pushed the already tense standoff into nuclear war.

'We can talk the blame game when everyone's safe on dry land,' Ryan said. 'Captain Holloway and his crew are out doing what we asked them to do. Let's get him on the horn. I want to talk to him.'

It took ten minutes for the communications specialist on watch in the Situation Room to reach the research vessel *Meriwether* and connect the captain with the Oval Office. Ryan put the call on speaker.

'Captain Holloway, Jack Ryan here.'

A screaming wind moaned in the background. 'Mr President.' Holloway's quiet voice barely cut through the static. He said something else, which was unintelligible.

Ryan fought the urge to speak louder over the phone. 'Do you have injuries, Captain?'

'No, sir,' Holloway said. He was obviously trying to hear himself above the wind – and likely the thump of his own heartbeat in his ears. The hissing connection made it sound as if were speaking in a strained stage whisper. 'We're all uninjured and accounted for, Mr President,' he said.

'Is there a way to repair the damage? Ryan asked.

'The fire was extensive,' Holloway said. 'My engineer is working to fix the problem, but it doesn't look promising. I want you to know we fully realize the gravity of this situation, sir. There are systems on the ship that cannot fall into Chinese hands.'

'That would be best,' Ryan said, wishing he could say otherwise.

'I have discussed using the life rafts and scuttling with the crew,' Holloway said. 'They will obey the order without argument, Mr President.'

'Hang on now, Captain,' Ryan said. 'We're not there yet.' He tried to imagine launching a rubber raft in gale winds and thirty-foot seas, let alone boarding the damned thing from a pitching ship. If the crew survived the deployment, and if the storm didn't shred the inflatable rafts, then their best hope for survival was getting picked up by a Chinese patrol. 'You take care of your people, Captain,' Ryan said. 'We'll get the cavalry heading your way with all possible speed.'

'Thank you, Mr President,' the captain said. The strain in his voice made it apparent that he was experienced and realistic enough to feel grateful for the President's outreach, without holding out some insane hope for an actual rescue.

Ryan ended the call and then looked at his watch. 'All right, gentlemen,' he said. 'It's half past two. Let's find out what we have in the way of a cavalry.'

Arnie stood. 'We'll have the NSC Principals Committee here inside the hour,' he said.

'Very well.' Ryan looked at the deputy national security adviser. 'It's early afternoon in Beijing. Robby, get with the duty officers downstairs and have them line up a Mandarin interpreter. Tell them we'll just need one. It'll be a fifteen-minute call at most. And get me the background sheet on President Zhao. I want you to set up a call with him as soon as humanly possible.'

'Right away, Mr President.'

Van Damm's head snapped around as if he'd been slapped. 'Oh, I'd urge against that, Jack.'

'I agree with Arnie, Mr President,' the SecDef said. 'We're not even sure the ChiComs know where this boat is.'

'And I don't plan to tell them,' Ryan said.

Commander Forrestal was already out the door. He had his orders, and the arguments of two advisers shouldn't slow him down. If the President wanted him to stop, the President would have to be the one to stop him.

Ryan was showered, shaved, and freshly suited in twenty minutes. Someone had rustled him up a cup of coffee and a Danish, and they were on his desk by the time he got back to the Oval. He took a bite and wondered idly what it would be like when he wasn't the leader of the free world anymore and magic coffee fairies didn't leave him pastries and Arabica roast when he most needed them.

It was just after four in the morning by the time USAF Major Jennifer Yi, the Mandarin speaker sent over by the Pentagon, entered the Oval Office ahead of Commander Forrestal. She was a tall, no-nonsense woman with a stern face that made Ryan think she probably voted for the other guy in the last election. Still, she was professional and looked him in the eye when she shook his hand. He didn't have to ask about her credentials as a simultaneous interpreter or her clearance. The NSC guys in the watch center would have handled all of that. By necessity, interpreters got to be a part of conversations that only a select few were privy to. Intense and often delicate negotiations hung in the balance of an interpreter's ability to pick up on what speakers meant to say and the words they chose to convey it.

Van Damm, Burgess, and Foley took seats on the couches while Major Yi moved her chair around behind the desk so she could be seated beside the President, closer to his ear. She would listen to the conversation via a headset, translating the Chinese president's Mandarin almost simultaneously. The effort required intense concentration, and she situated her chair so she faced away from the others in attendance, close to Ryan's ear but not looking at him. In addition to those in the room, the call would be recorded and monitored by a half-dozen aides and staffers.

Presumably, Zhao would have a similar situation on his end.

Forrestal picked up the handset on the President's desk, spoke to someone on the other end of the line for a moment, and then handed it to Ryan, giving him a thumbs-up.

'Mr President,' Ryan said. 'Thank you for taking my call . . .'

55

Arnie van Damm sat back on the sofa in the Oval Office after the interpreter had gone. 'I can't believe he agreed to hold off.' He breathed an audible sigh of relief. The phone call with the president of the People's Republic of China was straight from the Jack Ryan shoot-from-the-gut playbook. Unfortunately, that kind of shooting worked both ways, and brought with it the strong possibility of gut-shooting yourself in the process.

True to form, President Zhao had begun the call with an insistence that the United States affirm a one-China policy that denied the existence of Taiwan as an independent nation. It was a scripted verbal ballet, and once the two world leaders got past their respective parts, the call had progressed quickly. Ryan was his usual direct self, making statements that from the mouths of other men would have sounded like ultimatums but from him were just statements of cold, dispassionate fact.

It was apparent that Zhao already knew about the *Meriwether*'s predicament and geographic position. He had bristled at the incursion of yet another American vessel into Chinese waters at first. But in the end, he agreed to forgo intercepting *Meriwether* while she was in waters claimed by both China and Japan, adding, however, that his humanity necessitated that he 'rescue' the hapless research vessel the moment it entered waters not also claimed by the Japanese.

'I know exactly why he agreed,' Mary Pat Foley said.

Ryan nodded. 'The PLA Navy has already moved all their ships out of the path of the typhoon. He couldn't board the *Meriwether* if he wanted to.'

Burgess looked at his watch. 'That gives us roughly five hours,' he said. 'You can bet the ChiCom Navy is steaming out now. An American spy ship would be a grand coup for them in the media, not to mention the technology they'll glean if Captain Holloway doesn't have the sense to destroy it. We could be looking at another *Pueblo*.'

The USS *Pueblo* was the only commissioned US Navy ship to remain the captive of an enemy state. Many in the IC believed that the seizure of communications gear when the *Pueblo* was captured in 1968 had allowed the DPRK and the Soviet Union to monitor US Naval communications late into the 1980s. The *Pueblo* remained moored in Pyongyang at the Victorious War Museum.

Ryan looked again at the massive white vortex that was Typhoon Catelyn on Forrestal's computer screen.

'Five hours,' he said. 'That's assuming the sea doesn't take her first.'

The paramount leader of the People's Republic of China, Zhao Chengzhi, ended the call with Jack Ryan and leaned back in his chair. The talk had left him exhausted, but he believed he was hiding it well from the two female interpreters and the dozen other staff members who surrounded his desk.

Colonel Huang stood in his customary spot beside the door, eyes glinting in the muted light, flicking hawklike glances around the room as everyone filed out the door.

Admiral Qian, commander of the PLA Navy, was the last to leave. He was displeased with what he saw as the conciliatory tone of the phone call, but he had his orders, and would obey them.

'I plan to work a few more hours,' Zhao said to Huang when they were alone in the office.

'Very well, Zhao Zhuxi,' the CSB man said. 'Major Ts'ai will remain outside while I will see to the transition of the evening shift. I will return shortly to check in before I make the final security checks prior to our departure for Tokyo.'

Zhao removed his glasses and set them on his desk. 'I cannot help but feel that you would sleep here if I allowed it,' he said. 'Perhaps your wife would be my greatest threat since I take you away from her so often.'

Huang blanched at the sudden familiarity. 'My wife . . .'

'Forgive my candor, Huang Ju.' Zhao smiled. 'I am only joking. Perhaps my discussion with the American has made me overly emotional.'

The colonel gave a curt bow, suppressing a smile himself. 'If there is nothing else, Zhao Zhuxi.'

Colonel Huang knew each of the sixteen CSB protective agents on the oncoming shift by name as well as reputation. Fourteen good men and two equally stalwart women whom Huang had handpicked for the job from among hundreds of applicants. Each member of the detail had been working in their present capacity for over a year and the lack of new faces added a modicum of comfort to Huang's attitude. The evening briefing was held in the cramped basement Central Security Bureau squad room two floors below the paramount leader's office suite. Except for Huang, the rest of the day shift remained on station above until they were relieved. Huang relayed important logistical information about the early departure for the G20 and a number of protests that were expected in Japan regarding the Falun Gong and Tibet. Rules of engagement were reviewed, assignments discussed, along with a reminder that there would be cameras everywhere – and little ability to control the media.

Once the oncoming shift had assumed their posts – leaving a new officer outside the president's office – Huang walked his second-in-command, Major Ts'ai, to the gate. He wanted to discuss a few last-minute details about the Japan trip. Unlike members of the US Secret Service, even supervisory members of the Central Security Bureau's presidential protection unit did not have take-home cars. Most, including Major Ts'ai, did not mind, preferring to take the train over paying hundreds of thousands of yuan – the equivalent of thousands of dollars – for parking.

Two uniformed 1st Squadron, First Group CSB soldiers snapped to attention when they saw the two officers.

'Tomorrow morning, then, Colonel,' Major Ts'ai said as they reached the gate. 'I hope you are able to get some sleep.'

Huang smiled. 'I will sleep when the paramount leader is safely back in Chi –'

The pop of gunfire outside the gates caused the smile to vanish from Huang's face. Both he and the major drew their pistols, nodding to the uniformed guards.

Ever thinking of his first responsibility, the colonel

keyed the PTT button on his radio. He ordered the command post to keep President Zhao in his office and double the contingent of uniformed guards, forming concentric rings of protection.

'A mugging, perhaps,' Major Ts'ai said, Taurus pistol in his hand as he peered around the edge of the employee man-door through the walls of the highly guarded grounds.

'Perhaps,' Huang said, feeling in his gut that the shots signified something even more sinister.

Captain Fu Jiankang, another member of the president's primary detail, spoke in a halting voice over the radio, proving Huang's suspicions. Even wounded, the man retained his priorities. He gave his position – a location half a block down from the gate – and asked for medical assistance, as the victim of an apparent robbery. He demonstrated remarkable devotion to duty when he reminded his comrades to 'see to the safety of the paramount leader first.'

Colonel Huang's instinctive and completely human inclination was to rush to the aid of his friend, but training made both him and the major turn immediately and rush back to the president's office. On the street, gunfire popped and snapped. Another member of the detail called out that he was hit. And then another. Four minutes after the skirmish started, Colonel Huang stood with his back to President Zhao's door, listening through his earpiece to the sound of his men as they died.

56

Japan turned out to be one of those Unless Otherwise Directed situations when it came to carrying a firearm. Lisanne Robertson faxed arrival documents to passport control – along with payment information for the roughly five thousand dollars they would have to pay for the privilege of landing at the facilities, but Japanese officials rescinded permission to land at Haneda Airport nearer downtown Tokyo, instead sending the Hendley Associates Gulfstream to the larger Narita International – almost an hour outside the city. Narita's Business Aviation Terminal accepted only fifteen planes a day, so they were lucky to get a spot. The Premier Gate was glitzy and comfortable, but it shunted arriving bigwigs over and through the same shoe-disinfecting rug, body temperature scanner, immigration, and customs stations as every other visitor to Japan.

The Campus operators took the chance of raising a few eyebrows by packing the comms gear and granddad pocketknives in their luggage, but carrying in firearms would have been impossible. The pistols and larger blades remained hidden in the bulkhead compartments of the airplane.

The pilots and Lisanne stayed at a hotel close to Narita while the team made the forty-five-minute trip from the airport to Tokyo Station. Lisanne had been able to find them rooms at the Marriott near the Ginza – no small feat with attendees of the G20 packing the city. Luckily, all the venues appeared to be on the opposite side of the station – geographically close, but worlds away in a city as densely populated as Tokyo.

With nothing to go on but the fact that Vincent Chen and his cohorts were in Japan, Chavez told everyone to get settled and stand by to move. Ryan decided to grab a quick shower and change into his last pair of clean clothes. The rooms were small, as business hotel rooms were in Japan, with just enough floor space to turn around in at the foot of the bed. The tub was deep, meant for soaking – and Jack thought he would put it to good use when he had more time.

With his comms batteries changed and feeling uncharacteristically light without his pistol, Ryan walked through the automatic glass door to meet the other operators in the fourth-floor lobby of the Marriott. Midas read a copy of *The Asahi Shimbun*, the English-language edition, while Adara looked at their phones. Ryan sat down by Adara, who filled him in on the latest about Clark's injuries.

'He's doing fine,' she said. 'Still under guard at a hospital in Fort Worth. This female FBI agent appears to want to arrest Dom, too.'

'Like to see her try,' Adara groused.

Ryan sighed. 'Nothing from Gavin yet?'

Midas lowered the newspaper and peered over the top. 'Ding's still in his room, on the phone with him now,' he said. 'Hopefully he'll have –'

Chavez came over the net, cutting him off. Apparently, he'd just put in his earpiece. 'Saddle up and meet me in the lobby,' he said. There was an urgent calm in his voice that a seasoned hunter gets when he first spots his prey. 'We're going to a place called Shinjuku. Adara, jump on your phone and see what train we need to take.'

'Copy that,' Adara said. 'My buds and I blew some of our liberty walking around Kabukichō during a port call in Yokosuka. I could have guessed Chen would end up in a place like that.'

'So are we going to Shinjuku or Kabukichō?' Midas asked.

'Shinjuku is the area,' Adara said. 'Kabukichō is the red-light district in that area. Scads of pachinko parlors, love hotels. Everywhere you turn there's some yakuza tout trying to drag you into hostess clubs where girls in baby-doll costumes will flirt with you and charge exorbitant prices for alcohol, among other things.'

'*Chicas peligrosas,*' Jack muttered.

'You're right about that, *'mano,*' Chavez said. 'Anyway, the number Dom got from Lily Chen's phone pinged at a restaurant in Shinjuku three hours ago. It's quiet now, so he's either dumped it or turned it off. That's something. He doesn't know what we look like, so we may as well go have a look. Jack, you should probably call your new girlfriend and let her know what we have.'

'She's not my girlfriend,' Ryan said.

'You say so, *'mano,*' Chavez said. 'Let's be ready to roll in five.'

'We're all in the lobby,' Adara said. 'Ready to go, boss.'

Chavez gave a quiet chuckle. 'Copy that,' he said. 'I'll be out as soon as I can figure out the buttons on this Japanese toilet.'

Jack called the number on the card Yuki had given him. It usually irritated him when he got someone's voice mail, but he found he was oddly happy to hear Yukiko speak. She gave her number with no name or business affiliation, which was common in this business. There wasn't much to tell, so his message was short. They were looking for an Asian man in the busiest area of the most populated city in Asia – or the world, for that matter – because his phone said he'd been there three hours earlier.

The hotel was less than two blocks from Tokyo Station, and the team quickly fell in with the river of Japanese commuters, seemingly going in all directions at once. Ryan was no stranger to world travel but he'd thought the station was busy when they'd come in on the Narita Express at midday. Rush hour started late in Tokyo but was in full swing by six-thirty. The station itself was a sprawling shopping mall with tens of thousands of commuters passing them throughout the day. Women in brightly colored uniforms and young men in large costume hats shouted and cajoled – always in the most polite and deferential tone – inviting the captive audience to try their cake, fruit, waffle, fish, or countless other products.

Eccentric hairstyles and outlandish clothing could be seen here and there – the odd peroxide red, a blue Mohawk, and even a pierced nose or two. But Japan remained a place where you could buy a white shirt and tie at the corner convenience store. Conservative dress and demeanor were lauded, and for the most part, Tokyo Station was a sea of dark hair and dark suits – for men and women alike.

Adara and Ding both spoke a smattering of Japanese, so they led the way to platform 1, where the team jammed themselves into the 6:38 Chuo Line train for Shinjuku – which arrived precisely on the minute. The car proved to be shoulder-to-shoulder and chest-to-chest. Unlike China and some other countries where Jack and the others had worked, the trains in Japan seemed to have the same rules as libraries or urinals. No eye contact, no talking. And, Adara warned them, if the men were lucky enough to get a seat, under no circumstances should they offer it up to a woman under fifty who was not pregnant. Fortunately, the 6:38 Chuo was so crowded he barely had room to stand, let alone a seat to give up.

Four stops and fifteen minutes later, the train disgorged the team into a seething mass of evening commuters at Shinjuku, more crowded even than Tokyo Station. Chavez motioned everyone behind a row of coffee vending machines in order to not get run over while he checked his phone for the address Gavin had given him. With a basic idea of where they were going, he navigated them across the street toward a garish red neon sign that ran up the side of a building, reading in English: 'I "heart" Kabukichō.'

'We should have brought umbrellas,' Midas said, looking up at the boiling clouds in the night sky, reflecting red and orange from the neon lights. 'Would have given us some weapons.'

'It starts to rain, umbrella stands will sprout up all over the place,' Chavez said.

Adara had been right about Kabukichō. Touts ruled the narrow streets, venturing into the lighted streets from the shadows of their covered awnings only when someone promising walked past. On one, the clatter and ping of pachinko machines sounded above the nasal whine of shamisen music. On the next, men in white shirts and black bow ties beckoned anyone over eighteen into curtained 'information centers' to the decades-old hits of Olivia Newton-John. Crowds of tourists made the place seem slightly less sinister than it really was. Ten-foot-tall female robots waved their massive arms, and diminutive girls – many of whom spoke Korean – stood under strobing lights in skimpy costumes, handing out flyers that were written in characters Jack couldn't understand.

It was like Vegas in code.

'We turn right here,' Chavez said, pointing east on the grimy side street past the Robot Restaurant. 'It's supposed to be a couple blocks up that way.'

'Let me look at that,' Adara said, moving closer to Chavez. 'Ah, he was in the Golden Gai. This is making more sense by the minute.'

The Golden Gai, or Golden District, was roughly one large square block in size, bisected by narrow alleys and dozens of even narrower footpaths that cut between minuscule bars and cafés – most of which accommodated no more than seven or eight, and most of those regular patrons. The maze of ramshackle shanties with dim lights burning in the second-floor flats made it the perfect place to get lost. One sign read THE DOOR TO NARNIA; another proclaimed NO ENGLISH HERE!

The team split, with Ryan and Midas approaching the target address from the west while Adara and Ding walked parallel to circle around and come in from the east. Ryan and Midas slowed their pace, doing a little gawking while they gave the other team time to get ahead. American and European tourists roamed the shadowed alleys, staring into the tiny bars like they were visiting a human zoo. Ryan was just about to say something about it when he looked to his right and did a double take. Midas noticed and slowed to get a look himself.

'Is that –'

Jack nudged him forward. 'Come on,' he said. 'She's probably working.'

At the split pine counter of a cramped place called the Jazz Bar sat Yukiko Monzaki. She glanced up at Jack when he passed, then just as quickly looked away.

'You think we burned her?' Chavez asked after Ryan filled him in on who they'd seen.

'Our guy doesn't know what we look like,' Ryan said, still walking. 'Or, for that matter, that we're even after him.'

Two Asian men wearing light-colored golf jackets stepped out of a bar ahead, looked up and down the street, then turned down a small side alley to the left.

Ryan and Midas kept walking.

The sound of a sliding door and then a soft voice came from up the street behind them.

'Jack? What are you doing here?'

Ryan turned to find Yukiko standing in a pool of light beneath a red lantern outside the Jazz Bar.

Half a breath later, the door to the café in the middle of the block slid open and an Asian couple stepped into the street. It was the same door the two men had come out of earlier, between Yuki and Jack now. The man carried a leather satchel over his shoulder and was in the middle of lighting a cigarette. The burst of flame illuminated the face of Vincent Chen.

Ryan gave an involuntary start. Yuki took a half-step forward.

The woman with Chen shot a glance at Yuki and then back at Ryan and Midas before leaning in to whisper something. Chen looked up from his cigarette and hitched up the leather bag, walking toward Ryan. He made it two steps before darting left to disappear between two buildings where the earlier men had gone. The woman was right behind him. Three more men exited the same café before Ryan and Midas could follow. Amanda Salazar came out behind them.

'Chen and Kim Soo coming at you, mid-block,' Midas shouted into his mic. 'Two more Asian males ahead of them. Could be together.'

The last man out after Chen attempted to draw a long hunting knife from his belt, but Yuki came up from behind and gave him a brutal chop to the forearm with an expandable baton. He dropped the knife but wheeled on her immediately, still very much in the fight. Amanda screamed like a banshee and ran directly at Midas, clawing at his face. The two men came at Ryan in unison.

It was relatively early and Kabukichō was just waking up, but the few people on the narrow street jumped back, not sure if they should run or pull out their phones and start filming.

Grateful for the darkness, Ryan sidestepped the lead, moving into the entryway of a nearby bar, narrowing the possible angles his opponents had to mount their attack and forcing them to stack, one behind the other. Ryan faded back a hair, drawing that man in close before driving upward with a wicked uppercut, slamming the man's teeth together with a satisfying crack and setting him up for a quick left hook to the jaw that turned off his lights and left him sprawled on the pavement.

Ryan caught the glint of a blade in the hands of the second attacker, upping the ante. Undaunted by the quick defeat of his partner, this one was surely endowed with cold-steel courage brought on by the knife. He bent forward at the waist and rushed Ryan, shoulders stooped, blade out like a fencer on the offense. Ryan stepped sideways again, feeling the sickening scrape as the knife glanced off a rib. He grabbed a handful of golf jacket, taking advantage of the momentum to help the man run past. The man's head punched straight through the bar's flimsy hollow-core inner door, all the way to his shoulders. Blades and multiple opponents left little room for mercy. Ryan brought his elbow down on the back of the man's neck, crushing his throat against the edge of the door and ending the fight – for this one.

Seeing the mortally wounded man hanging half in, half out by his neck, two Japanese women in the tiny bar screamed and retreated to the far corners of the room.

Ryan moved his arms, chicken-wing-like, to be certain they still worked after the knife wound.

The quick *snap, snap* of fist to flesh came from Ryan's right. He turned in time to see Midas lift a screaming Amanda Salazar above his head and slam her to the ground. Blood poured from the big man's nose, revealing that the snapping sound had been Amanda hitting him and not the other way around. She moaned at his feet, writhing on the asphalt and bleeding from her ear.

Yuki stood over the body of the third man, clutching

her expandable baton. She bent quickly and handcuffed him to a standpipe next to the road.

'You okay?' Ryan looked at Yuki.

She nodded.

'I'm fine, brother,' Midas said, hand to his bleeding nose as he started for the alley. 'In case you were wondering.'

'Are you armed?' Ryan asked. He hadn't told them about his ribs, and hesitated to look down.

She nodded, producing a stainless SIG Sauer P230. 'You?'

Ryan glanced down at the man he'd knocked out and saw a small revolver in an ankle holster. He stooped and picked it up. 'I am now,' he said.

Yuki stepped in close, touching his side. 'You are bleeding.'

'I'm fine,' Ryan said, rolling his shoulders. 'Really.'

Lightning rent the sky above Tokyo, followed by a crack of thunder. The wind shifted abruptly to the north.

Adara's voice came on the radio, garbled and unintelligible. Ding shouted something next, on the net, but loud enough to hear from the next alley over.

The skies opened up, and it began to rain. More thunder echoed through the narrow streets. No, that wasn't right. It wasn't thunder at all, but the flat crack of gunfire.

57

Marine One took roughly seven minutes to fly from the White House to Joint Base Andrews. The HMX-1 helicopter flew in a formation of three identically marked Sikorsky Sea Kings, shifting positions constantly while en route to confuse any would-be attackers with their Presidential shell game in the predawn darkness. Identical helicopters had already been transported to Tokyo along with dozens of Secret Service vehicles (including two copies of the Presidential armored limo known as The Beast) aboard Air Force C-17s and C-5s.

Ryan saluted the Marine as he left the chopper and then walked approximately a hundred fifty feet with Special Agent Montgomery before returning the salute of the staff sergeant at the base of the air stairs leading to Air Force One. He paused halfway up the steps and looked at the big blue-and-white bird. The smell of jet fuel and tarmac gave Ryan the creeps, but if he had to fly, this was the plane to do it on.

Mary Pat Foley was waiting for him at the top of the stairs. Arnie van Damm followed him inside.

'MP,' Ryan said. It was a chilly morning and he wore his navy blue flight jacket with the Presidential seal.

'Good morning Mr President,' the DNI said. 'We have Captain Lim of the Taiwanese Coast Guard vessel *Taitung* on the line now.'

Ryan followed Foley amidships to the combination dining and conference room. Scott Adler was already there, along with the chief of naval operations, Admiral George Muñoz, and Coast Guard commander Jeff Carter. Gary Montgomery had already peeled off with the rest of the Secret Service detail to give the President his space.

A Chinese man in the blue uniform of the ROC Coast Guard looked on from the flat-screen television mounted on the bulkhead at the end of the conference table. He was slender, with high cheekbones and the pinched look of a man in the middle of a violent storm.

'Can he see us?' Ryan asked the Air Force staff sergeant from Communications.

'I can indeed, Mr President,' Captain Lim said. 'We are approaching your American research vessel now, but I must inform you that the PRC destroyer *Kunming* is twenty-six nautical miles to the west and closing rapidly.'

'How far are you from undisputed Chinese waters?' Ryan asked.

Captain Lim looked off screen and barked something in Mandarin. The pitch and roll of the ship were evident in the footage. 'Eleven nautical miles,' he said.

'Very well,' Ryan said. 'I appreciate your assistance – and I know the crew of *Meriwether* is even more grateful.'

With Ryan aboard, Air Force One began her takeoff roll almost immediately.

'We are almost in position, Mr President,' Lim said. 'I have explained to Commander Carter how we plan to attempt the rescue. I must ask to be excused as we get under way but one of my crewmen will attempt to video our efforts to the extent possible once we actually begin.'

'By all means, Captain,' Ryan said. 'Thank you again.'

Ryan nodded and the staff sergeant put the connection on mute.

United States Coast Guard Commander Jeff Carter sat at the table to Ryan's immediate right with a blank sheet of paper and a black Sharpie marker. Both Carter and the Four Star were on board Air Force One solely to be the president's subject matter experts regarding the *Meriwether* rescue. Both men would fly home commercially from Tokyo while everyone else on board attended to their duties at the G20.

'If I may be permitted, Mr President,' Carter said.

'Of course,' Ryan said.

Carter drew a small X in the center of the paper. '*Meriwether* is here, drifting toward undisputed Chinese waters at an estimated four knots.' He drew a second X. '*Taitung*, a thousand-ton Taiwanese Coast Guard patrol vessel, is approaching from the south. At eighty-seven meters, she can handle the seas, but she has a raised helicopter pad on the aft decks, giving her a large superstructure and making her susceptible to being shoved around a great deal in high winds.'

'And the *Kunming*?' Ryan asked. 'How soon will she be in range to be a threat?'

Commander Carter looked up from his drawing, deferring to the CNO.

Admiral Muñoz said, 'The *Kunming* is a threat now, Mr President. Her YJ-83 antiship missiles have at least a one-hundred-eighty-kilometer range, depending on the variant. As far as boarding, at best speed, she'll be right on top of *Meriwether* in half an hour, even steaming into the storm as she is.'

Ryan nodded, then waved at the paper. 'Please continue, Commander.'

'Yes, sir,' Carter said. 'Captain Lim will quarter the *Taitung* into the typhoon, putting *Meriwether* on her lee side while keeping enough standoff to prevent a collision. Once in position, the *Taitung* will deploy a small search-and-rescue crew of four with her Norsafe JYN 57 hard-topped lifeboat, which will come alongside *Meriwether*'s rubber lifeboat after they abandon ship.'

'And the *Meriwether* herself?' Ryan asked.

Commander Carter shot a glance at the DNI.

Mary Pat said, 'Captain Holloway destroyed any classified documents as soon as he realized the engine was unrepairable. There is, however, some highly sensitive hardware on the vessel. Most of it is modular and can be removed, but some is too large. Captain Holloway's engineers have rigged the ship to flood as they board the lifeboat.'

'Towing is out of the question, then?' Ryan said.

'I'm afraid so, Mr President,' the commander said. 'The *Meriwether* is a little too large for that in this present sea state. The Taiwanese cutter would almost certainly pull her through the face of a wave.'

'Will she go down fast enough?' Ryan asked. 'If she's scuttled, I mean.'

Admiral Muñoz nodded. 'We're usually worried about slowing down a sinking ship, Mr President. If Captain Holloway destroys all the through-hulls, those seas will take her in a matter of minutes.'

Ryan rubbed his eyes. 'Sounds simple enough – if they were on a calm lake and not looking at waves the size of houses.'

'The Norsafe can handle the seas, sir,' Commander Carter said. 'And if they have to, the lifeboat would be much easier to tow into friendly waters.'

'How about getting everyone back aboard the *Taitung*?' Ryan asked. 'If I remember right, those lifeboats leave a little to be desired as far as speed.'

'That's true,' Carter said. 'But theoretically, she'll be able to maneuver, and the *Taitung* should be about to come up alongside her and bring her in on the davit sleds. It'll be like threading a needle during a car wreck, but they'd rather do that than tow the lifeboat if they are able. Once the Norsafe is drawn in tight, the sleds should keep her from bashing against *Taitung*'s hull.'

'That's a lot of theories and shoulds, Commander,' Ryan said.

'Yes, it is, Mr President,' Carter said, giving a somber nod. 'But it is the plan. A better option would be for the *Taitung* to stand off until morning when a ship with a helicopter could arrive.'

Ryan shook his head. 'But *Meriwether* will be driven into Chinese waters in a matter of hours.'

The Air Force communications officer spoke up. 'Incoming message from SSN *Seawolf*, Admiral Muñoz.'

The chief of naval operations read the printed document and slid it across the table to Ryan.

'Captain Racher has positioned his submarine ten nautical miles west of the *Meriwether*, Mr President. Chinese communications would indicate that *Kunming* does not know she is there.'

'Very well,' Ryan said. 'Let's hope we can keep it that way.'

The *Seawolf* had been built as a replacement for the *Los Angeles*-class fast-attack submarine fleet. She was fast and well armed, but she was also expensive – too expensive for a post-Cold War Navy, so only three had been built. In destroyer-versus-fast-attack-sub battle, Ryan's money would be on the submarine – especially with the surface ship battling heavy seas – but the aftermath would be catastrophic.

Ryan said, 'Have *Taitung* advise the Chinese destroyer a rescue operation is under way and to stand off.'

The Air Force comms officer did so. There were several minutes of tense back-and-forth before he turned to Ryan.

'The Chinese vessel insists on rendering aid,' he said.

'In contested waters?' Ryan asked, cursing President Zhao under his breath.

The communications officer typed another message, and waited for the reply.

'Apparently so, Mr President,' the comms officer said three minutes later. '*Kunming* is two nautical miles from the imaginary line and doesn't appear to be slowing. Their captain says his orders to assist come directly from Admiral Qian, commander of the PLA Navy.'

All eyes looked at Ryan. 'Advise *Seawolf* to stand by, Admiral Muñoz. If the skipper of the *Kunming* presses me, I swear –'

Captain Lim's face appeared again on the flat-screen.

'Mr President,' he said, 'the crew of RV *Meriwether* is all safely aboard our lifeboat. We are rigging for retrieval at this time.'

'And the *Meriwether* herself?' Ryan asked.

'The aft deck is already awash, Mr President,' Captain Lim said, his expression somber. No sailor liked to see any ship go down, even if it was necessary.

'Thank you again for your assistance, Captain,' Ryan said. 'I'll be making my gratitude formally known to your superiors.'

'Thank you, Mr President,' Lim said, and like the leader he was, rather than basking in accolades, he asked to be excused to see to his duties.

Ryan put both hands flat on the table and heaved a sigh of relief. 'Have *Seawolf* shadow that damned destroyer awhile and keep her honest.'

'Yes, Mr President,' Admiral Muñoz said, typing in the orders personally with his authentication code.

'Good work, all of you,' Ryan said. 'You gentlemen get with the steward and enjoy your favorite beverage on me. Scott, Mary Pat, let's step back to my office for a bit.'

He didn't mention it in front of the military men, but both the DNI and the secretary of state knew they were about to dig into a strategy on what to do about President Zhao Chengzhi.

58

Jack Ryan, Jr, bowed his head against the driving rain and ran down the alley with Midas and Yuki, toward the sound of intermittent gunfire. He slowed as he neared the end of the narrow pathway, pulling up behind a broken vending machine to check the cylinder of the .38 revolver he'd taken from one of the bad guys. It was loaded with five, which, he decided, was a hell of a lot better than a sharp stick.

'Chavez, Adara,' he said. 'You guys copy?'

'Hold up, Jack,' Adara's whispered voice came back. 'If you're coming down the alley, Chen and his buds are to the right, just around the corner waiting for you.'

Ryan raised his fist but Midas had already stopped and was relaying the message to Yuki since she had no comms.

'Are you whole?' Ryan asked.

'Affirmative,' Adara said. 'We're pinned down in a bar across the street called the Albatross. A black stone front. Pretty sure Chen thinks we're armed, because he's not rushing us.'

'Copy,' Ryan said. 'Sit tight a minute. Yuki is armed and I have a little Chief's Special.'

'Yuki?' Chavez said.

'I'll explain later,' Ryan said. He turned to Yuki. 'You have backup anywhere nearby?'

'My partner is busy with the G20.' She shook her head. 'I stopped off here to interview a contact who knows Kim Soo. I did not expect her to be here.'

'Great,' Midas said.

'I did not expect you to be here,' Yuki said. Rain dripped from her nose. 'Any of you. In any case, gunfire is extremely rare in Japan. Ammunition is accountable here, not just firearms. Police officers are at this moment getting ready to converge on your friends. It would be best for me if we took care of Chen before the authorities arrive. Less explaining, if you know what I mean.'

Jack nodded, dabbed at the wound on his side. It would need a few stitches, but his rib bone had taken the brunt of the attack – doing what ribs were designed to do and protecting his heart and lungs. It would hurt like a son of a bitch when the adrenaline wore off.

Yuki was drenched and beginning to shiver. He considered giving her his jacket but thought it would offend her, considering the circumstances.

'You've got eight rounds,' he said, wiping the rain off his face. 'I've got five. That leaves –'

Adara's voice cut him off again. 'Jack!' she said. 'Chen and the girl are coming back your way.'

Sirens began to wail toward Shinjuku train station.

Ryan peeked around the vending machine to see Chen and Kim Soo sprinting toward him. Chen had his head down against the pouring rain, but the Korean woman saw Ryan and brought up a pistol, firing as she ran.

Rounds thwacked against the vending machine, just inches from Ryan's face. He shot twice, aiming center mass at Chen, who was also armed and in the lead. He hoped like hell the rounds stopped but didn't kill the bastard. They really, really needed to talk to him.

Yuki dropped to her knees as Ryan fired and leaned around the machine, shooting steadily, purposefully, dumping seven rounds and staying aimed in while she reloaded a fresh magazine from her pocket.

Both Chen and Kim Soo fell, their pistols skittering across the wet pavement.

More gunfire erupted from the other end of the alley.

'Talk to me, guys,' Midas said.

'We're good,' Chavez came back. 'Our two bad guys decided to engage the police. Are you guys all right?'

'We're good,' Midas said. 'Chen and Kim Soo are down.'

'Dead?' Chavez asked.

Jack put a hand to Chen's neck. 'Chen's still alive,' he said. Yuki did the same with Kim Soo but shook her head.

'Get them off the street if you can,' Chavez said. 'If you can manage to stop shooting, the cops might think these other dudes are responsible – at least until ballistics comes back. These idiots appear to be ready to go down in a hail of bullets, so they won't be around to question, either. I figure you got about five minutes while the cops still have their hands busy.'

Yuki picked the lock to the back door of a bar off the alley, leading into a storage room stacked high with boxes of wine and assorted liquor. Midas dragged in Kim Soo's body as well, in case any local police came up the alley from the other end to investigate. Ryan and Yuki leaned Chen against a stack of Suntory whiskey boxes and brought him around with a pinch to the underside of his upper arm. Shamisen music came from the thin door to the main bar along with a sliver of green neon. Otherwise the storage room was dark.

'Jack san,' Yuki said. 'You must give me the revolver.'

Ryan shook his head. 'Not yet. Still too sketchy out there.'

'I will return it if needed,' Yuki said. 'Possession of a firearm is seven years in prison in this country. No matter who you are.'

Ryan groaned and handed over the revolver, butt first. He took his frustration out on a moaning Vincent Chen.

'Tell us something, champ,' Ryan said. 'What are you doing in Japan?'

Chen put a hand to his shoulder, exploring the wounds, then looking to the floor at Kim Soo. 'I think the bitch shot me,' he said.

'I think so, too,' Ryan whispered. The gaping exit wound in front of Chen's chest indicated the shot had come from behind. 'Seriously, though, you some kind of bagman or what? I can get you protection if you help us out.'

'Protection would be most welcome,' Chen said. 'They will kill . . .' He began to cough up a pink foam, choking on his own blood.

'Damn it!' Ryan hissed. At least one of the rounds had punched through Chen's lung. He put a finger to the man's lips, grateful for the shamisen music. 'You gotta hush, dude, or they'll find us.' He had no idea who 'they' were, but Chen was scared of somebody.

'Gang . . .' Chen coughed again. 'F . . . f . . . four . . .

Ki . . .' He attempted another cough, but there was no energy in it. His words trailed off in one last rasping breath.

Yuki put her fingers to his neck. 'He is gone.'

'Son of a bitch!' Ryan hissed. 'They trail this guy all the way around the world, and now he dies spewing nothing but gibberish. 'Did he say "kill"?'

'Couldn't tell,' Midas said. 'He might have. Maybe "gang four-key" or "gang for kill." Hell, none of it makes sense.'

'Gang of Four?' Adara guessed over the net. 'That's got Chinese implications.'

'Could be,' Ryan said. None of this helped him figure out what threats might be facing his father. 'How's it looking out there?'

'One shitbird is down,' Chavez said. 'And the other has to be running out of bullets. You guys haul ass as soon as you're able. We'll sit tight here and play innocent bystander until things simmer down.'

'Copy that,' Ryan said. He grabbed Vincent Chen's leather briefcase, relieved to find a laptop computer inside. That was something anyway. With any luck, Gavin could link to it remotely and give them a little nugget to go on. Yuki took Kim Soo's ID and cell phone. Ryan draped the case over his shoulder and took a quick peek out the back door.

The police were still busy at the other end of the path. Rain pummeled the pavement, throwing as much spray back up as came down. If anything, it was raining even harder than before. They couldn't retrace their steps. There would surely be crowds gathered around the wounded – and possibly dead – they'd left behind. The police might even be there by now. Better to go straight out the front of this place.

The shamisen music stopped abruptly when Yukiko led them into the cramped six-by fifteen-foot bar, shouting like the place was on fire and pointing back at the storage room. Ryan didn't know exactly what she was saying, but he was pretty sure it was something about dead bodies and men with guns. They were out the door before anyone recovered from the shock.

Keeping east, they fell in with a fleeing crowd and were shunted through the red *torii* gates of the Hanazono Shinto shrine by a line of police officers staffing a barricade.

'You were right,' Ryan said as they slogged through the rain, over the gravel courtyard of the shrine. 'A female brought down Vincent Chen.'

He looked at Yuki, rain pressing a pale shirt to her shoulders, dripping from her bangs. Long tresses clung to her cheeks. A woman would probably be his downfall as well.

59

Protocol dictated that the paramount leader of China should arrive last, just prior to departure. Support staff and Colonel Huang had timed the ride to the airport so they could lift off moments after President Zhao was seated. The plane was a Boeing 747 used by Air China as a passenger jet when it was not pressed into service to fly the Chinese president on international trips. Prior to becoming China's version of Air Force One, the 747, usually one of two, was fitted with more luxurious furnishings, including beds, sofas, and plush seating. Madame Zhao enjoyed flying in such comfort. She had wanted to accompany him to Japan, but present circumstances made that an imprudent idea.

Zhao was not surprised to see Foreign Minister Li's motorcade already on the tarmac as his armored Hongqi L5 limousine came to a stop behind the uniformed military escort. He was, however, surprised to find Minister Li speaking with that detestable General Xu of the Central Security Bureau. The sun was up, a dull orange disk through the greasy pall of haze to the east, but lights illuminated the base of the plane and the length of red carpet rolled out from the air stairs.

The gaggle of men around Li and Xu snapped to attention when they saw the president approaching. Li gave a slight bow. Xu, a bow that was even slighter.

'Good morning, Zhao Zhuxi,' Li said. He gave Colonel Huang a look of uncharacteristic sympathy. 'I was sorry to hear about your men. The criminals responsible will be captured and punished to the fullest extent, I am sure.'

Colonel Huang thanked him for his courtesy, but looked nervously up and down the tarmac.

'Zhao Zhuxi,' General Xu said, 'the attack on your protective staff is what finds me here to greet you this morning. I have seen personally to providing three replacements from among our very finest at the Central Security Bureau.'

Zhao nodded thoughtfully. 'I was under the impression that the very finest would be assigned to the paramount leader in the first place.'

'Just so,' Xu blustered. 'But CSB has many talented and skilled officers. Is that not correct, Colonel Huang?'

'It is, General,' Huang said.

Zhao turned to him. 'Do we need more personnel?'

'General Xu is correct,' he said. 'We should not travel without a full complement.'

'Do you know these replacements, Colonel?' Zhao asked.

'I do, sir,' Huang said. 'By name and reputation. I have not had the pleasure of working with them.'

'You know best, of course, General,' Zhao said.

'Is something wrong, Zhao Zhuxi?' Li asked.

'No.' Zhao shook his head. 'The timing is unfortunate. That is all.'

'Please,' Li said. 'Allow me to offer three of my security detail. They are accustomed to working directly with Colonel Huang and his men. The three new officers may assume responsibilities for my protection.'

General Xu started to object, which made Zhao more prone to accept the offer.

He raised an eyebrow. 'This seems quite outside the norm.'

Li bowed again. 'The timing, as you say, is unfortunate. It would be my great honor to second Colonel Long Yun and two others. The best of my best.'

'I could not,' Zhao said.

'Your safety is paramount,' Li said. 'Please do me this honor.'

Colonel Huang's jaw muscles flexed. He was obviously surprised at the news.

'Very well,' Zhao said. He put a foot on the bottom step and then turned to the other two men. 'Have either of you been in contact with Admiral Qian? I wish to speak to him, but his staff said he is incommunicado.'

General Xu shrugged. 'Perhaps inspecting one of our submarines, Mr President.'

'Perhaps,' Zhao said, and bounded up the stairs.

I must go,' Li said as soon as the paramount leader was out of earshot.

'What is this business with Admiral Qian?' Xu asked. 'I have not been able to contact him, either. That man has disappeared.'

'I'm sure it is nothing,' Li said, turning to climb the stairs. The steward at the top waved him forward with a white glove, telling him, the foreign minister, to hurry. Li purposely slowed, taking his time up the last few steps, then noted the steward's name as he turned to find his seat.

Li took his spot in premium seating directly aft of the paramount leader's office and quarters. He took his mobile phone from the pocket of his suit jacket before handing it to a steward – not the idiot who had rushed him – and pressed the number for his wife. Oddly, there was no answer, even at this early hour. She'd been awake when he left. He tried his son, still reaching nothing but voice mail. He smiled a tight smile, fending off the inevitable worry of a man with many enemies who was leaving town.

The flight was just over three hours. He would try again when they landed.

60

If there was one fortunate thing about being tired all the time, President Ryan knew, it was that he could usually nap at any given moment. It hadn't always been that way. The Threat Board being what it was – urgent and stacked – it had a tendency to keep thinking people up at night. But as he spent more and more time with the sword of Damocles suspended over his head, Ryan's brain and body formed an uneasy truce, allowing thoughts on topics such as nuclear destruction or a fragile economy to simmer in the background instead of boiling over the moment his head hit the pillow. Cathy said he dreamed more now, tossing and turning and mumbling nonsensical things in his sleep. Ryan rarely remembered his dreams, which made him believe there was a God, and that He was merciful, because the dreams of a powerful man with any conscience at all were, by necessity, bad dreams.

He woke to the change in pressure in his ears as Air Force One began a gradual descent over Japan. Hopefully, the four-hour nap would get his body clock somewhere in line with Japan time. They would be wheels-down at Yokota Air Base at nine-twenty a.m. local – giving him a full day of meetings when his brain told him it was eight-twenty p.m. in DC. It was going to be a long one, so he shaved and put on a clean shirt and a midnight-blue tie. Cathy said the color made him look serious, which, he thought, was appropriate considering his upcoming meeting with President Zhao.

Though surely terrifying for the crew, the business with RV *Meriwether* had proven a litmus test for the power struggle that appeared to be going on inside China. Either Zhao was a liar or he didn't have control of his military. The former, Ryan had come to hope. The latter would be a nightmare.

Special Agent Gary Montgomery sat on the sofa outside the President's office and gazed out the windows at the ocean below. He didn't much care for water. It could kill you, but you couldn't kill it back. POTUS would be up soon, so Montgomery buttoned the top button on his white shirt and straightened his tie. He always brought two ties to work, a red one and a blue one – so he'd not be wearing the same color as his protectee. It was weird, Montgomery admitted that, but it was something he did for luck – well, that and countless hours at the range and in the gym. The President had been wearing a red power tie when they left Andrews, and Montgomery was happy he'd chosen a blue Brooks Brothers for today. This was his first flight with President Ryan, and he wanted everything to be perfect. His years in the Secret Service had taught him that if something could go wrong, it would. Montgomery didn't relish the idea of having a man he respected as much as Jack Ryan standing over his shoulder when things inevitably turned to shit.

The Japanese took a dim view of firearms and strictly enforced who could and could not carry for all but the agents immediately surrounding the President. Even these were warned of Japanese gun laws, but no one stopped the President of the United States or the dozen close-protection agents who arrived in the motorcade with him. Montgomery had been told it was a wink-and-a-nod sort of agreement, with the Japanese not doing very much winking – or nodding.

Yeah, Tokyo was touted as the safest city in the world, but the President of the United States had enemies, and it took only one devoted son of a bitch to ruin your whole day – especially if half your team was standing around holding nothing but air when they should be holding SIG Sauer pistols.

Most of the heavy-weapon portion of the vehicle package would be staffed by Japanese police, yet the Secret Service still had two armored limos and a number of their own follow-ups and staff vehicles. When they did move on the ground, the motorcade would be a staggering forty-three vehicles long – not including the motorcycle escorts that would provide rolling roadblocks prior to every intersection. The helos from HMX-1 were already on the ground as well, with backup air support in the form of two CV-22 Ospreys that had recently been stationed at Yokota.

The fifteen-minute trip on Marine One from Yokota Air Base to downtown Tokyo would be a hell of a lot better than a forty-minute drive. Mitzi Snelson, lead advance for the detail, advised that the Palace Hotel – the location of POTUS's bi-lat with the Chinese president – was buttoned up tight. She would meet them on the roof.

Montgomery looked at his watch and then knocked on the office door.

'Mr President,' he said. 'Wheels down in five minutes.'

Ryan's voice came back through the door. 'Very well. Everything good to go on the ground?'

'We're all set, sir,' Montgomery said, though he couldn't help but feel like he was forgetting something. Decades on the job and this trip had him feeling like a damn rookie.

'Good,' Ryan said, opening the door. He was wearing a midnight-blue tie instead of the red one he'd had on when they left.

Montgomery bit his tongue and forced a smile.

Ryan saw his change in mood. 'Is something wrong?'

'Not a thing, Mr President.'

The Akasaka Guesthouse is very secure,' Yuki said. She was sitting beside Jack Ryan, Jr, on the Marunouchi subway line, heading back toward Tokyo Station and the Palace Hotel. Ryan's chest needed stitches, but Adara had fixed him up with some superglue and a sticky bandage that stopped him from bleeding through his shirt.

The team had almost nothing to go on, aside from some cryptic phrases about a gang – and possibly the word 'kill,' which was chilling in and of itself, if that's what Chen had actually been saying. The fact that Chen was in town at all was bad news, and Jack tried to console himself that the man's cadre was dead or in jail. Yuki's superiors had told her the second gunman had survived and was in intensive care. Amanda Salazar and the man Ryan had knocked out were in police custody, refusing to talk. Their respective embassies had been notified and both would probably be released after all the visiting dignitaries left town – unless Yuki's organization could find a reason to hold them.

'Thanks,' Ryan said. 'I know you have plenty of work without me here having you run down a bunch of dead ends.'

Yuki smiled. 'We have a saying here in Japan: *Nokori-mono ni wa fuku ga aru*. Luck is in the leftovers.'

'I'm not sure what that means —'

'It means,' Yuki said, 'that we must keep going. We find our luck by working through to the last.'

'I hope my friends have some luck with Chen's computer.'

'I would be severely reprimanded for letting you tamper with that,' she said. 'If my superiors were to find out.'

'I know,' Ryan said. 'And like I said, I'm sorry to put you in this spot.'

The train rumbled to a stop at Kasumigaseki. They were two stops from Tokyo Station and the cars were getting crowded.

Three middle-aged women boarded and held the suspended rings in front of Ryan as the train began to move. His dad would not approve of his lack of chivalry.

'Japan has a load of cool proverbs,' he said. 'But I don't care for the custom of men sitting while women stand. I think I'll offer one of these ladies my seat.'

Yuki put her hand on his arm and left it there. 'Please,' she said. 'It is more polite for you to sit.'

'Seriously?' Ryan said. 'Because I might offend some other dude that didn't think of it first?'

'No.' She smiled, leaning in close to share a secret. 'You take up too much space.'

Ryan looked at her. She still hadn't moved her hand off his arm, and he was fine with that. 'Too much space?'

She squeezed his arm now, flirting a little, maybe. 'You are quite bulky compared to most Japanese. I am embarrassed to say that some might think you *kebukai yabanjin* – a hairy barbarian.' She raised her eyebrows. 'I do not think so, of course.'

'Of course.' Ryan gave her a slow nod, but he kept his seat until the train stopped at Tokyo Station.

Yuki led the way out of the Marunouchi tunnel. They opened their umbrellas against a steady rain and walked almost due west, past a water garden on the right, toward the Imperial Palace moat. Lots of water. Ryan had a lot of personal experience with the Secret Service. He was sure they'd already had scuba divers check the water features and run a couple dozen waterborne Attack on the Principal drills back on some lake near Beltsville.

They passed a small shrine, and a white castle across the water, the colors and edges of everything muted by the rain and mist.

'This country looks amazing when it's wet,' he said.

'I think so as well,' Yuki said. 'You must be careful, Jack. When you try to leave Japan, *ushirogami wo hikareru* – it will always tug at the hair on the back of your neck.'

'I can believe that –'

Chavez's voice came over the net. He was still at the hotel babysitting Chen's computer while Gavin Biery worked to break the passwords and encryption so he could conduct a remote assessment of its contents. Midas and Adara had been going from place to place, looking for any needles in the haystack of G20 venues. They all planned to link up around the hotel, across the street from the Imperial Palace and grounds.

'I've been trying to call you, 'mano,' Chavez said. 'Gavin got in.' His voice was far from happy.

'Okay,' Ryan said. 'An assassination plot?'

'Gav's still going over files,' Chavez said. 'But not so far. Just as Eddie Feng suspected, Chen is connected to the Beijing subway bombing. He was paid a nice sum for that one. But get this. Did you read about the soldier getting killed in Chad and an attack on a Navy vessel somewhere over near Bali?'

'Yeah,' Jack said.

'Chen received payments around the time of those attacks – and, of course, the bombing in Argentina.'

Ryan pondered the ramifications. 'Taiwan?'

'Not even close,' Chavez said. 'Foreign Minister Li. Gav got some weird hits checking some back channels. First he thought the connection was just because Li was a victim in the Argentina thing, but Li and a PRC general named Xu own shares in a diamond mine in West Africa. Get this, Vincent Chen's sister, Lily, is a minority partner in the same mine.'

Ryan stopped in his tracks. 'So Chen and Foreign Minister Li are connected? Maybe the sister hired Chen to kill her business partner.'

Yuki turned around to listen to Jack's half of the conversation.

'We have to pass this up the chain,' Jack said.

'Gerry's getting it to our friends at the Crossing now.'

He meant Liberty Crossing, home of the Office of the Director of National Intelligence – Mary Pat Foley. She would know if there was anything in the works regarding Li.

'I'll get back to you,' Chavez said. 'Gerry's calling.'

Ryan filled Yuki in as they crossed Uchibori Street, which was blocked off to vehicular traffic for the entire block in front of the hotel. They were able to walk north, along the Imperial Garden moat.

Yuki stopped with the gathered crowd directly across the street from the hotel. A dozen uniformed police officers and security guards in white hardhats formed a polite but unyielding skirmish line along the sidewalk, allowing people to look as long as they were empty-handed. Photography, or even holding a phone, was strictly prohibited.

Three helicopters thumped in the gray sky overhead, two peeling off while the third hovered over the hotel roof, settling in for a landing. Marine One. Jack felt his gut twist, knowing that his father was stepping into some serious unknowns.

'You needn't worry about the President,' Yukiko said. 'The Wadakura fountains and ponds form a natural barrier to the south of this venue and the police have closed the roads around the entire block.' She nodded toward a large white tent at the end of the street. 'Any delivery or staff support vehicle – even those of the police – must be screened with mirrors and explosive-detection canines. Pedestrians, including security, must show their credentials at that point, and then again inside the building, passing through metal detectors at both locations. It is like the layers of an onion. Concentric rings, countermeasures to thwart bombings, armed assailants, missiles, biological and chemical attacks, and crazy people with samurai swords. You see, it appears that every conceivable attacker has been covered.'

'Even *kebukai yabanjin*?' Jack said.

'Especially the hairy barbarians,' Yuki said.

Sirens yelped and a motorcade of fifteen cars turned off Uchibori and into the security tent half a block down.

The black Toyota sedan behind the police lead vehicles bore the red flags of the People's Republic of China.

'Zhao,' Ryan mused.

The motorcade proceeded under the hotel portico, out of the rain. Men in dark suits sprang from the two follow-up sedans, facing outbound as they surrounded the limousine. Some of them would be Japanese SPs – Security Police – but like the United States, China preferred to bring a relatively large contingent of her own personnel.

Ryan took a half-step forward in order to get a better look. It was hard to be certain in the rain from so far away.

'Do those two guys look familiar?'

Yuki moved up beside him. 'I . . . think so.'

President Zhao exited his limo, purposely shielded from clear view by the vehicle and the pillars in front of the hotel entry. He and several members of his security detail disappeared into the hotel. The motorcade pulled forward and then stopped again. More security men got out and surrounded a second protectee.

'Foreign Minister Li,' Yuki said. 'I know who those men were.'

'Me too,' Ryan said into the microphone on his neck loop.

'Hey, guys . . . We got a problem.'

61

Jack looked up at the twenty-three-story hotel. His father was somewhere up there right now. He fought the urge to pace back and forth. 'Everyone going in has to be credentialed, right?'

'Correct,' Yuki said. 'We can check the photo database.'

She took out her cell phone but a barked command from one of the policemen sent her and Jack to the end of the block.

Ryan held her umbrella while she worked.

'Are you sure they were Li's guys?' Midas asked over the radio.

'Pretty sure,' Ryan said. 'At least two of them were with him at the restaurant bombing in Argentina.'

Chavez weighed in. 'All the ChiCom bigwigs get protection from the CSB. It's like our Secret Service and Diplomatic Security Service combined.'

'True,' Ryan said. 'But the change at this point is too big a coincidence. Chen's getting paid to whack people, maybe even by Li, and then Li's protective detail moves over to Zhao – on the same day he's meeting with my dad. Yuki's right. This place is completely buttoned up – from everyone except the close-protection agents. It's impossible to guard against the guards.'

'You're right,' Chavez said. 'We need to alert the Secret Service.'

'Wait!' Ryan said. 'Let's think this through a second. Yuki might be able to get us upstairs.'

She shook her head. 'I am not credentialed to go in. I could get approval, but it would take time.'

'That's a no-go, then,' Ryan said. 'But if it is an assassination plot, these guys smell an alarm and they'll just open fire. The Secret Service won't know what's going on. No matter who the target is, everybody in the room will be sitting ducks.'

Yuki held up her phone. 'You are correct,' she said. 'Three new officers from the Central Security Bureau were credentialed for President Zhao's protective detail, including a man named Long Yun, the former agent in charge of Foreign Minister Li's security team.'

'Bear with me here, guys.' Jack passed the umbrella to Yuki and began thumb-typing feverishly into his cell phone. He copied the text, then hit send. Pasted the text, hit send again. Pasted the text once more, then sent it a third time. 'Okay,' he said, heaving a tense sigh once he'd sent the last text. 'When I was a kid, my dad missed one of my baseball games because he had to work. It really tore him up. He made this deal with all of us that if he was physically able, it wouldn't matter if he was with the Queen of England herself, he'd answer a call after three hang-ups in quick succession.' He blew out a heavy breath, nerves wound tight. 'Trust the guy on the ground, right, Midas?'

'Roger that,' Midas said.

'Well,' Jack said, 'Dad's the guy on the ground.'

'What did you send him?' Adara asked.

' *"Three bad guys new to Zhao's detail. Violence likely."* He'll know what to do . . . I hope.'

*

The two presidents had elected to conduct the short bilateral meeting alone, but for a single Security man each. Gary Montgomery had forty pounds and five inches on Zhao's man, but the Chinese Security agent appeared to vibrate with intensity. Neither were about to let anything – even a slight – happen to their respective charges.

The two other members of each protection detail waited in the slightly larger anteroom beyond a set of double doors. Ryan was seated in one of two chairs to the right of the Chinese leader. They were close, less than three feet apart, quartering away from a floor-to-ceiling window. A washroom was to Ryan's immediate right in the corner of the small, ten-by-ten-foot room.

Interpreters and other staff would assist them later, but for now, each saw the necessity of sitting down face-to-face and speaking candidly. Advance staff from both delegations had agreed to a small room off the back of one of the larger ballrooms. Politicians from around the world met in this hotel often, and there were several such private spaces, small enough for quiet conversation, and with a slightly larger, private antechamber beyond double doors that could be opened to form a room large enough for interpreters, additional staff, and photographers requisite for such a meeting.

Zhao had spent a year at Dartmouth and spoke excellent English. Ryan found him to be quiet, with the almost impenetrable façade common to people who must always guard their words. The best way to break through something like that was a direct approach – something Ryan had always preferred to pussyfooting around.

'Your assistance with our research vessel was appreciated, Mr President,' Ryan said.

Zhao gave a polite smile and started to say something, but Ryan kept talking. 'I was, however, extremely concerned with Admiral Qian's disregard for your orders.'

Zhao took a deep breath through his nose. There was no easy reply. 'Admiral Qian is in custody,' Zhao said. 'Surely even the United States has endured rogue commanders from time to time. There is no house of cards in China. The party is in complete control.'

'True enough,' Ryan said, sensing Zhao wanted to say more, and giving him time to do so. Silence, he'd learned, was often the least used and most needed ingredient in good statesmanship.

Zhao folded his hands in his lap. 'The container ship *Orion* –'

Ryan's cell phone began to hum in the pocket of his coat. At least he'd remembered to put the damn thing on vibrate. He ignored it, and it stopped. Then it buzzed again a second later. Stopped. And buzzed a third time. Ryan closed his eyes. His kids were grown – all of them old enough to know the importance of what he did – the delicate nature of his meetings. Damn it. That was the point. Of course, they knew. None of them would use the family code to bypass normal protocols if it weren't important.

Ryan reached into his pocket and held up the offending cell phone. 'I apologize, Mr President,' he said, scanning the message.

It was from Jack.

Ryan kept his face passive, motioning Montgomery

over with a slight flick of his hand. Colonel Huang came off the wall a half-step at the movement, but a look from Zhao kept him in place.

Ryan said, 'Gary, I'm going to show you something, and you have to promise to hear me out before you do anything.'

Everyone in the room was surprised to hear the President speak to his security agent so informally.

'Mr President –'

'This is crucial,' Ryan said.

'Yes, sir,' Montgomery said, sounding extremely unconvinced.

Ryan read the text, whispering in the event anyone in the anteroom happened to be listening. Both agents immediately put themselves between their protectees and the double doors, pistols in hand, making themselves as large a target as possible.

'New additions to your detail?' Ryan asked.

'Mr President,' Montgomery interrupted. 'I need you to step into the bathroom.'

There was no way out but the double doors.

Colonel Huang nodded. 'Such a move would be prudent, Zhao Zhuxi.'

The two presidents complied with their experts.

Once they were in the small washroom, Zhao said, 'Three new officers were transferred to my team.'

Colonel Huang said something in Chinese, presumably a curse. 'Long Yun is outside now.'

'And the other two new ones?' Montgomery asked.

'Downstairs,' Huang said. 'But Long Yun is extremely fast and accurate with his sidearm. I do not care for him, but honestly, he would be a very dangerous opponent.'

'Okay,' Ryan said. 'Members of my intelligence community believe your foreign minister may be in the process of launching a coup against you, or an assassination attempt against me. In either instance, unless you are personally involved, we will both be killed.'

'I assure you –'

Huang interrupted his boss, ready to protect his person and his reputation. 'Long Yun is from Foreign Minister Li's protective detail.'

'I believe you,' Ryan said. 'There is evidence to implicate you in this – far too much evidence, in fact. Piles of it. Too easy to find. I disagree with you and your government on most things, President Zhao, but I would imagine a stupid man would not rise to your office. You are many things, but inept is not one of them.'

Zhao pushed back his glasses but said nothing.

'Someone,' Ryan said, 'has been attempting to convince me that you are a very bad man.'

'They want you to invoke your Ryan Doctrine,' Zhao mused, saying the words as if they tasted bad. 'To punish me personally for actions against your nation.'

'Precisely,' Ryan said.

Montgomery spoke next. In any other circumstance of threat to the principal, protocol would be to sound off, cover, and evacuate immediately. So far, he'd done none of the above. 'Mr President –'

Ryan raised his hand, cutting him off. 'We're good for a moment, Gary. The attack won't happen until we walk outside. Here's what I propose . . .'

Colonel Huang was seething by the time President Ryan finished explaining his plan. He could not leave the paramount leader in the care of the Americans. That was insane.

'I'd go,' the burly Secret Service agent said. 'But your guy would sense a trap and start shooting as soon as I went through the door by myself.'

'Perhaps we could summon the agent I do trust,' Zhao offered. 'Isolating Long Yun among your Secret Service agents.'

'There is no lock on those double doors,' Ryan pointed out. 'If Long smells a rat –'

Montgomery was already briefing his three agents outside via their earpieces. They were surely having a difficult time controlling their emotions. Huang knew he would have to move quickly. Reinforcements would flood the room at any moment, and more than a few innocents would die in the ensuing gun battle.

The two Secret Service agents – one woman and one man – regarded Colonel Huang warily as he slipped through the double doors and nodded to Major Ts'ai, the only agent he trusted completely, asking for a break. Colonel Long stepped forward to volunteer, but the female American agent casually body-blocked him.

Ryan's plan had been for Huang to arrest Long Yun, but Huang had seen the other man shoot. Reaction being slower than action, Colonel Huang Ju decided on his own plan, one that would ensure the survival of the paramount leader. Smiling, he swept the hem of his jacket and drew the Taurus. His finger found the trigger as he rocked the muzzle toward Long Yun, firing two rounds from less than four feet away. Long took a half-step back, going for his own pistol. He wore a ballistic vest, but the nine-millimeter rounds stunned him enough to stagger him, slowing him down for the fraction of a second it took for Huang to rock the Taurus upward and fire two more rounds on the heels of the first volley, catching Long in the throat and above his right eye.

Colonel Huang dropped his pistol immediately, raising his hands high above his head to show he was no threat to the armed Japanese officers that poured through the door at the sound of gunfire.

Three Secret Service agents, including Gary Montgomery, formed a protective phalanx around Ryan and hustled him through the anteroom and past Long Yun's body to meet another half-dozen of their cohort and escort him straight to the roof and a waiting Marine One.

The President had wanted to wait and see to Zhao, or even scoop him up in the protective bubble – but at some point, those decisions stopped being up to the President. He would understand that. Probably. Maybe.

Ryan sent a text to Jack Junior as soon as they were airborne letting him know he was safe. He'd call later, catching up as much as he could. He wondered if he'd ever know exactly how Jack had figured out about Zhao's detail – and what had led him to look into it in the first place. Some things, Ryan decided, were probably best left unsaid, for the time being, at least.

He called Cathy, in case she happened to be watching the news. She wasn't, but it was good to talk to her anyway.

Arnie and Mary Pat met him at the Akasaka State Guesthouse and they drafted a press release that named an unidentified gunman and extolled the fast work of Japanese authorities. If Zhao decided he wanted his name involved, that was up to him.

'So,' Mary Pat said, 'it sounds like Foreign Minister Li had some sort of relationship with a provocateur named Vincent Chen. He along with three others in the party were involved in a coup to oust Zhao and have Li installed as the new president.'

'I'm surprised Zhao would let it get this far,' van Damm said. 'He's steady, but from the outside looking in, he seems to rule with an iron hand.'

Ryan rubbed a hand across his face, feeling the effects of jet lag and the ebb of adrenaline. 'While we were lying on the floor, waiting for them to take care of Long Yun, he confided that he had suspected the foreign minister for some time. He considered the plot was intended to get me to invoke the Ryan Doctrine, but he admits he didn't believe Li would attempt to have him killed directly.'

'Just how was it supposed to work?' Mary Pat asked.

Ryan shrugged, holding out his hand, watching it tremble slightly. 'Long Yun shoots Zhao and Colonel Huang and my security detail – and me. The guy was apparently an impressive shooter. Five or six head shots. It would have been over in a heartbeat – especially if no one was suspecting it. He'd just blame the assassination on us.'

'Still,' Arnie said, 'I find it odd that a man who's risen to Zhao's level could be duped like that.'

Ryan said, 'I wouldn't move Zhao out of the sneaky-bastard category just yet. He admitted to me that he did not expect the attack to happen so quickly after arrival in Japan. He intended to meet with Li later in the day and let him know his wife and son had been in "protective custody" since early this morning.'

'I'm sure the foreign minister and his cronies will all be granted fair trials and speedy executions,' Arnie said.

Mary Pat gave a smug nod. 'Sounds legit.'

Ryan turned to Montgomery, who stood against the wall, unwilling to let the President out of his sight.

'So, Gary,' Ryan said, 'you told Colonel Huang you would have gone to handle it yourself if that were possible?'

'Backing your play, sir,' Montgomery said.

'So you wouldn't have?' Ryan mused. 'Left me with the Chinese, I mean, while you took care of it.'

'No, Mr President,' Montgomery said. 'Not in a million years.'

62

Magdalena Rojas insisted on going to the hospital to see Eddie Feng and thank him for his kindness that night at Parrot's party. Callahan could hardly say no to the request, considering all the poor kid had been through. She and Caruso stood with her beside Feng's bed.

The whites of his eyes were still red with pronounced petechiae from the attempted dead-leg hanging, but his ridiculous fauxhawk was combed down and he wasn't quite so twitchy, since he'd been off energy drinks for the better part of a week.

'I'm sorry I stole your thumb drive,' the child said.

Feng scoffed. 'I'm not,' he said. 'Not if it got you out.'

Magdalena leaned over and gave him a hug. He squirmed and looked up at Callahan and Caruso, not knowing what to do.

'I want to thank that other man, too,' Magdalena said. 'Is he still in the hospital?'

Callahan shot a narrow look at Caruso. 'He should be,' she said. 'But someone checked him out.'

'He saved me, you know,' she said. 'And I heard he saved Jo, too. She was one of Parrot's girls. And Paula and Leticia at Matarife's place.' She shivered at the mention of the name. 'He saved us all. I would like him to know we are grateful. What is his name?'

'His name is John.' Caruso smiled. 'I'm sure he knows.'

A guardian from Child Protective Services put her arm around Magdalena and led her into the hall.

'What happens to her now?' Eddie Feng asked, genuinely concerned.

Callahan sighed. 'I'm not going to lie to you. Lots of counseling, rehab for any drug habits, treatment for STDs, and foster care.'

'As long as you don't send her back to her mom,' Feng said. 'From what she told me, that lady is evil.'

'Oh, no,' Callahan said. 'I'm already working on a way to pinch that awful woman for international human trafficking.' She removed the leg irons that kept him chained to the bed. 'Get some rest, Eddie. You're a weirdo, but you're apparently not a pedophile.'

Feng threw his head back against the pillow and began to cry. 'That's the nicest thing anyone's ever said to me.'

Callahan spun on Caruso once they were outside the room. 'I'm guessing you're going to disappear now as well.'

He sighed. 'Yep, into the sunset . . .'

'Seriously, Dom, I'm not a heartless bitch. I know your friend saved those kids, but that kind of stuff is . . . it's just old-school.'

'That it is,' Caruso said.

'Someone just came in with a writ of habeas corpus and waltzed him outta here,' she said. 'Did you know his fingerprints don't come back to anyone?'

Caruso shrugged.

'Come on, Dom, tell me who he is. It would be nice to know what he's all about.'

'Oh, Kelsey,' Caruso said. 'Some things are nice to know – and some things are just nuts to know.'

Yuki's credentials had enough juice to get her and Ryan past security and into the business-jet departure lounge. The others had already cleared Japanese immigration and gotten the exit stamps on their passports. Reid and the other pilots were already waiting aboard the Gulfstream.

Chavez stood at the door leading out to the tarmac with a duffel in his hand.

'Sure you don't want to fly back with us?' Ding prodded. 'It's more comfortable than commercial – even business class.'

'I'm good,' Ryan said. Yuki stood right beside him. She wasn't holding his hand, but she may as well have been. 'You know I've been wanting to work on a second language. Think I'll start with Japanese.'

'I am glad you stayed, Jack-san,' Yuki said as they walked out to her car. They'd considered taking the train, but Yuki had decided she wanted to take him for a drive, into the mountains. It was still raining, and they shared an umbrella, which, Jack realized, was even better than holding hands.

'Me too,' Ryan said. 'Can I ask you something?'

They stopped and she turned to face him under the umbrella. She was half a head shorter than him, and looked up, blinking dark lashes. Mist from the rain dampened her face, despite the umbrella. He considered asking about the scratches on her cheek but decided this wasn't the time. Too heavy.

She continued to peer up at him. 'Yes?'

'When did you know that my dad was the President of the United States?'

'When I saw you in the sewers,' she said.

'I'm serious.'

'So am I,' Yuki said. 'I am, after all, an intelligence officer. I have a trained eye.'

'And you didn't say anything about it?'

She stood and looked at him for a long moment and then, seeming to come to a serious conclusion, said, 'We have a saying here in Japan.'

'Oh, really?' Ryan said. 'And what's that?'

She was on tiptoe now, her lips just inches from his, her voice hoarse and breathy.

'Sometimes,' she said, 'it is better to shut the hell up.'

He just wanted a decent book to read ...

Not too much to ask, is it? It was in 1935 when Allen Lane, Managing Director of Bodley Head Publishers, stood on a platform at Exeter railway station looking for something good to read on his journey back to London. His choice was limited to popular magazines and poor-quality paperbacks – the same choice faced every day by the vast majority of readers, few of whom could afford hardbacks. Lane's disappointment and subsequent anger at the range of books generally available led him to found a company – and change the world.

'We believed in the existence in this country of a vast reading public for intelligent books at a low price, and staked everything on it'
Sir Allen Lane, 1902–1970, founder of Penguin Books

The quality paperback had arrived – and not just in bookshops. Lane was adamant that his Penguins should appear in chain stores and tobacconists, and should cost no more than a packet of cigarettes.

Reading habits (and cigarette prices) have changed since 1935, but Penguin still believes in publishing the best books for everybody to enjoy. We still believe that good design costs no more than bad design, and we still believe that quality books published passionately and responsibly make the world a better place.

So wherever you see the little bird – whether it's on a piece of prize-winning literary fiction or a celebrity autobiography, political tour de force or historical masterpiece, a serial-killer thriller, reference book, world classic or a piece of pure escapism – you can bet that it represents the very best that the genre has to offer.

Whatever you like to read – trust Penguin.